BLOOD
ON THE
TRACKS

BLOOD
ON THE
TRACKS

BARBARA NICKLESS

THOMAS & MERCER

This is a work of fiction. Names, characters, organizations, places, events, and incidents are either products of the author's imagination or are used fictitiously.

Text copyright © 2016 by Barbara Nickless
All rights reserved.

No part of this work may be reproduced, or stored in a retrieval system, or transmitted in any form or by any means, electronic, mechanical, photocopying, recording, or otherwise, without express written permission of the publisher.

Published by Thomas & Mercer, Seattle

www.apub.com

Amazon, the Amazon logo, and Thomas & Mercer are trademarks of Amazon.com, Inc., or its affiliates.

ISBN-10: 1503936864
ISBN-13: 9781503936867

Cover design by Christian Fuenfhausen Design

For Steve, Kyle, and Amanda.
And for Cathy, who was there the longest.

THE BURNED MAN

His life wasn't worth spit in a hard rain.

For two weeks he'd been camping under the 7th Street Bridge, smoking and dozing next to the slow roll of the Los Angeles River. Through the misery of dry-heat days and blue-neon nights, he listened to the roar of traffic overhead and wondered how a man could shed the perilous weight of memory.

Time and again, he imagined climbing the crumbling pylons of the bridge, folding his uniform neatly over the rail, and stepping naked onto the highway to let that roar take him down.

After fifteen days, and with his mind made up, he was standing on the bridge when his phone rang. His woman, calling from Denver.

"I miss you, Tucker. Please come home."

"I can't," he said. "Bad has filled every part of me. There ain't room for nothing else."

"Please, Tucker. I love you. I've thought about what you said. I've thought about nothing else." A pause, while the sound of her breath filled his ear. "I will marry you."

Her words fell on him like rain, coming down sweet and clean, washing away the dust devils of Iraq. He ran his hands over the remains of his face and felt the memory of her fingers there from when she'd last touched him. He realized, to his surprise, that even constant pain left room for love.

"I'm coming," he told her. "A week, I'll be there."

"A week," she said, "I'll be done with everything else."

He backed away from the road, packed all he owned into his ruck, and thumbed his way to the rail yard.

Hopping trains was brutal. A split second of distraction or carelessness or just pure bad luck could cost you your fingers or hands, a leg or your life. You could be arrested, jailed, beaten, robbed. Murdered as you slept, your body tossed into a ravine somewhere between nowhere and nohow.

Worse for the Burned Man: everywhere he went he took his face, a haunted-house mask that never came off no matter how many surgeries they gave him in the burn unit at Brooke Army Medical. A face not even a mother could love, as his mother had proved when she'd up and left, the door of the ICU slamming closed behind her, somewhere between his sixth surgery and the tenth.

But his woman loved him.

Loved him even with this face. Loved him even when he called her dumb and crazy and all the other shit he'd thrown at her when she said she loved him still, loved him before the war and loved him after, even with all that the war had done to him. He told her it was pity, not love, and you damn sure couldn't make a life out of pity. She'd pushed right back, telling him now he was being the stupid one, tossing away love like they sang about on the radio.

"Look at me," he'd yelled, shoving his face into hers. "Look at what I am!"

But she'd only raised her fingers to the ruins of him, pressed her palms against the ravines and overhangs and gullies that mapped out his face and said she cherished his new geography. That was the word she'd used—*cherished*. The hills and furrows of his body were as close to traveling as she was likely to get, she said, and as far as she had a care to go.

"Come home soon," she'd said the last time he'd run off.

The Burned Man had never been one for staying put. Even before the war he'd been riding trains, putting out his thumb on highways, working whatever crew would take him this way and that. After the war it got worse—the ghosts more shrill, the demons unrelenting.

But maybe it was finally time to float down and let the world reclaim him. If he didn't grab hold of this woman, he would drift away in a delirium of grief and rage until he ended up back under the 7th Street Bridge.

Then standing on top of it, waiting for that roar to take him down.

So the morning after she called, in a predawn blue flecked with stars, he caught out. He went north in a boxcar to the cold fog of Olympia and the long rolling call of the ocean, took a gondola carrying steel pipe across the pine-choked wilds of Montana, and finally into Wyoming, where he jumped aboard a coal train clattering south toward Denver and the warmth of his woman.

He spent the Wyoming days crouched between the hoppers so that the wind was in his teeth and his eyes burned with cinders, then roughshodding over miles of ballast looking for unwatched locomotives in which to pass the nights. The wide land brought him some peace, hinted that maybe God was around after all, buried deep in the details and ready to let him be. Maybe God no longer kept a ledger against him of dead friends and dead Iraqis, no longer wanted to punish him with a face that opened a door to the dead every time he looked in the mirror.

Smack between Shawnee Junction and Wolf, sitting solo in a snowy hobo camp, he ran into some trouble. He usually did—some skinhead tramp taking exception to his face. But he managed okay; a few bruises, one long scrape. Pain, as his sergeant had said, was weakness leaving the body. He'd given the other guy a fair dose of it.

In Cheyenne he got a tattoo on his upper arm, on a piece of flesh as smooth as a baby's skin. He'd been drinking with a repair crew on the north line, and when he talked about his face and the constant hassle, an old German told him if he had a tattoo of a double lightning bolt no one would mess with him.

"Face like that, you don't need to do a damn thing," the German said as they sat on a dead tree trunk pulled up next to the campfire. "They give you any grief, you let 'em see the tat. It'll send 'em off, tail tucked."

"Don't this mean I killed someone?"

"You did, right? In the war?"

The Burned Man looked away, out into a darkness shot through with trailing embers. "Yeah."

"So there you be."

"What if I run into a real banger?"

The German spit a long stream of tobacco into the fire. "You're white. You're a vet. You look like the devil threw you onto his personal bonfire. You'll be good."

That night the Burned Man dreamed that roots grew from his feet, going deep into the earth, and his hands reached toward the sky like saplings. It was him, growing up and growing old alongside his woman.

By the time he got to Denver, his heart was swept clean. He washed up and changed into his uniform in a gas station bathroom, walked to 38th Avenue, then stuck out his thumb and caught a ride north on Pecos with a guy on a milk run. In exchange for the lift, the Burned Man helped deliver the bottles, leaving the milk on narrow stoops while on the other side of walls, radios clicked on with morning shows and dogs scratched at doors. In the driveways, SUVs and minivans lumbered out of the dark, perspiring frost. A man drove a rumbling pickup down the street, a boy tossing newspapers from the bed.

The Burned Man looked at all this and thought maybe he could have it, too.

4

The milkman dropped him off at 47th. Here the city smelled of old things, like nature gone quiet. Wet earth and decaying leaves and the thin, waiting scent of dormant trees.

He walked three blocks past Victorian-style homes a hundred years past their youth, then turned north and at long last stood on the wide, root-cracked sidewalk in front of her rooming house, his eyes red with road dust, his ruck stiff with diesel oil, his boots worn from a thousand miles of desert sand and railroad rock and plain hard times. A glow of gold showed through the blinds in her second-floor apartment. Next to her window was the stick figure of a cat.

Hobo sign.

"Elise," he said, releasing her name from the tight place he'd held it.

The main door squeaked as he opened it. The hall was lit by a single bulb from an overhead light. Hot, dry air from the radiator filled the quiet space. A rug of faded roses lay damp and wrinkled on the floor, a single muddy boot print on the edge. The Burned Man stared at that print, and the heat of the desert curled in his bowels like a snake nesting.

I am home, he reminded himself.

I am safe.

The stairs creaked as he walked up, wood so old it sank in the middle, white-painted rails touched for over a hundred years by people coming in from the road.

On the landing outside her door, a night-light burned below the table where Elise kept a vase of fresh flowers. The petals had dropped, the water low in the glass and smelling of mold. The Burned Man went still, tight with the same unease he used to get approaching a neighborhood in Fallujah when nothing was out of place, not a single damned thing, but everything was *wrong*.

After a moment, he shook himself, set his ruck on the scuffed wooden floor, and knocked.

Silence. On the window to his right, looking out over the brown front lawn, ice that had glazed the glass overnight thinned under the warmth of the rising sun. Pale light crept into the hallway.

He tried the door. The glass knob turned readily under his hand. He picked up his ruck and walked in, his boots soundless on the tan carpet. A waft of chill air greeted him.

"Elise?" he called.

The front room was neat and tidy, dominated by the scarred oak table where tramps often sat to eat and talk. Two glasses of milk—one half drunk, the other untouched—sat on the table.

She's been busy, he thought. Too busy to clean.

A week, she'd told him, *I'll be done with everything else.*

In the kitchen, morning light splayed across the linoleum. A third glass was overturned on the counter, a dribble of milk splotched down the side of the sink. Seeing that glass, the Burned Man tried to close his hands around the stock of a rifle he no longer carried, his sense of wrong growing until it lifted the hairs on the nape of his neck. He grabbed a knife from the drawer near the stove and walked down the hallway beyond, telling himself maybe she wasn't here. Maybe she had changed her mind about him and fled before he arrived.

The air grew colder. In Elise's small guestroom, the bed was made, a stuffed Tweety Bird staring blankly from a mound of gingham pillows. From the nightstand he picked up a picture of himself and Elise taken before his deployment, her smile sweet, his expression cocky—unlined, unmarred, unscarred.

Back then he'd believed nothing could touch him.

Some instinct made him slide the photo, frame and all, into his ruck. As if already she was slipping away from him, and he had to grab this one thing. He went back into the hallway. Wind rattled the closed door of Elise's bedroom, and a draft came through, making his heart race. He closed his eyes before he opened the door.

"Elise?"

He walked in.

"You did this!" the man shouted through the Iraqi interpreter. He pointed at the dead woman lying in the street. Her body was stiff and fly-ridden, like she'd been there for a day or two.

"You killed her! I saw you!"

"Wasn't me, man." Tucker looked at the 'terp. "Tell him. We wasn't anywhere near here."

But part of him wasn't sure. They'd driven a patrol down this same street yesterday, and he'd opened fire from the turret of the Humvee when he heard a sharp click and thought maybe someone was triggering a bomb. Everyone was so damned afraid of the IEDs, those fucking human incinerators that ripped a man to hell and left him there.

So Tucker had reacted to that loud, metallic click. Or not so much Tucker, but his trigger finger, which didn't need Tucker to give it instructions. It knew how to survive.

"It wasn't me!" he shouted. "Wasn't me!"

"Wasn't me," he sobbed.

He looked down. In his hand was a knife, bloodied. Nearby, a filthy urinal and a dripping sink and a sign by the door telling employees to wash their hands.

Where *was* he? And where was Elise? What—?

What had he *done*?

The old, familiar shakes came on until his teeth rattled in his head and his vision danced, and he let out an animal cry. There was blood on his clothes and on his boots, and a buzzing noise as a fluorescent light flared on and off, on and off, and there was blood, no-blood, blood, no-blood as his back hit the wall and he slid down the tiles, plunging into an abyss of sand and shit and sweat and noise, and finally into a darkness that closed up after him and swallowed him whole.

Chapter 1

Our job, the duty of the Marines of Mortuary Affairs,
was to go in after the fact.
Once the grunts and the gunners and the insurgents had
done their job or died trying, we went in to pick up the HR—
the human remains. We cleaned up after the IEDs and the
armor-piercing ammo and the 81-millimeter mortar rounds.
We used gloves and tarps and scrapers. Sometimes just our
hands, scooping up flesh and pouring it into body bags that
sloshed as we carried them to the reefer.
                    —Corporal Sydney Rose Parnell. Denver Post.
                                        January 13, 2010.

Clyde and I left the house early, forced out by the dead private who was sitting, as he did most mornings, at my kitchen table. My grandmother, who could neither see nor hear the dead man, finished washing the dishes under the private's watchful eyes and placed the bowls in the side sink.

"I gotta go, Grams," I said.

Ghosts are the guilt we carry, a fellow Marine once told me. For what we did. For what we didn't do. For making it out alive. They're not real. Most of us get over it.

Grams wiped her hands then kissed my cheek with her paper-dry lips.

"Love you, Sydney Rose," she whispered. Then, as she said every day, "You be tough out there, girl."

I kept my eyes on the private as I picked up the paper bags on the counter and backed out of the kitchen, my K9 partner, Clyde, pressing hard against my thighs. Grams followed us into the hallway and held out my coat. As I pulled it on over my railway police uniform, she pretended to point to something out the front window. I pretended to look while she sneaked last night's leftover hamburger to Clyde.

"You'll get fat," I told Clyde as we stepped out onto the porch.

He ignored me, his black-and-gold face stoic, his Malinois ears swiveling as he took in the morning.

The air was crystalline, poised to snap, the temperature just below freezing. The wind had died, and our breath hung in the stillness. I yanked on my duty belt, pulling the strap to the last notch. It still sagged low on my hips, even with the leather keepers snapped to my uniform belt. Grams would slip me cold hamburgers if I'd take them. But I hadn't eaten much of anything for eighteen months. Not since the war.

Not since the ghosts.

"Survivor's guilt," I said to Clyde. "Remember that."

He yawned and licked his chops.

I loaded the paper bags into the back of my railway-issued Ford Explorer and tossed my college textbooks into the backseat before whistling Clyde into the front. I started the engine, flipped on the defroster, and Clyde watched while I scraped ice off the windows. By the time I got back into the cab, the interior smelled like anxious dog.

"Bath tonight," I told him.

He huffed, his breath a fog in the still-cold cab.

Backlit against the rising sun, Denver shrugged into the morning. Buildings and parks and bridges shambled into familiar forms. Neon signs still buzzed from the night before, their light anemic in the rising sun. To the east, the gold dome of the capitol building hung in the morning air, a glittering reminder of Denver's gold rush days. The city ran over and through me; its smog filled my lungs, its February chill pressed cold fingers to my face. For his part, Clyde watched out the window with an intentness only a former military dog can muster.

"Easy, boy," I said. "Just a regular Saturday."

Clyde's war had been hard, too.

At Hogan's Alley near the intersection of Denargo Street and Arkins, I parked the Explorer in a patch of dirt twenty feet off the road and surveyed the transient camp through the windshield. There was Trash Can's blue tarp and, a few paces beyond it, an unfamiliar military-green pup tent. The cottonwoods along the South Platte River—their branches glittering with frost—obscured the rest of the camp.

"Fucking suck of a time to be homeless," I said to Clyde.

I pinned up my braid and tucked it inside my ball cap, then stepped out into the morning. I strapped on the thigh holster with my backup sidearm and retrieved the bags from the back. Clyde hopped out of the cab after me. He sniffed at the bags in my hand and gave me his best look.

"You had yours, Clyde. And a hamburger to boot."

He looked away.

"Eating isn't how you solve your problems." I locked the car. "Let's go, boy."

The camp was silent as we approached, everyone still rolled in their blankets, sleeping off the night's drunk or trying to find the last slender shred of warmth. The fire in the middle of the camp had gone to ashes.

I stopped outside Trash Can's tarp roof and looked at the army blanket he'd hung over a low branch and duct-taped to the tarp for privacy.

"What are you doing back, Trash Can?"

A rustle from the other side of the blanket and a string of curses.

"You know I'm supposed to roust you guys," I went on. "Why you still here? You got a hate on me?"

"Agent Parnell," Trash Can said, relief in his voice.

"Your pancakes are getting cold."

The camp stirred to life, tent flaps lifting as worn, ragged forms emerged, blinking in the light and scuffing toward me across the dirt and weeds like extras in a zombie movie. I set the bags on the picnic table and laid out Styrofoam plates and plastic forks. The other police—those who knew about my weekly visits, anyway, Nik and the captain—thought I was crazy. But I had taken on debt in the war and had very little coin with which to pay it back.

Most everyone nodded in my direction, and all of them gave Clyde a respectful clearance. Everyone seemed twitchy today, eating fast and keeping their heads up. I saw Melody Weber, thought *shit*, and searched for her daughter, found the eight-year-old huddled under a blanket nearby. Melody had a three-inch cut across her chin.

I settled on a tree stump and waited. When Melody finished eating, I waved her over and studied the cut with a clinical eye.

"Again?" I asked.

She shrugged, her plump shoulders shivering under a dirty red sweatshirt. She held out her fingers toward Clyde, who sniffed them and allowed her to scratch behind his ears. Clyde didn't care for strangers, but he'd gotten used to our weekly visit to the camps, and he tolerated the touch of Melody and a few others.

"The world does enough to you without you staying with him," I said. "What about Liz?"

"He wouldn't never hurt her." Melody stared me down, defiant. "He loves that girl like she was his own."

"She'll grow up thinking it's normal for a man to beat the shit out of his girlfriend. You want that for her?"

"I teach her better than that. She knows." She was shivering hard enough her teeth chattered.

"Where's your coat?" I asked.

"I got it. Don't worry. I didn't lose it."

"Can't keep you warm, you don't wear it."

She glared, daring me to question her. "It's in the tent. Liz got cold."

I held my sigh. "I'm going to call a friend at Human Services. She'll pick you up, take both of you to the women's shelter."

"It's the ones who love us, hurt us the most, you know."

"What he does to you isn't love."

Melody shrugged. "You don't know everything."

"Dammit, Melody, you aren't helpless."

"Easy for you to say, being a cop and all." She dug a wad of fast-food napkins out of her jeans pocket and blew her nose. "What do you know about being trapped someplace and you can't get out?"

I flashed to our base in Iraq—the mortars, the gunfire. "Not much, I guess."

After I'd phoned and made arrangements with my contact at Human Services, I gestured for Melody to sit on the stump.

"You want me to fix up that cut?" I asked.

She nodded.

"Wait here."

Clyde followed me to the Explorer. As I came up the hill, I saw a short, skinny man standing near my truck, leaning over the hood and peering through the glass.

"Help you with something?" I asked.

He startled and glanced my way. Blue eyes gleamed within the shadow of his hoodie amid a tracing of tattoos. Chronologically, he was a teenager, just getting started down the road of his life. But the flat expression in those blue eyes was miles older. He must have hit some pretty deep ruts already.

He flipped me the bird.

"There's food down at the table if you're hungry," I told him. "But I need you to move away from the car. Dog's pretty possessive."

His gaze flicked to Clyde. Wordlessly, he spun on his heel and headed toward the road. I watched him until he was well away before unlocking the truck. Hard world sometimes, turning kids into jerks before they had time to do the job themselves.

Back at the camp with my first aid kit, I knelt on the frozen ground and donned a pair of latex gloves. Everyone had finished eating and most were heading out, moving fast and with glances all around.

"It just me, or is everyone skittish today?" I asked.

"Some, maybe."

Melody gathered her dishwater-blond hair in a fist and pulled it back while I worked. Her daughter watched blankly from the picnic table. Usually the little girl was all over Clyde, but today she had drawn into herself, knees pulled to her chest, chin tucked, a tight ball of heartbreak.

I poured hydrogen peroxide onto a cotton ball. "What's got everyone spooked?"

"The Burned Man's back," she said.

"He here now?"

"Not so's I know. Saw him early this morning when the train come through, but he didn't stay."

The Burned Man. A former Marine I'd seen once before. Never got a chance to talk to him. When I saw him, I thought, *Poor bastard.* I'd seen enough of his kind of injuries to wonder if he would have been better off dying.

Then again, I'd spent enough sleepless nights with the dead to be sure I had no right to ask.

I cleaned the cut, then applied antibiotic ointment, gauze, and finally white tape. Melody bore it all without complaint, her gaze somewhere I couldn't follow.

I sat back on my haunches, surveying my work and looking for other injuries. "The Burned Man hasn't caused any trouble, has he?"

She freed her hair. "He's like one of them monsters from the movies. Like the incredible melting man. He makes Liz cry."

"He ever threaten you?"

"Nah." She lit a cigarette, inhaled it like it was the Second Coming.

"Go freak on you, run around without his clothes?"

"Nah. Keeps to himself, mostly. Heard he got a mean temper."

"You ever see him get angry?"

"Nah." She shook her head. "Never seen him do much of anything."

"So, why so jumpy? Someone else roll in?"

She seemed to be deciding whether or not to answer when my headset buzzed. I excused myself, stripped off the gloves, and turned away to answer. My day shift had started more than four hours ago, at 3 a.m., and this was my work phone.

"Senior Special Agent Parnell," I said.

"Agent Parnell, this is Detective Cohen. Mike. Your captain told me you were on duty."

"I am, sir. What can I do for you?"

"You don't remember me. We worked a jumper together a year ago."

"I remember." I pulled his face up in my mind. Michael Walker Cohen, Denver PD, Major Crimes Division. Nice enough guy, but . . . weighted. Like he'd seen too damn much and didn't expect the world to show him anything different. He didn't blink when I led him over to the jumper's corpse. Body parts everywhere, and he didn't even put down his coffee. He just looked tired.

"You got another jumper?" I asked.

"We got a deceased white female cut to pieces in her own home. There are weird symbols all over the place, inside and out. We're thinking it might be hobo code. The crime scene guys are about finished, and the ME has already called the body snatchers. I was hoping you'd take a look first, though. Tell me what you see. I'm not exactly up on the code of the road."

"Hold on."

Clyde and I moved up the slope, away from the camp. The wind kicked a whorl of dirt into the air and flapped the makeshift tents.

Indifferent flakes of snow swirled by. A watery sun found a path through the clouds and flattened long shadows across the ground.

We got a deceased white female.

I curled my fists, feeling that panicked scramble between when you see the flash of a tracer round, dive for cover, and then—despite all your efforts—feel the bullet bury itself in your astounded belly. Down by the river the Sir, who'd been my commanding officer during the war, gave me a nod with his ghostly head. I could imagine what he would say to me if he had a tongue with which to speak: *There's no escaping death, Corporal Parnell. Not for any of us. Not even when you're young.*

Not even when you come home.

I squeezed my eyes closed. *Survivor's guilt.* When I opened them again, the Sir was gone.

"Parnell?"

"I'm here, Detective." I glanced over at Clyde, whose ears were pricked as he, too, looked toward the river. I brought my hands together and pressed until my knuckles went white. "Give me the address."

CHAPTER 2

In Iraq, the dead stay with you. You can't walk outside your tent or drive into the desert without feeling them all around. Americans will think I'm lying about this. Or I'm crazy. But it's true. In America, we don't know how to listen to our ghosts.

But they're here, too. They're everywhere.

[Pause] I shouldn't have said that.

—*Corporal Sydney Rose Parnell. Denver Post.*

January 13, 2010.

The victim's house was on a quiet, shabby street with root-cracked sidewalks and a scrim of dirty snow clinging to the curb from last week's storm. The bare oaks were twice my girth, the packed dirt beneath littered with a mat of decaying leaves. I'd patrolled here before; our track runs five hundred yards behind the east-side row of houses. Not a terrible neighborhood. But not one where I'd want kids playing after dark, either.

The house, a sprawling Victorian, listed gently. Scratched next to an upper-floor window was the stick figure of a cat.

Four police units were parked at the curb in front of the house, along with half a dozen unmarked cars. In a squad car with the engine running against the cold, a plainclothes cop interviewed an elderly woman. The woman wore a white knit hat and smoked furiously, the gray cloud rising like a smoke signal through a lowered window. Her face was red and knotted, wet with tears.

I parked on the other side of the street, popped a couple of Xanax from the bottle I kept in the glove box, and ordered Clyde into the heated crate in the back. He settled quickly, his head on his forelegs, watching me. Unhappy.

"You hate cadavers." I touched his head, and he thumped his tail. "I won't be long."

I grabbed my bag and crossed the street. On the sidewalk, the death fear hit me like a sucker punch. I bent over, waiting for the nausea to pass, glad that I hadn't brought Clyde with me; my fear would have traveled right down the leash to him.

The door opened and Detective Cohen stepped out. "Special Agent Parnell?"

I straightened fast and wiped my mouth with the back of my hand. "Shitty breakfast."

"Hear that," he said.

Our gazes met. Cohen, a tall, thirty-something man with too much experience in his eyes, was built like a junkyard dog—lean and hungry and ready to run with it. He wore a nice suit, but his hair looked like he'd cut it with manicure scissors. He needed a shave and his eyes were shot with red.

He struck me as a man who didn't much care what tried to get in his way. He'd keep moving forward until something gave.

"Need a minute?" he asked.

"I'm good."

I sucked in air and followed him up the steps.

"I saw your interview in the *Denver Post*," he said, making conversation as we walked through the house. "I had no idea about Mortuary Affairs."

"Most people don't." It was why I'd agreed to the interview. But as soon as I saw my name in print, I'd regretted it. People still didn't understand. And I'd said too much.

In the hallway outside the apartment, I signed the log offered up by a patrolman and reached for a pair of cloth booties to pull over my shoes.

"She's in the back bedroom," Cohen said.

"Got an ID on her?" I asked.

"Driver's license found in a purse in the kitchen is for Elise Hensley, age twenty."

Holding a bootie and balancing on one leg, I looked up at him. "Well, fuck."

"Know her?"

"Yeah. We weren't close, but yeah. She's niece to one of the men in my department. Senior Special Agent Nik Lasko. Elise was a good girl. Did well in school, never caused trouble. Did some modeling for a while. Works at Al's Diner on 36th." I snugged the bootie in place. "Worked."

Cohen looked away, the bones of his face shifting toward something heavy. Hard week, I figured.

Hard weeks pile up in his line of work.

"I'm sorry, Parnell," he said.

"You do a next-of-kin notification?"

"Not yet."

"Mind if I do it?" This would kill Nik. He loved Elise like a daughter, much as he had always loved me. His two orphans. Better the news came from me.

Cohen finally nodded. "Give me fifteen minutes inside first. Then the body crew can move her. You let Special Agent Lasko know, and we'll follow up with him later."

"Thanks."

The first thing I noticed was that the apartment was cold. The front room was full of people, none of whom I knew. Plainclothes Denver PD and detectives from the crime lab, probably. I might have been in training with some of these people but, if so, their faces hadn't registered. They nodded and went back to their work.

"There's a lot I want you to see in her bedroom," Cohen said. "First, though, take a look at some of these photos, see if you know any of these people."

There were framed photographs arranged throughout the living room and more covering the refrigerator door in clear, magnetized frames. I began a circuit, studying each picture. I noticed a Bible open on the dining room table, passages highlighted. A cross hung on the wall next to the largest collection of photos.

"Take your time," Cohen said.

I shot him a glance to see if he was being sarcastic, but he was writing something in an oversize spiral notebook.

I came to a stop in front of the refrigerator.

"Anything?" Cohen finally asked.

"They're hobos. All of them. Nik never shared this, but my guess is Elise was what is known as a kindhearted lady, someone who feeds the rail riders. That's what the drawing of a cat outside the window means. She probably helped them in other ways, too. Clothing. Jobs. Medical care if they needed it, rehab if they'd take it. Sometimes these women try to save them, in the Christian sense of the word. They're soul catchers."

"Soul catchers? You mean like some sort of voodoo thing?"

"Only if you consider the mysticism of the Holy Trinity a black art. Elise probably preached to them, tried to get them to accept Jesus in their hearts and return to their families."

"These guys have real homes?"

"Some of them. But often the families don't want them back. People who ride the rails usually have problems of one kind or another.

A lot of them are pretty antisocial." Something I understood. I shoved my hands in my pockets. "I'm ready to see the bedroom."

"One more room, first."

He led the way down the hallway. Our feet whispered on the plastic runner laid by the crime scene guys.

"This room," he said. "See anything in here?"

I took in the neatly made bed with its feminine quilt. A battered oak nightstand. On the bed was a bright-yellow Tweety Bird. I pointed it out.

"From one of the traveling carnies," I said. "Maybe Elise liked to go to those."

"We'll look into that. Last carny, though, would have been back in, what, August?"

"September. They came in on our trains." I raised an eyebrow at him. "Something here I'm supposed to notice?"

He shook his head. "Just wanted you to see everything."

I was turning away to leave when I noticed a disruption on the nightstand's thin veneer of dust. I turned back and crouched so I was eye level with the surface.

Within the fine dust was a clear patch about eleven inches long and two inches deep. "Someone took something," I said.

Cohen squatted next to me. "Framed photo, maybe." He went out and came back with a detective to take a photograph.

"Why take this photo and leave all the others?" I asked. "If a tramp killed Elise, he'd likely be in some of those pictures, too."

"This picture being right next to the bed," Cohen said. "It was probably someone special."

The detective placed a yellow marker on the nightstand, shot his photos, and left.

"I'm ready to see the body," I said.

Cohen stood, suddenly awkward. He glanced toward the door, as if making sure no one was there, then back at me. "Look, Agent Parnell, I want to thank you for your service."

I rose as well, shoulders stiff. "Where you going with this, Cohen?"

"It's a fucking mess in there. Whoever did this had a lot of rage. I'm sorry to spring this kind of body on you. Especially someone you knew, for Christ's sake. I know what you did in Iraq and—"

"Don't be an asshole, Detective." I held up a hand and mentally counted to five. "Look, I'm sure you mean well. But I'm a cop, okay? I'm not going to jump when someone says boo. That stuff you read about vets and PTSD and flashbacks and all? Mostly it's not true."

"No." He looked down at his shoes. "I see that."

But I'd caught the expression in his eyes before he looked away. No doubt he knew damn well how my nights went. I might as well get the fucking T-shirt.

While Cohen asked the three people squeezed in the back bedroom to give us a moment, I did a quick meditation, the way the VA counselor had taught me.

I am not here. I am far away. Nothing can touch me.

"Parnell?"

The others had cleared out. Cohen was looking at me again.

I took a breath; the Xanax unfurled in my blood like a roll of velvet. I stepped to the doorway.

The killing had been savage, leaving the victim no dignity even in death. Elise Hensley had been sliced and diced, her stomach opened, her bare arms flayed. The walls of the room were sprayed with arterial blood, her hair matted with it. From the wreck of her face, her eyes stared at the ceiling.

Everywhere along the walls, written over the blood and smearing it, were symbols drawn in what looked like black Sharpie. Circles and arrows, hatch marks. A stick figure of a cat.

The work of a madman.

"Damn," I said, thinking that this had to have been done by one of my homeless guys. By someone I *knew*.

"When we first saw these, we thought it was some sort of cult thing," Cohen said.

I shook my head. "You were right about it being hobo sign. Like the cat outside."

"What do they mean?"

"The circle with two arrows across it means to get out fast—hobos aren't wanted here. The circle next to the square means a bad man lives here. Elise have a roommate?"

"Not according to the landlady. An on-and-off boyfriend. Maybe the guy in the missing photo. What about the next sign, the one that looks like a snowman holding a ball?"

"It means sucker. Someone who is easy to catch."

"The killer describing himself in all of these?"

"Could be. But the cat means this is the home of a kindhearted woman. So why kill the kindhearted woman?"

"Beats the fuck out of me," he said. "Maybe because you're a bad-hearted man." A tic started in his jaw and his eyes went hollow. Could be murder cops get PTSD, too.

We put on masks and entered the room. Air coming in through the half-open window chilled my face.

"Left open to hide the odor?" I asked.

"Might buy the killer a day or two. But someone phoned it in."

"Who?"

"Anonymous call. A kid, sounded like. Teenager, maybe."

I bent down and looked under the bed.

"Your guys look under here?"

"Yeah. A couple of beads, right? They'll bag 'em when we're done."

I pulled the Maglite from my duty belt and played the beam beneath the bed. A cluster of dust bunnies shivered in the far corner. Three carved wooden beads had rolled against the baseboard, their colors bright. "Hobo beads. In case we weren't sure about Elise's connections. Your crime scene guys reach under the bed?"

"Only photos so far. Why?"

"The dust has been disturbed. Maybe the necklace broke in a struggle, and the killer tried to collect the beads and got scared off." I straightened, returned the flashlight to my belt. "You find any other beads?"

"One. Against the wall there."

He waited while I snapped my own pictures. I didn't ask permission, and he didn't ask what I was doing.

"Anything else you want me to look at?" I said. "I need to call Nik."

"That's it. Thanks, Parnell. Appreciate it."

Following Cohen out of the room, I stopped and made myself turn back. Elise had been a beautiful woman, with bright-blond hair and porcelain skin. The sweetest smile this side of the Mississippi, Nik always said.

Automatically, because cleaning up the dead had been my job for fourteen months, I made her beautiful once more. In my mind, I closed her wounds, washed away her blood. I shampooed her hair and combed it, arranged her slashed hands upon her breast. Then I did what no mortician could. I rebuilt her shattered face and restored the flush to her cheeks, the pulse to her throat. I made her smile.

In my mind, I made her whole.

"I'll hold you here," I whispered, touching my hand to my heart. It was what I said to all the dead.

Maybe that was why they crowded me so.

CHAPTER 3

The United States rail system has 140,000 miles of track. About half of these tracks are un-signaled, meaning conductors operate using written instructions and their watches. Operating a train in this so-called dark territory means driving blind with no way to detect other trains, misaligned switches, broken rails, or runaway rail cars. Any one of which might kill you.

—Sydney Parnell, ANTH 2800,
The Nature of Language

Back in my vehicle, I let Clyde into the front seat and watched as the medical examiner backed her van into the driveway. A small crowd of neighbors had gathered. It was a mixed crowd—mostly elderly couples and very young families, with a handful of middle-aged yuppies whose money had been gentrifying some of the nearby neighborhoods. I wondered if this murder would drive them away, send them reeling back to the suburbs or the safety of their downtown high-rises.

I called my captain and told him about Elise Hensley's death, that it had been ugly, and that I had been requested at the scene because of the hobo code.

"The victim was Nik's niece," I said, finishing.

"Goddamn." The meat of his fist connected with something. His desk, or maybe a wall. "I'll go with you to break the news to Nik."

Deputy Chief John Mauer—we called him Captain—came to Denver from Chicago. A decent man and a good chief. But we hadn't been stitched together at the hip like a lot of the railroad families, and Nik was private. The last thing he'd want was for Mauer to witness the first raw slap of his grief.

"It's probably better if I go by myself, sir."

"Don't need a Chicago boy tagging along. Right. Give Lasko my sympathies. Tell him anything he needs, I'm here. I'll cover your shift and let the rest of the agents know. Fuck, this is the worst."

"Yes, sir. Thank you, sir."

I hung up thinking Mauer had just gone up in my estimation.

Nik Lasko lived in the Royer district, a low-rent urban blot where a lot of railroading families had addresses when they weren't out on the line. My family had moved away from here eighteen years ago, when I was nine, after my dad had a falling-out with some of the union guys. When my dad walked out six months after that and my mom went to prison a year later, Nik took me under his wing—a long-ago promise he'd made to my parents. So Grams and I came back often, alighting like migrating geese for birthdays and anniversaries. Royer was the home that sang in my blood. My dad had been born and raised here, the son of a dispatcher and a brakeman; I had been suckled on the stench of diesel and the clatter of wheels, brought up on tales of union strikes and derailments and—to my childhood terror—stories of ghosts that followed the railmen home from distant lands. Ghosts that lingered in attics and cellars haunted the smoky confines of Joe's Tavern and stirred a cold wind in the alleyways.

The houses in Royer were older than my neighborhood, boxed in on two sides by warehouses and boom-then-bust factories. On the third side was I-70, swollen with traffic. Maybe everyone here slept better than my family did—surrounded by kin, lulled to sleep by the river-roar motion of wheels. No matter that some of those wheels glided on pavement instead of iron; they heeded the call to move, always move, rocking us to sleep with dreams of the white-line fever.

Royer had donated sons and daughters to the wars, more than its share. From Korea and 'Nam to the Gulf War and Operation Enduring Freedom. Probably back to the great wars, when a lot of these folks fled here from the poverty of Appalachia. Faded, weather-blotched ribbons fluttered in front yards as I drove past, and the cars on the street sported yellow ribbon decals and bumper stickers exhorting everyone to *Support Our Troops*.

I slowed as I turned onto Navajo Street. Five boys and a single, fierce-faced girl played soccer in the street leading to Nik's cul-de-sac. Beat-up orange cones served as goals; the curbs worked as the outside lines. The kids' faces were vaguely familiar from one of Nik's block parties. For all I knew, I was going to deliver bad news about someone they were related to—there was a good chance Elise was an aunt or cousin or a years-back babysitter. They glared at me as I drove past. With the exception of Nik, in Royer the law was an authority recognized only as an object of contempt. But the girl saw Clyde sitting in the passenger seat, and her face fell into an openmouthed gape of longing. I made a mental note to stop and let her meet him on the way out.

I parked in the driveway and stared at the single-story house with its recently painted green shutters and the white siding Nik had installed last summer with the help of his son and some local boys. A sturdy picket fence lined the front yard, and an American flag filled half the front window.

The Ford's engine ticked as I shut it off, pinging in the cold air. From the backyard, Nik's Doberman, Harvey, barked a couple of half-hearted woofs then lapsed into silence.

I draped my arms over the steering wheel and closed my eyes.

Nik was fifty-nine, but he hadn't slowed much with age. Still strong as a bull and with the same calm stubbornness. Grams had raised me, but Nik had shaped my life. He'd mentored me through boyfriends and algebra, through stolen cigarettes and faithless friends and my disillusionment with community college. He'd tried to talk me out of enlisting and, when I signed up anyway, he'd tried to listen when I came back broken.

That was hard for him. Nik was more of a fake-it-till-you-make-it kind of guy when it came to dealing with tough times and dark thoughts. After my tours, he bought me whiskey down at Joe's Tavern and told me we all had ghosts to carry. I wanted to ask him if his ghosts sat at his kitchen table or followed him around at work. But I didn't want him thinking I was certifiable. I drank my whiskey and kept my mouth shut. Nik went on to say that the anger and the memory problems and the nightmares would eventually stop, and that it was best not to talk about them because that gave them weight. "Weight with a capital *W*," he'd told me. "The hardest pounds you'll ever work to shed." Nik had been a grunt in 'Nam; he knew what he was talking about. So I listened and learned, did my best to be as stoic as he was. When I told him I wanted to be a railroad cop, one of the first women to do so, he'd clapped my back, and we'd switched from Johnnie Walker to Macallan.

In the Ford, I lifted my head. In a few short minutes, Nik would have Weight again.

A sudden gust rocked the truck like a reminder that I couldn't wait forever. Clyde gave a delicate, inquiring bark. I opened my eyes and scratched behind his ears.

"Right, boy. No time like the present."

Nik was waiting for us at the door. He'd been smiling as we came up the walk, but when I didn't smile back, his expression went flat.

"This can't be good," he said.

I looked down. Someone had scratched a line through the word *Welcome* in the doormat, slicing right through the plastic. Nearby were the remnants of a swastika someone had spray-painted on the concrete.

"What the hell?" I asked.

"Punks. Hit a bunch of the houses here."

I looked up and caught his eyes. "Nik, it's—"

But he shook his head. "Let's do this right, whatever it is. Come inside, Sydney Rose."

He led Clyde and me to the kitchen and poured coffee without my asking. He put nondairy creamer on the old pine table next to the sugar bowl, then sat across from me and shook a couple of antacid tablets out of a bottle. He'd obviously just begun his day: the coffee was fresh and his hair was wet from the shower. He had a piece of tissue stuck on his cheek where he'd cut himself shaving. Nik still used a straight razor, or so his wife had told me. "The man shaves like he's making penance," Ellen Ann had said. "I offered to buy him a horsehair shirt, but he said he'd make do with the razor."

I nodded at the tissue, tried to make my voice light. "You still haven't gotten the hang of that?"

"Hands aren't as steady as they used to be."

More Weight.

Clyde tolerated Nik petting him for a minute, then took up a post at the back door. Nik's Doberman barked once through the door, Clyde growled, and they were done with the territory thing.

"How's school going?" Nik asked.

I accepted the delay. "We're still on winter break. Just picked up my books for this semester."

"Good. That's good. Don't quit, Sydney Rose."

"No." I stirred sugar into my coffee. "I needed this. Thanks."

"You're welcome."

He didn't meet my gaze, so I gave him some time. I looked around the tidy little kitchen with its rooster-themed wallpaper and blue countertops. I'd sat in this kitchen, at this table, hundreds of times. Doing homework, eating Ellen Ann's Appalachian stew, filling out the paperwork for my Marine enlistment. Often other people were here, too, railroad employees come around to ask Nik's advice or sample Ellen Ann's cooking or just shoot the breeze. Sometimes Grams came with me to chop vegetables or knead bread dough so that she and Ellen Ann could talk.

The wooden pendulum clock on the wall filled the silence with its thick, syrupy voice. *Tick . . . tock . . . tick . . . tock.*

I'd traded words with Elise now and again at this table. But there was a gap of almost seven years between us, and we had little interest in each other. She was still just a big-eyed, scrape-kneed kid in a training bra when I left for Iraq.

I glanced out the window over the sink, into the dead yard with its scattershot rim of dormant poplars. Overhead, the sky was washed lead. A jet stitched a line down the middle.

Nik cleared his throat. "I figured the railroad would be downsizing."

"What? Oh. Nik, it's not your job. We all have our jobs. Our jobs are fine."

His hands went still, wrapped around his coffee mug. "Tell me."

My courage failed. I opened my mouth. Closed it.

"Sydney Rose." His voice held a warning.

"It's Elise."

"She hurt?"

"Worse."

"An accident?"

"Homicide called me."

He made a small noise that seemed to originate in his chest and swell through his throat. His eyelids lowered slowly over the blue irises and lifted just as slowly. As if he were moving from the first act of his life to whatever might lie beyond.

"Wait," he said.

He got up, opened the cupboard over the refrigerator, and pulled out a bottle of Johnnie Walker. He poured a generous amount into his half-empty coffee cup. When he raised the bottle again, I hesitated only a moment before pushing my cup toward him.

He poured almost as much in mine.

We drank in silence for a few minutes, the whiskey lighting a welcome fire I'd managed to avoid for two weeks now.

Do you drink more than one alcoholic beverage a day? the VA questionnaire asked.

On my good days.

Do you take street drugs or abuse prescription meds?

Not as often as I should.

"Where is Ellen Ann?" I asked.

"With her sister. Spent the night. They do a sleepover the last Friday of every month, like they were still girls. Watch movies, eat popcorn." He drained his cup and poured more whiskey in, not bothering with the coffee. When he moved to pour more for me, I waved him away.

He set the bottle down and rubbed his hand hard over his face. "I've been worried about Elise. Letting all those tramps into her home. Welcoming them like they were good men who just needed a taste of God to set them straight. I told her. Goddammit, I told her."

He sank his face into his hands.

I knew better than to touch him. I waited him out while he gathered himself into that tight, controlled place where he spent so much of his life. I waited and listened to the clock until I thought its steady tick would drive me mad.

Finally he looked up.

"What happened to her? Tell me everything."

I told him. Some of it. About Cohen's phone call and going to Elise's and the hobo sign scrawled on her wall. But not all of it. He didn't need to know what some madman had done to his girl.

When I finished, he stood and cleared our coffee cups, rinsing them before setting them in the sink. He cranked the window open a couple of inches to let in some air, then stood for a long time, gripping the edge of the counter and staring out the glass.

"I am so sorry, Nik."

"You let them move her?"

"The medical examiner was ready." Nik said nothing, and I got defensive. "Wasn't my call."

"So you didn't think to pick up the phone and say, 'Nik, get your ass down here right now' and give me the chance to see her?" His voice cracked. "Didn't give me the chance to know exactly what was done to her, what she suffered?"

"It's not how you want to remember her."

He slammed the sideboard. "Damn it, Sydney Rose, she's *family*. It isn't about what I want. It's about what she deserves. We *do* for each other."

I flashed to what Detective Cohen had said before he took me in to see Elise. How patronizing I'd found him and how angry his words had made me, even though I now realized his intentions were good. "I should have called."

He gave me his back a few minutes longer. When he finally turned around, he was calm.

"Who's working it?"

"Mike Cohen. And his partner, I assume."

"Cohen the guy you worked that jumper with?"

"Yes."

"What are your thoughts on him?"

He's haunted, I wanted to say. Tired. "Decent sort. Works hard. Seems sincere enough."

"*Sincere.* What I mean, Sydney Rose, is what kind of cop is he? What's his record? How many perps have walked under him?"

"Nik, I don't know. We worked together all of two days before he ruled the case a suicide."

"You agreed with his assessment?"

"Yes."

"Any chance he'll do that to Elise?"

"Rule it a suicide?" I held his gaze. "No."

We both jumped when the front door banged open and a cheerful male voice called down the hall. "Dad? Is Sydney here? Where's Clyde?"

"I'll tell him," Nik said quietly, just before his son walked into the kitchen.

Gentry Lasko, Nik and Ellen Ann's golden child. The center of their universe, for whom they'd sacrificed everything to put him through law school. Brilliant, cheerful, with a tall and sturdy build, Gentry was the kind of guy who took over a room just by walking in. A handsome brute—as he called himself—who'd e-mailed me every day while I was in Iraq and earned my undying love for it.

I stood to hug him.

"Syd! I knew that was your unit parked in front." He hauled me into a bear hug then pulled away and kissed both my cheeks. "Damn, girl, you look good. Pale, though. You need a few days on the beach. Am I right? Where's Clyde?"

Clyde had been waiting for Gentry to notice him. He barked and wagged his tail, his tongue hanging as he hopped up on his back legs. Gentry bear-hugged Clyde, too, then hauled him down to the floor to alpha-roll him. Other than myself, Gentry was the only person—man, woman, or child—whom Clyde genuinely loved. I figured it was because Gentry so resembled Dougie, who'd once been the love of Clyde's life.

And mine.

For an instant, I could *see* Doug Ayers standing in front of me, grinning at something I'd said. Tall and blond and raucous, in my face and full of life. Looking at him, I laughed, too, and took his hand.

Three of his fingers were missing, the stumps oozing blood. I lifted my eyes to his, but they'd gone dead.

I blinked.

Gentry play-wrestled Clyde for a few minutes, then rose and turned toward his father. Immediately he froze, the merriment leaving his face as if someone had doused him with ice water.

"Dad? What's happened? What is it?"

Nik kept his eyes on Gentry. "Give us a minute, Sydney Rose."

I whistled to Clyde, and we went out to the porch. I looked for the kids playing soccer, but they had vanished, leaving behind one partially crumpled orange cone. I hunched against the wind, eyeballing the remnants of the swastika on Nik's porch and wishing I'd brought the whiskey. Clyde pressed close against my legs, and I laid my hand atop his head, finding comfort in his steady presence.

From inside the house, Gentry's voice rose in a raw cry. Clyde barked. I heard Nik's low rumble, another cry, and then Gentry slammed out through the front door. He gave me a wild-eyed stare and ran to the curb.

"Gentry!" I hurried after him. "Wait!"

But he threw himself into his cherry-red muscle car, started the engine, shifted into gear, and punched the gas, screaming away from the curb. The orange cone flew up from his wheels, bounced into the gutter. Seconds later he turned the corner and disappeared.

I went back inside to find Nik in the hallway, fists balled, looking like he'd been pistol-whipped. I walked him back to the kitchen, and this time I was the one who poured the whiskey.

Nik opened the kitchen window wider then rooted in a drawer and dredged up a pack of cigarettes even though I knew he'd promised Ellen Ann he had quit. He offered the pack to me. In the chill air, we sat at the table and lit up with matches from Pete's Diner on Colfax. I hadn't had a cigarette in a month, and the nicotine hit felt even better than I remembered. I pulled smoke hard into my lungs.

"He'll be okay," I said, knowing the words to be a lie.

Nik used an empty glass as an ashtray. "I know who did this."

I thought of the photos in Elise's living room and kitchen, the hundred or so faces staring out through the lens of the camera.

And the hobo sign in her room. *A bad man lives here.*

"How can you know?"

"Elise had taken up with a kid named Tucker Rhodes," Nik said in a flat voice. "Born and raised in Montana, but he landed in Denver after a tour in Iraq. Kid was hurt bad a few days before his tour ended. Trapped in a Humvee that ran over an IED. Third-degree burns over thirty percent of his body. The VA tried to do everything for him, but after a few surgeries he walked away from any kind of help. The Corps hit him with a dishonorable discharge."

"For skipping out on the surgeries?"

"For going AWOL. He took to hopping freights, catching work here and there. Basically a bum. Don't know what Elise saw in him except something hurt that needed saving."

Tucker Rhodes. The Burned Man. Had to be. What Nik hadn't said, although I knew he was thinking it, was that Tucker Rhodes was a coward for walking away from whatever help the military might offer. Counseling. Medications. Ways to mitigate the pain. Help that might have saved both him and Elise.

Something obstinate rose in me. "Getting help from the VA isn't always easy."

Nik gave me a steely stare. "You are *not* defending him."

"No. If he did this, then he deserves whatever the law throws at him. I'm just saying there isn't as much help to be had as people think. Nor do we know he's guilty."

"He's a killer."

We're all killers, Nik, I wanted to say. All of us who have seen combat. Some of us haven't figured out how to turn from killers to suits when we come back to the land of plenty.

I knocked ash into the glass. My hand shook on the cigarette. How many mangled bodies had I pulled from Humvees and tanks and the slow-moving five-tons with their five-hundred-gallon water buffaloes and loads of Meals Ready to Eat? How many men and women had I touched, Marines missing limbs and eyes and ears, their intestines spilling into the dirt, their faces blank with shock or white with terror?

If the Burned Man had brought that back with him, how responsible was he for making a mess of his life? For Elise? I'd danced on the edge myself more times than I wanted to count, found myself looking across that thin red line at something monstrous.

"Why do you think it was him?" I asked.

"Twice he hurt her. Twice I know of. Popped her in the face. I didn't hear about it until he'd run off and left her." The words came out like talking hurt. "Then she goes and talks him home. She was going to marry the son of a bitch."

"They were in love?"

Nik went to stand by the window. "Elise didn't much separate her feelings for a stray cat with how she felt about the man she planned to spend her life with. She felt sorry for Rhodes. She thought she could fix him."

"If he loved her, then why would he do such terrible—why would he end her life?"

Nik was suddenly breathing hard, his lungs going like bellows, and I knew he'd heard what I'd almost said. *Why would he do such terrible things to her?*

"Nik, I didn't mean—"

He talked over me, uninterested in apology or explanation. "Maybe Elise had come to her senses. Maybe she told him she couldn't marry him, and he flipped out."

"You're making a pretty big leap. Guys hit their wives, their girlfriends. Sometimes the woman hits back. But it doesn't usually end with—"

My throat closed as the past rose up like a fist. *Murder*, I'd almost said, before thinking of my mother and the man she'd taken up with even before my father left. The man the law said she'd shoved in front of a train during a drunken spat. The judge had sentenced her to twenty for second-degree murder. But she'd been dead of cancer before she'd served a year. With my dad still MIA, I'd effectively become an orphan.

Nik saw it immediately. "Ah, hell, Sydney Rose. I'm sorry."

I looked down and forced together the ragged edges of my childhood, zipping closed old wounds. After a minute I said, "It doesn't make Rhodes guilty."

"Well, maybe I'm wrong. I hope to God I'm wrong. I hope the last thing Elise saw before she died wasn't the face of someone she—"

He stopped. Blinked.

"Fuck of a day," I whispered.

We waited. Smoked. Let the roar of our pulses calm enough to allow in the sounds of the clock and the traffic.

Nik said, "Tucker's the most likely, isn't he? We're usually betrayed by those who claim to love us best."

I felt my own Weight. "He was in camp this morning. At Hogan's Alley. One of the transients saw him."

Nik crushed his cigarette out in the sink, closed the window. "He still there?"

"Not when I was, as of 0800. He'd come in on a freight and walked out." I pulled out my cell phone. "I'll tell Cohen."

"You do that. But I'm going to find him first."

"How do you plan to do that?"

"I'll start with the camp. Maybe he told someone where he was going. Maybe he's back there. Or he could have caught out already and someone saw him. I'll find him."

I dropped the phone back in my pocket. "This can't be about vigilante justice."

"I'm not saying that's what I mean to do. But I will not let this man go. I will not let him ride into another jurisdiction and disappear under some overworked sheriff's paperwork. Rhodes could be halfway across the country by now. You know that. So you go ahead and call Cohen, but I'm not waiting on Denver PD. If he's caught out, he's mine."

"We aren't murder police."

Nik stared at the whiskey bottle for a long time, as if contemplating finishing it off. Instead, he capped it and returned it to the cupboard above the refrigerator, out of easy reach. He squared his shoulders at me. "How long you been on the force?"

"Just over eighteen months."

"I've been working the trains longer than you've been alive, Sydney Rose. Forty years, the last twenty as a railroad cop. Since I was sixteen I've worked the lines. The only time I took off was a stretch in the Corps when I was nineteen. I've worked jumpers and gangbangers and serial killers. I've handled bombers and thieves and dealt with the general scum of the earth. I'm a Level I POST-certified peace officer like every goddamn cop in Denver, and have been since before your city detective got his ears wet at the academy." He stabbed a finger at me. "Now you sit there and tell me that I am not qualified to track down this piece of shit. You tell me that, Sydney Rose, and I'll put my feet up on the desk and stare down at a belly grown fat, and I'll sit that way until I die."

I took in his anger, understanding it. But I was shaking. I didn't want to be dragged into another death investigation. I'd left that behind in Iraq. I didn't want to go to the autopsy, give up Tucker Rhodes's name, embroil myself in Elise's death. I didn't want the *Weight* of Elise's soul.

I would hold her in my heart. But I didn't want her at my breakfast table.

As if reading my mind, Nik said, "I don't need your help on this. You call your detective then go into the office and tell the captain I'm searching for a trespasser. I'll do this on my own time."

"Nik—"

He held up a hand. "I'm police and I'm kin. No one knows the lines and the yards like me. If Rhodes caught out, I've got a better chance than anyone of finding him. If he's sitting on a siding somewhere or hiding in a DPU, he's on railroad property, and that makes him mine."

I drew a deep, shuddering breath. "They won't talk to you."

"What?"

"The transients. They won't tell you anything."

"They'd damn well better."

"That's just it, Nik. You're too old school. They're afraid of you."

"Then get me started."

I saw in his eyes what he wouldn't say. He needed me to do this more than he'd ever needed anything from me.

I looked out the window. The crows had flown away. There came a lull in the traffic. The world lay empty. Even the ghosts I'd brought back with me were gone, although I could hear the whisper of their passage across the pale, dead grass in Nik's yard. I looked for the Sir in the tangled scrub oak in the field behind Nik's yard, but there was only the rattle of the wind.

I turned back, the familiar nausea in my gut. "Just this one thing, Nik. I'll talk to the people at the camp. But we notify city police. And as soon as we have a lead, we step out, let them handle it. Deal?"

He nodded. "That's the way you want it."

But he was lying, and I knew it. Nik wouldn't let this go. He'd track Tucker Rhodes to the ends of the earth. He'd hunt the boy down every rail line and road and dirt track until one of them finished it.

Chapter 4

Why did I re-up? Because when I came home, I didn't know how to be home. Didn't know how to fit in anymore. Didn't know what to do with myself. I missed the order. The adrenaline. The sense of larger purpose.

War is a drug; it'll call you back until it kills you.

—Corporal Sydney Rose Parnell. Denver Post.

January 13, 2010.

The sky had lowered when Nik and I emerged from his house. Slow, fat flakes fell and melted on the asphalt. The air was raw. I opened the rear door of the Ford and Clyde jumped into his carrier. I got in behind the wheel. Nik stood on the other side of the truck, his forearms on the roof as he leaned into the closed door and stared at the curb where Gentry's car had been parked thirty minutes earlier.

Through the glass and the swirl of snow, Nik's face looked as if someone had bulldozed the foundation of his cranial bones, the skin pocked and falling like a ruined house. It hit me that Nik was no longer young. And that maybe sometimes age comes in an instant. Nik had been fifty-nine years young right up until I sat at his kitchen table and told him about Elise.

Now there was nothing young about him.

After a moment, he slapped his open palm against the metal roof and climbed into the cab. I started the engine and backed out of the driveway as snow gathered on the grass. The warmth from the whiskey had fled, and I was both tired and painfully sharp, the way I had felt in Iraq after a shift processing the dead. In Camp Taqaddum, I'd walk outside into the 3:00 a.m. night, always with company because sometimes the male Marines weren't my best friends. We'd stand outside and smoke, me and Bailor or Tomitsch. Sometimes the Sir. Whoever'd been with me on shift. We'd listen to the passage of ghosts, our senses scraped raw after handling flesh that would never know of our touch.

"The hardest pounds," Nik said.

I glanced over, saw the Weight collect on him as he began his own walk with the dead. His hand cupped mine for an instant.

"Glad it was you who brought the news, Sydney Rose."

At Hogan's Alley, I pulled into the same patch of dirt where I'd parked that morning and turned off the engine. The snow hadn't started to fall here, yet. A light wind blew. Trash Can's tarp and the green pup tent were gone. I zipped my coat and grabbed my bag.

"Wait here," I said. "You'll just intimidate everyone."

"To hell with that."

I shrugged and said, "Your show."

This time I leashed Clyde. On a lead or not, he'd feel my anxiety, and I didn't want him deciding on his own if someone was a threat. It's easier to call a dog out than to call him off.

The camp was empty save for one person, a black woman in her forties with the road name Calamity Jane. Calamity Jane had been hopping trains for eight years; she had to be one tough bitch to have survived. Blacks on the rails were rarer than hen's teeth, women near as scarce. A black woman stood out like a crow trying to hide in a flock of pigeons.

Jane sat atop the picnic table, hunched over with forearms on thighs as she slowly swayed, a ratty quilt draped over her shoulders and a homemade cigarette hanging from her lips. She was whip-thin under her gray sweat-shirt and blue jeans, her long feet thrust, sockless, into filthy Keds. Her hair was greasy and shot through with gray, her eyes at half-mast.

We stopped next to the table.

"Morning, Jane."

She blinked at me. Recognition filtered in like light through a dirty window.

"Senior Special Agent Parnell. And Clyde." She squinted. "Your first name Bonnie?"

I smiled and shook my head. "How's life treating you, Jane?"

"Rough here. Rough there." She barked a phlegmy laugh. "Rough all through. So who cares?"

Her voice was husky, tattered, as if her vocal cords had been scraped raw. She pursed her lips, blowing cigarette smoke up into the skies, then knocked ash on the ground. "Heard I done missed your pancakes."

I gave her a chocolate bar from my bag. She tucked it into the pocket of her sweatshirt.

"You can get food at the shelter," I said, my voice soft.

"Yeah." She snorted. "I get me a steamed hot dog, then some shit be wanting head as payback. I done with that."

Nik had had enough of the pleasantries. "We're looking for someone."

Her eyes cut to him, and she used one skinny fist to gather the blanket at her throat. "Yeah?"

"A bum known as the Burned Man. You seen him?"

"He been around. Came in early, when it all still dark. Took off near as fast. What you want with that poor boy?"

"He's a material witness."

She waved a hand dismissively. "We all material witnesses. Only we ain't got none of the material." She cackled.

"You heard anything about where he might have gone?"

"He didn't do no check-in with me, that what you asking."

Nik exhaled sharply, his last bit of patience a single thread in a fraying blanket. "What *do* you know?"

"Maybe I seen him."

"Where?"

She shrugged, coy. "Then again, ain't nobody paid me to watch him."

Nik leaned in, putting his cop's eyes on her. "You want to tell the same story down at the station?"

"You can't arrest me 'cause I don't know where that boy is."

"Loitering. Vagrancy. Illegal drug use. Vandalism. Trespassing." He put his hands on the table and stepped in until his face was inches from hers. "I can haul you in for ass-fucking a rabbit if that's what I decide you did. You get my drift, you piece of filth?"

Nik. Old school all the way.

Jane dropped the blanket. She looked ready to take a swing at Nik, and I began to get an idea of how she'd lasted on the rails.

"Ah, Jesus, Nik." I grabbed his arm, yanked him back, out of earshot. It was his show, but that didn't mean he had to throw it all away. "You're going about this all wrong."

"She knows where he is."

"Maybe. Give her a chance to share. These people, it's all about honey. They get enough shit from everyone else. You really want to find Rhodes, be smart about how you do it."

He looked at my hand on his arm, and for a moment it was like he didn't see me at all, just something standing in his way. I released him and gave him my own cop's eyes. "Nik."

It took him a moment, but he came back. "Right." He moved back toward Jane and nodded at her. "Sorry."

Jane lifted her chin and shoulders, pissed off and righteous. "There no call for him to be talking to me like that. I ain't some trash he can shit on."

"We just want to have a little chat with the Burned Man," I said. "A bad thing went down this morning, and he might have seen something. You notice when he came and when he left?"

She kept her eyes on Nik, but relented. "Don't know 'xactly when he come in the first time. Just heard people goin' on about his face. But I was here when he come back. One, maybe two hours ago. Left on a freight after that."

"Going which way?"

For the first time, she seemed uncertain. She lifted her hands, dropped them, then finally jerked a thumb over her shoulder, pointing north.

"You sure?" I asked.

"Yeah." She didn't meet my eyes. "I'm sure."

"Powder River," Nik said. "Bastard's leaving the state."

"What else, Jane?"

"What you mean?"

"Something's got you nervous. What aren't you telling us?"

"Nothing." She kept her eyes on the ground. "Ain't nothing else."

"Jane. C'mon, help us out. If there's something you know—"

"Ain't *nothing*. I told you what I know." She shot me a defiant look. "Believe whatever make you happy."

"Okay." I blew out a breath. "You happen to see what part of the train he caught?"

"Just that most the dragon done gone by."

"He set up camp at all?"

She shrugged. "Spent time in his usual spot. Started a fire. It got quiet, so I up and took a look. He just sitting there. Thought he was drunk asleep, too tired even to lie down. Soon as that train come, though, he moving like the Devil after him."

"Show us where he camped," Nik said.

Some fire came back in her eyes. "Tell me why I should help, you talk to me like that."

Nik spread his hands. "Bad day. Nothing personal."

She sniffed. "Well, then."

She squashed out her cigarette and hefted herself off the table. We followed as she pushed through the brush and shuffled down the slope toward the riverbank. She stopped under a cluster of cottonwoods and pointed toward a cleared space that held a fire pit in the middle of a twenty-by-twenty-foot patch of dirt. To one side of the cleared area was a heap of trash, neatly scraped into a pile and weighted down with rocks. Next to that, a small stack of canned food—hash and tuna and peaches. On the other side of the clearing, Rhodes or someone had dragged a fallen tree to a place where a man could sit and watch his food warming on the fire and think about what he'd done with his life, what he still might do.

I thanked Jane, gave her a twenty-dollar bill, and she turned back the way we'd come. I heard her crash through the underbrush, then silence.

I led Clyde to a patch of ground away from the camp and ordered him to stay. He watched me curiously, waiting for me to give him something to do.

Nik squatted on the edge of the cleared area and surveyed the camp. I stood over him.

"There was no need for that," I said.

"We missed him by an hour."

"I mean it. This isn't a good idea. You shouldn't be here."

"Won't happen again."

"Good." I tugged off the pins holding my braid and stuck them in my mouth while I tucked stray strands back into the plait and re-coiled it under my cap. "You want to hold this area while I call Cohen and lead him here?"

But Nik was staring at the pile of cans. "Why'd he leave all his food?"

"I don't know. Maybe he wasn't thinking clearly. Maybe he wanted to go light."

"You got gloves in that bag? And a camera?"

"We have our lead, Nik. We're done here."

"We're right on top of his camp." He stood. "Let's give the regulars a little more than a possible lead from a strung-out bum, okay? Let's pretend we're cops a few minutes more and give your detective something to work with."

I glanced down the river, toward the snarl of cheatgrass and thistle where I'd seen the Sir that morning. I let Nik's nastiness go. It was grief talking. And grief was why he needed to see things through. I got it.

The dead can be very compelling.

Plus I'd never been able to stand up to Nik. Going along with him now would cost me something with Cohen. But Nik was essentially family. And in Royer, family is always first.

I shrugged. "You're pushing it," I said, just to make my point.

He knew he had me. "Appreciate it, Sydney Rose."

I opened the bag and handed him the box of latex gloves. I removed the camera and took shots of the camp and the surrounding area, stepping carefully around the periphery of Tucker Rhodes's jungle as I photographed from all angles. The packed earth held few footprints, but I took shots of what was there. Snapped a lot of zooms of the fire pit and the trash.

When I was done, I hung the camera around my neck.

"You want the trash or the pit?" I asked.

"I'll take the trash."

We got to work. I found a broken branch and knelt on the ground, the cold pressing through my uniform. I began carefully sifting. Rhodes had shoveled dirt into the fire pit, but heat still rose from underneath. The warmth hit my face, welcome. I thought of Rhodes, crouched in a rear locomotive or maybe freezing in a gondola rattling open to the sky. I wondered if snow was falling on him, if he saw blue sky or gray.

I pulled out a tin can, cut neatly in half and still full. Pinto beans. So he'd eaten a little. Or started to eat. I hooked the stick into the can and set it aside.

"A note," Nik said from the other side of the cleared space. "In Elise's handwriting."

I looked over. Nik held a piece of paper. It was worn and creased, as if Tucker had read it over and over.

"She's asking him to come home," Nik said.

"Bag it," I told him, keeping my voice detached. I watched him for a moment then went back to work.

The cold crept up my spine. I flexed my frozen fingers and turned back to the fire. Underneath the can of beans was another layer of ash. As I pushed it aside, the air turned hot. Whatever was in there was still smoldering.

A piece of fabric emerged. A tan-and-brown pattern I recognized from Iraq. I dug faster. A couple more minutes, and I had enough fabric free of the pit to see that I was right. It was part of a Marine desert camouflage uniform.

From over by the trash pile, Nik made a noise. He was holding up a picture frame made of ceramic clowns. The glass was cracked, the frame empty. He stared at the frame as if he'd caught a rattler by the tail and was waiting for the thing to swing around and bite him.

I flashed to the dust-free spot on Elise's bedside table.

"It's Elise's," he said. He stood rigid, as if everything soft had gone out of his body. "She had a photo of her and Rhodes in it. Why would he kill her and then keep their picture?"

I shook my head, tilted my face up to the frigid air.

I did not want to look at that uniform, afraid of what it might reveal. For a moment, the Colorado cold disappeared, replaced by heat and flies and sand, and I was standing in our bunker, in the processing room, washing a body. Carefully I cleaned away the blood and dirt, the pieces of gray matter and spatters of internal organs that might or might not belong to the dead man. This particular body had no feet. No left hand.

The back of his skull was gone.

What about the missing parts? I asked as I made a diagram of the body. *Color them in*, said the Sir. *Shade them black.*

"Sydney Rose?"

I blinked. "His uniform blouse is here. In the pit. He tried to burn it."

This time Nik held the camera. I grabbed another stick and used the two pieces like tongs to tug the fabric free. Rhodes's entire uniform was in the pit. Blouse, trousers, and cover, folded tight. When I had the articles free of the pit, I used the sticks to unfurl them. They were tacky and gave way reluctantly. We saw why when I had the blouse and trousers open on the ground.

"Elise's blood," Nik said, looking at the red-black blooms on the desert camouflage. He wobbled on his feet and I caught his arm.

"Let me get the pictures, Nik. Take Clyde and go for a walk."

But he shook me off. "I'll do it."

"I'm calling Cohen."

He didn't respond. I watched him for a moment as he held the Lumix up and began snapping pictures. When I was sure he was steady, I stripped off my gloves and went to stand next to Clyde. Clyde moved close and looked up into my face.

"Good boy, Clyde," I said. "We're almost done here."

I dialed Cohen.

"It's Parnell," I said when the detective answered. "Elise Hensley's uncle ID'd a possible suspect for her murder. Said she was engaged to a war vet, a homeless man. There were a couple of domestic violence incidents. We're down at his camp now. Word is he came in this morning, early, then caught out maybe an hour ago."

"You got a name?" Cohen asked.

"Tucker Rhodes. Marine Corps vet. Originally from Montana. His uniform is here. He tried to burn it. Looks like blood all over it."

"Where are you?"

I gave him the cross streets.

"Hold on," he said. I heard talking in the background, then he came back on.

"My partner and a couple of uniforms are on their way. What do you mean he 'caught out'?"

"It's a hobo term. It means that if our witness is right, Rhodes hopped an empty coal train heading north. He could be halfway to the Wyoming border by now, depending on whether the train hit any delays. I can find out exactly where."

"I'll run him. Can you stop the train?"

"If that's what you want to do. Let me find out which train and where it is. I'll call you back."

I hung up and called NOC, the National Operations Center in Fort Worth. The Colorado chief dispatcher and I ran down a list of possible trains until we hit the one Rhodes had likely caught. Dispatch gave me the train symbol, the engine number, and a mile marker.

"You want me to stop it?" the dispatcher asked.

I heard the reluctance in her voice. Trains were only profitable when they had velocity—when they ran smoothly and stuck to their timetable. The crews, too, were on a strict schedule. Once they'd put in their twelve hours, they were dead on line, and you had to get them off the train. Didn't matter where they were. Top of a mountain pass in the middle of a blizzard, you had to get them off that train and back to town.

"I'll let you know," I said.

I disconnected and studied Rhodes's small jungle. The uniform, the uneaten beans, the clown picture frame, and the pile of canned food sitting in the open where any hobo could help himself to Rhodes's trove. There was something final in his actions. Not just that he didn't mean to come back here, to Denver. More like he was going someplace he wouldn't ever come back from. Burning his uniform made sense if he was hiding evidence. But it also made sense if he was severing his last ties to the world.

Nik finished with the pictures and came to stand with me and Clyde.

"He's going home, Nik. He's going to kill himself."

"You don't know that."

I gestured to the train tracks. "This line leads to Montana. He's going home to die."

Nik's face went hard. "I won't let him do that."

My headset buzzed. Cohen. I put my phone on speaker so Nik could hear.

"I found a Lance Corporal Tucker Rhodes of Shelby, Montana," Cohen said.

"That's him."

"No priors, no extraditable warrants. Dishonorably discharged after going AWOL from his treatments at a residence in Texas near Brooke Army Medical."

Meaning he had no right to wear the uniform. But as badly as he'd been hurt in the service of his country, who could blame him for feeling the uniform was still his?

"You find the train?" Cohen asked.

"It's outside Fort Collins, fifty miles south of the Wyoming border."

"He could have hopped off in Fort Collins," Cohen said.

"Have the police there put out an APB. But I think he's going home. To Montana."

"What makes you say that?"

"Call it a hunch."

"Okay." Cohen sucked in breath through his teeth; I heard the hiss. "He could also be trying to get as far north as he can. Canada won't expedite arrest warrants against Americans who risk the death penalty. If Rhodes knows that, he might be trying to make a run for the border."

"Could be."

"But you don't think so."

"I think he plans to kill himself. And I think he wants to do it in Montana."

"Based on what?"

"He shed his stuff. Food. Personal belongings. His uniform."

"Classic. Okay. But if he's going to kill himself, why wait until he gets to Montana?"

"You spend a lot of time on the other side of the world, watch your best friends get blown apart there?" My gaze traveled toward the river where I'd seen the Sir earlier. "You go through that, then you want to be home when you call it in."

"You think that's the way he's working it, that's what we'll run with," Cohen said. "We'll set up an ambush. I'll contact the Larimer County sheriff's office. We need a place along the line where SWAT can hide."

Nik identified himself. "There's an abandoned fertilizer factory ten miles south of the Wyoming border. It's a couple of miles west of the interstate, and the terrain is pretty flat, so even if he runs, he'll find it hard to hide. There's still a usable road leading directly to it, so SWAT won't have any problem getting in."

"How long before the train gets there?"

"Forty-five minutes, give or take," I said.

"That's tight."

"We can buy you some time," Nik said. "Have the crew stop on the tracks until the sheriff has his men in place."

But I shook my head. "Too risky. By now he figures there's a good chance we're looking for him. Anything out of the ordinary, he'll jump. We can slow the train down, buy another five minutes. Maybe ten. But I wouldn't stop it."

"Make it ten," Cohen said.

Nik took a few steps away and I heard him on his phone, talking to dispatch.

Cohen told me to hang on. Muffled voices whispered unintelligibly through the phone connection. Then he came back. "We're notifying the sheriff now. So this camp of his. Someone ID'd it as his personal camping spot?"

"Yes."

"Wish you'd invited me to the party."

I heard the anger in his voice and knew he was right. But I stuck by Nik. "You wouldn't know about the guest of honor without us."

"I'll call for an arrest warrant. Give me five." He hung up, called back in three.

"We've got the right judge handling warrants. Should go fast. You two want to be there when this goes down?"

"You want the victim's uncle to be part of the ambush?"

"He's a pro, isn't he? It's how we usually play things. And it's railroad property. Your arrest, if you want it. I don't believe in waltzing in on someone else's territory."

I ignored the dig. "Doesn't matter. There's no way we can make it. Not even if we push it all the way north."

"You gotta learn to think outside the box, Parnell," Cohen said. "How you guys feel about helicopters?"

Nik watched me over the hood of the Explorer while we waited for Cohen and the chopper. Cohen's partner, a dour-faced mountain of a man by the name of Len Bandoni, was already down at Rhodes's camp. A pair of uniforms was stringing up crime scene tape. The snow had finally arrived, falling steadily.

"You don't need to come, Sydney Rose," Nik said. "You gave what I asked."

"And you didn't. The deal was to get a lead then hand things over to regular police."

"We pulled Cohen into it."

"That wasn't what we agreed."

He shook out a cigarette. "It's Elise, for Christ's sake."

"I know." I poured water in a bowl for Clyde and watched him drink. "I know, Nik. I understand. It's the reason I'm not yelling at you. But you're too close to this. You almost lost it with our witness."

He lit the cigarette and flicked the match away. "I'm not going to shoot him."

"So you say."

He came around the hood of the Ford. Clyde was instantly up and standing between us.

"Out," I said to Clyde, giving him the command to back down. Reluctantly he went to heel, but he kept his eyes on Nik.

"I need to do this," Nik said. "And Cohen invited me personally. Once Rhodes is in custody, I'm good, okay? I'll let the law do what it needs to do."

I folded my arms.

Nik said, "But I was wrong earlier. What I said about you going back to the office. I want you to come."

"No."

"Clyde could use Rhodes's uniform."

"What?"

"To smell him out. If Rhodes slips out between the searchers, Clyde could track him from the scent of his uniform."

"The sheriff has K9 teams."

"You ever know an air scent dog good as Clyde? Or a dog as likely to stay the course?"

"Damn it, Nik."

"You will make me beg, won't you, Sydney Rose? Fine. I'm begging. We're talking about *Elise*, for Christ's sake. If Rhodes slips through this ambush, he could disappear forever into Canada. If he ends up killing himself, justice will never be served."

"Not our justice, maybe."

He inhaled, blew smoke. "There isn't any other kind."

I heard a steady *whop-whop* high above us. I glanced up to see the police bird approaching.

"I'm asking," Nik said.

"Damn it."

His face was made of stone. "Please."

A shadow moved in the trees near Rhodes's camp. At first I thought it was Len Bandoni. Or maybe Calamity Jane going after Rhodes's discarded food. But then I caught a flash of fair skin and the gleam of blond hair matted with blood.

Elise.

When you acknowledge the dead, you call them to you. I hadn't yet figured out how to send them away. *Most of us get over it*, the Marine had told me.

I kept reminding myself of that.

"Ah, shit." I pushed my face into Nik's. Clyde gave a low growl, but this time I didn't call him off. "You have no idea what this is costing me."

"I think I do."

"No. You don't. You have no *fucking* idea because you never want to hear about it. I will do this because I love you, Nik. But you have used up every single karma point you had with me. You understand?"

"I'll never ask you for anything else," Nik said.

Heat rose in my face. "Damn straight, Nikolas George Lasko. You will never ask again."

He blinked. "I got it, Sydney Rose."

I turned away so he wouldn't see the tears burning my eyes. Something had broken between us that I wasn't sure we could fix. The worst kind of Weight.

I picked up Clyde's empty water dish, locked up the Ford, and shouldered my bag.

The chopper came straight down, dropping a path through the snow, throwing a dim gray shadow over us and the truck.

Down by the river, Elise moved from tree to tree, drawn steadily toward her lover's lingering aura. She looked toward me, blue eyes meeting mine beneath a veil of blood, and I turned my back on her and Nik and the whole damn world. I fisted my hands in Clyde's leash.

The chopper landed.

CHAPTER 5

In modern warfare, people disappear. Not because they run off, or go native, or get taken prisoner. I don't even mean that they're gone because they're dead. I mean they vanish. One second they're right there, standing next to you, as bright and alive as they will always remain in the eyes of their parents, wives, children. Maybe they're talking about how the Broncos just put some whup-ass on the Raiders or how they're going to start a computer repair business when they get home or maybe just about how sweet that first post-dawn cigarette tastes and would you like one, too?

And then they take a few steps and the bomb goes off, and when the pink mist is done soaking into the dust, all you're left with is a single boot and the guy's hand. Or maybe just his rucksack spewing his med pack and his lucky rabbit's foot and his last clean pair of underwear across the field.

And there you stand, scared all to shit and grieving like you've never grieved.

But fuck if you aren't happy, too. Because part of you is like, sweet Jesus, that could have been me.

—Sydney Parnell. Personal journal.

Cohen waited, arms folded and jaw tight, while I ducked against the downdraft and hoisted Clyde into the helicopter before Nik and I scrambled aboard, dropping into the forward-facing seats across from the detective.

Cohen shook our hands briefly in turn then closed the chopper door.

He donned headphones and gestured for Nik and me to do the same so that we could talk over the sound of the rotors.

"Be just a minute," he said. "Checking our clearance with Denver Approach."

"That train's chewing up iron," Nik said.

"Won't be long."

Cohen dropped back into his seat and busied himself writing notes in his large spiral book. Up front, the pilots shared a laugh on their private channel. The smell of hydraulic fluid rose from the floorboards, and the chill air held the stink of jet fuel. In an instant, my skin grew hot, my pulse jumped, and sweat beaded at my temples as memories from Iraq burst like mortar fire across my brain.

The Sir. The bomb. Gurneys full of the dead.

I pressed my hands to my face. PTSD. The gift that keeps on giving. I'd been furious with Nik because of Elise's ghost. But it looked like the helicopter ride was going to be a bonus.

Clyde pushed up against me. He'd been trained for helicopters, but he didn't look happy, either. He laid back his ears and furrowed his face.

"Easy, boy," I said.

I held out some kibble from the bag in my pocket and stroked his head, leaning over to whisper into his ear.

"We're still good."

He ignored the kibble and watched my face. Dogs sniff out fear and anxiety the way a street thief finds a mark—quickly and without effort. I had to convince myself we were okay before I could convince Clyde.

Still holding out the treat, I relaxed my shoulders and drew in deep, regular breaths the way the VA counselor had taught me. I looked into

Clyde's anxious eyes and envisioned sitting with him in a mountain glen somewhere far away, the two of us basking in the sunlight, watching clouds drift overhead.

We are here, we are here, we are here. Nothing can harm us.

After a minute or two of silent interrogation, Clyde's ears came forward and his brow smoothed out. He took the kibble from my hand then settled himself on the floor near my feet.

I scrubbed behind his ears. "Good boy."

One small victory.

I straightened and looked over at Cohen. "Detective?"

He kept jotting notes. "Yeah, Parnell?"

"We were just doing our job. Down at the camp."

Cohen lifted his head; his eyes met mine like a fist to the face. "That how it seemed to you? Because it seems to me that was my scene. My case, my scene."

Nik broke in. "We couldn't be sure we had anything," he said calmly. "Time was wasting. I made the call."

"My sympathy for your loss, Lasko. But it was a bad call."

"Could be we pushed the line a little. But if we'd waited for you to drag your ass down there, we wouldn't be after Rhodes now."

Cohen ignored the jibe. "You think how it will look if this goes to trial? You think about what the judge is going to say, you digging around the camp of the man who—"

"Look," Nik said, "we weren't trying to piss on your hydrant. But we've got to catch the guy before we can try him. We were there. You weren't."

Cohen's face went harder. "Why bring a perp in if you can't keep him?"

"You sound like a DA."

"And you're what, the Lone Ranger? Or did I just miss the memo? When did you become a murder cop?"

"Around the time you decided to sit on your ass while a killer got away."

"Stop," I said.

Nik looked at me. Cohen kept his eyes on Nik.

I glared at both of them. "Can we quit with the territory crap and focus on Tucker Rhodes?"

"Right," Nik said softly.

"Right," said Cohen. Still pissed.

The pilot's voice came over the line. "We're cleared to go."

The sound of the rotors deepened as they bit the air. Clyde gave a soft whine, and I pulled him close. Together we stared out the window as the chopper got light on her skids then lifted into the snow-dappled air.

Denver dropped beneath us. Distance swallowed first Cohen's partner in his dark overcoat and then the bright gleam of Elise's hair. The tents and tarps of the hobo camp disappeared behind the cottonwoods as we swung north.

For the next few minutes we flew in and out of pockets of a half-hearted storm; blue-gray sky whipped by, mottled with pale sunlight. The pilots chatted privately. In his corner, Nik sat like a man braced against a hard wind. Across from me, Cohen kept writing in his notebook.

"Detective?"

He didn't look up. "What?"

Ground glass in his voice.

"You invited us along. How can we help?"

He tapped a finger on the metal spiral then put aside his anger like a man shrugging off a heavy coat. "Tell me about the train."

"Engine 158346. It's a mixed string of a hundred and thirty-eight cars. That translates into a lot of length."

"How much length?"

"Almost a mile and a half."

His eyebrows shot up. "There a way to narrow that down?"

"Our witness at the camp said he caught out somewhere on the back half of the train. Chances are good he's in a rear DPU—"

"Which is?"

"Distributed power unit. Otherwise known as the rear locomotive. Hobos like it because it's warm and it has a bathroom. This train has two rear units."

"Okay. We'll put men in place along the tracks so they're close to those units when we stop the train. Where else could he be?"

"Can I borrow your notebook and pen?"

When he passed them over, I flipped to a blank page. Then I called up the train consist—the string of cars—from my 3:00 a.m. memory when I'd checked into work from the computer at home. My laptop was still in the shop. A replacement hadn't materialized.

I started sketching.

"Mostly we've got empty coal hoppers," I said. "They're too deep to climb out of, and the bottoms are angled into a chute. Hobos don't ride them because they're death traps. We won't find Rhodes there."

"What else?"

I kept scribbling as I ran down my mental list. "Sixteen or seventeen closed hoppers strung together two-thirds of the way down the train. Rhodes could be riding a hopper platform or tucked into the cubby. If that's where he is, it will be easy for him to make a fast getaway when the train stops. You'll have to get men on those quickly."

"And hoppers are what exactly?"

The edge in his voice made me lift my head. Cohen's face held a hungry, open-ended curiosity. A need to know everything I knew, and yesterday was too late. I'd seen the look on Doug Ayers's face a thousand times. Usually when he met with someone involved in whatever covert ops he was working.

The resemblance between the men was so startling that for a second I couldn't breathe.

Tell me everything, Dougie would say to his source.

The memory shot through me with the kick of a sniper's bullet. Dougie, sitting at a metal folding table in a grove of gum arabic trees, his long legs stretched in front of him, his left hand waving away the droning flies as he chatted with an old tribesman while Clyde and I kept watch twenty yards away. Dust rose languidly into the air and hung there, white as talcum in the desert light. Dougie's face carried its habitual expression of curiosity and impatience as he twirled the old lion's head ring he wore on braided leather around his neck.

"Tell me everything," he said in Arabic.

"Na'am," said his source, the Iraqi elder, and poured more tea.

Dougie lifted his cup, saluted the old man.

"Salâmati!"

The old man raised his own cup. *"Salâmati!"*

Ten days later, Dougie's broken body lay on my table in Mortuary Affairs, his eyes and face powdered with that same fine, white dust. The day after that, someone left the old man's head outside our gates.

Tell me everything, Dougie, I'd whispered to his body. *I need to know.*

"Sydney Rose?" Nik's voice came from the far end of a long tunnel. "You okay?"

I shook myself, my hand going to Dougie's ring where it now hung around my neck. Through my coat, I touched the heavy gold. "I'm fine."

Nik eyeballed me.

I flushed. "I *am*, Nik. I'm fine."

His eyes narrowed at the lie, but he nodded and went back to his window.

"Hoppers and cubbies." Cohen's expression had softened. "You know that I have no clue what the hell you're talking about."

"Right. Sorry. A hopper is a car used for carrying bulk items like corn or wheat—products that have to be protected from the weather. The front and rear walls angle in from the top to the bottom, leaving room at each end of the car for a metal platform that sits directly over the wheels. Like this." I drew a quick sketch. "One platform is taken up with the brake system. But the other platform is open. Perfect for hobos."

"And the cubby?"

"It's a hole cut into the end-wall of the car, here"—I pointed—
"above the platform. Not roomy, but a great place to hide."

"Okay. I got the hoppers. Go on."

"A few flatcars. No worries there—they're filled with loads that
make riding them too risky. But we've got twenty-three gondolas spread
out along the train." I made another sketch. "A gondola is essentially
a roofless boxcar sliced in half horizontally so it's only about six feet
higher than the wheels. On our train, thirteen of the gondolas are
empty, which means he could easily be inside. The only way for us to
know is to climb up inside each car and take a look."

"What about a flyover? Could we see him that way?"

"Depends. If he's in one of the gondolas, sure. But if he's on a platform or in a cubby, he'll be impossible to see from the air. And we run
the risk of alerting him if we do a flyover in a police chopper."

Cohen nodded. "Sounds like the work will have to be done from
the ground."

"How many men do you have?"

"Larimer County is putting their SWAT team in with twenty-one
men plus a commander. We've got ten deputies, the sheriff, and two
K9 teams. State's giving us another twenty-five men. So sixty plus us."
Cohen rubbed his eyes as if only now realizing how tired he was. "You
got suggestions on how we should use everybody once the train stops?
Your witness placed him near the rear of the train?"

"Right."

"Your witness is a drug addict, right?"

"Doesn't matter. Rhodes has enough experience catching out to
know that the back half of a train makes for a better ride. I'd recom-
mend focusing your manpower on the cluster of closed hoppers and
empty gondolas in the last third of the train."

I showed him the consist I'd sketched. "Here," I pointed. "And
here. Plus the rear DPUs. If you stop so that the forward third of the
train is across the bridge north of the fertilizer plant, you'll be able to

place men on the roof of the building to look into the open hoppers and the gondolas and to watch for him if he makes a run for it. Put some men on perimeter near the front of the train and at the bridge. Just in case. And tell the guys on perimeter that if Rhodes gets wind of what we're doing, he might jump as soon as the train slows."

"We need to tell the sheriff exactly where he should place his men along the track."

"Mark off the track in hundred-yard segments. So you'll have men in these places." I drew tiny markers on the paper.

While Cohen passed the distance indicators onto the sheriff's dispatcher, I asked the copilot to patch me in with the Fort Worth operations center so I could talk to Engine 158346. The engineer was Dan Albers, a brute of a man with the temper of a cornered badger. When on duty, he kept a Bowie knife strapped to his calf and a sawed-off shotgun next to his chair. He once single-handedly took down a trio of purported members of an FTRA gang who tried to hop his train. The Freight Train Riders of America are violent thugs with a take-no-prisoners mentality. Albers coldcocked two of them before they knew he was there, and he had the third cowering in a boxcar at gunpoint by the time police arrived.

Something to be said for taking care of your own problems. But with his temper, Albers wasn't who I would have chosen to be driving this particular train.

"Bastard's on my train," he said when dispatch put me through.

"Albers, don't get in the middle of this," I warned him. "Stay in the cab."

"Bastard's got no business being there."

"Albers."

"Shit, Parnell."

I waited.

"Long as he don't cross me," he said finally.

"Keep the air up on the brakes," I said. "We want him to think you've just stopped for something on the track."

"I got it. Don't get yourself hurt, okay?"

"Thanks." I hung up.

Cohen glanced at his watch. He looked gray with exhaustion.

"Long day?" I asked.

"Not long enough to fix anything."

I said nothing. I was unfairly angry at him for making me think of Dougie. Plus, I had no patience for complaints of exhaustion or lack of time. I'd set my standard by the Sir, who was years older than Cohen. The Sir would take seventy-two-hour shifts dodging IEDs and terrorists, spend the next forty-eight up to his elbows in gore, and top it off with back-to-back meetings with grieving Iraqi families. After all that, he would muster up a smile for his crew and a murmured "We're still good."

"Parnell?"

"What?"

Something must have showed in my face because a gleam of amusement shone through Cohen's exhaustion.

"You think I'm a pussy."

"What do you care what I think?"

"What if I do?"

That stopped me. I noticed again the sharpness of his winter eyes, the rime-edge of intelligence gleaming there. And something else in his gaze, something as far from the ice as night from day. Something I might have labeled compassion if I'd been in a more generous mood.

I frowned. "To be honest, Detective, I don't have any opinions about you. Good or bad."

Cohen leaned back. "You don't mince words, do you?"

"Sorry. I'm more honest than I should be."

He winced.

"That came out wrong," I said. "I—"

"No. It's okay. I probably deserved it." He laughed. "I'm out of practice, but you're pretty good at the shutdown."

"A gift from the Corps."

"I'll bet," he said, but it wasn't unkind. He scrubbed his face with both hands and shook off his fatigue. "Railroad property. I assume you want to be part of the takedown. You and the sheriff can duke it out as to who makes the arrest."

"No, thanks. If it works for you, Clyde and I will get on the lead engine. Stay with the crew and make sure they're okay." And make sure Albers didn't shoot his own brakeman.

Nik came back from whatever mental ride he'd gone on. "I'll go with SWAT on the rear DPU."

"Not this time," Cohen said. "I need you to stay on the roof with the SWAT commander and the sheriff."

Nik's eyes went flinty. "No point in bringing me if you aren't going to use me."

"It was a courtesy," Cohen said. "Situation's a little too hot to have you on the ground, Lasko. Things don't go well, we don't want the jury asking the wrong kind of questions. Like, what the hell you were doing so close to the suspect when you have every reason to want to rip off his fucking head."

Nik balled his fists on his thighs as his shoulders came up. I'd never seen Nik this angry. Not even with Calamity Jane. He looked wound so tight that I thought maybe the only way for him to uncoil was to let it all fly free.

"Nik," I said.

Nothing.

"Nik."

I put everything into his name, using my voice on him the way I'd used it on Clyde when he and I were first alone together after Dougie died. Back when Clyde was so lashed with grief I thought he'd rip out my throat for the singular sin of not being Dougie.

Nik didn't look at me. But he didn't fly apart, either. He drew in a deep, ragged breath and flattened his hands on his thighs. The anger fell away, replaced by a grief that pulled his face to wreckage.

After a minute, he nodded in Cohen's general direction.

"Got it," he said and turned back to the window.

Cohen watched him a moment longer, then opened a file folder and pulled out a sheaf of papers stapled together and handed it to me.

It was a summary of Tucker Rhodes—his service in the Corps, a list of his injuries from the IED, a brief investigation after his disappearance from Brooke. Parents were Ken and Melissa Rhodes, divorced, mom now residing in Florida, dad still in Shelby, a rancher. No siblings. I flipped through the pages, found a standard-issue Marine Corps induction photo. At the time of his enlistment, Rhodes had been a startlingly handsome man with dark hair and a look of cocky self-confidence. The expression in his green eyes didn't reveal a single chink in the armor of his good looks.

I stared at those eyes, remembered the taste of rust like nails in my mouth.

I knew this guy. Somehow, somewhere. Maybe nothing more than a passing glance in the chow line at one of the forward bases. He was good-looking enough that he would have caught my eye, even when I was with Dougie.

But the twist in my gut said our encounter had been something more, even if I couldn't place when or why our paths had crossed.

I shivered. Where . . . ?

Cohen's voice brought me back. "Guys hopping trains usually carry a gun?"

"A few do," I said, shaking off the déjà vu. "Handguns. Something they can conceal in a backpack. But you're more likely to find knives or a length of pipe. Most of these guys can't afford firearms."

"A vet, we should figure he's got a gun," Nik said.

Cohen nodded.

Nik went on. "Warn your SWAT guys that if he's armed, he might try to provoke a fire fight."

"Suicide by cop?"

"It's possible."

Cohen pointed his chin toward a pair of Kevlar vests stowed in mesh pockets in the rear of the chopper. "When we land, why don't you put those on?"

"Sure."

Cohen packed away the papers and his notebook. He glanced at his wristwatch.

"So, Parnell," he said, "what do you think he'll do when we try to stop him?"

"He might see us as mere obstacles to his goal of reaching Montana and do everything in his power to eliminate us. Or could be he'll—" I stopped. "You know, right, that my service in Iraq doesn't give me any special insight into what Rhodes is thinking?"

The detective raised an eyebrow. "I think maybe it does."

I looked down at the floor. Maybe. I thought about what kind of ugly might be in Tucker Rhodes's head. Either he had killed Elise, or he'd found her torn up like that. Either way, he was a man in a world of hurt. He was likely to be scared—of himself and of us. Scared with the kind of fear that makes a man half wild and all crazy. Scared enough to shoot up half the state's police if they got in his way.

A strand of sunlight made its way through the window and fell across Clyde where he lay on the floor. He thumped his tail and looked at me.

Then again, maybe Tucker Rhodes had had his fill of battle. Maybe too much death had turned him into a dove who wouldn't fight even to defend his own life.

I'd seen both kinds of crazy in Iraq.

I raised my head. "He might decide to bait us, go for that suicide-by-cop scenario Nik mentioned. Seems entirely possible. My gut, though, is that he'll try to run and hide, wait for another chance to make his way north. He's lost everything except his home. I don't think he cares what happens to him once he's in Montana. But I think he wants to get there."

"Okay," Cohen said. He went back on the radio.

I looked at my watch. We had twenty-five minutes to land and get into position.

Nik pointed. "There's the place."

I reached for the binoculars. The storm hadn't reached this far north, and from the air, the fertilizer plant was a hive of activity. Deputy's cars, state police vehicles, an ambulance, and two SWAT vans sat in the lot. Men jogged down the track, moving into the approximate positions we had given them.

"They'd better move the cars," I said. "If Rhodes is sitting where he has a visual, he'll either run or be waiting for us."

Cohen got on the radio again. Shortly, a handful of men emerged through a door and began moving the vehicles around to the north side of the building.

Nik slid next to me, placed his hand on mine in a rare gesture of affection. "You ready for this, Sydney Rose?"

I worked not to pull my hand away. "Whatever you need, Nik."

I told myself I could do this. When we landed, I would not throw up or scream or crawl on my hands and knees to the nearest shelter to hide from an enemy on the other side of the world. I would not press into the ground close enough to eat dirt, or throw myself over Clyde. I would convince my body that we were safe, and my mind would follow suit.

Two minutes after that, we were on the ground.

CHAPTER 6

*After your buddy gets blown to bits, it's your job to clean
up whatever's left. You busy yourself trying to find anything
more than a hand and a boot so the family will have something to bury and because you don't want to leave a fellow
Marine behind.*

*You work all day to find what you can, and all the while
your head hurts and your gut's locked down tight, wondering
if there's another bomb out there with your name on it.*

*Then darkness falls, and you get back to the FOB with
that boot and the hand and an ounce of flesh and you're so
nauseous you can't eat and so tired you can hardly stand and
the Sir tells you to shade it black.*

*And you say, Yes, sir, and you look down at the gurney—
at that hand and that boot and that ounce of flesh.*

And you wonder how the fuck you're supposed to do that.
                              —Sydney Parnell. Personal journal.

The Larimer County sheriff was a tall, lean man in his mid-sixties with
a sunburn, a nest of crow's-feet, and an attitude for city folk radiat-
ing off him like stink from a stockyard. He met us at the door of the
abandoned factory with his feet planted and his arms folded across his
narrow chest.

"Thanks for pitching in on this," he said to Cohen and Nik after quick introductions. He didn't look at me. "Our men are in place. I've got two K9 teams here, ready to go if we need 'em. You got something the dogs can scent on?"

"I have the suspect's uniform," Nik said. "And Clyde here is one of the best air scent dogs around."

The sheriff gave a slow "hmmm" that said, *We'll see about that*, and handed me a Kevlar dog vest.

"K9 guys thought you'd want this."

He pushed the vest into my hands. I felt like an ass for leaving Clyde's vest and mine behind in our truck in Denver.

"Yes, sir. Thank you."

An angry flush rose in the sheriff's neck when his eyes met mine. He was the sort of guy who'd never taken to the idea of women pushing into the brotherhood. Probably he was wondering who I'd slept with and whether my incompetence would get one of his men shot.

His eyes swept past me to Clyde.

"Dog looks a little sick. Not much for chopper rides?"

Heat rose in my own face. "He's fine, sir."

"You're not looking so peachy yourself."

"Happens when I encounter an asshole. I'll feel better soon."

"Why you little—"

Cohen's mouth twitched.

Nik jumped in. "As soon as the train starts to slow down," he said, "your men should be prepared for Rhodes to jump."

The sheriff ripped his gaze from me, taking skin with it.

"Miles ahead of you, Lasko," he said. "State troopers have set up as much of a perimeter as they can. Kinda like trying to lasso a bronco with a piece of string and a whistle." He nodded his chin toward the distant horizon where clouds hung, fat with snow. "We got a big storm coming. We don't catch your guy in the next couple of hours, we'll have to shut down before our asses are hanging in the wind."

He gave us radios, told us what frequency to use, then clapped his hands together, a single, harsh sound in the cold-chapped air. "Let's get this show on the road. Agent Parnell, I assume you want a ride up to where the engine will stop."

"We'll jog up there, sir."

Another narrow look. I grinned at him, baring my teeth. The sheriff spun on his heel and disappeared into the building.

"You be careful, Sydney Rose," Nik said to me. "And watch that temper of yours. The sheriff is on our side."

Some of the wildness had gone out of his eyes, replaced by bone-tired.

"And you stay on the roof," I told him.

He nodded. "Yeah."

He followed the sheriff inside, and I was left facing Cohen.

The detective stared past me at the prairie, his eyes slitted against the wind. "That hold you up much at work, that temper of yours?"

"Stupid, eh? Zero to pissed off in, what, twenty seconds?"

"Seven." His eyes came back to me, amused. "For that, maybe we'll call the whole crime scene ownership thing a wash."

I mustered a smile. "Good."

"Yeah." He ran a hand over his cropped hair, needlessly smoothing it, another gesture that reminded me of Dougie. Was this detective what Dougie would have looked like ten years down the road, if he'd made it home? The same lines around kind eyes, the same weariness in the set of his mouth? Would Dougie, always larger than life, have become this worn down and cynical?

"I wondered if . . ." he started.

"What?"

But he shook himself. "Be careful, Parnell."

"You too, Detective."

He followed the other men inside.

I unsnapped Clyde's lead and coiled up its length. He looked at me expectantly.

"Let's go, boy."

Away from the shelter of the building, the wind was biting; it felt good on my face as we took off. Clyde and I jogged lightly north next to the tracks, heading upwind toward the bridge, our breaths puffing in front of us. The winter sun threw faint, flat shadows over the ground. Two miles away, pale sunlight glinted off cars and trucks on the interstate.

A jackrabbit with comically large ears darted across our path. Clyde cut sharply after it, his head down and intent. I called him back.

"Clyde, you know better," I scolded. "We're on a job."

Clyde looked longingly after the rabbit bounding away across the prairie.

"C'mon, boy."

Clyde had once been the canine equivalent of a Navy SEAL. His training had gone beyond even the rigorous preparation given a normal military multipurpose dog and made him worth a small fortune. I'd only been able to adopt him because Dougie's death had so destabilized him that he'd been declared unworkable. Now as a railroad K9, he had decent training. But I had not kept his skills to the level he'd once known. It had never seemed necessary. Nor did he enjoy the work anymore.

Something was broken inside of Clyde. I doubted he'd ever be the dog he'd been with Dougie. Any more than I would again be the bright, fearless woman whom Dougie had loved.

Chasing rabbits, though. That was a new low for us both.

At the suspension bridge, we picked up our pace. The viaduct hung over a sand-choked gully that had been carved out by flash floods. Clyde and I fell into a rhythm as our feet hit the ties.

Half a mile on the other side, we cut right. Twenty feet from the tracks, I gestured Clyde down and then lay flat on the ground next to him. The earth was still damp from the last snow. The Kevlar vest ground into the soft flesh under my chin, and Dougie's ring dug into my breastbone. I wriggled around, trying to get comfortable.

Clyde settled himself companionably next to me, tongue lolling, happier than I'd seen him in a long time. His Kevlar vest didn't bother him at all. Business as usual for a military dog.

"This is like a vacation for you, isn't it, Clyde?"

He yawned.

"That rabbit means we're losing our edge. Getting soft. We need to start training again."

He paid me no attention whatsoever.

We waited. The smells of damp earth and sage wafted up, mingling with the sharp tang of creosote from the railroad ties. A lone crow circled overhead, and I followed it with my eyes, feeling some part of me up there with it, remote and unattached, free of asshole sheriffs and nightmare memories and war-shattered vets. Free of Weight.

"Five minutes," the dispatcher said in my ear.

From the south, Engine 158346 was now visible, her headlamp and ditch lights burning brightly in the clear day like a star hooked to a workhorse. She was a four-thousand-horsepower war-bonnet, twelve feet wide, fifteen tall, and weighing two hundred tons. Part of the Powder River run, she'd been built to build America.

But she was also a danger. Flat-out, she could go sixty miles an hour. Get too close, and her slipstream would drag you under her wheels. Cross her path, and her driver would not see you. And even if he did, it would take him a mile and a half to stop.

By then, there would be nothing human about you except your DNA.

I could hear her now. The steady thrum of her engine, and beneath that vibrant hum, the clack of her wheels like blood thumping in iron veins. The radio burst with static as everyone down the line confirmed their position. Next to me, Clyde tensed. I resnapped his lead and pulled him close, wrapping an arm around him.

Railroad dispatch buzzed in my ear. "One minute."

The tunnel vision of combat closed in, shutting out everything but the train. No smells or sights, no sound or sense of touch other than what rolled in with Engine 158346.

Our Lady squealed over the bridge, tossing off velocity, shrieking to a halt in a way that said stopping was all wrong, that the rhythm of the tracks should never be disrupted. Her steel sides swept by like a leviathan breaching, her wheels screaming in fury. Sparks kicked up from the rails and it looked like she would sail right on past. Stopping wasn't what she was built for.

But, finally, heavily, she conceded. She dragged to a halt, her brakes whooshing. The air stayed up, just as Albers had promised, and Clyde and I sprang to our feet. We sprinted across the grass then bounded up the stairs and into the cab, me shouting my name as I ran so the crew wouldn't think I was a trespasser.

Albers was sitting in the console behind the controls, his shotgun leaning against the wall within easy reach. The brakeman, Greg Walters, sat to his left, wide-eyed and pale. Walters rose and grabbed my arm as soon as I entered the cab.

"Who is this guy, Sydney?" he asked. "I think I saw SWAT out there."

"He's just a trespasser," I told him. "No worries. But we're going to be cautious. I want both of you down, out of sight."

"What? Why?" Walters asked even as he crouched on the internal stairs leading down to the head.

"Bullets will be flying," Albers answered gleefully. He clearly itched to be part of the action. But when I glared, he complied with my order, hunkering near Walters on the stairs and snugging the shotgun up to his chest like a lover.

"Don't even think of using that," I told him.

I removed Clyde's lead and gave him the order to stay with the men. Then I clambered to the top of the locomotive so that I could watch for anyone approaching.

Atop the engine, I shaded my eyes. The wind rippled through the prairie, spreading flat and desolate to either horizon. North of me, two deputies stood in full protective gear, scanning the southern terrain where Engine 158346 cleaved the land like a zipper.

I listened to the running commentary on my radio as the sheriff and the SWAT leader talked to their teams. Men were clearing the DPUs and the gondolas; in the pristine silence of the flatlands, the clang of their boots on rusting platforms and metal ladders echoed like rifle shots.

The searchers found an abandoned bedroll, a paperback mystery novel, three porno mags, fifteen empty whiskey bottles, a deck of cards, and what sounded like a dumpster's worth of trash.

But of Tucker Rhodes, there was nothing. The rear DPUs sat empty, the gondolas contained mostly snowmelt.

"He must have jumped," said the sheriff. "Probably back in Fort Collins. But let's take a look-see closer to home as long as we've still got daylight. Once that storm hits, it's gonna be darker than a rattler den at midnight."

The SWAT commander came on. "Let's clear this train, gentlemen. Car by car. Use the mirrors where you need to, and sweep each car before taking the next. Teams three and four, move from south to north, and take the K9 teams with you. Teams one and two, stay on perimeter. Keep twenty yards back in case we rattle something loose. State troopers on perimeter have nothing so far, so could be our guy is still around. We've got less than an hour before that storm hits. Move fast, but be smart."

"Agent Parnell?" The sheriff again. "You awake up there?"

"Sir."

"How about you take your dog and start searching from the north? Don't worry about clearing the cars. Just see if your dog can pick up a scent. If he does, back off and hold tight until I can get more men up there. Team five, stay on her ass, give her some cover."

"Pleasure, sir," came a male voice.

My lucky day.

I climbed down to the platform and whistled Clyde out. We hopped to the ground and watched the two deputies approach. As soon as the men got close enough for Clyde to make out the protective gear—their Kevlar-inflated bulk and face-concealing radios—Clyde lowered his neck, tucked his tail, and slunk behind my legs.

I knelt and took his face in my hands, trying to instill the same calm we'd managed together on the chopper.

"Clyde," I whispered, aware that the deputies were now right behind me. "No bombs. No snipers. We're still good."

Clyde studied me again; again he bought my line.

"Sit."

He sat.

"Good boy."

"He okay?" asked one of the deputies.

I rose to my feet, forced a smile. "Sure."

The deputies introduced themselves as Ed Kohl and Scott O'Malley. We shook hands. But when I tried to introduce Clyde, he refused to participate. He stayed obediently by my side but ignored the men's outstretched hands.

"He won't bite, will he?" Kohl asked.

"Only if you stay on my ass."

The deputies laughed and the moment passed.

Both Kohl and O'Malley had run searches with their K9 teams and knew the drill. Clyde and I would walk point. The deputies would follow a few paces behind on my right and left so they could, as the sheriff so delicately put it, cover my ass.

I faced south. The wind pushed into my back, tugging strands of my hair free and whipping them into my face.

"Lousy search conditions," I warned the deputies. "Moving with the wind means we could walk right past Rhodes before Clyde catches his scent."

"Just don't get more than a couple of paces ahead of us," O'Malley said. "Keep it tight. Clyde alerts or you see or hear anything, drop so we have a clear line of sight. Don't worry. If Rhodes moves, we'll get him."

"Didn't you say that all we got up here are coal cars and that he wouldn't be in a coal car?" Kohl asked.

"Coal cars and flatcars," I said. "Not likely to be on either of those. But let's make your boss happy."

I attached Clyde's lead then showed him his favorite ball, a bright-red rubber chew toy called a Kong. Clyde's ears lifted and a sparkle came into his brown eyes. Work was play for Clyde, and even after everything he'd been through, he still loved to work. I pulled out the bag with Rhodes's military cap. All I could smell was smoke from when Rhodes tried to burn it. But Clyde would pick up the human scent underneath.

Clyde sniffed the cover, wagging his tail. When he had what he needed, his eyes went to my face. He was ready to rumble.

"Seek!"

Clyde lowered his head and began sniffing in the dirt near the tracks, his tail up and straight back like a flag. He moved steadily down the track toward the bridge, his step jaunty, his ears pricked. Now and then he lifted his head to sample the air. I kept the lead relaxed, letting him focus.

The deputies fell in behind us.

We crossed the bridge, left it behind. Our dull gray shadows stretched eastward, lumpy and distorted on the uneven ground. Clyde made all the noise of a ghost. But stray ballast and dead grass crunched beneath my boots and those of the deputies, and our breaths sounded like a bellows as we worked to keep up with Clyde. The temperature had dropped probably ten degrees since we'd arrived, and out here in the wind my face and ears quickly went numb, my nose running with the cold. My hands, cupped around the lead, turned stiff. I thought regret-fully of my hat and gloves, left behind in the truck in Denver, along with our vests. Apparently I'd forgotten everything I'd been taught.

One of the deputies stumbled and muttered a quick "goddamn," but I didn't look around.

Twenty cars past the bridge, Clyde slowed. His breathing changed as he trotted back and forth next to the train, taking in more air. A few seconds later he sat down next to the tracks.

He had a hit, and the scent hadn't gone any farther from the train than where we stood.

I tugged on Clyde's lead, silently calling him back. Wordlessly, the four of us jogged fifteen yards back from the train and crouched behind a slight knoll. I downed Clyde while I studied the train.

"I thought you said—" Kohl started to protest.

I raised a hand, silencing him.

It didn't look promising. The flatcar Clyde had alerted next to was the kind of ride Rhodes would never risk, not if he wanted to get to Montana. It was exposed and—with a load of rebar that would constantly shift—treacherous. I looked for any indication that the load had been moved around to create a hiding place, but from our vantage point, everything looked normal.

I ran my gaze over the coal cars; on the forward car was a series of scratches along the inside edge. The scratches were still shiny. Probably left when the latest load of coal was dumped in El Paso. But it wasn't the sort of mark a hobo would or could make. And anyway, no hobo with any kind of experience would grab that ride. Even a guy looking to die probably didn't want to do so trapped in an empty hopper.

I narrowed my eyes in frustration. The train sat silent and stubborn in the failing light, the cars shadowy and silent.

Dogs make mistakes. Maybe a farmer was burning corn husks somewhere, and Clyde had alerted on a few molecules of smoke brushing by on the wind. Or maybe a rabbit had denned nearby. Clyde's earlier pursuit of the rabbit told me I hadn't been working him enough. He'd become distractible.

The first fat flakes of snow skittered down as the sky folded in on itself. The wind shrilled in the bridge's suspension cables. The promise of violence filled the world as the storm approached.

Kohl shifted around, scratched himself. "Did your dog find something or not?"

"Hold on."

The last thing I wanted to do was call out the sheriff's cavalry on a false alert.

"I once shot a tramp near here," Kohl said in a voice barely loud enough to hear over the wind. "Fucker had a meat cleaver. His buddy'd made a batch of wood alcohol and mixed it with soda. Pink Lady, they call it. But he wouldn't share with Mr. Cleaver. Mr. Cleaver got pretty pissed about that. He chopped off his pal's arm and was getting ready to take a whack at the other arm when I dropped him."

"Kohl, you talk too much," O'Malley said. "You guys hear anything?"

"Nah," Kohl said. "Not over this damn wind. You really think he's here? Maybe Clyde caught an old scent or something."

The snow was falling heavily now, turning the train into a ghost. My eyes kept going back to that bright line of raw metal at the top of the forward hopper like it was some kind of sign. Either Clyde had it wrong, or my assumptions about where Rhodes wanted to die were wrong.

I was betting Clyde had it right.

"Radio the sheriff," I said to the deputies. "Tell him we have a possible."

O'Malley tapped his radio.

"Sheriff, looks like Parnell's dog found something in one of the cars. Want us to see if we can spook anything out?"

"Dog alerted, did he?"

"Yes, sir."

"Well, tell Parnell not to get her panties in a twist. I just heard from Fort Collins PD. Our suspect was spotted there. They're closing in on him now." He switched to the general channel. "All units, report back to the factory. Suspect has been located in Fort Collins. Looks like today's little exercise is over."

I stared at Clyde in disbelief. He stared back with furrowed brow, reading the disappointment on my face and wondering what he'd gotten wrong.

Over the radio, groans and cheers sounded up and down the line.

"Jesus, about time. My dick is an icicle," said one of the men.

"You always were a cold prick, Mathers," said dispatch.

Laughter.

O'Malley touched my shoulder. "Hey, no worries. It goes like that, sometimes."

"No," I said. "They've got the wrong man. He's here."

O'Malley and I looked at the silent train, the cars which I'd said myself were the kind Tucker Rhodes would never ride. Clyde had definitely caught a whiff of something. But maybe not Rhodes. I've always been a big fan of Occam's razor, so I had to ask myself—what were the chances that Fort Collins PD had stumbled across a second hobo with severe burn scars on his face?

O'Malley looked so sorry for me, I wanted to punch him.

"We all make mistakes," he said. "Part of being human. Or canine. No big deal."

"Yeah." I couldn't meet his eyes. "Thanks."

Kohl stood with a grunt and unkinked his neck. "What a gaggle fuck."

Angry and embarrassed, I looped up Clyde's lead. O'Malley was right. Mistakes happen, even with the best-trained men and dogs. But if Clyde had given a false alert, the error wasn't his. It was mine for not keeping up with his training. My fault that he'd gone after that rabbit earlier. And my mistake for not working him through his war-induced anxieties so that he didn't slink away when faced with lawmen in body armor. I'd let him down in every way.

"I'm ready for a whiskey and a hot shower," O'Malley said.

"Whiskey?" Kohl scoffed. "You drink that paint thinner? Ain't you an American, O'Malley?"

"Irish, boy, and proud of it."

The deputies turned in the direction of the fertilizer plant, now invisible behind the swirling snow.

"Coming?" O'Malley asked me.

I shook my head. I didn't feel up for the good-hearted banter the others would be sharing at the fertilizer factory. And I didn't want to face the sheriff.

"Be there in a minute," I said. "I'm going to see this train off."

O'Malley squatted down and gave Clyde a friendly look. "It happens, pal. No worries. You'll get your man next time."

The men walked away, disappearing into the storm. Clyde looked up at me, ears back in embarrassment. I stroked his head.

"Not your bad, boy. I own this one. We are back in training starting ASAP. Either that, or I'm going to get a job pouring shots at Joe's Tavern, and you can be my bouncer."

My headset buzzed. Nik.

"Well, that's that," he said.

"Looks like."

"Clyde didn't alert?"

So it wasn't yet general knowledge. "He picked up a scent just before the sheriff gave us the news. But we couldn't find anything."

"You sure? It's not like Clyde to give a false alert. Maybe Rhodes—"

I sucked in a breath and released it. "They found him, Nik. Clyde and I made a mistake. I'm going to release the train and come in. We'll have to get a new crew on in Cheyenne. Albers and Walters have been cooling their heels for most of their shift. Can you tell the captain?"

"I'll call him. And I'll ask around, see if I can get us a ride back to Denver. That chopper won't be coming back."

"Okay. Good." I was tired. And cold. All I wanted was to get home, have a drink or two, take a shower, and crash. "See you in a few minutes."

I called Albers, told him he'd be clear to head out shortly. Ten minutes later, with all of the sheriff's men accounted for, I gave Albers the go-ahead.

A *chunk-chunk-chunk* rattled down the line as the brakes came off the wheels. A few minutes later, cars clanged and rattled like cannons firing as the slack in the couplers was taken up or buffeted out. Taking the slack out of a string was a lengthy process; it would be several minutes before any motion reached the flatbed near where Clyde and I stood. Albers's engine would travel seventy-five feet or more before the last car in the string even began to move.

An old yardmaster had once told me that a train is Newton's first law etched in steel. An object in motion tends to stay in motion. Ditto for an object at rest.

The couplers quieted, which meant that all the slack had played out. Wheels shrieked on iron. The train was under way.

While Clyde trotted restlessly back and forth at the end of his lead, I followed the train with my eyes as it dug a slow path through the falling snow, watching that series of bright-silver scratches on the coal car until they winked out in the gloom.

Nik called again. "You coming in, Sydney Rose? I've got us a ride."

"On my way."

I hung up. Stared at the darkness. Clyde whined and pulled on his lead, no doubt as ready as I was to get out of the storm.

"C'mon, boy, let's go home."

He trotted toward me then spun around and darted toward the train, the suddenness of his leap jerking the leash out of my numb hands.

"Clyde! No!" I lunged after him. "Come!"

Clyde paid me no mind. Without a sound, he disappeared beneath the wheels as Engine 158346 rumbled north.

Chapter 7

In a moment of crisis, your body takes over. It knows what it needs to do to keep you alive, and that's exactly what it does.

This instinct for survival comes from your reptilian brain—the most basic, simplistic part of who you are. Your reptilian brain breathes for you. Digests and defecates for you. Watches out for you.

And—if it deems the threat high enough—it kills for you.

—Sydney Parnell, ENGL 0208,
Psychology of Combat

I dropped to the ground and peered under the train.

Clyde had vanished into the snowfall on the other side of the tracks, chasing whatever scent he'd caught.

I sprang to my feet. Narrowing my eyes against the pelting snow, I first took note of my distance from the bridge and then zeroed in on a landmark as it flashed into and out of sight between the cars—a twisted piñon pine bent over a shattered pile of sandstone.

I turned and sprinted south, running against the direction of the cars. Clyde was my partner. As long as we were separated by a moving train, his life was at risk. No time to tell Albers to stop—if Clyde decided to come back, he could be crushed many times over before the train settled.

Learning to catch out isn't part of a railway cop's education. All we hear in training is to stay clear of a moving train. Want to survive until your retirement? Then do not get in an argument with fourteen thousand tons of steel. Handle whatever needs handling after the train stops.

The instructors never said what to do if your partner was trapped on the other side of that rolling steel.

The wheels rat-a-tatted on the rails. Four cars down, a hopper glowered in the dreary late-afternoon gloom, her platform sitting empty on the north end. I estimated the engine's speed at twelve miles an hour. Another two minutes, the train would be going more than eighteen miles an hour. Jumping then would be nothing but suicide.

But I'd made a promise to Dougie. And to Clyde. I put on more speed, slid sideways in the first slick fall of snow, and caught myself. My duty belt banged and rattled, my bag bounced on my hip.

Five trainees in my class gave catching out a try—got drunk and tried to hop a southbound freight. Results were mixed—a broken wrist, two broken ankles, and a sheered-off thumb. Those still in one piece spent the next two weeks running calisthenics and watching endless safety videos.

The guy who lost his thumb took a job as a mall cop.

Next to me, the train filled the horizon, looming like a mountain against the sky. I kept my eyes on the platform and on the dark cubby above it.

In the far distance, Clyde barked, a single sharp sound. *Hurry up*, he was telling me. *I've got something.*

I put on a final burst of speed. I was my father's daughter, and unlike those cadets, I knew exactly what to do. Coming abreast of the hopper, I thrust my foot onto the metal stirrup, grabbed hold of the ladder like a penitent reaching for God, and swung onto the platform.

The motion of the train slammed me onto a steel floor slick with snow. I went skittering across. The skin split on my cheek and peeled off my palms. My brain bounced in my skull with a sickening jolt.

I scrabbled for a hold on the icy floor. My feet shot out over the other side, and I felt the suck of gravity and the grinding tug of the wheels. I reached for the ladder on the far side, was jerked away with the train's motion, and grabbed again.

Then, like grace descending, my body reached the tempo of the train. My hands closed on the ladder, and the world quieted.

I hauled myself to a crouch and looked at the ground hurtling by. A landscape that had seemed harmless when walking was now a minefield of sharp ballast, thorny acacias, and vast fields of cactus.

I saw my landmark—the piñon pine and limestone scree—and leapt.

The earth slammed into me and I rolled along the ground with the momentum of the train, pitching to a stop against an acacia bush. I lay still, momentarily stunned, blinking up into the leaden sky. Snow burned my wounded face.

Then Clyde was on top of me, tail wagging fiercely, sweeping the snow from my skin with his tongue.

I rose to my knees and threw my arms around him, burying my throbbing face in his fur, heedless of the pain, my pulse thundering in my ears from adrenaline and the fear of losing him.

Clyde tolerated my embrace for a moment or two before he wriggled free and danced around me, sniffing my jacket pockets for his Kong, still on the game.

I stood and grabbed his lead and held it as tightly as I could with my injured hands.

"Game over, boy. I don't know what you think you've found, but it's time to get the hell home."

But Clyde trotted away from me, moving west as far as his lead would allow. He looked back at me over his shoulder, ears cocked and tail jaunty. His tongue lolled.

Game ON, he seemed to be saying. *Are we going to get this guy or what?*

I whistled him back. Reluctantly, he obeyed.

"They got the guy, Clyde. In Fort Collins. Or almost got him. He isn't here."

Clyde looked up at me, then at my coat pocket where his Kong was stashed.

The first worm of doubt raised its head. I pushed it down. "There's nothing here, Clyde. Look, this is all my fault. You're the best damn dog around, and you and I both know it. We'll get your shine back."

Clyde waited.

"Ah, hell, boy. What are you trying to tell me? That you got it right and the Fort Collins PD are full of shit? I am not going to walk into a blizzard to track down a phantom. How do I know it's not a rabbit or groundhog or some farmer burning corn? How do I know it's Rhodes?"

Clyde nosed my jacket. I ignored him. The scrapes on my face and hands throbbed in the cold. My back and shoulders ached. My left calf burned, and when I looked down, I saw that dozens of cactus spines had pierced my pant leg and punctured my skin.

I hugged myself and stared out over the brown prairie with its thickening shroud of white. The wind had backed off, and the sky shook loose a light and steady fall of snow. The snow tossed the dying sunlight back into the air, a secondhand radiance filled with the ancient scents of musk and sage and fallow soil. Far away, a herd of pronghorn stood with their heads up, alert, like a series of exclamation points against the swollen clouds, alarmed probably by the approaching storm.

Or maybe by a man, walking nearby.

After its first harsh breath, the storm had retreated. But the promise of violence twined like razor wire into the silence. When the storm let go again—probably when the sun dropped behind the distant mountains—it would be a full-on Colorado fury.

"And so what if it *is* Rhodes? He *wants* to die, Clyde. It's why he was trying to get home." I was sure of that now. It wasn't asylum in Canada that Rhodes sought. It was the kind of sanctuary found only in death.

Probably he'd wanted a final meeting with his dad, maybe to say farewell to a beloved pet or an old girlfriend. Then . . . peace.

"And if he killed Elise, and now he wants to die, too, well, maybe it's what he deserves. Did you think about that?"

Clyde, of course, said nothing. He kept his ears and tail high, the perfect picture of confidence as he nosed for his Kong.

The wind ticked up, sharp with threat. The pronghorn quivered and bolted. The sky lowered, and a thick, clotting snow began to fall in earnest. I was shivering hard now and couldn't seem to stop.

"*I* don't want to die, Clyde. You've got a fur coat, in case you hadn't noticed. If he's out there, we'll find him in the morning."

Clyde abandoned his search for his Kong and sat quietly, looking west, waiting for me to get my act together and do what I needed to do.

Military working dogs, especially ones like Clyde, train differently from K9 units. In wilderness police pursuits, you back off if your target becomes all but impossible to find and your men might get killed due to poor conditions—usually bad weather or darkness. You wait for conditions to improve, knowing that your bad guy is going to have to wait it out, too. The sheriff had been following protocol when he called us in before we'd finished searching the train. Especially after hearing from Fort Collins.

But in war, a dog is tracking enemy soldiers or terrorists. Men who, if they aren't caught, disappear into their rat holes and spend their free hours planting IEDs or taking sniper shots at your men. Military dogs and their handlers don't call it a day when the going gets tough.

For Clyde, the game wasn't over until he found his man.

I puffed out a long breath of air. Could it really be Rhodes? He would have heard us searching the train, then the announcement over the radio that we'd found our guy in Fort Collins, and finally the sound of everyone leaving. He must have known he was safe in the coal car, at least for the moment. But maybe he figured that as soon as we realized Fort Collins had the wrong guy, we'd be waiting for him in Cheyenne.

So he'd used whatever method he'd devised to get out of that car, a rope or a grappling hook, and—as Grams would say—gone while the getting was good. Maybe he was heading toward the ruined homesteader cabin that sat on railroad property a few miles west. Tramps sometimes squatted there. Maybe he figured he could wait out the night and the storm in that dubious shelter.

My mind went to those silver scratches on the coal car.

So maybe Clyde was right. But if we waited until morning, we'd be hunting a dead man. Much as I didn't want to admit it, I knew from listening to Corpsmen in Iraq that with the kind of injuries Rhodes had sustained in the war, even if he made it to the cabin, he wouldn't last the night. Severe burns make a person hypersensitive to extremes in temperature, particularly the cold. Rhodes might have underlying muscle or organ damage as well.

And the cabin wasn't much more than three walls and half a roof.

I squatted and looked Clyde in the eyes. "I swear, if this is a rabbit, I will give you to a little old lady who lives in an apartment in Manhattan and never leaves home except to drive you to the pet groomer. They'll shampoo you with lilac soap and clip your toenails and tie a bow around your neck."

He looked back at me patiently. The war and Dougie's death might have broken Clyde's heart, but not his spirit.

I stood. "You're a better man than I am."

I pulled up my hood and tied it, snugged up my zipper and checked my Sam Browne belt to make sure everything was secure. I showed Clyde his Kong, then gave him a whiff of Rhodes's cover. Clyde's nostrils flared, and he quivered with anticipation.

"Seek!"

Clyde took off west, angling away from the tracks. I held tight to his lead and jogged after him.

Far to the north, the train gave a final blast of its whistle. Albers saying farewell. I caught a glimpse of the train's running lights on the rear DPU as the last of the train swept behind us, and then the leviathan vanished, swallowed whole by a swell in the sea of grass.

Clyde trotted on, and I jogged after him. I warmed up as we moved, and my shivering eased. Soon I broke a sweat. I focused on the rhythm of our movements, holding the lead lightly but with a sure touch, trailing confidently after Clyde and keeping my gaze just below the horizon to watch for obstacles.

After we'd gone three quarters of a mile or so and climbed down and back up a couple of dry arroyos, I made Clyde stop so I could take a directional reading. I pulled out Dougie's old military Wittnauer compass and popped it open. Motes of Iraqi sand sparkled in the scuffed metal housing. I noted our precise heading, then we were off again.

A minute later, my headset buzzed. Nik. Angry.

"What's keeping you? The state patrol guys have been cut loose, and almost everyone's gone. The sheriff's almost done closing down. I've got one anxious deputy willing to give us a ride back to Denver if we hurry. But that storm's getting worse. Much longer, we'll have to bunk down near here."

"Where's Cohen?"

"He went to Fort Collins to pick up his suspect. I insisted on going with him, but he shut me down, the goddamn punk."

My heart dropped. "They got Rhodes?"

"Still in pursuit is what I heard. But Cohen figured they'd have him by the time he arrived. Should have let me go with him. Those douche bags can't find their own asses without a flashlight and a mirror."

"Nik, Clyde's acting like he's got a lead on our suspect."

A pause. "He scented off Rhodes's cover?"

"Yes."

Another pause, longer this time, and I could almost imagine the war going on inside him. The need to hunt down Rhodes and finish it and restore some balance to the world. Against that, the need to protect me as he'd always protected me.

When he finally spoke, his voice sounded like someone was using a pair of pliers to yank out each word. "It doesn't matter. If he's out there, we'll find him in the morning. Or find his body. Your teeth are chattering. And the radio says the worst of the storm is heading our way fast. You need to get inside."

"Clyde is sure."

"It doesn't matter, Sydney Rose. Get back here."

"Look, Clyde is confident. But I haven't been working him enough, and he went after a rabbit earlier. Let me look around a little bit more, see if I can find footprints or some other indication that someone came this way. If I don't find anything, I'll turn around."

"Ten minutes. You find something, make a mark. Then turn around anyway. You know how bad I want this guy, but I won't give you up. We can start again in the morning."

"Got it."

I hung up and gave Clyde his head for another couple of hundred yards. He slowed and then stopped, circling around as if he'd lost the trail.

"Shit, Clyde. Can't lose him now, boy."

An orange glow shimmered in the west: the last threads of tattered daylight. I'd been so focused on the ground and following Clyde that I hadn't realized how dark it was getting. I pulled the flashlight from my duty belt and took another reading on the compass.

Clyde found his scent, tugged on his lead.

"Let's just take a look, boy."

I downed him then looped his lead around my wrist. I played the beam of the Maglite along the ankle-high grasses. About three or four inches' worth of snow had fallen, but the wind had whirled a lot of it away before it could settle. Still, bent grass and faint impressions showed what might be footprints heading west. Running perpendicular to them was a set of rabbit tracks, explaining Clyde's momentary loss of the scent cone.

The orange glow faded to lavender, and the snow now came at us so hard and fast that it was like looking down the hyperdrive tunnel in a science fiction movie. The temperature plummeted. The only sound was the wind, filled with teeth.

"Sad place to die, Rhodes. If you're out there."

I shone the beam along the ground again. Already the tracing of footprints had vanished.

A phantom. Chasing ghosts in winter's gloom.

But ghosts were one thing I got.

I keyed the radio.

The sheriff sounded plenty pissed off. "Agent Parnell, why haven't you returned to the factory as ordered?"

"Sir, can you call me on my cell, please?" I didn't want to have this conversation in front of dispatch and any of the deputies who might still be monitoring transmissions.

But he ignored my request. "What the hell are you doing?"

"Sir, I'm approximately a mile and a half west of the tracks and a quarter mile south of the bridge. My dog appears to have a lead on Rhodes."

"Fort Collins PD spotted Rhodes more than an hour ago. Or did you somehow miss that, Agent Parnell?"

"Can you ask them to check, sir?"

"What?"

"Can you verify with them that the man they're tracking is Tucker Rhodes? Do they know he's burned over thirty percent of his body and that he's almost certainly dressed in civvies? Or did someone pass along his Marine induction photo and now they're chasing some train bum in camo? A lot of the hobos wear old military uniforms. Sir."

"Jesus."

I waited.

"Oh, Christ. Of all the—" Another pause. "How sure is your dog?"

"Very, sir."

He dropped his voice as if that would keep dispatch from hearing. "If you make me look like an ass, Parnell, I swear you will never play with real police again. You got me?"

I remained silent. I'd already told him once that looking like an ass came naturally to him.

A muttered curse. Then, "Stop your pursuit and stay where you are. Sheriff out."

The radio went dead.

I crouched next to Clyde, ducking my head against the wind and pressing my body to his reassuring heat. Several minutes ticked by before the sheriff's voice again crackled over the radio.

"They're still in pursuit, Parnell. I passed on what you said. About his injuries and his being in civvies."

"Thank you, sir."

"I need you to come back in. Even if it *is* Rhodes, I'm not sending men out in this."

"The snow and wind'll take away his scent by morning, sir."

"Then we'll find it again."

"Also, sir, because of his injuries, Rhodes has no way to regulate his internal temperature. We don't bring him in, he'll die."

Another pause. I could imagine the sheriff's jaw working as he tried not to say what he no doubt wanted to say. "God's truth, Parnell, you know the rules. My responsibility is to you, and to my men, who are mostly all home by now. I intend to leave them there. I will not risk their lives to search for some deranged nutcase wandering around with his dick in his hand. Not in this kind of visibility and with these temps. I can't get a vehicle out there, anyway. Terrain's too rough. Highway's already closed at the Wyoming border. Find something to mark your place so we can restart our search in the morning. Then turn around and get back here."

"I can bring him in on my own, sir."

"Goddammit, girl, listen to me. Never mind the weather, do you *know* what this guy did to the last little lady who crossed his path? Get back to the factory. That's an order."

The radio went dead.

"Yes, sir," I said to the silence.

Stiffly, I got back to my feet. I stomped in place and opened and closed my fists, trying to bring back the feeling.

In my mind's eye, I could see my living room. The worn, sagging couch, Grams's yellow and orange crocheted afghan. Clyde's bed in front of the fireplace. And the ancient coffee table with its burn marks from cigarettes years—decades—past. In my mental picture, a glass sat on that table, a tumbler filled with two fingers of whiskey, poured neat.

After watching what booze had done to my mother, I had not allowed alcohol to pass my lips until I went to war. In Iraq, I started sharing the airplane-size bottles of booze smuggled in by my fellow Marines. When I realized how good it was to be numb, I couldn't get enough.

Now, in the snowstorm, I swallowed hard at how much I wanted that drink.

But none of that mattered. I could not live with myself if I left Tucker Rhodes out here to die. Not even if he'd killed Elise. Not even if he'd run out here for the sole purpose of dying. He was a fellow Marine who'd given everything for his country and, whatever had happened since, I could not let him go.

I moved the phone around in my hand until I managed to get a signal and called Nik.

"Is the ambulance still there?"

"Just left. Where are you? You okay?"

"I'm fine. Ask them to come back, would you?"

"I can do that. You sure you're fine?"

"We're all good. Clyde and I will be there before you know it."

I hung up and tightened Clyde's lead.

"Let's go, boy. Seek!"

As Clyde and I staggered through the storm, heads lowered against the wind, I ran down a mental list of where my path might have crossed with Tucker Rhodes, who had served as a gunner. Kuwait, which had been our introduction to the Middle East; Al-Taqaddum, where we'd set up Mortuary Affairs; and all the sites in Anbar Province where the Mortuary Affairs platoon had gone to gather the bodies of the dead—Habbaniyah, Fallujah, Ramadi.

But of Tucker Rhodes, and who he might have been to me, I could pull up nothing.

My mind scrolled through the list again, the names rolling unspoken along my tongue with the rich, heady taste of olives and the acrid bite of sand.

When I'd first heard of places like Baghdad and Samarra, I'd imagined fantastic scenes from *Lawrence of Arabia*—Bedouins riding camelback across oceans of sand and a blazing sun pulled to earth by the muezzin's haunting call to prayer. As a child, I'd loved *Ali Baba and the Forty Thieves* and other stories from *The Arabian Nights*. I'd spent evenings on the couch with Grams watching silly musicals like *The Desert Song* and *Kismet*, pretending I would grow up to be one of those beautiful women, singing of love.

But Iraq—with its dead Marines, butchered civilians, and murdered idealism—the real Iraq with its twenty-first-century war, ground those youthful fantasies to dust.

As Clyde and I hunted through the storm, I pulled the distant warmth of the desert around me, repeating the romantic names like a talisman. If Iraq hadn't killed me, I reasoned, neither would a snowstorm.

With the descent of night, the storm worsened. I gave it the finger, then turned my radio off so it couldn't squawk and warn Rhodes of our approach. And so the sheriff couldn't again order me to return. I took another heading on the compass, wrapped Clyde's lead around my waist and looped it again around my wrist.

If I collapsed, Clyde would get me home. He would drag me there if he had to.

I fell the first time when we were climbing out of a shallow ditch, and my numb toes caught a rock. Clyde waited while I hauled myself back up and stumbled forward, only vaguely aware that I had fallen and that my pants were now soaked through. I fell again maybe fifty yards on. This time it took me longer to get back up.

Once, through the darkness, I glimpsed the Sir. My flashlight flitted across his grave face. But when I called out to him, he only shook his head and turned away. The dead private made an appearance, followed by Gonzo and a parade of some of the other Marines I'd processed in the bunker at Camp Taqaddum. I caught a glimpse of Elise, her hair like a light.

When Rhodes finally appeared, I thought he, too, was a ghost.

The wind had shifted to blow out of the east, carrying his scent away from us, and I think Clyde saw him at the same moment I did. Rhodes stood on a slight rise, his back to us, looking west. He wore jeans and sneakers, a watch cap, and a medium-weight parka.

I played the flashlight briefly over him, but I couldn't see his hands.

His erect bearing—shoulders up, back straight—made me wonder if he'd passed into a stage of hypothermia where he no longer felt the cold.

Silently, I downed Clyde so that he would make as low a profile as possible, dropped the flashlight, and fumbled for my Glock. I held it next to my leg, pointing down.

"Tucker Rhodes," I shouted. "Special Agent Parnell with the railway police. Show me your hands!"

He didn't move. Didn't so much as twitch.

"Rhodes!"

He turned his head to the side and said, "She's out there."

I risked a glance past him at the snow-studded darkness and suppressed a shiver. "Raise your hands, Rhodes."

"Elise." Her name came out like a prayer. "Waiting for me."

I blinked snow from my eyes. "Sure you want that, Rhodes? She's probably a little pissed at you right now."

"She understands."

"Really? She's feeling okay that you killed her?"

Another long silence. Then, "I'm pretty fucked up, aren't I?"

"We're all pretty fucked up, Marine. But you may top the list."

"Ma'am, I know you have a gun. You could do me a right big favor by using it. 'Cause I'm not going back with you. I'm either gonna die right here in the middle of goddamn nowhere. Or I'm gonna get to Montana and die there. Way I feel, I'd just as soon make it now."

"I leave you here, you won't make it to Montana or anywhere else. You want to see your dad again, right? And your mom? If you come with me, you'll at least have that."

He shook his head. "Someone once told me that you can take the boy out of the war. But not the war out of the man. My dad gets that. I know he does. But maybe he don't want to see it for himself."

"What about your mom? You want to see her, don't you?"

"My mom don't understand any of the shit I brought back with me. She just wanted her beautiful boy back. But he's dead. Elise understood. But now she's dead, too."

"Because of you."

He didn't answer. But I had my suspicions about what might have happened. Not the why of it. There is no why in killing someone you love. But sometimes the hurt rises up in you so hard you don't see it coming. Rhodes had grown up a rancher's boy, but war had forged him into someone else entirely. Lance Corporal Rhodes survived in Iraq by devouring Tucker Rhodes so completely that only a warrior remained. It happens to pretty much everyone who sees combat. It keeps you alive until you come home.

Then suddenly the enemy is the person you became in order to survive.

"Parnell," he said.

"Yes."

"Corporal Sydney Parnell? Of Mortuary Affairs?"

The hair lifted on my neck. "Yes."

I brought the gun partway up, ready, as he turned and faced me. He had a bandana wrapped around the lower half of his face, but the beam of my flashlight caught his eyes, those beautiful jade-green eyes.

Memory came like a blow.

Though we'd never known each other officially, and though I'd never seen any part of his face except his eyes, Rhodes and I had met the night when everything I believed in, or thought I believed in, exploded, sending shards of betrayal and revenge into everyone around us.

"Fuck," I said.

"Fuck all," he agreed.

The Sir had done everything he could to gather the shattered pieces and bury them. But as I stood with Rhodes in the middle of nowhere, I realized that if he went to trial for Elise's murder, the spectacular details of her death would draw in curious journalists and hard-charging pros- ecutors, all eager to dig up everything they could about the wounded war hero turned killer. And the story they would eventually uncover, the story from Iraq, would destroy not only Rhodes, but every single person who'd been involved.

"Habbaniyah," Rhodes said. "It was you that night."

Fury roiled under my skin. A pure and sharpened rage that whittled me down to bone and white-hot steel. Because the man standing in front of me was the biggest threat I'd known since returning to the States. Tucker Rhodes could destroy me and everything that mattered to me.

"You had no right," I said.

"No."

My body trembled, helpless against the rising tempest. Clyde came to his feet, barking. But I barely heard him. For a thought wailed in my brain like a siren.

Rhodes was a threat only if he lived long enough for the jackals to catch his scent. If he died, he would end up a tragic two inches of space in the local section of the paper. Within a day or two, he wouldn't even be that. He and Elise would disappear, another sad footnote to the war. Just another good vet gone bad, two more lives sacrificed to the cause.

My vision narrowed until it held nothing but my hand with the gun. And Rhodes.

The rage turned from heat to ice. I quieted Clyde.

"You were there," Rhodes said. "You know what bringing me back will cost you and the others. You'd do us all a favor if you'd use that gun."

The cold crept from my heart to my gun hand. "I'm not a killer," I said, even though I knew I was.

"You're a Marine. And Marines do the right thing, no matter the cost, right?"

"Except for Habbaniyah."

He dipped his head in acknowledgment.

He stood silhouetted hard against the falling snow, a dark bulk I could not fail to hit if I raised the Glock. My finger slid toward the trigger, brushed against the edge.

The cool, rational part of my brain egged me on. Shooting him would be something every other cop would understand. Some would even applaud. I would say I thought he had a weapon—and probably he did, hidden in the pocket of his coat. I would say I thought my life was in danger, and they would understand. I would tell them that he threatened to do to me what he'd done to Elise, and they would clap me on the back for my bravery.

Hell, they'd probably give me a medal.

My finger shook. But I kept the gun pointing somewhere near his feet. Had I really come out here thinking I would save him only to turn around and become his killer?

"Shit," I said.

"Please," he whispered. And I knew he was asking me, not to spare his life, but to end it.

Killing him would be easier than many things I'd done. And kinder.

"Shit," I said again.

"Do it," he said. "I ruined your life. Do it."

My hand came up of its own volition.

"Do it because it's the right thing," he said. "Please."

My finger slid through the trigger guard, bumped against the Glock's safe-action trigger.

Clyde barked.

Rhodes fell to his knees with his eyes locked on mine, then tipped to the ground. He rolled down the slope and landed, face up, at my feet.

The jade-green eyes looked at nothing for a long time, then closed.

CHAPTER 8

In war, you do things that people back home will never understand.

—Sydney Parnell, ENGL 0208,
Psychology of Combat

Clyde sniffed at Rhodes's still form.

I'd spent two tours of duty—a lifetime—carrying bodies in Iraq. The work had broken something inside of me. But it had also made me strong. I figured Rhodes probably weighed two hundred pounds to my hundred and twenty-five.

I could work with it.

I didn't bother checking for a pulse, because at this point it didn't really matter if he was alive or dead. I was taking him back. And I was going to do it on my own. As the sheriff himself had said, no vehicle at his disposal would be able to navigate the terrain I'd crossed on my way here.

I holstered my gun then searched his pockets for weapons. The only thing I found was a photo of him with Elise, snapped before the IED had done its dirty work; probably the one he'd taken from Elise's bedroom. I slid it back into his pocket.

He groaned when I rolled him onto his stomach.

"Hang in there, Marine."

When he'd fallen down the hill, I'd thought maybe I'd actually shot him. That I, too, had been swallowed up by my war-self. I had to sniff the Glock's barrel to be sure I hadn't fired.

I'd think later about whether I was glad about that.

Now I straddled Rhodes from behind, grabbed him beneath his arms then pulled him up to his knees. I had to work to get him to his feet. He was dead weight, and the ground was slick. For a few bad moments, I thought I wasn't going to make it and we'd have to ride out the storm here. But eventually we were both standing upright, Rhodes slumped against me.

I rotated him, squatted, then pivoted as his weight fell across my shoulders. I had to lean on Clyde to get back to my feet.

I staggered forward a few steps, then tried to orient myself with the compass. It took me way too long to read the dial in the thin beam of my flashlight. The compass face swam in front of my eyes, and I couldn't focus.

Hypothermia, settling in for the ride.

Clyde gave an anxious whine. Now that he'd completed his mission, he looked miserable despite his fur coat.

"This way, boy."

I talked to myself and Clyde as we stumbled forward, muttering old Marine cadences. When I ran out of the ones I knew, I made up my own. I never was much of a poet.

"We are marching through the snow. Will we make it, I don't know."

And a little later, "Rhodes, you know you weigh a ton. Carrying you ain't any fun."

Leave him, whispered a voice in my ear. *His life for everyone else's. No one need know. He could have been dead when you found him.*

The snow grew coarse and hard and hot, whisking us to the other side of the world as it morphed to sand that glowed like brass under a brown Iraqi sky. A molten sun threatened to burn our skin black and peel it like an orange. My tongue grew thick in the dry paste of my mouth. If I'd had a free hand, I would have unzipped my coat, shrugged it off.

"Any help is far away. We won't live another day."

The boiling sun set, yielding to the silver knives of moonlight that carved up Camp Taqaddum, slicing through the barracks and the rec center and the motor pool. Outside the barricade, someone fired an AK-47, the rounds echoing in the empty desert around us. Insurgents. Or maybe just a member of the Iraqi Security Forces letting off steam on the base at Habbaniyah.

I touched my sidearm in the thigh holster to make sure it was still there in case insurgents overran the barricades.

"We're safe," said Corporal Tomitsch. We called him Conan, because that's how he was built.

"You think?"

"Sure, Lady Hawk." My own nickname.

I bid him goodnight and ducked into my tent, curling into a fetal position on my cot and breathing in kerosene fumes from the canvas. I must have finally slept, because sometime later I was startled awake by the Sir, who knelt next to my bed, the red beam of his flashlight illuminating his face. He pressed his finger to his lips and tipped his head to indicate I should go with him. I reached for my uniform, but he handed me a pair of sweats and a hoodie, and I noticed that he was dressed in civvies. Uneasy, I pulled the sweats on over my T-shirt and shorts and followed him, weaving my way past my sleeping tent mates. Outside, the warm wind threw dust in our eyes while overhead, the Milky Way glittered like treasure from Ali Baba's cave.

The Sir said, "I'm going into Habbaniyah, Corporal Parnell, and I could use your help."

"This an order, sir?" Knowing something was off by his manner and our clothes.

"No, Corporal. Your choice."

"I'll come."

He knew damn well I would travel to Baghdad on my knees if that was what he needed me to do.

"Should I get Ayers, sir?" I asked. "For security?"

He regarded me with sudden alarm. I wondered if he'd just realized that because of Dougie, maybe I wasn't the right person for the job. My heart tripped.

"Doug Ayers? No," the Sir said. "No one can know about this. Especially not—no. Do you understand, Corporal? You can't tell Ayers."

"I won't, sir. But, sir, you're giving me a bad feeling."

"Good. Want to back out?"

"No, sir."

"I trust you, Parnell. It's why I chose you."

"Yes, sir. You can trust me."

"This way then, Corporal."

Clyde barked, and I jerked awake in the snow.

We stood on the edge of an embankment. I would have tumbled in if Clyde hadn't barked a warning. I backed away from the edge and took another reading on the compass. When it diverted from the path Clyde clearly wanted to take, I followed him.

The Sir led me to the area on base where equipment was stored and maintained. An Iraqi man, one of our interpreters, met us there. Everyone called him Mohammed, though that wasn't his name. Mohammed gassed up a dusty white van and drove us through the gate and out of the wire, down the plateau to the town of Habbaniyah, where someone had been firing a rifle earlier. After twenty minutes, he turned onto a narrow dirt street leading to a residential area in a part of town we wouldn't normally venture into without an armored caravan. Four men with rifles stood outside a single-story mud house. Moonlight etched shadows on the dirt street and against the far wall of houses, shimmered in the battered leaves of a grove of palms. The men wore street clothes; keffiyehs covered their mouths and noses. I thought they were Iraqi until I heard them whispering.

Americans.

One of them turned toward me as I climbed out of the car. He watched in silence as I wrapped a hijab around my head and throat. All I could see of him were his eyes, which were a startling emerald green. They were wide with worry.

The wind drove snow under my jacket, down the cuffs. Rhodes moaned. I had no idea how far we'd come, or how far we had left to go. Clyde was trying to push our pace; I hoped that meant that we were getting close. I clawed my phone free. No signal. I touched the radio. But I wasn't going to call the sheriff.

I followed the Sir and one of the Marines into the house.

In a back bedroom were two bodies, both naked, dead a couple of hours. A male Marine, castrated and beheaded, his head propped next to the gaping wound near his crotch, his penis and testicles where his head should have been. Next to him lay a pregnant female Iraqi, her face destroyed, her body battered until the skin had split.

In the front room was an Iraqi boy, ten or eleven, rocking and weeping on the floor.

Nauseated, horrified, I clung to the wooden doorjamb for support. I couldn't understand why the Sir had brought me to this place in the middle of the night. To these deaths and this weeping child. It wasn't how we operated.

"Let's get them out of here, Corporal," the Sir said to me.

And because he was my CO, and because I trusted him, I did as he asked. We lifted the corpses into body bags, placed them into the back of the van, and took them away.

I wondered—then and in the days that followed—why it was so important to hide the truth of how the Marine and the woman had died. But I never asked. The Sir said it was our job to protect everyone involved, and that had been enough for me. So I had covered up their murders, pretended that something altogether different had happened. The Sir told me it was better for everyone that way. And God knows, we meant well. But our actions—and those of the Marines involved—unleashed a fusillade of vengeance that spiraled out of control.

We could be court-martialed if the truth came out. The dead man's widow would learn she didn't have sole occupancy of her husband's heart, and the Sir's family would have to wonder if he really was a hero. But there'd never been any reason for the truth to come out. The four Marines would never tell.

And the little boy who was the *real* reason the Sir had brought me and not Tomitsch or Bailor, he had—

The wind slammed us hard, and I went down to one knee. Labored back up again.

Rhodes said in a slurred voice, "You can put me down, Corporal. I can walk to the Humvee from here. I ain't hurt that bad."

Three more steps, and I went down again. One knee, then the other. Rhodes slid off my shoulders onto the ground, and we lay together in a heap. I strung enough brain cells together to prop the flashlight so that the beam pointed eastward. Or maybe eastward. Clyde sat next to me and gave an anxious whine.

"We're still good, boy."

Some time passed. The victorious wind fell to a tuneless lullaby. My body grew heavy, sinking into the quiet earth as snow gentled a blanket over us. I stretched out, entangled with Clyde and Rhodes, and closed my eyes.

The Sir shook me.

Get up, Marine.

Can't, sir.

NOW, Marine.

No can do, sir.

Clyde was on his feet, barking a volley of deep-chested warnings that startled me back from the twilight of my thoughts. I lifted my head.

Nik. My flashlight had caught him, grim-faced and silent, in its beam. Snow swirled around him as if a flock of geese had exploded overhead.

I grabbed Clyde's lead, tried to find my voice.

Nik stepped away from the light. His calm, quiet voice came out of the darkness. "Rhodes, get away from her and stand up. Do it now, you goddamned son of a bitch."

Half on top and half underneath me, Rhodes twitched and groaned. He flattened his hands and pushed his feet along the ground as if he meant to obey.

I found my voice. "Nik, it's okay. I'm okay."

"Sydney Rose?"

"We're good."

"Are you hurt?"

"No."

Rhodes stopped trying to rise and crumpled back against me.

The flashlight soared into the air as Nik picked it up and turned the beam on us. "Move away from him, Sydney Rose."

But when he'd lifted the light, I'd seen what was in his eyes. And in his hand. I wrapped my arms around Rhodes.

"It's okay," Nik went on in the same gentle voice, as if he were approaching a trapped animal. "It's all okay, Sydney Rose. Just move away. Let me do what needs to be done."

"No." I struggled to gather my words. "Not up to us."

Sudden fury flashed in Nik's voice. "This man tortured and killed Elise. He is a disgrace to the uniform he tried to burn. The media will turn him into a victim, spew all that PTSD crap. But Elise is the true victim. Now move away."

"Not our call. Please, Nik." I panted with the effort of speaking. "No . . . gun."

Nik took two steps toward us, and Clyde darted in front of me. The beam of the Maglite swung toward him, followed by Nik's gun.

Terror clawed up my throat. "Nik, no!" My worthless hands scrabbled to find my own gun. "Clyde, come!"

Behind Nik, a pair of lights flared, and an engine revved as a vehicle labored up the rise. I tried to find my knees, floundered like a landed fish. Doors opened. Voices spilled out.

"Nik!" I pleaded. "Don't. Think of Ellen Ann and Gentry. They need you. You can't sacrifice them to kill Rhodes."

Backlit by the headlights, Nik shuddered.

"Don't take away your son's father," I said.

"Ah, shit." Nik lowered his gun. Sank to his knees. "Ah, Jesus. Elise. Oh, Elise."

More voices. The silhouettes of people climbing toward us. A sound that might have been Nik, weeping.

Clyde crouched next to me, head thrust forward as he snarled a warning to anyone who tried to approach.

"Somebody get the dog away from her," one of the voices said.

Nik's voice then, trying to call Clyde away. But Clyde dug in. I fumbled for his lead, ordered him down, curled into myself. I just wanted to sleep.

"Get a muzzle on him."

Clyde snarled as someone pulled him away.

Hands grabbed me, rolled me onto my back. Nik's face came into view, then the face of Deputy O'Malley. O'Malley pushed the hair back from my face and grinned at me.

"Fucking Marines," he said.

Doors opened and closed again and someone shouted for a stretcher, and then O'Malley had me in his arms and someone gripped my wrist and someone else asked if Rhodes was alive.

A woman said, "Doesn't look good."

"Alive," I whispered to whoever could hear me. "He's alive."

I was down again, but not on the ground. Someone placed a mask over my mouth and nose and warm air flooded my lungs and the Sir was there, saying we're all good, we're all good, and finally, with my hand in Nik's and the salt of his tears on my skin, they let me sleep.

CHAPTER 9

- I see dead people. Like in that movie. Ghosts that no one else can see. Except my dog. I think he sees them, too.

- Do these ghosts threaten you?

- No. It's not like that. They're just . . . sad. I'm sad. We're all sad together. Like something has broken, and none of us knows how to fix it.

- Corporal Parnell, do you believe these ghosts are real?

- Yes. PAUSE. No. PAUSE. I don't know if they're real. If I were still in Iraq, I'd say yes. They seem real. I mean, one of them sits at my kitchen table pretty much every morning. But here? I just don't know. Does this mean I'm crazy?

- I'm going to write you a prescription for alprazolam. It will calm you down, let you sleep. It will let your ghosts sleep, too. Maybe they won't bother you so much.

- What if they're trying to say something important? Not just to me but to everyone. I mean, maybe they haven't figured it out exactly, either, so they're just kind of . . . waiting. Maybe there's something we're all supposed to learn.

> *- Here's the scrip, Corporal Parnell. You can get it filled before you leave today. I'm going to be out of town next month, but we'll talk when I get back.*
> *—Interview Transcript, VA Assistance Office,*
> *Camp Pendleton*

Elise rode home with me.

In the back of the deputy's car, I sat slumped against the driver's-side door, one of the EMTs' blankets still wrapped around my shoulders. Next to me, Clyde took up most of the backseat, his head in my lap. I stroked his fur and whispered apologies. I know he too had nightmares of Iraq.

Iraq. Habbaniyah. A house of mud and stone.

Elise sat on the floor on the passenger side, her head in her hands, able to slide into that small space because, of course, she wasn't really there.

Clyde was careful not to let his paws dangle.

Nik rode up front with the deputy, Brad Perkins. I hadn't met Perkins before—he'd been part of the search teams on the back end of the train. Decent guy for hanging around and then driving us through this mess. Beyond decent. I heard Nik offer Perkins his spare bedroom if they closed the highway.

"Got a sister lives nearby," Perkins answered. "Appreciate it, though."

Nik turned in his seat.

"You still cold?" he asked.

I nodded. My teeth had finally quit chattering, but the cold went deeper than blankets or a car heater could cure.

"Should have let them take you to the hospital."

"I'll be fine." My voice sounded like Velcro ripping. "They sure Rhodes is going to make it?"

"Yeah. You want that coffee now?"

I nodded again. Nik passed a paper cup with a lid through the opening in the safety screen that divided the front seat from the back. My frozen fingers still weren't working, so I held the cup with my palms.

"I want you to stay with me and Ellen Ann," he said. "Grams is there now. You shouldn't be alone."

I could not bear Ellen Ann's grief. "The EMTs checked me out. I'm good."

"That's not what I mean. You look like you've seen a ghost."

I barked a little laugh.

"I have Clyde," I said.

"Clyde looks a little the worse for wear, too." Nik dropped his fist lightly on the seat back. "I'm sorry I dragged you into this."

I couldn't say what I wanted to say in front of the deputy. About how I understood what he'd done and why, and that it was okay. That I'd been that crazy before, too. That I totally got the rage and the helplessness, which were really two sides of the same coin.

I glanced over at Elise. "No Weight, Nik."

"No?"

"No."

"Okay." He cleared his throat. "We can talk more later."

"Sure."

"Tomorrow, maybe."

I turned toward the window and closed my eyes against his voice, slipping away again.

In the days after we'd taken away the bodies of the Marine and the interpreter, the dead Marine's buddies had made it their mission to hunt down his killers. The insurgents had responded with increased sniper fire and IEDs.

Before long, everything *had gone to shit.*

"What are we going to do about this, Sir?" I'd asked.

"It's a mess, Parnell. Jesus Christ. Wish I hadn't dragged you into it."

"I'm good, sir. But I'm wondering what we're going to do."

"You mean, like, are we going to tell everyone about how the insurgents killed Haifa and Resenko? And how after that some of our Marines went bat-shit crazy and decided to play Charles Bronson? And that now we're getting a taste of our own payback?"

"Bronson, sir?"

"Never mind."

He looked at me, eyes grim in his calm, soldier-leader face, a face I'd grown to love and trust. "You expect me to have the answers, Parnell. And you should. That's your right. But it's a gaggle fuck. The whole damn thing is a gaggle fuck. And there isn't a damn thing we can do except keep using our shovels to try and dig our way out." He raised his voice so everyone could hear. "Load 'em up and let's hit the road, Marines. We got bodies."

"Ah, Christ." Bailor. "Why so many bodies all the sudden? Damn ragheads got some real hate on us."

"No worries," Tomitsch said. "We'll kill every last one of them."

The sheriff's car swayed side-to-side as we hit traffic, and I jerked awake. Clyde lifted his head. The snow had stopped, and only a thin layer of white covered the ground. Maybe the storm hadn't hit very hard this far south. The blue-white glow of the city's mercury lights fractured on the car's ice-streaked windows.

Elise was gone.

"We left our duty vehicle right down here," Nik was saying to the deputy. "There it is."

The car eased to a stop, and Clyde and I had to wait for the deputy to open the back door—the backseat was meant for perps, so there were no inside handles. I tumbled out, still weak, and Perkins caught me.

"Easy there," he said in a big, gentle voice, his breath like smoke in the cold. "Ain't easy being a hero."

I tried to laugh off my embarrassment. "Right."

He set me upright. "You take care of yourself, okay?"

"Sure. Thanks for the ride."

"Anytime."

I felt Perkins's eyes on me as Nik came around. The men shook hands, then Nik took my arm and led me to the Explorer. When I was settled in the passenger seat, he let Clyde into the back, started the engine, and stepped back out to clear the windows. Perkins turned his duty vehicle around and headed north. He waved before he left.

Down near the creek, the hobo camp looked deserted in the cloud-reflected city shine. Tents and tarps were gone, the fire pit empty. Hopefully that meant everyone had managed to find beds at Saint Joseph's or Step 13 or another shelter.

Nik got back into the vehicle, put the engine in gear, and climbed the embankment toward the street.

"Sydney Rose—"

"I'm too tired, Nik."

"Just let me say my piece."

I stayed silent.

"I went a little crazy up there. I'm sorry. I wouldn't have shot Clyde. You know that."

"You don't have to explain."

"I just—" His jaw knotted beneath his skin. "I didn't know I could hurt so much. Thought I was too strong to hurt like this."

"It's not about strength, Nik. Jesus. It's about love."

"Love." A quiet, rueful snort. "Gives us feet of clay."

"And makes us strong."

He glanced at me, looked away. "Could be."

We stared out the windshield and waited for traffic to clear. Headlights from a passing truck carved Nik's face into arcs of bright and dark.

"I wish you had left him out there," he said.

"That so?" Anger sparked through the exhaustion. "I thought letting him freeze to death wasn't hands-on enough for you. Got the feeling you wanted something more personal."

He laid his eyes on me. "That were so, Sydney Rose, I wouldn't have told you to give up the search and come back."

"You knew damn well I wouldn't come back. Not without him. So don't give me that bullshit. I was your one shot at Rhodes. So you came after me, made sure you caught up to us where there weren't any witnesses. You'd of killed him if the deputies hadn't arrived when they did."

A long silence. Then, "Why'd you go after him?"

"You're asking me that? Jesus, Nik, you were the one taught me to never leave a fallen soldier behind."

I yanked open the glove box and rifled past sunscreen and lip balm and pills for a stray cigarette, desperate for the burn in my lungs to mask my sudden wounding. My heart hurt with what I didn't want him to say, with the fear that I was right about him.

He was so still and so quiet. It was as if he'd traveled to a place that didn't reside in the same dimension as the rest of the world. Some place so completely apart I couldn't follow him.

"Unless they've gone bad," he said.

"What?"

He returned with a start, suddenly back in the truck with me.

"Always my belief that if they've gone bad," he said, "you leave them."

He pulled onto the street, corrected the car when it fish-tailed on the ice, then eased into late-evening traffic. "My fault for not teaching you that."

At Nik's house, he pulled to the curb.

"You sure you're good to drive?" he asked.

"Yeah."

Nik got out, and I climbed over behind the steering wheel. Ellen Ann stood in the sallow light just inside the front door, wrapped in an old gray sweater and staring out through the screen, arms crossed over her chest. Her face was ashen, her hair in disarray. I gave her a small wave, and she raised a single, listless hand to show she'd seen me.

Nik leaned back into the truck, laid his hand on mine for a moment, then closed the door and walked up the drive, a man yoked to his grief like a single ox pulling for six. I left him to his wife and their anguish and drove home, steering along the icy streets with my wrists. A few blocks from the house, I pulled into the drive-through of a twenty-four-hour McDonald's and ordered ten cheeseburgers.

Only the porch light and a single, dim lamp in the living room pushed back the darkness when I pulled into the driveway. I let Clyde out and waited while he did his business. Something rustling in the deep shadows of the neighbor's trees caught his attention, a squirrel probably, but I called him back, and together we walked like ninety-year-olds to the house.

Inside, I shrugged out of my coat, tugged off my boots in the hallway, then closed and locked the front door. Clyde hurried down the hall ahead of me, his nails clicking on the linoleum. I heard him drink from his bowl. In the kitchen, I found a note on the table: "Gone to Nik and Ellen Ann's. Probably stay a few days. You need me, you call me. Love, Grams."

I turned on all the lights in the house, chasing away shadows and ghosts alike. I rinsed and cleaned Clyde's water bowl and refilled it, then dug out his cheeseburgers and placed them on the floor, buns and all.

I found a yogurt in the refrigerator and opened a can of peaches.

Clyde wolfed down his burgers, then came over to the kitchen table to see if I was eating anything interesting. I let him sniff the yogurt, and to my surprise, he scooped out a big dollop with his tongue. I placed the yogurt on the floor and watched him eat.

I picked up the phone and called my boss, Captain Mauer, at his home. I filled him in on the day—he already knew most of it from dispatch.

"The sheriff called to lodge a complaint about you, said you disobeyed orders and endangered his men."

I said nothing.

"He said women had no business playing at being cops."

I closed my eyes.

"I told him if he wanted to whine about you saving his ass, he ought to take his complaint to the media, see what they make of the story."

"Thank you, Captain."

"Take tomorrow off, Parnell."

"Thank you, sir. But if it's all the same, I'd just as soon get back on schedule."

"Not this time. What you did today finishes off your shift. We'll see you back here next week. From what I've heard, your body's gonna need the rest."

"Sir—"

"That's an order, Parnell."

"Yes, sir."

"You did good today," he said and hung up.

I pulled off my headset and leaned my forehead against the plaster. After a minute of trying to talk myself out of it, I pulled the whiskey down from the cupboard, poured two fingers into a glass and drained it. Then I poured some more and lit a cigarette. I took the pain meds the EMTs had given me from my pocket and set them on the counter. I looked at them for a long time before turning away.

I watched the news while I finished the cigarette and the whiskey. Nothing about Elise.

The memory of Tucker Rhodes's jade-green eyes stayed with me as I grabbed sweats and a T-shirt from my bedroom and, trailed by Clyde, went down the hallway toward the bathroom where I hoped a hot shower would wash everything away. Elise's brutalized body. Nik's Weight. Rhodes's pain and grief. And his jade-green eyes, once arrogant, now lost.

Clyde trotted into the bathroom then whimpered and came back out.

I reached in through the doorway and flipped on the light.

Elise stood in the center of the tiled floor. Behind her, a naked man, headless and still, his body burned.

"Survivor's guilt," I said to Clyde. "That's all."

Gently, I waved Elise and Resenko into the hallway, a breath of chill air kissing my cheeks as they passed by. Clyde and I tumbled into the bathroom, and I closed the door, leaned against it. Clyde sniffed at the gap between the door and the tiles.

Only silence from the hallway. I turned the lock.

"We're still good," I told Clyde.

I set the whiskey on the sink and ordered him to lie down.

"Roll over, boy."

With meticulous attention, I went over every inch of his body, looking for any injuries, paying special attention to his paws. When I was sure he was clear, I gave him a good belly rub, then turned my attention to my own weary body.

I stripped off my uniform and dropped it on the floor. In a drawer, I found a pair of tweezers, closed the toilet lid, and propped my left foot on it. It took me half an hour to pull out all the spines. Clyde watched at first, then settled himself with a yawn against the bathroom door. The skin on my leg was angry and red, and I set out the bottle of hydrogen peroxide to use after I showered.

I unwrapped the bandages on my hands, decided the scrapes weren't too bad. My face was another matter. From my jump onto the train and subsequent slide across the platform, I looked exactly like someone who'd taken on a freight train and lost. The cut on my cheek was larger than I'd realized, offset by a bruise that grew as I watched. Both my eyes were puffy, and it wouldn't surprise me if they were black by morning.

Well, it wasn't as if I had anyone to impress.

In the shower, I wielded the washcloth fiercely, ignoring the pain from my bruised back and shoulders as I scrubbed my body then rubbed shampoo into my scalp. I didn't want to think about Iraq. I didn't want to think about dead people and wounded people and sad and guilty people. I didn't want nightmares or ghosts or flashbacks to bodies torn apart by IEDs. I didn't want Tucker Rhodes. I didn't want to think about my parents. I just wanted to be a regular twenty-seven-year-old woman, holding down a decent job, enrolled at the community college and studying whatever caught my interest while I tried to figure out my life. Maybe later I'd want something more, but all I cared about right now were the simple things—my grandmother and my dog and a roof over our heads and not losing all of that because of something that went down in another life on the other side of the world.

I toweled off, combed out my hair, pulled on the sweats, then eyeballed Clyde. He lowered his ears with perhaps the first warning of what was coming.

"Bath," I said.

I filled the tub with a few inches of water and poured in baby shampoo. I brought out towels from the linen closet and set them in a heap on the floor.

I pointed to the tub. "Get in, boy."

He hauled himself to his feet like an old dog. I helped him scrabble into the tub and began rubbing soapy water into his fur. I took my time, scratching him in his favorite places. He wasn't too big on baths, but he seemed to be enjoying this one. He stood in the water with his eyes closed and fairly purred as I ran his brush through his wet fur.

When I finished, I rinsed him off with the shower nozzle, then ordered him still while I toweled off as much water as I could before the inevitable full-body shake. I helped him out of the tub, and he curled up on the bath mat. I sat on the floor next to him.

The bathroom was warm, small, safe. The furnace clanked comfortingly through the vents, the mirrors were foggy and moist and opaque—they didn't make me look at anything I didn't want to see.

And outside in the hallway . . .

I grabbed my whiskey glass from the sink, drank. Then, gently, I laid my hand on Clyde's head and began scratching him with the brush behind his ears, talking to him in the high-pitched singsong voice dogs love. I knew we were thinking about the same thing—about Dougie and his last day and whatever mission he'd gone on that had required him to leave Clyde with me. Clyde, who loved me because Dougie loved me. And who couldn't forgive me when Dougie didn't come back.

"I am sorry I didn't trust you today, Clyde."

His ears came up.

"I promise, from here on out, you are my go-to guy. Okay? Partners through thick and thin."

He placed his chin on my thigh. As my fingers found the tender spots, he curled into me. He looked almost happy.

"But we're going to get serious about our training. And the whole PTSD thing. We'll have to figure that one out together."

He yawned. Closed his eyes.

"Good boy," I told him. His tail thumped on the tile.

I cleaned up the bathroom, then used the hydrogen peroxide on my face and hands and calf, put a butterfly bandage on my cheek, and smeared a light coating of petroleum jelly on my hands, followed by more bandages.

At the door, I braced myself. But the hallway lay empty.

Clyde followed me on my rounds as I checked doors and windows and turned out the lights, then went with me to the room at the end of the hall—my childhood bedroom, which Grams had kept exactly the same since I'd been a teenager. When I returned home from Iraq, a decorated Marine, it was to this girl's room with its painted white furniture and polka-dot comforter, the turquoise-blue walls covered with the peeling posters of indie bands. Other than bringing in my Marine stuff and a couple of mementos from Iraq, I hadn't changed anything. Maybe because I needed to hang on to the girl I'd been. Or because I didn't know how to move on.

I touched the photo of Dougie propped on the nightstand then turned on the bedside lamp and slid under the sheets.

"Goodnight, Clyde."

I waited for him to take up his usual post outside my bedroom door. But for the first time since he'd come back with me from Iraq, Clyde settled himself on the faux zebra rug next to my bed. A minute later, he was snoring.

I smiled even though it hurt. "Goodnight, Clyde."

I read a few pages of Homer's *Iliad* for my upcoming class then turned out the light and fell into a tortured sleep.

In my dream, I stood in the desert at night, under the glittering band of the Milky Way, watching Doug Ayers as the wind riffled his blond hair. The alarm on his watch beeped over and over, and I kept telling him we needed to be quiet. That insurgents were nearby. He finally turned around and looked at me. He nodded his head as if making up his mind about something.

"Go on, Rosie," he said. "It's okay."

"Go where, Dougie? And it's not okay. Don't tell me it's okay. What were you thinking?"

"Take care of Clyde. Someday he'll save your life."

"Why didn't you take him with you that night? He might have saved *your* life."

"Couldn't. You know that. But you can. Take him with you. And keep him trained, Rosie. You keep working it, too. And I don't mean just what you're doing in the reserves. That's not enough. You guys are only as good as your training. I need to know the two of you are okay here."

"They'll send me to jail, Dougie. Because of Rhodes. Then what will happen to Clyde?"

He tilted his head back, looked up at the stars. "You know what you need to do, Rosie. Now's the time to be strong."

His alarm kept pinging over and over until I woke up enough to realize it was my cell phone as someone rang, hung up, tried again.

Still half in the dream, my heart leaping in panic, I scrabbled across the nightstand for the phone.

"Dougie?"

"Um, this is Detective Cohen. May I speak with Special Agent Parnell?"

I closed my eyes against the fresh wash of grief.

"Speaking," I said after a moment.

"It's Mike. Sorry. Did I wake you?"

I turned toward the red glow of the clock face. 1:27 a.m. "No. I was reading."

"Insomnia?"

"Guilt."

Silence.

"Sorry, Detective. Sometimes I don't think before I speak."

"S'kay. I have a lot of those nights."

We were both silent for a moment. Then he said, "Thanks for doing my job for me while I sat on my ass in Fort Collins. Everyone says you're a hero."

I wasn't going to play that gig. "I'm guessing you didn't call me at one thirty in the morning to sing my praises."

"No. It's Rhodes. He's asking for you."

I sat up, fumbled on the nightstand for a cigarette. A pounding ache began behind my eyes. "You're at the hospital?"

"Headquarters. The ER doc released him, and we brought him here."

"He's okay?"

"He's got some old bruising and other injuries. Says someone jumped him in Wyoming. But the hypothermia wasn't too bad, I guess. His heart's good, he's clearheaded. All tests come back normal. Doc says if he'd stayed out there, though, it would have tipped the other way. You saved his life."

I brought the cigarette up, found some matches, swung my feet to the floor. My body protested, and I sucked in my breath at the pain. "Don't tell Nik that."

"Yeah. Rough spot, that one. Hold on." A pause while Cohen covered the mouthpiece and said something to someone. He came back on. "Look, if you're not sleeping anyway, think you could come down to headquarters? Rhodes says he'll talk to us, but only if he can talk to you first."

"He ask for me by name?"

"Yeah."

"He say why?"

"Probably some jarhead Marine shit."

I lit the cigarette, inhaled. Clyde got to his feet and padded over to the window.

"Can't this wait until morning?"

"Rhodes is ready to talk. We don't want to give him time to change his mind or think too much about his story or call in a lawyer. Look, I know it's a lot, but we'd appreciate it, Bandoni and me."

I bent down and shook out my boots, a standard routine in Iraq when you had to make sure scorpions hadn't crawled into your clothing while you slept. I stopped with the left boot cradled in my injured palm. The dream must still have had its hold on me.

"All right," I said finally, thinking, *And so it begins.* "Give me a half hour or so to get there."

"Thanks, Parnell."

I hung up and rose painfully to my feet, the whiskey a whisper in my veins. I crossed to the window next to Clyde and pushed aside the curtain, looking out on the blue-white landscape. The storm had gone through and the night sky was clear. Moonlight irradiated the yard. I looked for the Sir, the man who'd brought me into this. But the yard lay empty.

I smoked. Touched Dougie's ring beneath my T-shirt.

It is true that life gives us the very thing we fear the most. After the war and after losing Dougie and after everything else that happened, life was handing me Rhodes and our deadly, mutual past in Habbaniyah. Lest I forget my debts. Lest I try to put them behind me.

The ravens of war always come home to roost.

Clyde put his front paws on the windowsill, maybe wondering what had caught my attention. His breath left a fog on the glass.

"We're in it now, Marine," I said.

He dropped back to the floor and trotted out of the room. A moment later I heard him in the kitchen, rifling through the empty McDonald's bag.

CHAPTER 10

In war, your fellow soldiers become everything to you. Brother, sister, father, son. These are the women and men who have your back. Who hold your life. Whose lives you hold.

Loyalty rises above everything else. Above compassion for civilians, above right cause, above command orders. Loyalty rises even over self-preservation. It's why men throw themselves on grenades to save their buddies.

In war, loyalty is the one thing you can count on. This is what the Marine motto, Semper Fidelis, is all about: Always Faithful.

—Sydney Parnell, ENGL 0208, Psychology of Combat

The Denver PD Major Crimes unit is located in the headquarters building in the Capitol Hill area of Denver, ten blocks from where Elise was murdered. I parked in a police slot on 14th Avenue, entered the lobby, and showed my badge to the officer at the bank of windows.

"Detective Cohen is expecting me."

"I'll buzz him." The officer pushed a clipboard in my direction. "Sign here."

Five minutes later, an elevator pinged, doors whooshed open, and Cohen appeared on the other side of the walk-through metal detector wearing the same button-down shirt and rumpled charcoal suit I'd last seen him in. The previous twenty-four hours sat on him with the kind of weight that could bend bones. He looked two inches shorter.

"Hey," I said.

"Hey."

He waved me through the detector, then took in my injured face. His eyes went narrow.

"Rhodes do that?"

"No."

"Then what?"

I heard a familiar tone in his voice—affronted manhood. I'd heard it a lot in Iraq. No Marine wants to see a buddy hurt. But when a female is involved, the male Marines get proprietary about it. It used to piss me off. But coming from Cohen, it seemed okay. Less knee-jerk and more personal.

I tried a smile. "You can't worry about me, you know."

"Not what friends are for?"

"So we're friends now?"

"Just feel like slumming is all," he said.

"Thought you'd get enough of that working here."

Even his laugh was tired.

I followed him through the door, up the elevator to the second floor, and then down a hall past conference rooms and through multiple doorways. Even a police station gets quiet in the middle of the night. Or some parts of it. Our footsteps scratched on the carpet, rapped back at us off the scuffed white walls. Somewhere, water was dripping.

"Clyde doesn't like police stations?" Cohen asked over his shoulder.

"He doesn't like cops."

I'd left Clyde sprawled out and snoring on the kitchen floor, sated with bath and burgers. Alone with my thoughts as I'd driven over, I'd stared into the white-frosted night, the gamut of my emotions ping-ponging around like a checklist for the mentally disturbed.

First, I had anger. A lot of it.

Then sorrow, running through the anger like a black thread. Mostly for Elise, whose brutalized body had taken residence in my mind even as her ghost haunted my home. And there was grief for the living, too. For Nik and Ellen Ann. For Gentry. And even for Rhodes, who had lost everything.

Third came pity. Rhodes might have signed up for the war. But he hadn't signed up for what happened to him there. I'm sure he would have hated my pity if he'd known about it. Probably hated it every time he saw it in someone's face. But there it was.

And finally, a jagged, icy fear. A fear that reached through all the meds the docs had prescribed for me—the antianxiety tablets, the antidepressants, the pills for anger and insomnia and hypervigilance and for the long string of days when I just didn't give a shit. The fear that pressed against my throat like a blade.

Fear of the rage that had almost made me shoot a man.

And fear of Iraq. Of Habbaniyah.

Cohen waved me through a door marked *Homicide Division* where at last some life showed. A handful of detectives were on third watch or still working on something they'd started earlier. Cohen's partner, Len Bandoni, waited for us at a desk near the windows, shredding an empty Styrofoam cup while his eyes skimmed a file lying open in front of him. He'd hung his XXL suit jacket over the back of his chair and rolled up the cuffs of his gray button-down. He looked as tired and rumpled as Cohen, his shirt creased and stained, his tie wadded up and stuffed between a couple of framed family photos.

At the sound of our approach, he rose, brushed the Styrofoam remnants off his pants, and offered a massive hand. His walrus mustache bristled as he said my name. His grip was a dime's edge from bone-crushing. Even tired, he looked like he could tear down a mountain without breaking a sweat.

"Those'll be shiners in a couple more hours," he said, releasing my hand. He reeked of cigarettes.

I resisted the urge to massage my fingers. "Saves on eyeliner."

"Thanks for working the crime scene for us. Saved us hours of work we would have spent doing it right."

I worked not to flinch.

"You're right," I said. "Our bad."

"You sometimes forget you're a railway cop? Maybe forget forensics and due process and all those other unimportant formalities that we in the Denver PD like to consider part of the job?"

"Look, I—"

"So busy cleaning up graffiti you think it's your job to clean up a crime scene, too?"

Cohen said, "Bandoni."

My face flamed. "You ever forget what it's like to lose someone you love?"

From a desk ten feet away, a detective talking on the phone covered the mouthpiece and glared at us. "It the Mutt and Jeff show over there? Keep it down to a dull roar, maybe?"

Bandoni gave him the finger.

Cohen pulled out a chair for me then perched on the corner of the desk. He toed open one of the drawers and rested his feet on it.

I ignored the chair. "Where's Rhodes?"

Bandoni leaned against his desk, arms folded. "Cooling his heels in an interview room."

"You read him his rights?"

"We've taken him into custody," Cohen said. "But we haven't arrested him."

"I thought you got a warrant."

"We don't want him to lawyer up." This from Bandoni. "But he won't talk."

"Really? Two of Denver's finest can't get a grieving boy to admit he went a little crazy?"

"He just keeps saying he can't remember anything." Bandoni's voice rumbled like a subway. "Keeps saying he wants to talk to you."

"How sure are you that he's good for Elise's death?"

"About like Brutus with Caesar," Bandoni said. "We got his bloodied uniform. We got a bloodied knife found in the bathroom of a 7-Eleven a block from the vic's home. We got a video of Rhodes going in and out of said bathroom in said uniform. The landlady tells us a man wearing military camouflage came in early this morning and went upstairs. Rhodes tried to burn his uniform, and then he fled the area. Most incriminating, we got what my gut's saying."

I bit. "What's that?"

"That there's a reason our boy has nervous eyes."

"Everyone who's come back from Iraq has nervous eyes."

He gazed at me speculatively. "We don't need the eyes."

"Sounds like everything's cut-and-dried then. So why am I here?"

"You mean other than as a favor to a fellow Marine?" Cohen asked.

"I figure you guys aren't in the habit of dispensing favors to murder suspects."

"We're hoping he'll open up to you."

"Get a guy with amnesia to confess to a crime he can't remember?"

Bandoni shook his head in disgust. "He doesn't have fucking amnesia. He fucked up big time, and now he wants to weasel out of it. We need you to get him to tell you what happened. One Marine to another."

"Just like that."

"And get it on tape," he added.

"Makes everyone's job easier," Cohen said. "He confesses, and the physical evidence backs him up, the DA will probably offer him a plea bargain and we won't have to go to trial."

"I thought you guys liked to go to trial. The reward for all your hard work."

"That's after we've done a lot of hard work."

I reached behind me for the chair and sat down. My heart gave an eager little flutter that shamed me. If Rhodes confessed, Elise would get her justice, but there would be no need for a trial. There would be no media circus, no eager journalists or determined prosecutors digging into Rhodes's past. No news personalities looking for what had turned a man into a butcher.

No Habbaniyah.

"I'll talk to him," I said.

"I want more than a confession," Bandoni said. "It can't be something the defense can throw out as speculation or a false confession. We can't have Rhodes saying later that he was taking you for a monkey ride. I need him to show enough awareness of his crime that the best public defender in the world can't turn it into an insanity plea. I want details. I want him to say he took that knife into the apartment. I want proof that he remembers every single goddamn thing he did to that girl."

Bandoni resumed his seat. The chair squealed.

"What if he really has amnesia?"

"You're kidding me, right?"

"By itself, amnesia doesn't grant incompetence," Cohen said. "But in combination with other factors, such as his war experiences, a judge could rule incompetency or take an insanity plea."

"So what would happen to him then?" I asked. "Same result, right? No trial, but an indictment."

Bandoni dropped the remains of the shredded coffee cup into the trash. "Judge rules incompetency, Rhodes won't do a day of jail time. He'll spend a couple of years in a cushy nut-job facility, then get released when some do-gooder psychiatrist decides he's redeemed himself."

I narrowed my eyes. "It cross your mind that might be exactly what he needs?"

"Please," Bandoni drawled, extending the word to two syllables. *Puh-leeze.* "You saw the girl."

"I know what war can do."

He looked like he might throttle me. "She's some relative of yours, right?"

"Family friend."

Bandoni yanked a photo out of the file on his desk and slapped it on top of the other papers. A picture from the crime scene with a close-up of Elise's ruined body.

"Don't," I snapped. "Don't pull that manipulative shit on me."

"I'm sure you can imagine what her last moments were like. The terror she felt. The pain. Trapped in that room with her killer. Him coming after her with the knife, and her with nothing to do but put her arms in front of her face and beg."

"Stop."

Bandoni leaned forward in his chair and got in my face, peering into my eyes like a priest seeking proof of remorse. When he spoke again, his voice was almost gentle. "Does having him get out in a couple of years seem like justice to you, Special Agent Parnell? You really okay with that?"

"Okay, Len," Cohen said. "Back off."

I dropped my forearms to my thighs and stared at the stained blue carpet, turning Elise's brutal death over in my mind, like trying to polish a jagged stone. How do you decide between insanity and culpability when someone's brain has been slammed around like a soccer ball? How different was Rhodes now from the man he'd been before Iraq? How responsible was he for his actions? When he took the knife to the woman he claimed to love, how much was Rhodes the man really present? And how much was he the beast that war makes?

Can you let war split a man in two, then turn around and expect the pieces to fit back together?

I sat up. The two detectives regarded me, Cohen with a distant concern, Bandoni with angry hopefulness. But I had something bigger to protect. Whatever happened, whatever Rhodes wanted to say to me, I couldn't let them know about Habbaniyah.

"I'll talk to him," I said. "But no camera or recorders."

Bandoni's neck flushed. "Excuse me?"

"Rhodes asked for me. Maybe what he wants to talk about's got nothing to do with Elise. Maybe he wants to talk about Iraq. Or about his family and how they don't get what he's been through. Maybe he just wants to spit on me for bringing him back. None of that is relevant to your case. I want to talk to him privately first."

Bandoni's face went red. "Fuck me."

"Turns out he does want to confess, then I'll switch on the recorder. But not before then."

A vein pulsed in the middle of Bandoni's forehead. "You're a goddamned railroad cop, not a homicide investigator. You have no fucking idea what you're doing. You could let a lot of important stuff go by, sail right past your ears. Jesus, please. Just turn on the fucking recorder. We promise not to listen to the part where he's crying about not being understood."

"Or I could just go home."

"You smug little—" He whirled on Cohen. "Whose idea was this? Whose idea to bring in a fucking *railroad* cop?"

"No. It's okay." Cohen kicked the drawer closed and slid off the desk, looking at me. "What you're saying is reasonable. As long as you're willing to turn on the recorder if he gives you anything about Elise's death."

Bandoni's eyes went to Cohen, and some signal passed between them. The older detective huffed once and returned to his file, giving us the immense expanse of his back, like closing the gates to the Wall of Jericho.

"Knock yourself out," he said without turning around.

CHAPTER 11

No one can understand war like those who have been in it with you. And no one is closer than those who have suffered with you and died next to you.

Those who have protected you, and whom you have protected, are bonded more closely even than by blood.

—Sydney Parnell, ENGL 0208,
Psychology of Combat

Cohen took a small digital recorder from another desk—presumably his—and showed me the basics. I dropped the recorder in my right pants pocket, then followed Cohen down another hall and past a series of closed doors. He stopped in front of a door with the number three on it.

"Video and microphone are on," he said. "I'll turn them off from the observation room. When you're ready to leave, or if you run into a problem, there's a buzzer on the wall near your side of the table. Once I turn off the audio and visual, I'll be right outside."

"Thanks."

"Don't wreck the case for us, Parnell."

"No," I said.

He unlocked and opened the door. A uniform stood and nodded at Cohen and me, then stepped out.

The interview room was an eight-by-ten holding cell decorated in peeling plaster. A single window broke up the far wall, the glass reinforced with black wire. In the middle of the room was a metal table, bolted to the floor, and two metal and vinyl chairs.

I paused in the doorway.

Rhodes sat in the far chair, his left hand fisted against his cheek, staring off into a distance that went far beyond the confines of the interview room. His right wrist was handcuffed to a metal ring welded to the table. His fire-scarred face, yellow and pink in the pitiless lights, made me clutch for Dougie's ring where it hung beneath my turtleneck.

"Fucking suck of a war," I whispered.

At the sound of my voice, Rhodes startled and came back from wherever he'd been. Cohen warned him to behave himself and left, closing the door behind him.

Rhodes watched in silence as I shrugged out of my coat, dragged a chair to the camera in the corner, climbed up and draped my coat over the lens. I took off my scarf and wrapped it around the microphone. I then removed my own digital recorder, which I'd brought from home. I set it on the floor near the muffled microphone and hit play. The buzz of a busy restaurant filled the room. The clatter of cutlery, the murmur of voices. Someone calling up orders. It was an old recording I'd made when I once inadvertently hit the power button at the diner where I was eating breakfast. I'd kept the recording because when I was in one of my dark moods, the innocuous sounds of people going about their day soothed me. A lonely person's white noise.

Satisfied that anything we said would be sufficiently distorted, I dragged the chair back to the table and took a seat across from Rhodes. I held up a finger to warn him to remain silent for a few minutes longer to see if there would be any reaction to my maneuverings. When three or four minutes went by with no response from Cohen, I gave Rhodes a nod.

At first he said nothing, only continued to study me. The emerald eyes glittered in his ruined face. When he finally spoke, his voice was quiet. "It *is* you. I can tell even with those shiners. The woman in the yellow scarf. From Mortuary Affairs."

"Yes."

"All the way from one side of the world to the other, and here we are again."

"With another dead woman between us."

He didn't flinch. But something in his eyes pulled away. "You remember me?"

"Yes."

"Even the way I am now?"

"All I saw of you that night were your eyes."

"Yeah. 'Course." He ran the thumb of his free hand along the table. His skin came back gray. "My mom used to say I had girls' eyes. Wasn't fair, she said. Me having girls' eyes." He rubbed the grime onto his road-filthy jeans. "Miracle they didn't blow all to hell, too."

He'd been a kid when that IED set his vehicle on fire and engulfed his life. Was still a kid. Right about now he should be deciding whether he wanted to go to school or find a job. Spending his days helping his dad on the ranch while he figured things out. Spending his Friday nights drinking beer with his friends, his Saturdays with a girl.

"I'm truly sorry for what happened to you."

"Yeah?" He shrugged, Marine tough. "Not me sitting in that seat, would have been someone else."

"Is that what we could say about Elise? She'd been someone else's girlfriend, maybe this wouldn't have happened?"

He held my gaze. A vein throbbed in his neck. "You shouldn't have brought me back from out there. You should have left me in the storm. Elise and me, we'd be together now."

I waited.

"I didn't kill her."

I stayed silent.

"I *worried* that I might. You go through that sometimes, right? Worry the pressure is gonna build and build until it screams out of you like a bomb going off?" He turned his manacled wrist back and forth. "Then you'll just be some killing machine. A fucking terminator."

Bandoni would shit himself that I wasn't recording this.

"I know what you mean," I said. And I did.

In ancient times, soldiers called it going amok—a descent into the battle craziness that took you out of yourself and dropped you into the warrior's world of blood and darkness. Going amok was a form of insanity prized by the Greeks and Spartans and Vikings—it made for great warriors. Thus did Achilles slay Hector, Beowulf defeat Grendel.

But unless you bring your heroes back to themselves—with a ritual purification or with a journey of some sort, like Odysseus's long struggle home or World War II vets taking weeks to sail back across the sea together—there is a price to pay when the bloodied warrior returns. These days, soldiers return from Iraq and Afghanistan alone and in a matter of hours. We drop them back into society as if they were widgets that have simply gone missing for a while. But a lot of the widgets are bent hopelessly out of shape.

I put my hands in my pockets. "Is that what happened, Rhodes? You snapped? Elise said something, told you to leave maybe, and you went off on her?"

The stink of oil and sweat lifted off his grease-stained flannel shirt and jeans as he shifted around.

"I was so scared of that blackness," he said, "that I up and left her a couple of months ago. Scared of myself. Scared for her. But then she called me, said she'd marry me. I knew then that she didn't care about me being a monster. She loved me. We thought maybe that was enough to, you know, kill the beast. I'd get counseling. Finish up my surgeries. Get the pain under control with something other than drugs and booze.

I heard they got some new computer program, some video game that you play and it helps."

I'd heard of it, too, but I hadn't looked into it. Booze killed the pain, too, and it was a lot easier to find.

"Elise and I—" His eyes grew red, and he sucked in wet, clotted air. "I thought maybe we could have something together. Something good and real. A family. A little girl. A little boy."

"Would you hit your kids like you hit her?"

"I *never* hit her. No matter how mad I got."

"You're lying to me, Rhodes."

His shoulders came up like walls. He let go a few ragged sobs then slowly exhaled, flattening his free hand on the table and breathing like he'd just outrun a locomotive.

"I didn't hurt her. I *never* hurt her. I couldn't have killed her."

My fingers touched Cohen's recorder, pushed it further down into my pocket. "Then what did happen?"

"I don't know. Honest to God, I can't remember. I was standing outside the door to her bedroom, and I got a bad feeling. Then . . . nothing. Came to in a bathroom somewhere. Then I was gone again until I was on that train."

"You had a knife."

"That's what they told me." He ground the heel of one hand against his forehead. "I swear to God, I don't remember."

"Last night you told me Elise understood what you'd done, like she was okay with it. Then you told me how fucked up you were." I kept my face hard. "Losing your freedom bring a little clarity on what you were admitting to? Make you change your mind?"

Beneath his rigid skin, his jaw bunched. "I don't blame you for thinking the worst. But things have changed since last night."

"How's that?"

"She came to me. When they were bringing me here in the ambulance. And I don't mean like in a dream. I mean like she was as real as you. I could feel her breath on my cheek, see her eyes looking into mine. She always—" He looked toward the window, the set of his jaw like a wall brooking no access. "She always loved my eyes. My stupid girls' eyes."

I followed his gaze. Streetlamps burned along the street below, lonely, feeble glows.

But Elise was with *me* last night, I wanted to say. In *my* car. But if our ghosts are our guilt, I guess there's no reason we can't share.

"Nice of her to drop in," I said. "I don't suppose she told you who *did* kill her."

"She didn't say nothing. But I know she was trying to tell me that we're still together. Still a team. And she wouldn't have felt that way if I'd just—if I'd hurt her, right? She was saying it wasn't me who did that to her."

I thought about Bandoni's need for details. For proof. "Did what, exactly?"

His eyes came back to mine. "They said . . ." His voice turned thick again. "They said I sliced her to pieces. Like I was butchering a calf, is what they told me."

"That's about right. Exactly what you learned to do on your dad's ranch, right?"

"Not like that."

I moved in for the kill. "Elise was a devout Christian?"

"What?" He pinched the corners of his eyes. "Yeah."

"So maybe she came to see you last night just to let you know she forgives you."

His face went south suddenly, and what little fire had been in his eyes faded to dull embers.

Feeling like an executioner, I went on. "Did you kill her, Rhodes? Do you think maybe you *might* have killed her? Marine to Marine. I need to know. It will affect everything else we say to each other in this room. It will affect everything that happens from here on out."

Rhodes jerked his bound hand, yanking the chain so hard that the table, still bolted into the floor, trembled. I leaned away from the agony in his face.

"No," he said. "No. That isn't what she meant. That isn't why she was there. She came to tell me she's waiting for me. And that before me and her can be together again, I have to fix things."

"You sure that's how you want to play it? Think carefully, Rhodes. If you confess, it will make things a lot easier on you. You won't go to jail. They'll put you in a facility. You'll get the help you need. You'll get your life back."

"You know what they used to call us? Beauty and the Beast. People would say to her, 'Why don't you kiss him, see if he turns into a prince?' Elise wants me to make sure people don't think they were right about me and her. That they don't think this is how our love ended."

"That the Beast slew Beauty," I said softly.

He turned as far away from me as he could get, which wasn't far with the cuff around his wrist. But when he buried his face with his free hand, we were a million miles apart.

Even more softly, I said, "None of us came back from that war the same, Rhodes."

He just shook his head, and I waited him out. The only sound in the room was his ragged breathing. From beyond the heavy door came the faintest murmur of voices and a high trill that might have been a phone ringing. A faint thump sounded against the wall. Cohen moving around, maybe.

After a while, Rhodes wiped his eyes on his sleeve, straightened his body toward the table, and came back to me. I sensed he had found a place to put the pain.

"Do you know why I asked to see you?"

I jerked a thumb toward the door, reminding him of Cohen's presence in the hallway. Quietly I said, "Habbaniyah."

He nodded. "Elise kept a key under the rug at her front door. So anyone could have come in and hurt her. But why? Everyone loved her. The hobos. The people at that diner where she worked. I been asking myself, who ever hurts a saint?"

I didn't point out that saints were usually martyrs. "What's this got to do with Iraq?"

"Just listen. I know the street, and the street's got nothing to say about Elise. No one's pissed off at her, no one has anything against her. So I get to wondering if it's just some—some random thing that happened. But I can't accept that. You know? Can't bear that someone just got a few screws loose, wandered in, and—and did that to her. Don't make any sense."

"Sometimes that's the way it happens," I said.

"I can't buy that. So I got to thinking. Maybe this is about Iraq."

"I don't follow."

"Elise knew. About what happened over there. I'd been holding it all inside, but I was starting to unravel. So I told her. No secrets, right? Not between two people who love each other."

"Dammit, Rhodes, we all took an oath. Remember that? We all swore we'd never talk about Habbaniyah."

"I couldn't do it anymore. Couldn't hold it."

Anger popped through me and just as quickly faded. How many times had I wished for someone to share the story with? Someone to tell me it had all been for the best. "And now you think she talked and someone got scared?"

"You gotta understand the kind of woman Elise is." Breath. "Was. Elise said there ain't none of us hasn't done something we feel bad for. She said we should confess our sins and make amends. To save our souls. To save *ourselves*, she said. She wasn't all self-righteous about it. She just really cared. A life's no good, she said, if it's a lie."

"So maybe she told some tramp he should confess about something, and it pissed him off. Or scared him into wanting to shut her up."

"Probably it did. But not in the way you're thinking. She'd of told me if there was someone like that, someone she was scared of. I'd of heard about it." He shook his head. "I think it was Iraq. Elise wanted everyone in our platoon to come clean. A lot of them had figured out at least part of what had happened. Or at least that we'd pissed off a lot of Iraqis."

"The whole *platoon*?" I gaped at him. "Did you tell her what would happen if the story came out?"

"'Course I did. Told her everybody'd been through enough and deserved a chance to put it behind them. She argued with me at first. But when I told her all that would happen is a whole lot of pain for a whole lot of people, she let it go. She understood." He smoothed a hand over his scarred scalp. "I thought that was that."

"What's changed your mind?"

"I got a call from Jeezer."

"Jeezer."

"Jeremy Kane. Our fireteam leader. He and I joined the Marines at the same time. Signed up for the buddy program and deployed together. He called and told me Elise had dropped by."

"To talk about the war."

"She told him the same thing she'd told me. That he needed to come clean."

"When was this?"

"Three, four days ago."

"Shit." I closed my eyes, gathered myself, finally looked at Rhodes again. "Elise talk to anyone else in your team? In your squad?"

"Honest to God, I don't know. She didn't say nothing to me. I thought we was done with that." His jaw worked. "The last time we talked, she told me that she'd be done with everything in a week."

"You know what she meant by that?"

"Figured it was one of her projects. She had a lot of those. Helping people with this or that. I never guessed it might be Habbaniyah."

"So this Jeremy Kane. He lives in Denver?"

"Littleton."

"Would he—?"

"No. Not Jeezer. He wouldn't hurt a fly. And why tell me about her visit if he was gonna, you know, shut her up? Not any of the other guys in our squad, neither. He just wanted me to talk to her."

"What about your platoon? Why did she think the entire platoon needed to confess?"

By now we'd leaned in so close to each other that our faces were inches apart.

"The platoon didn't know any details," Rhodes said. "But they knew we was all the sudden getting hit hard and that it had to do with our team, something we'd done. They were pissed at us, at least at first. But they were more pissed at the Iraqis. They backed us up—we all went a little crazy when it came time to clear streets and houses. We wasn't exactly worried about hearts and minds."

"Okay." I considered this. "If your platoon didn't know the story, then they'd have no reason to kill someone to keep it quiet. The fact that some of us weren't saints over there isn't breaking news. Every American in Iraq was pissed off at the insurgents."

He nodded.

"So who, then?" I pressed.

"I'm thinking she found someone to talk to who has a lot more to lose even than me and Jeezer and the others. After we found Resenko in that house, it was Sarge who handled things. He's the one called your CO. But we always figured there was someone higher up. Someone who'd, you know, be in a hell of a bad place if the truth came out about how Resenko and Haifa died and that, after, we'd been ordered to keep it on the QT. I asked Sarge about it. He just gave me a funny look and told me to shut up. Do my time, go home, and keep my pie hole closed. Then the IED happened." Tucker cleared his throat. "I went home, all right."

I'd believed the same thing. The Sir wouldn't take orders from a sergeant. And he didn't know anyone in Rhodes's fireteam well enough to do them a personal favor of this magnitude. Someone else was involved. I'd just never understood why it mattered to any of the brass that Resenko'd had an affair, even if the woman involved was Iraqi.

I placed the flat of my hands against my neck. "How would Elise find that person?"

"I don't know. But she was smart. She could've maybe talked to Sarge, gotten a name from him."

The headache nudged its way deeper into my brain. I pushed back from the table and went to lean against the wall with my arms folded. The pain in my hands and face popped alive as if I'd hit a switch.

So who *would* the Sir have taken an order from? Or maybe not even an order. Maybe a request he felt honor-bound to answer. Maybe it wasn't someone in his chain of command, but someone else he respected or trusted.

Was it possible that this unknown person figured hiding the truth was worth one more death?

A flicker of white-hot anger broke through my exhaustion. All of this for what? Because some corporal couldn't keep his dick in his pants?

"Tell me one thing, Rhodes," I said in a harsh whisper. "Did the Marine they killed—"

"Dave Resenko."

"Did he love her? Did he love Haifa?"

He looked surprised. "You know her name?"

"I processed her body, Rhodes. Remember that? I might have lied about how she died, but I still handled her remains. I *altered* her remains and Resenko's to cover up how they died."

And I took her son.

"Hell yeah, he loved her," Rhodes said. "Haifa was our 'terp. Rode with us everywhere, brave as a Marine. Braver, because she didn't have a gun or armor or nothing. Resenko, man, he had it bad for her. His wife was sleeping with some guy she met at a fucking Home Depot, told Resenko she wanted a divorce. So Rinks was gonna bring Haifa back with him. The US State Department was offering special visas for people like her. Staties made a shitload of promises. But it was all lies."

There'd been a lot of cases like Haifa's. The Iraqis helped us, working as interpreters or mechanics or administrators. Then were killed for it by their own people when we mustered home.

"They were gonna bring Haifa's son, too," Rhodes said.

I looked down so Rhodes couldn't see my face. "Malik. Yeah. I heard."

Malik, the boy crying in the front room. Malik, whom I'd wrapped in a blanket and placed in the front seat of our van while the body of his mother bled into a body bag in the back. Malik, who'd crept into my heart and made a home there.

I'd tried with everything I had to bring him back with me. I'd worked with USAID, the State Department, Christian charities, the List Project.

But I'd failed. In the end, I'd had to choose between home and Iraq. Between Malik and Grams. Between having a life and giving one up.

I returned to the table. "So the insurgents killed Haifa and Resenko for sleeping together, or maybe just for loving each other. And then our own private war started, didn't it? You and your buddies went after the men you thought killed Resenko. And their friends retaliated by going hard after every Marine in the area."

He didn't look at me.

"And now, if you don't confess, you're going to go to trial for Elise's murder. And everyone in the world will learn what happened over there."

"I didn't kill her."

"So you say." I placed my wounded palms on the table and leaned in until I could see the blood vessels in his eyes. "Now you've asked for me, and here I am. What is it, exactly, you want me to do? Find the high-ranking officer you think is behind all this and beg him to confess? Not only to lying about Resenko's death and covering it up, but to murdering Elise? That's what you want from me?"

Rhodes's face showed both defiance and regret. And something that was kissing cousins to anguish. "Yes."

"Anything else?"

He shook his head.

"You do know that if I find this phantasm and arrest him, *he'll* go to trial, and Habbaniyah will still come out."

"Maybe it's time," Rhodes said. "Maybe Elise was right."

I glared at him. Thoughts like that kept me up at night.

"Corporal Parnell, I don't want to go down in history as Elise's killer. I don't want to have *this* face on everybody's TV. I don't want to sit in a courtroom and look at pictures of her—" He broke a little here, and I waited. "Of what was done to her. I don't want the media swarming in front of my dad's house or to have to watch my dad's heart break in two. And I most especially don't want Elise's killer to walk free."

His eyes followed me as I moved to the window. "You helped us before. I need your help again."

At the window, I rested my forehead against the glass. "No."

"Marine to Marine."

"No."

"Corporal—"

"Goddammit, Rhodes." I whirled on him. "I still don't know that you didn't kill her. The knife. The blood. The timing with you riding into Denver when you did. Hell, it's about as textbook as it gets. Maybe all this talk about some mysterious officer is just some crazy conspiracy theory you've cooked up to make yourself look innocent. Everything points to you, Rhodes. Everything."

"If someone wanted to set me up, would you expect any different from whoever handled Resenko's death?"

"This mystery man didn't put blood on your uniform or a knife in your hand."

"No. I probably—I probably picked her up. Held her. So this guy, this killer, he gets lucky because my head's not straight."

I ignored the thumping in my chest and waved my hand dismissively. "It's too crazy. I don't buy it."

"Please. Just talk to Jeezer. Ask him if he's heard anything. And the Sarge—Max Udell. See if they know anything. After you talk to them, you can think about what to do. If you do anything at all."

"Shit."

"Please."

I stared at those lonely lights burning along the street two stories down. I remembered one of my favorite sayings, about how it's better to light a single candle than to sit and curse the dark. I'd used that one a lot in Iraq.

Malik had been the candle I'd tried to light, and look where that got me.

"I'll think about it," I finally said, turning back to him. "That's as much as I can give you right now."

The desperation in his face flattened to despair. But he took it like a Marine.

"Thank you, Corporal. For whatever you can do."

I grabbed my coat and scarf and recorder. "You want me to call your parents?"

"Not my mom. She's busy with her own life."

"Your dad, then."

He looked out the window for a moment, finally shook his head. "He's got cancer. He's dying. He don't need anything else on him."

"I'm sorry, Rhodes."

"Yeah."

I hit the buzzer, waited for Cohen to let me out.

"Hope your life turns out okay, ma'am," Rhodes said. "Whatever you decide. Jeezer and me and the rest, we'll always owe you one from the war."

Cohen opened the door and held it for me, told Rhodes he'd return in just a minute. The uniform went back into the room. Suicide watch.

I found myself turning back as the door fell shut. Rhodes had once again clasped his arm across his chest as if to hold in the pain. He didn't look well. I wondered if maybe the docs had released him too soon.

I craned my neck for a last glimpse, some final insight. But Rhodes's scarred face was a mask, showing nothing.

"Pretty smooth, Parnell," Cohen said. "Covering the audio and visual."

"Marine business."

"Go okay?" he asked.

"Went like shit."

CHAPTER 12

Any Marine will tell you the hardest thing to live with once you're home is the guilt. Guilt over what you did or didn't do when the bombs exploded and the mortars shrieked into the road and enemy snipers picked off everyone standing.

Did you run? If you ran, did you go back for your buddies? Were any of your squad mates trapped in an Abrams or Humvee, screaming for help while flames raced toward the fuel tanks?

Worse, did you not go out of the wire that day at all? You were having a bad morning so someone went in your stead, and now they're bringing him back in a body bag, and in your nightmares he keeps asking why you let him die.

It was your turn, he says as he sits in the tank night after night after night. Burning.

Your turn.

—*Sydney Parnell. Personal journal.*

Cohen led me back to Homicide.

Len Bandoni stood and watched our approach with furious eyes. When we were still ten feet away, he addressed me around an unlit cigarette tucked in the corner of his mouth.

"You two have a nice little chat?"

"Gone better with a couple of cocktails."

"He gonna confess?"

"Says he didn't do it."

"Shit." Bandoni plopped in his chair and stared at his gut like it was one more thing weighing on him. Like he wasn't sure how all the beer and burgers had come to this. "Him and Ted Bundy. Innocent as the day they were born."

Cohen resettled himself on Bandoni's desk. "He give you anything?"

"Not really. He says he remembers standing in front of the door to her bedroom and having a bad feeling. But he can't remember anything after that until he reached the 7-Eleven. Then he blacked out again until the train."

"A bad feeling," Bandoni scoffed. "Was it an I'm-gonna-butcher-my-girlfriend kind of bad feeling?"

"I don't think so."

"How'd he explain the blood?" Cohen asked.

"He thinks maybe he picked her up after he found her. Held her."

Cohen chewed on that. "And the knife?"

"Says he has no idea."

Bandoni moved the cigarette to the other side of his mouth. "You got all this on tape, of course."

"No." I pulled Cohen's recorder out of my pocket and placed it on his desk.

Heat rose in his neck. "You gonna tell me why not?"

"That was as much as we talked about Elise's death, Bandoni. He's genuinely grieving, you ask me. But he's scared, too, doesn't want people thinking of him as her killer. He's not going to confess."

"Douche bag shoulda thought of that twenty-four hours ago." He jiggled the recorder in his hand. "You know, Special Agent Parnell, you're not making any friends here."

"It's not why I came."

"Yeah, I know. Semper Fi and all that shit."

A sudden tiredness washed over me, a wave so high and wide it nearly flattened me. I sank into the chair. "I don't know if he's guilty or not. But I'd swear he doesn't remember. If it turns out he killed her, his lawyer will go for an insanity defense and probably get it."

"Not gonna happen," Bandoni snarled, his face purple. "I won't *let* it happen. Trust me, I've seen the best goddamn liars the world has to offer. But you hit 'em with enough evidence, and eventually they cave."

He held up a piece of paper where he'd jotted down a list and popped the paper with each word. "Knife. Bloody uniform. A longstanding relationship with the vic. Hobo sign. We got that picture frame missing from her house that he buried in his camp, and him carrying the photo. Witnesses at the house and in the camp. Known PTSD case."

"You don't worry much about being wrong, do you, Bandoni?" I asked.

"Because I'm never wrong."

"Don't lose much sleep, either, do you?"

"Only time I lose sleep is when I let the bad guy walk. So mark me on this. I need my beauty rest. Rhodes ain't gonna walk."

The man, I realized, was an avalanche. An entire mountain ready to roar down on you, prepared to entomb you with his lists and his gut and his thoughts about your eyes. The righteous cop.

He'd bury Rhodes.

Maybe that was exactly what made a good murder cop.

I glanced at Cohen, who looked like he had a year ago when we were standing by the jumper's body. Like a gateway had opened up to somewhere he didn't want to go. He took a drink of something out of a plastic cup and avoided my gaze.

"You're white as a ghost, Parnell," Bandoni said abruptly, giving me the eye. "Pastier coming out than you were going in. You were in there a long time, even without cocktails. How long does your Semper Fi crap take?"

"Well, you know. Railroad cops are notoriously slow. It's not like we know what we're doing."

An eyebrow went up. "Finally. Something we can agree on."

"Fuck you, Bandoni."

He opened his hands. "Sure. Just don't take an age to do it."

I pushed my hands in my pockets so I wouldn't wrap my hands around his throat. I hunched my shoulders against a sudden need for sleep, an excruciating desire to fall into unconsciousness. Almost twitching with guilt, I forced myself to my feet. "Can we trade insults later? I need to get some air. And a smoke."

"Sure," Bandoni said with a small, knowing smile. "Take your time. Think of something good."

"I'm not a suspect," I snapped at him.

"I read that interview you did in the *Denver Post*. All that stuff about ghosts and everything. You really believe that shit?"

I tried one last time. "You know, Bandoni, I like a good fight, same as you. But aren't we on the same side here?"

"Are we?"

Cohen jumped in. "You can smoke outside. On the plaza."

He was scrutinizing me, too. Like maybe our buddy-buddy days were over. Lesson for the day—it doesn't pay to go against murder cops.

"When you're done," he went on, "why don't you come back up and watch us chat with Rhodes? Maybe you'll catch something we miss."

"Okay. Sure." I looked at the cigarette in Bandoni's mouth. Thing about being a smoker fresh off the wagon—you can want to disembowel a guy and still hope to bum a cigarette from him. "Got an extra?"

With that same tight smile, Bandoni pulled a crushed pack of Salems and a plastic lighter from an inside pocket. "Keep 'em. I'm trying to quit."

"I need an escort back out?"

Cohen stood. "I'll walk you to the elevator."

"And, Parnell," said Bandoni. "Don't go wandering off, right? Got a few more things to go over."

I shrugged and moved away. Turned back. "One thing you guys should know. Rhodes says Elise always kept a key under her doormat. Wanted hobos to feel welcome, even when she wasn't home."

"A key," Bandoni said. "Ain't that convenient for our forgetful little killer?"

Outside, a pearl-gray line smeared the eastern horizon just visible between the glass and steel silhouettes of downtown Denver. I sat on a bench in the wide concrete plaza and shivered in my coat, staring at the fallen officer memorial as I smoked Bandoni's cigarettes. Five of them. One after the other, like a junkie, until the nicotine gave me the shakes.

Dawn is a favorite time for ghosts. Perhaps because we mortals are at our most fragile then, sleep-wrecked, bleary-eyed, still lost in a world where only moonlight leads the way. But perhaps it is also because we are at our most hopeful in the morning, trailing Wordsworth's intimations of immortality into a new day. We awaken with a full allotment of light stretching ahead of us before night closes in again.

This witch's brew of vulnerability and fear and hope makes dawn the time when we can best hear whatever it is our ghosts are trying to tell us.

But not today, apparently. I sat alone in the courtyard, shivering, smoking, watching the pearl of sunrise spread to a gray swath without a whisper of gold in it, listening to the growl of traffic climb from the mewling of kittens to a lion's roar. Today might devour me, and neither the Sir nor Elise nor my faithful private were there to offer any clarification.

Fair-weather friends.

I knocked ash on the ground.

If Rhodes was innocent—a big if—and if he were right that Elise's death had something to do with Habbaniyah and Resenko and Haifa, then exposing the killer meant I'd be hunting for what amounted to my own suicide. If the entire truth came out—everything we'd done while we still wore the uniform—there'd be a court-martial and jail time. Loss of honor. Loss of my job and my benefits, which were my only means of supporting Grams and Clyde. I'd lose my education reimbursement and flush away the future I was trying to imagine for myself.

But if this mysterious officer had killed Elise and framed Rhodes for it—and if he'd done a good enough job of it that he'd buried Habbaniyah as well—then Rhodes would take the fall for all the world to see and judge. He would forever be the beast who slew Beauty.

Let him go down, some part of me urged. Let him go down and then shovel the dirt in after him *and* Habbaniyah. Close the hole and be done.

"Fucking suck," I said to the baleful windows of DPD headquarters.

Who was it that said once you save a life, you must keep that life safe forever? How was I supposed to stand back and let Rhodes go down, watch him pay for the sins of others? Pay multiple times. Once by going off to war. Again by covering for Resenko. Then a third time by taking the rap for the death of the woman he loved.

Especially, I realized, when my heart could not believe Tucker was guilty. Maybe *needed* for him to not be guilty. Because if he could kill the woman he loved, what did that say about the rest of us wounded warriors? What were any of us capable of when the monster took hold?

I finished my final cigarette and crushed it beneath my foot just as Cohen came out bearing two Styrofoam cups. The sun found a break in the mercury denseness of the sky and lit his face with sudden warmth. The light should have made him look older, with his unshaven chin and his face like a rumpled sheet. Instead, he looked younger. Vulnerable. I noticed again that his suit, as worn and scruffy as his face, was expensive, his overcoat stylish, his shoes of good leather. Maybe that's where he put all his money. He certainly hadn't put it into a haircut.

"You didn't come back." He sat next to me and handed me one of the cups. "Coffee with lots of cream and sugar. I figured you could use both after doing my job for me yesterday and bringing in Rhodes."

We exchanged small smiles. Cohen's was the dry, cynical smile of a cop. Mine probably looked the same.

"Thanks for the coffee."

Another smile, this one a little more real. "So did he appreciate your saving his life? Or did he want to kick your ass?"

"He isn't happy with me."

"He give up anything we can use? Anything at all?"

I slid into the lie like a seal into water. "Other than what I told you, we just talked about Iraq. You and Bandoni learn anything?"

His eyes narrowed, and I got the distinct feeling he'd seen right through me. That he'd taken note of my transgression and filed it away for later.

"He *is* pretty convincing," Cohen said. "Whatever he did or didn't do, I think he really believes he's innocent. Bandoni's not buying it, though. Figures he's faking the memory loss."

"Seems to me everything you've got is circumstantial."

"Until we get the ME's report."

"Then it becomes evidence."

"Evidence is pretty much what we hang our hats on."

I took a big swallow of lukewarm coffee, frowned at the sweetness of it. "Give me something, Cohen. Some little piece of evidence that'll give me a gap I can slide my foot into."

"You want your Marine to be innocent." He rolled his neck. His spine popped. "There is one possible ray of sunshine."

"Yeah?"

"Remember the hobo beads? We showed them to Rhodes, told him they were found near his girlfriend's body. He freaked out. We had to wait for him to settle. Then he says they look like his beads—one of them even has *Screw Iraq* carved on it. But he claims his were stolen in Wyoming. And also that a lot of hobos wear them, including vets. So they might or might not be his. That true?"

"It's true."

I dropped my elbows to my thighs, kept my face blank as I ran through the list of possibilities. Another tramp, one who'd served in Iraq. Tucker's thief. Or our mysterious officer, planting evidence. "Does he know who stole them?"

Cohen sighed like it hurt. "Assuming we believe him?"

"Assuming that."

"Says he was asleep. But he claims some skinhead jumped him in Wolf, and it was that night his beads went missing. I asked why the Nazi went after him. He says it just happens like that sometimes—he gets jumped because people don't like his face. Doc backs up his story to the extent that Rhodes has a nice set of two- or three-day-old bruises and a pretty good scrape."

"Who won the fight?"

"Rhodes says it was close, but he'd of won on points."

"So it's payback time? This guy, this random, angry asshole, gets to Denver first and takes out his hate on Elise?"

Cohen shrugged. "That's one theory. Seems thin. How would the Nazi even know about her?"

"The word on the rails. Pretty easy to find out who's connected. Can you get a sketch artist?"

"Miles ahead of you, Parnell."

"There any witnesses? Hobos, I can run them down."

"No. But Rhodes has a fresh tat on his arm, a double lightning bolt. It's—"

"Used by the white-supremacist jail gangs. He spend any time in prison?"

"No." Cohen frowned. "Claims he's not a racist, either. Says some old German, a railroad man who works on the lines, did it for him after Rhodes took a beating. The German told him no one would bother him with that tat."

"He's probably right. There're a lot of white power skinheads riding the rails. Rumor has them killing hobos as a form of initiation. With transients and miles of empty space, it can be months or even years before someone is reported missing. If they ever are."

Something small and distant switched on in my memory like a feeble light bulb. I tried to follow its faint glow, but nothing came.

We sat in silence. The wind flicked a random backhand at us, flapping open Cohen's overcoat and sending a swirl of dust around the courtyard.

I straightened, pressing my palm against the small of my back where a muscle had locked. "So if what he says is true, if he's innocent, how do we help him?"

"Whoa, Parnell. You may live in a world of innocent until proven guilty. But I tend to take the long view. You want to play Fairy Godmother, be my guest. But my job is to find a killer."

"Who says those are mutually exclusive? We look for someone else who could have been at Elise's Friday night. Verify Rhodes's story about the key. See if it's still there and—"

"We checked. It's not. If it ever was."

"—and find the guy who jumped him. Dig for motives. Talk to family and friends and coworkers to see if she was afraid of anyone or fighting with anyone."

He caught his errant coat, buttoned it. "Christ, Sydney. This may not matter worth a shit. The ME says what I think she'll say, none of us can do a damn thing for him. My captain will hand Rhodes off to the DA and that'll be that."

"How will that make you feel?"

He set his cup on the ground. Another flutter of wind blew it over, and he grabbed it before it could roll. "You know, he's probably good for it, no matter how sorry we feel for him. ME connects all the dots for me, I got no choice. I gotta move on."

"Bandoni's already connected the dots."

Cohen shrugged. "Len can act like an ass sometimes, but he's a good cop. Best partner I've had. He won't shut this case down just because doing so would give us a win. But his instinct is usually dead-on, and right now his gut is sending up warnings like a five-alarm fire."

"And my gut says he's innocent."

"We've got means, opportunity. Maybe a motive."

"PTSD isn't a motive."

"So you don't like it. That doesn't make it go away."

"Do you really care about these people, Cohen? Or are they just stats on a spreadsheet?"

He didn't say anything for a while. Finally he smiled that cynical smile. "If you knew me, you wouldn't need to ask me that."

I gave him a long, hard look. "You really think my life would be better if we were friends?"

"Just saying."

"Jesus, let it go already. For your own sake. I make a shitty friend."

"That what you told Rhodes?"

"He's not looking for a friend. He needs a Marine."

Cohen tossed down the dregs of his coffee and flattened the cup. "Don't overstep, okay, Parnell? You're a cop, and I suspect you're a good one. And we really want your help on this. But you aren't a murder cop. Don't lose sight of that."

I couldn't think of anything to say to that, so I downed my cold coffee. Between the nicotine and the caffeine and the sugar, I wondered if I'd ever come back to earth. I held myself still and listened to my heart complain at the extra work I'd ladled on.

I said, "You going to run him by the doc again? He acts like he's in pain."

"We'll have the EMTs take a look at him. He was pretty tired. Why we cut the interview short. But he was against going back to the hospital."

A small, ugly voice inside me pointed out that if Rhodes were to die, the worry about Habbaniyah would die with him.

I'd heard this ugly little voice a lot in Iraq. My survivor voice. What kind of shit excuse for a world is it when you have to choose between honor and survival?

"You need to keep him on suicide watch," I said.

"We've made it official and arrested him. Now that he's in the system, we can take his belt and anything else he might use. We'll have someone watching him."

"I'll find the German," I said. "I'll want that sketch as soon as you have it."

"Should be later this morning. Want me to text it to you?"

"Sure."

I was already forming workarounds to avoid bringing Cohen into my piece of the investigation. But if the skinhead proved to be our perp, I wouldn't have to worry about Habbaniyah or the mysterious man behind it, whom I was starting to think of as simply the Alpha. The skinhead offered all of us—Rhodes, me, his squad mates—a way out.

A flutter of hope stirred in my chest. Or maybe it was the sugar.

"I'll ask around the camps, too," I said. "And the homeless shelters. See if there's any talk about someone carrying a hate for Elise."

"Or maybe unrequited passion. She was a beautiful girl."

"Yeah." I stood. "I'll bring whatever I learn to you."

"Including our German, right?"

I rose and busied myself with an errant strand of hair so I wouldn't have to meet his gaze. "Of course."

His expression was quizzical. "I'm not feeling the love, Parnell."

"It's not about love. It's about faith."

"Whatever," he said, trailing me across the plaza toward my truck. "I'm not feeling it."

"You need to learn to trust, Detective Cohen."

"Give me a reason, Special Agent Parnell."

I turned and looked him straight in the eye. "I promise. I'll tell you everything I know."

"Dante placed liars in the eighth circle, you know."

"An educated murder cop. Don't forget he put traitors in the deepest pit of Hell."

One eyebrow shot up. "An educated railroad cop. You thinking of betraying someone, Parnell?"

"Not you." I stopped at the curb. "I'm thinking of someone else entirely."

CHAPTER 13

Do not call us heroes. Not if you are calling us that in order to absolve yourself of guilt over sending us off to an unwinnable war. Some of us are heroes. But some of us never had the chance. And some of us got slammed face-first into the fact that when we looked inside, we found nothing heroic at all.

—Corporal Sydney Rose Parnell. Denver Post.

January 13, 2010.

When I got home, Clyde greeted me at the door, light on his paws and ready to rumble. I pulled out the donut I'd lifted from a box at the police station.

"Last one, buddy," I said. "You're going on a working-dog diet starting in about thirty seconds."

He ate the donut in one gulp and licked his chops.

"Okay, ten seconds."

I started the coffeepot, took a few minutes to clear the driveway and steps, then called the personnel office at Denver Pacific Continental. Nik would probably know right away who the German was. But I didn't want him to know I was working the case.

"It's Special Agent Parnell," I said when Ted Rivers picked up.

"Ah, our hero. Good job, bringing that perp in."

"This mean I'll get a hero bonus in my next paycheck?"

"Settle for a bag of M&M's?"

"Throw in some kibble for Clyde. Look, Rivers, I'm trying to track down a man on one of our repair crews."

"Sure thing. You got a name?"

"A name is what I need. All I know is he's German, probably over fifty, and he was working near Wolf, Wyoming, two nights ago."

"Roald Hoffreider," Rivers said immediately. "Guy's been with us for thirty-some years. You want his cell number?"

"Rivers, I could kiss you," I said after I'd jotted down the phone number.

"Name the time and place. I'll be there, lips puckered."

I laughed despite myself and hung up. I dialed Hoffreider's number and left a message when he didn't pick up, asking him to call me.

I poured a cup of coffee then went into the tiny dining room, which I'd converted into a study of sorts, and sat at the computer. First I did a little digging to see if I could find Rhodes's chain of command. Nothing. Since 9/11, those sites have been locked down tighter than a maximum-security prison. I turned to pulling information on ex-Marine Jeremy "Jeezer" Winston Kane.

Married and with a daughter, Kane worked as a night stocker for the Costco Warehouse in Littleton. From an adrenaline-charged soldier risking death every day to a man driving forklifts of Pampers—I wondered how well he was making the transition.

Especially given that before the war, he'd been a premed student at the University of Colorado. Tough change in career plans. Why hadn't he gone back to school on the GI Bill?

I called the Costco, pretended to be a friend, and learned Jeremy had gotten off work at six a.m. I whistled to Clyde, and we headed to the door. If I moved quickly, I should be able to catch Jeremy before he went to bed.

Littleton is a fourteen-square-mile municipality on Denver's southwest side. It's a surprisingly quiet place, given that it's home to the gravesite of America's only convicted cannibal and shares a zip code with the site of one of the deadliest mass shootings in US history. I drove south out of Denver's downtown congestion—heavy even on a Sunday—and then west on 285. I kept the window cracked, trying to keep myself awake. A few miles away, the Rocky Mountains gleamed with silver indifference under clear, cold skies.

The Kanes lived in a split-level set halfway down the block of a lower-middle-class neighborhood, where the homes looked mean and the yards amounted to postage stamps. I pulled over near the crumbling curb and studied the house.

At just past eight o'clock, it was quiet, the drapes half drawn. The porch light still burned and a newspaper lay in the driveway, its plastic cover sparkling with frost. The snowy front yard held an abandoned wheelbarrow and shovel; it looked like someone had been scooping gravel into a border. An old Ford pickup sat in the driveway, filthy with mud from the recent storms. A *Beware of Dog* sign hung on the chain-link fence.

I left Clyde in the heated dog crate and walked up the drive, picking up the paper as I went by. No dog barked from the yard. At the scuffed front door, I paused and listened for people moving or talking. A faint sound of singing came through the wood—a children's television show. I caught the smoky aroma of bacon frying.

I took a breath and rang the bell. Act One of my subterfuge. From inside, a dog unloosed an artillery of deep-throated barks. A sharp command from a female voice, and the dog immediately quieted. A house with discipline.

The woman who came to the door was in her early twenties, with long blond hair and an open, pretty face. She was six or seven months pregnant and dressed in loose-fitting sweats and a Broncos hoodie.

A muscular pit bull/grizzly bear mix strained against her legs where she held him by his collar. She jerked the collar hard and said, "Ogre, sit."

Ogre sat. But he didn't look happy about it.

The woman took in my uniform coat. Her gaze flicked past me to the Denver Pacific Continental truck at the curb then back to me, settling on my black eyes and bandaged cheek.

"Can I help you?"

I lifted her newspaper—a peace offering—and showed her my badge. "I'm Senior Special Agent Parnell with the Denver Pacific Continental Railway. Are you Mrs. Kane?"

"I'm Sherri Kane, yes."

"I need to talk to your husband. Is he home?"

A crease marred her pretty forehead. "He's watching *Dora the Explorer* with our daughter. It's the only show she's allowed. Could you come back in half an hour?"

Very disciplined.

"I'll be as brief as I can."

The crease deepened, matched with a frown, and I thought she might refuse. Cross a mother bear by threatening her child's happiness, and it likely won't go well. But I needed Jeremy Kane off-guard and tired.

"It's official business, Mrs. Kane."

She shook her head and sighed. Her ponytail danced. "Let me just put Ogre in back," she said. "He's not big on company."

A minute later and the dog was barking at me from behind the *Beware of Dog* sign. He looked like he hadn't had his breakfast yet.

Sherri Kane returned to the front door and unenthusiastically waved me in.

The house opened into a living room with cheap, new-looking furniture—matching sofa and love seat, oak coffee and end tables, and a curio cabinet filled with ceramic animals. Sherri led me through the room and into a hallway. At the kitchen she paused to turn off the stove, then went down a short flight of steps to the family room. A man and a girl two or maybe three years old sat with their backs to us, snuggled together on a couch watching *Dora* on the small TV.

"Jeremy," Sherri said.

The man glanced over his shoulder, saw me, and got to his feet. He was tall and athletic looking, with bright-blue eyes, sandy red hair, and a trim beard. Like his wife, he had an open, friendly face, which I decided on principle to mistrust.

The little girl hung with the television show.

"I'm sorry," Kane said. "I thought it was our neighbor again, back for more coffee."

"I'm Special Agent Parnell with DPC," I said.

"The railroad?" Jeremy Kane's brow furrowed much as his wife's had. But he came around the couch and offered his hand. He walked with a slight limp. "What's this about, Officer?"

"I'm here at the request of Tucker Rhodes."

Kane blinked. "Tucks? Why didn't he come himself?"

"He's not free to do that, Mr. Kane."

I watched Kane connect the dots. Hobo. Railway cop. "Damn, he's not under arrest or something, is he? Not hurt, or anything?"

"Why would you think he'd be under arrest?"

Kane flushed. "Well, trespassing, I guess. No secret about him and trains."

"Mr. Kane, could we talk in private?"

Kane and his wife exchanged glances.

"Um, sure. Honey, can you take Haley to our bedroom? She can watch TV up there."

Sherri gave me her angry mommy face, but she scooped up the little girl with another cheery swish of her ponytail and pushed past us. Haley watched me over her mother's shoulder with dark, liquid eyes as she and Sherri climbed the stairs and disappeared into the hallway.

Kane clicked off the TV. "Get you some coffee?"

"No. Thanks."

He gestured me toward the couch.

"What's going on with Tucks?" he asked after we sat down.

"Mr. Kane, Elise Hensley came to visit you a few days ago."

For the first time, Kane looked uncomfortable. His long fingers drummed the legs of his jeans. "Yeah. She wanted to let me know Tucks was on his way back to town."

From upstairs the floor creaked and then came the murmur of the TV.

"Some reason she came by instead of calling?"

He shrugged. "She said Tucks had gotten his hobo beads stolen. She wanted to see if Sherri would make him more. She's going to surprise Tucks with them."

That sidetracked me. "Sherri makes hobo beads?"

"Yeah. It lets her stay home with Haley and still make a little money. She sells them at boutiques and craft fairs. Amazing what people will pay. But of course she doesn't charge Tucks for his."

I filed this information away. "Does Elise come by often?"

"Sure. Usually when Tucks is in town. Elise and Sherri aren't the best of friends, but Sherri knows I need to spend time with my old buddies. She's good about it."

"But this last time Elise came alone."

Another affable shrug. "Sherri and I tell her to come as often as she can. Watching out for Elise is just something we do. Tucks likes to know she's being taken care of."

"You stay in touch with any other guys from your platoon?"

He blinked at the change in topic. "My squad, sure. A few others." He kept drumming his fingers. Still friendly but growing cautious. "What's this about?"

"Mr. Kane, did Elise's visit upset you?"

Another blink. "Um, no. Of course not."

"But she came to talk to you about Habbaniyah, isn't that right?"

Kane's eyes dropped and his fingers stopped their fidgeting. His body twitched once then went still as a mannequin's. The only thing that gave him away was his Adam's apple sliding up and down as he swallowed.

"What do you know about that?" he asked in a soft, careful voice.

"Before I worked for the railroad, Private Kane, I was a Marine with Mortuary Affairs. I processed the bodies of Haifa and Resenko."

His eyes came back up, taking me in. "Yes." He nodded to himself. "I remember you now, even with those shiners. We used to talk about you. The lady with the yellow hijab."

"What did Elise want, Mr. Kane?"

For the first time I saw his intelligence shining through the friendly demeanor like lamplight cutting through fog. A premed student, I reminded myself. Probably good with a knife.

"I always figured you hated us for what happened," he said. "Are you really here as Tucks's friend?"

"More as an interested party. And I need to know, Mr. Kane. Why did Elise want to talk about Habbaniyah? And who else did she talk to?"

Another bob of his Adam's apple. "Special Agent Parnell, I don't think I have to tell you anything. You're not regular police. You have no authority here. I don't know what dirt you're trying to dig up, but you tell Tucks that if he wants to talk to me, he needs to come himself."

Hoping I wasn't doing something that Cohen would rightfully want to shoot me for later, I said, "Elise was found dead in her apartment yesterday morning. Rhodes is under arrest for her murder."

Kane went white. "What?"

"Where were you Friday night and Saturday morning, Mr. Kane?"

"Me? What?"

He stood so suddenly that his knee caught the flimsy coffee table, flinging it over. Books and coffee mugs and magazines spilled to the floor. Overhead, footsteps thumped on the floor. Sherri.

"Does she know?" I asked. "Does your wife know about Habbaniyah?"

"What? No." He looked at me in panic. "You can't think I had anything to do with—with Elise being killed. Oh, my God. And poor Tucks. Not another one."

Sherri appeared at the top of the stairs. "Another what?"

Jeremy looked at her, eyes wild. "Sherri, no. Go back with Haley."

But Sherri came on down the stairs, a matriarchal elephant. She looked at the toppled table and then at her husband.

"Jeremy? What's going on? Why are you—what's wrong?" When he didn't answer, she whirled on me. "What did you say to him?"

Kane found his voice. "Elise is dead. She thinks I killed her."

For a moment, the room was utterly still. Ogre's tags jingled from the backyard as he paced the fence. Upstairs, *Dora the Explorer* and her friends sang, *We did it!*

Sherri shoved her face into mine.

"Get out of our house," she whispered harshly. "Get out!"

"No, honey, it's okay." Kane took his wife's arm, tried to pull her back. She shook him off. Eyes still on me, she said, "What is she talking about, Jeremy? Is Elise really dead? How can she think that—"

Gently he took her arms again. "Sherri. Be quiet, okay? This is important. I need you to go back upstairs and wait with Haley. I'll take care of this."

"No."

"It's about the war, honey. Okay? Marine stuff. Agent Parnell doesn't really think I did anything. It's about Tucks, okay? So, please, go upstairs. Everything's going to be fine."

Sherri shook him off again, took a step back. Her face flushed and she seemed about to argue, but then abruptly she turned and hurried back up the stairs, her hands holding her pregnant belly.

Kane watched her go. "She knows stuff happened over there. And she wants to support me. She really does. But to be honest, she'd rather not hear about it." He turned back to me. "She likes things to be nice. To be . . . orderly. It's why she doesn't like Elise. Elise couldn't let stuff go. Sometimes I was almost jealous of Tucks. He shouldn't have told her things, but Elise wanted to know. She wanted to *understand*."

"You haven't answered my question. Where were you?"

He knelt on the ground, started gathering the books and magazines. "I was at work. I'm a stocker at Costco. I was there all night."

"I'll check that."

"Go ahead."

"What did you mean, 'another one'?"

"Guy from our squad was just arrested for taking a baseball bat to his wife. But I didn't mean it that way. Tucks isn't like that. No way he could have—have hurt Elise."

I helped him right the table. "Why not?"

"Tucks had enough killing in the war. He came home, he couldn't go hunting with his dad anymore. Hell, he can't squash a spider. He might freak out a little sometimes. Anyone would, they went through what he did. But, he'd hurt himself before he'd hurt her."

"They've got a lot of evidence against him."

"I don't care what they think they have. I'll bet everything I own on Tucks."

We returned the books and magazines to the coffee table. Kane carried the empty coffee mugs to the kitchen and came back. He stared blankly at the coffee stain on the carpet.

"What's this got to do with Habbaniyah?" he asked.

"Maybe nothing. Who else did Elise talk to, Kane? Who might have felt threatened by what she knew?"

"If Elise talked to anyone else, she didn't tell me about it. What does Tucks say?"

"He doesn't know, either."

"The only other guys who know what happened over there, besides you and your CO, are Crowe and Sarge." He sank back to the couch.

"Shit. We took an oath not to tell anyone. Not *anyone*. Why did Tucks have to go and tell Elise?"

"Your sergeant didn't ride with you guys. Who was the fourth member of your team?"

"Dave Tignor. He was back home with his folks in Omaha. Killed himself a couple of months ago. What about your CO?"

"You didn't know?"

"Know what?"

"He's dead." The words, so rarely spoken, made me wince. "Do you know who gave the original order?"

"None of us knew that. Except your CO. And maybe Sarge." He looked up at me, panic on his face. "Do you really think Elise was killed because of Habbaniyah?"

"That's what I'm trying to find out."

"If Rhodes goes to trial, the whole story will come out, won't it?"

"Probably."

"Things won't be nice for Sherri then, will they?"

"No." I looked around at the clean, tidy house, the carpet now splotched with coffee. I remembered what Bandoni had said about having seen the best liars the world has to offer. Maybe Kane was one of them.

But I was starting to warm up to him. To trust him, even. Could be I was more like Bandoni than I wished, going with my gut and watching the eyes.

"You guys look like you're doing okay," I said.

"You think?" He snorted. "We're barely hanging on. Sherri's stayed with me, but it's been a bitch of a ride. She thought she'd be a doctor's wife by now."

"She loves you."

"Yeah." He gave a rueful headshake. "I had two ambitions for my twenties. I mean, outside of marrying Sherri and raising a family."

"Yeah?"

"I wanted to become a surgeon, like my dad. And run some marathons. That's it. Two things that I could work hard for and actually do. I wasn't asking for the moon. Wasn't asking for any favors or any help. But instead I got all patriotic. Dropped out of school and signed up. Came home with a pin in my leg and a traumatic brain injury that has done fuck-all with my memory. That and the joy of seeing Tucks burn all over again, every goddamn time I close my eyes at night." He glared at me. "That sound like I'm doing okay?"

"I'm sorry."

"They tell me I'm a hero and thank me for my service. You ever try taking that to the bank?"

"Every day."

"How's it working for you?"

I laughed, then we fell quiet, lost in thoughts of loss.

"You didn't go back to school because of your memory problems?" I asked after a time.

"Oh, I'm going back. It'll be the hardest thing I've ever done, but Sherri and I are together on this. We're just trying to save enough money so that I only have to work part-time once I finish my undergrad degree." A bleakness settled over his face like the arrival of winter. "The stuff about Habbaniyah comes out, it'll be all over. They could court-martial us, right? Because of—"

"Are you in the reserves?"

"No."

"Then, no," I said. "They can't court-martial you. Tell me how to find Sarge and Crowe."

"Crowe, it'll take a while. Last time I saw him was after Tucks's fourth surgery. He calls every blue moon. Travels a lot. He's from Detroit, but says living there is worse than being in Iraq. I don't have a number for him, or an address. Best I can do is give you his sister's number."

"You ever give that number to Elise?"

"Nah. She never asked."

So chances were good that Elise couldn't have tracked him down, either. "What about Sarge?"

Jeremy glanced at the watch on his wrist. "You want to talk to him right now?"

"He lives around here?"

"Moved to Denver maybe three months ago. Met a girl in California, and she dragged him here. See him every couple of weeks."

"And he's never said anything about Elise?"

"No. But Sarge is pretty closemouthed, even with me. He's never uttered one word about Habbaniyah."

"So he wouldn't have appreciated Elise's efforts to get everyone to confess."

Kane shot me a glance. "No. But he wouldn't have killed her, either."

"Okay. No time like the present, then."

Kane grabbed a cordless phone from the kitchen, punched in a number, and pressed the speakerphone button. I heard a man's voice, then realized it was a recording. Kane disconnected.

"Sometimes after Saturday night he's pretty hung over. I go over and make him coffee, throw him in the shower. He has to be at work by noon."

"You. Not his girlfriend."

"Sarge and Amy break up and make up every couple of weeks. When she's around, she usually needs waking up, too." He stood. "You up for driving over there? He's only fifteen minutes away."

"You lead," I said. "I'll follow."

Sherri met us at the front door, her eyes wet and red. Kane kissed her and told her he was going to Sarge's, that he'd be back in an hour.

"Is she going with you?"

"She needs to talk to him." He touched her cheek with a gentle finger. "You about done with those beads for Tucker?"

She turned her face into his touch. "Almost."

Kane spread his open hand across her belly as if for good luck then pushed out the front door, heading toward his truck. I moved to follow him, but Sherri stepped into my path.

"If you're looking for dirt Elise might have dug up," she said, "there's a lot of places to look besides my husband."

"What do you mean?"

She glanced over her shoulder. Kane was unlocking his truck.

"Elise was nosy," Sherri said, turning back. "Poking around, stirring up a hornet's nest of trouble. She didn't worry who might get stung."

"Sounds like you know something."

She looked down. When her eyes came back up, fear sparked the defiance in her green eyes. "Look, my husband's a good man. And Elise was nothing but trouble. You think you're some hotshot investigator? Maybe you ought to look at whoever she upset and not bother those who tried to help her."

"A name or two would get me started."

"I don't know names. Just those people Elise hung out with. Those tramps."

"She made trouble for them?"

"She made trouble for everyone."

"Okay." I pulled out my car keys. "I'll keep that in mind."

"You do that."

I gave her my card. "Call me if any names come to you."

Sherri Kane's eyes stayed on me as I opened the door and walked down the driveway. From behind his sign, Ogre cranked up his bark.

This time, Sherri didn't tell him to stop.

Chapter 14

Ask most people in America what "normal" is, and they'll
tell you it's a roof and three squares a day. It's a decent job
and good health and a marriage that's going along just fine,
thanks. It's the middle-class version of the American Dream.
What no one wants to admit is that this idea of normal
isn't really normal at all. It's a fantasy.
Normal is whatever we've gotten used to in our own pri-
vate universe. It's war or cancer or poverty. Hopelessness or
pain or fear. It's the cigarette burns on the coffee table and
bone-deep exhaustion and the stink of booze and the black
eye from—you tell everyone who asks—running into a door.
Normal is the devil-ridden quiet of three a.m. when
you're eyeball-to-eyeball with God, and you know you won't
win because the deck is stacked.
Best you can do is fold.
—Sydney Parnell. Personal journal.

Sarge and his on-again, off-again lady friend lived a few miles north in
what could generously be called the un-gentrified part of town. As I
followed Kane's truck, the lower-middle-class residential area gave way
to dispirited strip malls and fast-food joints, which, in turn, surrendered

to a zone of apartment complexes designed with the lower ten percent in mind.

Hartstone Village sat on the very outskirts of Littleton across the highway from a small, winter-brown field. Maybe the field had been intended as a park, but now all it held were weeds, a broken-down jungle gym, and a clutch of trash blown in from the fast-food places. I veered around a pothole the size of Delaware and pulled into Hartstone, parking next to Kane. He sat in his cab chatting on his cell phone; when I looked over, he held up his index finger, telling me to give him a minute.

I killed the engine and stared out through the dirt-streaked windshield.

Hartstone had never been the Taj Mahal, but it had seen better days. The chipped and peeling paint, cracked asphalt, and narrow balconies cluttered with cast-off furniture and rusting barbeque grills—all of it gave the place the feel of a refugee camp. A dreary stopover for people on their way up to something better. Or maybe on their way back down.

I had a pretty good idea in which direction Sarge was headed.

Despite the cold, the complex was Sunday stay-at-home busy. Cars pulled in and out of the parking lot in a steady stream. A man worked at repairing a motorcycle on a front sidewalk while, nearby, a pair of bored-looking women huddled together on a wooden bench, watching him. Kids underdressed for the cold played on a set of swings to the west of the L-shaped block of buildings. Two teens ran past my truck and darted across the road, horns blowing in their wake. They leapt over the curb, laughing, then stood in the weeds with their backs to the wind and smoked.

Nothing but normal. So why was my gut sending up a five-alarm warning?

Clyde, either feeling his own anxiety or picking up on mine, pressed next to me and gave a whine that sounded exactly like a dog's version of *what the hell?*

"I hear you," I said.

Kane had finished his phone call and was locking up his truck. I stepped out, and Clyde hopped down after me. A cold wind rattled the chains on the swing set and flapped a plastic US flag hanging next to a second-floor apartment. I snapped the leash onto Clyde's collar, and we followed Kane, who was already heading up the stairs toward the second floor.

On the drive over, I had called the Costco and verified that Kane had been on-shift the night Elise was killed. Each shift had two fifteen-minute breaks and half an hour in the middle for a late-night snack. Unless a witness said Kane had taken a long, unscheduled break, it looked like he was in the clear.

One suspect down. A lot more to go, if Sherri was right.

Unless Sarge told us something I really didn't want to hear.

Clyde and I caught up with Kane at the door next to the flag; he was searching through keys hanging from a tiny plastic replica of an AK-47.

"I've been trying to call him all the way over here," Kane said. "Nothing. He gets into a real bender, he doesn't hear the alarm, the phone, not anything."

I cocked my head at the sound of voices and music coming faintly through the scuffed door. "You already knocked?"

He gave me the eye. "I graduated salutatorian from Thomas Edison High School."

So yes.

"What about the TV? You're saying he'd sleep through that?"

Kane sucked in a breath, huffed it out.

"Sarge doesn't watch TV. He bought it for Amy. But she's supposed to be in Lubbock this weekend, visiting her mom."

He found the key and undid the deadbolt, then slid a different key into the main lock. Before he could turn the knob, I pulled him back.

"Clyde and I'll take the lead," I said and drew my gun, holding it with the barrel down.

Kane stared at the gun then cast an astonished glance at me. "It's probably just Amy, changed her mind about the family thing. Passed out while she was watching TV."

"Maybe."

Kane's face went stubborn.

"It's Amy," he said. "What else could it be?"

"Elise is dead," I reminded him. "Someone made her that way while her landlady was sitting in the room right below."

"But here? Shit, there's a million people around."

I waited.

"Shit." But Kane finally nodded his agreement, turned the knob to unlatch the door then stepped behind Clyde and me.

I nudged the door open with my foot.

"Max Udell? Amy?"

The door swung open to a dumpy front room with a sagging sofa, a rickety-looking coffee table covered with beer cans, and a top-of-the-line television set. The TV was tuned to a show about land mines in Serbia; as we walked in, the tone lightened from somber to merely serious, and a celebrity appeared, urging anyone watching to get life insurance while there was still time.

Not a flesh-and-blood person in sight. But there was something here. I could feel it like ice against my skin.

Kane closed the front door behind us and turned off the TV. In the sudden silence, the wind smacked the building. Down in the parking lot a horn honked, and someone hollered for their kid.

"Sarge?" Kane called. "You here, man?"

Nothing.

Kane opened a tiny closet next to the front door and glanced inside. "His rifle's gone."

"He one to get trigger-happy?"

"Never known him to."

We made our way through the living room to the kitchen, calling Udell's name. The kitchenette was in a worse state of disarray than the front room, with overflowing trash and a counter covered with empty pizza boxes stained with grease. More beer cans rounded out the bachelor décor. The place stank like a Dumpster.

"Is it always like this?"

"Maybe not quite this bad."

A cockroach skittered across the floor and disappeared beneath a cabinet. "Has he ever talked about ending it all?"

Kane had started stacking the empty pizza boxes as if he meant to tidy up out of sheer habit. Now he froze.

"You mean kill himself?" He dropped his hands. "Do you know anyone who's seen combat who hasn't talked that way sometimes?"

"Sure," I said. "A lot of guys. Which side of the fence would you put Sarge on?"

"On the never side."

"Okay."

But I watched him mentally hitch himself up. Preparing.

We moved into the hallway. A bathroom on our right was empty. The hall was a scant ten feet long and ended in two closed doors.

"Door on the left is his bedroom," Kane said. "He uses the room on the right as a study."

"Doors usually closed?"

"The study, yeah. He doesn't let anyone in there. His bedroom, I don't know. I think so."

I raised my voice. "Max Udell, this is Special Agent Parnell with the DPC railroad. I'm here with Jeremy Kane. My dog and I are coming to talk to you. That sound okay?"

The wind drew a breath, and in the sudden quiet we heard a creaking sound.

I edged forward. "Udell?"

Behind me, Kane said, "Sarge, it's me, man. You there?"

"Keep an eye on the door on the right," I told Kane. "I'm going in the left."

At his nod, Clyde and I glided down the rest of the hallway. Just outside the door, Clyde's ears came up and his tail lifted like a flag. We pressed against the wall to the left of the door, and I reached over, turned the knob, then kicked the door open, going in with my gun arm raised.

A man, tall and tanned and bearded, stood at the window, staring out at the bleak February day. His white button-down shirt and black slacks were rumpled and dusty. In his hand he held a manila file.

Winter light filtered softly through him.

My gun hand trembled as he turned to look at me. The light glimmered in his blue eyes. He gave me a nod.

"Udell?" I whispered.

Clyde whimpered.

I raised my voice. "Kane? What's your sergeant look like?"

Kane's reply came from the second bedroom.

"Shit, is he in there?" Panic in his voice and the creak of the floor as he moved.

"No. It's all clear."

Kane appeared in the doorway, glanced around, then gave me a bewildered look.

"Why are you asking what he looks like?"

"Humor me."

"Black man. Not too tall. Built like a tank. There are photos of him in the other room if you want to see."

The man at the window, fair-skinned and well over six foot, turned his back to me, stepped toward the window, and vanished.

"Shit," I whispered.

"What is it?" Kane moved closer. "Geez, Parnell, you look like you've seen a ghost."

I waved Kane away and holstered my gun. Where the hell had this guy come from? If I'd processed his body in Iraq, he must have been missing key parts. Like a face. So how had I conjured him out of incomplete memories?

Maybe it was time to go back into counseling. Before I started building entire armies of the dead.

◆　◆　◆

While Kane started in on the study, I set Clyde to guard the front door then took my time searching Udell's bedroom for any indication he'd been in touch with Elise or threatened by the mysterious Alpha. I looked in drawers, between the mattress and box springs, then under the bed frame. I wasn't sure what, exactly, I was looking for, but I figured I'd know it if I saw it. A letter or a scrawled note. A token from Habbaniyah, something like the embroidered name tape from Resenko's uniform or maybe a photo. With meticulous care I went through the clothes hanging in the closet—expensive-looking jackets and brand-name sweaters—and rifled through the piles of papers and books on the shelf. I played back the recorder on his phone, but any messages had been erased. I finished in his bedroom by looking for a place where the carpet might have been pulled up.

Nothing.

I checked out the kitchen, the bathroom and linen closet, the living room, and the tiny entry closet. I found a high-quality camera and a pair of binoculars that looked like they'd cost more than I earned in a year. But nothing else. I went back down the hallway to the second bedroom. Kane stood in front of a four-drawer metal filing cabinet, reading through the folders in the top drawer.

"Anything?" I asked.

"Sarge has got some weird shit in here. Studies on neurology and psychosis. Self-help articles. Articles about spies. Old *National*

*Geographic*s. And a ton of maps. But I've been through every file, and there's nothing about Habbaniyah. I even pulled out every map Sarge has of Iraq, looking for writing or marks of some kind. Nothing."

"And nothing about whoever might have ordered the cover-up? Newspaper articles about senior officers, say?"

"Nada."

"How about something weird like a bomb fragment or a war-trophy? Something someone might have mailed to him as a threat."

The corner of his mouth ticked. "Like an ear, you mean?"

"Exactly like that."

"Those were confiscated when we mustered out," he said, deadpan.

Unsure whether I felt relieved or disappointed at the lack of any apparent links to Habbaniyah, I leaned against the doorjamb and took in the room.

Max Udell's study was a shrine to his time in the Marines and especially Iraq. In contrast to the rest of the apartment, this room was clean and organized. Floor-to-ceiling shelves on three walls held novels and nonfiction books about the Middle East, about Sunni and Shia cultures, about Islam and Mohammed. Neatly displayed around the books were Bedouin daggers and clay pots, alabaster cups and broken cuneiform tablets. A woolen prayer rug hung on the wall next to the window; beneath it, a stone cheetah snarled at me in eternal silence. A table covered in a red cloth held a filthy tactical vest, Udell's helmet, and an NCO ceremonial sword in a black sheath.

I gaped. "Do you know where he got all this stuff?"

"Off eBay, mostly. Bought some shit from other guys. Stuff's fake. You know, replicas. Or a lot of it is."

"You sure of that? It's damn freaky."

Kane turned to look at the shelves as if seeing everything for the first time. But after a moment he shook his head. "Sarge doesn't have the money to be a collector. And he isn't a thief. The rug is real. Some of the pots and the dagger. But mostly it's fakes. And it's not freaky. It's just Sarge. Most of us try not to think about Iraq. But for Sarge, it was the biggest part of his life."

Maybe it still is, I thought.

Kane went back to the files. I started at the top of the left-most bookshelf and went through everything. I was especially attentive with the books, but they were all as pristine as the day they were printed. Maybe this really was a shrine. A place to hold memories, not examine them.

When I finished with the shelves, I turned to the most personal thing in the room—an entire wall of photos thumbtacked directly into the drywall above Udell's desk. Color photos, mostly, although there was the occasional black and white. The pictures seemed to be arranged in no particular pattern. Photos from boot camp were interwoven with scenes from Iraq and other shots I guessed to be from Udell's childhood. Pictures of Rhodes taken before the bomb, cocky and handsome. Of Kane and Rhodes and the murdered Resenko along with two other men whom I took to be the missing Crowe and the recently deceased Tignor. These alternated with 1970s-ish wedding photos of a young black couple and even older photos of people I assumed were Udell's grandparents.

There was also a scattering of photos taken after the suicide bomber hit our forward operating base, our FOB. Looking at those photos, I felt a muscle jump below my left eye.

Worst among all the photos were a handful of snapshots featuring dead Iraqi soldiers and insurgents, their bodies burned or riddled with bullets. A victory cry or a penance? Just owning them was probably a violation of half a dozen war crime laws.

I crossed to the window and stared outside for a minute or two, waited until my breathing evened out. Then I returned to the wall.

Given the orderliness of everything else in the room, the photos looked like a crazed mosaic created by a singularly bewildered man—one who made no distinction between the past and the present.

In the very middle of the wall was a photo of Sarge with Haifa's son, Malik. The boy I'd tried to save. Udell and Malik stood with the dead man I'd just seen in Sarge's bedroom. In the photo, the then-living man wore traditional Iraqi dress rather than the suit I'd seen him in. His beard was longer. He looked confident, even arrogant. He and Udell were squinting into the desert sun, the boy standing between them and holding a soccer ball. All three were smiling like they'd just won the lottery.

It didn't surprise me to see Sarge with Malik. The boy had become something of a camp mascot, as wrong as it sounds to say that now. But who the hell was the other guy? And why had I imagined him in the other room?

I took down the photo and flipped it over, hoping for a clue on the back. Nothing.

"Who's the white guy?" I asked Kane, holding out the photo.

Kane placed his finger in a file to hold his place and looked at the picture. "Not sure. Saw him around the FOB from time to time, a couple of times with Sarge. Usually wearing native garb. Rumor was that he was CIA, but that didn't make any sense. Guys I knew in intelligence would never let anyone snap their photo. And no reason why Sarge would be hanging out with a spook."

"No," I murmured, staring at Malik's shining face. "No reason at all."

"You think that guy might have something to do with what's going on?"

"I don't know. Mind if I keep this?"

Kane shrugged. "Not my call. Keep it for now, and you can take it up with Sarge when he gets back from wherever he's gone off to."

"You've tried the girlfriend?"

He gave me the look I probably deserved.

"Right," I said. "Salutatorian."

When he went back to the files, I slid the photo into an inside coat pocket. I looked for other snapshots featuring either Malik or the spook. I found one more with the dead man in it. Still wearing native dress and standing in front of an Iraqi market.

Behind him and to his right stood a second man, also dressed like an Iraqi. This man's face was in shadow and hard to make out. At his side he wore a curved Kurdish dagger tucked in his belt. I knew that dagger. The carved hilt, the heavy silver sheath. I'd been with the man when he bought it off a Bedouin coming in from the wadis of the Syrian desert.

The man standing in the shadowy background was Douglas Reynauld Ayers.

Dougie.

After Kane had finished searching the filing cabinet, and I'd finished with the desk, we traded places and went through everything once more. Kane tried calling Sarge and his girlfriend again and fielded a couple of calls from an irate Sherri. We then put everything back the way we'd found it and converged at the front door, where Clyde sat patiently guarding against any would-be intruders.

"I hate doing this, Kane," I said, "but I need you to turn your pockets out."

"What?"

"You searched Sarge's files before I did. I need to make sure you didn't take anything."

He glared at me. But he offered no resistance as I did a quick search. Nothing.

Salutatorian, I reminded myself. He could come back any time to take whatever he wanted, so long as Sarge was still AWOL.

"Okay," I said, stepping back.

Kane offered his hand to Clyde, who ignored it.

"He's on duty," I said by way of explanation.

Kane folded his arms at me. "Tucker didn't do it."

"You said that."

"It's true. No way in hell he would ever hurt her."

"He hit her, Kane. More than once."

"He tell you that?"

"No." Nik's face rose in my mind. "Heard it from someone close to Elise."

But Kane shook his head. "I don't believe it."

"That's why he left. He was afraid he'd hurt her again."

"No." Kane stared out the front window, his jaw tight. "He left because he thought he was damaged goods, and she was . . . pure." He turned from the window, his blue eyes searching mine as if wanting to make sure I understood what he was trying to say. "Tucker told me that Elise was the best person he'd ever known. 'True of heart,' is how he put it. The opposite of all the shit we saw in Iraq. She was like those crazy movies where an angel comes down to earth and pretends to be human so she can help people."

"Your wife tells a different story."

"Yeah." He stuffed his hands in his coat pockets, jangled the keys. "Sherri's a good woman. But life has made it kind of easy for her to be good, if you know what I mean. Up until now, her life's been a cakewalk. She's smart and beautiful and she has rich parents who think she can do no wrong. She's succeeded at everything that mattered to her."

"Okay."

"Then all the sudden she had to deal with me being gone and then coming back not quite right and she's not going to be a doctor's wife anymore. Still, she was good. Right up until we started hanging with Tucks and Elise."

I waited.

"Now suddenly there's this woman," Kane went on, "who *didn't* have it easy growing up. Who never had a silver spoon anywhere near her mouth. And suddenly she's everyone's sweetheart. Hell, even Sherri's *parents* fell in love with Elise."

"So you think what your wife's telling me is more jealousy than truth."

"She probably told you Elise was a troublemaker. She's said that often enough to me. And I know women sometimes see things in other women that men don't see. Men can be blind when it comes to a pretty woman. But as much as I love my wife, I wouldn't put too much stock in what she says about Elise."

"What does Sherri know about Habbaniyah?"

Kane rubbed his jaw. "Nothing. Like I said before. For Sherri, life is still pretty much shopping malls and lattes and playgroups for Haley. The war doesn't really figure into that."

"Did she know that Elise was trying to get you guys to come clean?"

"Nah." His eyes narrowed. "What are you driving at?"

"Nothing." I held up my hands at the sharpness in his voice. "Back to the hobos. You've never known Elise to have run-ins with that crowd?"

"Only the crazies. And everyone has trouble with them, according to Tucks. But even that isn't quite right. Elise could usually calm the crazies, find whatever in them was still working and focus on that."

"Usually?"

"Usually. Maybe always. I don't know."

"Tell me about the hobo beads, Kane."

"What do you mean?"

"Rhodes called Elise, told her his beads had been stolen?"

"That's what she said."

"She say how it happened?"

"Just some asshole jumped Tucks in Wyoming. He loved those beads. Wanted 'em back. Or ones just like them, anyway."

"Has Sherri made them yet?"

"She's almost done with them, I think. Why does this matter?"

"Probably it doesn't."

My headset buzzed and I glanced at my phone; it was a number I recognized. I apologized to Kane and went into the kitchen.

"Hey, Cohen," I said.

"Parnell," he said. "I'm sending a photo of the sketch of Rhodes's assailant to your cell phone. I've got uniforms showing the sketch to Elise's neighbors and Bandoni's talking to coworkers. The drawing has been released to Crime Stoppers, so it'll hit the ten p.m. news."

"Nothing so far?"

"We're just getting started. Why don't you and I arrange to meet somewhere? I want to hand out flyers to your hobo crowd."

"You want me to show myself around the camps with a homicide dick?"

"Worried your reputation can't take the hit?"

"I'm worried yours can't. Look, I'm in the middle of something. Can I call you back?"

"Sure. Take your time. It's not like I got a murder case going or anything."

"Smart-ass," I said and disconnected.

We let ourselves out of Sarge's place, and Kane locked the door. We walked toward the stairs.

"You'll let me know when you hear from Sarge?" I asked. "Or Amy?"

"Sure."

At the top of the stairs, I took Kane's arm, bringing him to a stop. Everyone had disappeared as the weather worsened. The guy with the motorcycle had vanished, the playground sat empty. Tumbleweeds skittered through the parking lot. The entire apartment complex groaned under the frigid gale, which seemed to be building toward something momentous. In the sudden emptiness, it was as if Kane and I were the last two humans on Earth.

"Kane, how do you feel about Habbaniyah? About what you guys did after they killed Resenko and Haifa?"

He stared across the street toward the never-quite-a-park. Maybe seeing it. Maybe seeing nothing at all.

"I don't regret any of it," he said, finally. "Not what we did to start, anyway. Those bastards deserved to die. Killing them felt . . . righteous. Then they set that bomb and Haifa's brothers died, and that's when I realized we'd brought down something bigger than all of us. We'd brought down God's law."

"Biblical justice?"

"Maybe more like the law of the universe. Newton's law. For every action, there is an equal and opposite reaction." He turned his eyes back to me, and I held still against the bleakness of his gaze. "After that bomb went off, I finally understood what we'd set in motion. What Resenko and Haifa had started without meaning to, and which we'd followed blindly, like picking up Hansel and Gretel's bread crumbs. Only those crumbs weren't leading us home. They were leading us straight to the witch."

He started down the stairs, his tread heavy, his limp making every other step clang like the tolling of a bell. His words floated back to me on the wind.

"I never forgave myself for that bomb."

CHAPTER 15

7:00 a.m. Camp Taqaddum.

The sun low in the sky, its light spreading like a fan across the FOB. The wind rustling tent flaps and furling flags. Usher's "Burn" quiet on someone's boom box. A yelp of laughter and the clatter of cutlery and the rasp of sand against my boots as the Sir and I walk toward the mess tent.

Then a burst of light, and the air comes apart like cloth ripping.

People drop. Debris tears past. Dust roils up in a great clotted cloud and swallows the light.

In the ringing silence that follows, Marines clamber to their feet, yelling voicelessly as they look for their brothers, their comrades, their leaders.

I roll onto my side, and there is the Sir, lying next to me. He looks fine. Just a little vague, staring over my shoulder. As if his attention has been caught by something I can't see.

As it turned out, it was something none of us could see.

—Sydney Parnell. Personal journal.

I drove across the street to the field where the teens had gone to smoke, pulled up over the curb, and parked in the weeds. I let Clyde out to do his business, gave him some water, then we jumped back into the truck and out of the rising wind. While Clyde curled up to nap, I watched the storm rolling in over the mountains. When the clouds hit the sun, I huddled in the gloom and picked through my thoughts like a cook sorting beans.

Maybe Kane's wife was a jealous liar. But she was right about Elise's interest in the lives of others. Nik had told me that, in addition to her work with the homeless, his niece was the first to volunteer at the soup kitchen and the first to start a Christmas toy drive. That she organized and ran a weekend Bible study and that, at the diner where she waitressed, she'd started a fund drive for the sick child of one of the cooks. In her copious spare time, she volunteered at a shelter for victims of domestic violence.

Like an angel come down to earth, per Jeremy Kane.

The question of the moment was whether any of these humanitarian pursuits had been the cause of her death. If her savage end had nothing to do with Tucker or the war, but only with her kindness.

I frowned. I wasn't a big fan of irony.

The wind rocked the truck, and Clyde whimpered in his sleep. Any other dog, I'd figure he was dreaming about rabbits. But not Clyde. His paws twitched in pursuit of some Morphean monster.

"It's all good, boy." I reached over and stroked his head until he quieted.

I leaned against the door and pressed my face to the cold glass while I considered what we'd found at Sarge's place—the photographs of dead Iraqis and young Malik and a mystery man who might or might not be CIA.

I thought, too, about what we hadn't found—any indication whatsoever that Sarge had been contacted or threatened by the Alpha. Any sign at all that Tucker Rhodes's fear of an Alpha had any bearing. For all I knew, whoever the Alpha was, he might have died in the bomb blast too. That was an irony I could appreciate.

I pulled out the two photos I'd taken from Sarge's wall and set them on the dash. In the first photo, the one taken with Malik and Sarge, the unknown man had been all smiles. Malik, too, looked happy. Joyous, even. As if he'd just gotten some very good news.

I touched my finger to Malik's beaming face, blinked back the moisture in my eyes.

After I'd returned to the States, I'd continued to work for months to bring Malik to Denver. As his application ground through the State Department, where it eventually died, I'd stayed in touch with Marines still in Iraq. Malik was fine, they'd assured me. He missed me and Clyde, asked for us every single day. But he was doing okay.

Then, suddenly, he was gone. No one knew where. He'd simply disappeared. The most logical explanation was that he'd found his family, or they'd found him, and he'd gone back to where he belonged, taken in by an aunt or a grandparent. That he was not only safe but happy.

I fervently hoped this was true. But my gut would have none of it. My gut said that the rage over Haifa's affair with an American had extended to Malik, and that he'd been kidnapped and killed by the same insurgents who'd murdered his mother.

I picked up the second photo. In this shot with Dougie, the unknown man was also smiling. But his smile looked strained. Even through the lens of a camera, worry weighted his eyes.

Dougie wasn't smiling at all.

I looked away from the picture and out the window again, watched as the storm circled around, tracking north.

Dougie had bought the Bedouin knife two weeks before he was killed. That narrowed the time frame of the photograph to the days between everything going to shit over Resenko and when Dougie's body had been found in the desert. I'd never even considered that Dougie's death might have something to do with our cover-up or its aftermath. I'd assumed his murder was part of the general surge against us, and particularly against people like Dougie who went out amongst the people without a show of guns, without any armor and only a bodyguard or two. Talking to the sheiks man to man. Hearts and minds.

Could be I was wrong.

I returned my gaze to the photo, wanting nothing so much as just one more hour with him and the white-hot knowledge that it would be our last.

"Did you know you'd leave me without a chance to say good-bye?" I whispered. "Without a chance to say any of the things that needed saying? *Tell me everything*, you used to say. But I never had the chance."

In sudden, anguished fury, I dropped the photo and slammed my injured palms against the steering wheel. Clyde startled awake, coming up fast on his feet.

"Why don't you ever visit me, Dougie?" I shouted. "Everyone else does. All the fucking time. Every single dead person I processed in Iraq has come to see me. Every person I've tried to piece back together in my mind. They come to me when I'm reading in bed or sitting on the couch or taking a fucking shower. But not you, Dougie. Not you. Not ever. Not once."

The tears rolled down my face, splashed on my throbbing hands.

"I never had the chance to make you whole."

When they'd brought in his mutilated body, the lion ring still on its leather braid around his neck, I'd collapsed on the floor, curled up fetal-tight and vomited. White as ash and crying without making a sound, Gonzo told me later. I stayed that way until the Sir came and pulled me up and away, out of Mortuary Affairs, out to the edge of the FOB where he'd left me in the company of two MPs. He kept me out of Mortuary Affairs until he and Gonzo and Tomitsch were through with Dougie and my beloved was just a shape in a body bag.

Clyde thrust his nose into my face and licked my chin. I pulled him close.

I'd never asked Dougie what he did in Iraq. I knew it was all hush-hush, and to be honest, I didn't want to know. It didn't matter.

I trusted him, and that was enough. The man I loved wasn't about torture or blackmail or illegal manipulation. He believed in what he was doing, and he did it with integrity. I was sure of it, and that was enough for me.

I pulled out his ring on its silver chain, held it dangling in the forlorn light.

What would the VA counselor make of the fact that the one ghost I didn't seem to be haunted by was that of the man I'd loved? The man I still loved.

After he'd died and the Sir had given me Dougie's ring, I tried wearing it on my thumb. But even my thumb was too small to keep the ring in place. So I'd hung it on the chain with my dog tags. When I got home, I moved it to my dad's old silver chain, the one he'd worn every day then left on my dresser right before he walked out.

Now I held the lion tight in my hands, squeezing it hard until it bit into my palm.

It occurred to me that perhaps I should let sleeping lions lie. That if I nosed into the link between the mystery man and Malik and Dougie, I might find out things about Dougie that would destroy the fragile peace I'd built for myself, the acceptance I'd finally reached. And I might learn that Malik wasn't living with family, safe and happy.

Maybe wasn't living at all.

More immediately, trying to track down the identity of a spook, even a dead one, could bring down more wrath than letting the world know about Habbaniyah. Right now I worried about being court-martialed. Get tangled up with the CIA or DIA or DHS or whoever the hell this man worked for and I might end up dead. I had no illusions that the life of a single Marine would count for anything to people bent on protecting America at all costs.

On the other hand, Tucker's reputation, even his life, might lie in that black space between what I knew and what I thought I knew. If

I didn't close that gap, I'd have to live with myself while Tucker once again paid the price.

"Not much of a choice is it, Clyde?"

He looked at me with furrowed brow.

"We gotta go for it."

I'd stayed in touch with a few of Dougie's friends. One of them, Hal Beckett, worked for the Company. Hal had been a lot of comfort in the days after Dougie died. He'd shown up within hours of Dougie's death and sat with me outside Mortuary Affairs. He'd personally escorted Dougie's body back to the States. He'd also helped me get Clyde's status changed from unadoptable—which was a death sentence—to stateside adoption. On top of that, Hal had made sure Clyde had never gone into an official foster program but instead had come straight to me. Hal knew the right people, could pull the right strings.

All I had to do was figure out how to ask him questions without arousing his suspicion.

Or maybe go out on a limb and trust him. Dougie had. I dialed.

"Well, son of a bitch," came Hal's Boston voice. "Sydney Rose Parnell!"

Hearing him made the tears rise again, and for a moment I couldn't say anything.

"Rosie? You there, girl?"

"Yeah." I cleared my throat. "How's life, Hal?"

"Pretty quiet these days. Can't say I miss the war, but I miss the thrill. And you? You doing all right?"

We chatted for a few minutes, swapping inconsequential things. Finally I got to it.

"I'm trying to ID someone from a photo, Hal. I'm hoping you can help me."

"Someone from Iraq, I'm guessing."

"Yeah. Some guy who was with Dougie a week or so before—"

"Where are you going with this, Rosie?"

"I'm a railway cop now, investigating a murder. Could be it has something to do with things that happened in Iraq."

"You are shitting me, right?"

"I don't know. Probably. Maybe. The victim was the fiancée of a Marine who served in Habbaniyah. I've been told that before she was killed, she was asking around about what exactly her fiancé did over there. And this guy I'm asking you about, he's in a few photos, laughing it up with the Marine's sergeant."

"I don't see how there could be any connection. But text me the photo. I'll call you right back."

I hung up, snapped a picture of Dougie's photo, and sent it. Hal called me back a minute later.

"I can't tell you his name because that's classified. But I can tell you this guy's got nothing to do with your girl's death."

"How can you be—"

"Where did you say you got this picture?"

"I didn't say. But it came from the home of someone we're investigating. The man's got a whole shitload of photos up on his wall. Several of them featured this guy."

"This guy shouldn't be in *any* photos. Who the hell are you investigating?"

"I can't tell you that, Hal. He's not a suspect."

"Ah. Of course." Hal accepted my refusal so quickly that I knew he had his own way of finding out, if he chose to do so. "But he can't have had anything to do with your victim."

"Because he's dead?"

A long pause. "What makes you think he's dead?"

I opened my mouth. Closed it.

Because . . . if I hadn't seen his dead body at some point, he wouldn't be haunting me. That was how it worked. Our ghosts are our guilt.

"I don't," I finally said. "Just misconnecting my dots."

"What are you not telling me, Rosie?"

Um, I see dead people. "Nothing. Forget it, Hal. My bad."

Silence. Then, "I can swear to you this guy's got nothing to do with your victim. He isn't even in the country. He's about as far away from here as you can get—"

Understatement of the year.

"—and he can't possibly be involved in your murder case. Does that help?"

"Sure. Yeah." I looked out the window at the storm clouds trailing north. "Did he work with Dougie?"

"Oh, my young friend. Tell me you're not dreaming up connections that don't exist."

"No. I just—"

"How much time do you spend thinking about Dougie?" His voice was so gentle that the tears once again found a way out, slid down my cheeks. "You need to move on with your life. It's what Dougie would want."

"I did. I am."

"Then stop looking for things that take you back to the war, okay? You don't need to look to the other side of the world to find your killer."

"Right," I whispered.

We talked a little longer, Hal's voice soothing, reassuring. He promised to call me soon, just to see how I was doing. I told him that would be nice. I didn't add that by then I'd probably be locked away in a padded cell.

At least I would have the dead to talk to.

After we hung up, I started the engine and flipped on the heater, colder now than I had been. I found a stray cigarette in the console, started searching for matches.

Was I going crazy? Were Tucker and I just a pair of warriors without a battle to fight, trying to stir up some excitement by imagining the war had come home with us? By imagining the *dead* had come home with us? To each his own insanity. Maybe Tucker had killed Elise, and

when he couldn't face what he'd done, he'd created an entirely different scenario out of whole cloth. And I'd jumped right into the game
because anything was better than thinking Tucker's war-broken heart
had cost Elise her life.

A dark memory uncoiled—the fury I'd felt only yesterday. When
I'd aimed my gun at Tucker, wanting so badly to shoot him that I could
taste blood in my mouth.

I found an old lighter and lit up, cracking the window to free the
smoke.

"But I didn't," I said to Clyde. "We're still good."

Clyde huffed out a breath.

My headset buzzed. Cohen. I waited it out, not ready to find my
voice. A moment later the phone pinged with his text.

A text I could deal with. I opened it and stared at a photograph of
the sketch artist's rendition of Rhodes's assailant.

The drawing showed a white kid in his late twenties with a shaved
skull and deeply sunken, sullen eyes and a chip on his shoulder the size
of the moon. Looking into the man's face, I felt as if someone had just
pressed an ice cube to the base of my skull.

Other than the fact that the punk looked like a hundred other
hostile, pissed-off, twenty-something punks—and I'd seen a lot of
those in the Marines—this face was unfamiliar. But the facial tats were
something I'd seen before. Recently, in fact. It took me a moment to
remember exactly where, but when I had it, the hair lifted on the back
of my neck.

That kid I'd seen near my truck at Hogan's Alley, looking through
my windshield. Was it only yesterday morning? I'd caught just a
glimpse of his face in the shadow of his hoodie, but he'd been sporting
these same tats. Nothing so overt as a swastika, or I likely would have
thought of him when Cohen first mentioned Tucker's assault. But the
tattoos had been screaming Nazi all the same, if I'd taken time to think
about them.

On the forehead of both the punk's face and now the assailant's was the number 88, representative of the *H*, the eighth letter of the alphabet. For white power skinheads, eighty-eight stands for Heil Hitler.

On their respective chins, both men also sported the number 14, for the fourteen-word creed of skinheads everywhere: "We must secure the existence of our people and a future for white children."

Finally, on the right cheek of the man in the sketch were three interlocking triangles, the symbol of the Nordic afterlife. Called a Valknot, it means a willingness to die for the cause. I couldn't be sure if the kid I'd seen had the Valknot. But it seemed likely.

I put out my cigarette and dialed Cohen.

"Classic skinhead tats," I said when he answered.

"Yeah. The question is, do they belong to the face of a real person?"

"I saw a kid yesterday morning at the homeless camp. He was nosing around my work vehicle. He had tats just like these."

I could almost hear him sit up straighter.

"He look like this guy?"

"No," I said. "Too young. But it could mean something larger is at play here."

"Like what? Skinheads knock the homeless around. But are they rail riders?"

"White punks are. So are college kids, for what it's worth. Hopping freights never goes out of style. And there are some who claim that FTRA has neo-Nazi elements."

"Fat-ra who?"

"Freight Train Riders of America. A gang linked to a lot of railroad vandalism and thefts and more than a few deaths. But their connection to a neo-Nazi movement is pretty tenuous. My guess is that a few of these skinheads have decided to break into new turf. They do that now and again. Killing innocents like Elise could be an initiation."

Even as I said it, I felt that same stir of memory that had tickled my mind back at police headquarters. Hadn't something like this happened ten or twelve years ago? I chased the memory down like tracking a shooting star. A young girl had disappeared and never been found. She'd delivered lunch or dinner or something to her brother who worked in the rail yard. Then, according to the Royer rumor mill, as soon as she was out of her brother's sight, she'd been dragged away from the yard by a group of skinheads. After that, she'd vanished. The talk among us kids was that she'd been a gang sacrifice. There'd been some worried speculation among the grown-ups, and a lot of my friends were told by their parents to steer clear of the yard and the rails and the camps. The little girl's brother worked for DPC, but in all other ways the family—black and not locals—had been outsiders. When months went by and nothing emerged from the investigation, the girl was dismissed as a runaway. Never mind that little black girls don't usually run away with white supremacists.

Cohen was talking. "Hardly a fair battle if these skinheads are going after hobos. And why pick on white folks like Rhodes and Elise?"

"Oh, any number of reasons," I murmured, my brain still racing.

"What kind of reasons?" Cohen asked.

"Detective, do me a favor. See if you can pull up a missing persons report from the fall of 2000 or 2001. Little girl named Jazmine. With a 'z' I think. Don't know the last name."

"You wanna tell me how this relates?"

"Jazmine was a little girl who disappeared from the rail yard. Rumor was she'd been taken away by a group of skinheads. It was all the talk for a while, but nothing ever came of it, as far as I know."

"And this connects to Elise Hensley's death how?"

"I don't know. I'm looking for patterns."

"They've killed people associated with the rails before, they might do it again? That's pretty thin, Parnell. It's not like Elise was a hobo."

"Didn't you say it sounded like a kid who called in Elise's death? Maybe one of the punks got a case of the guilts."

"Hmm," Cohen said, unconvinced.

"Elise spent so much time working with these guys, it could be she learned something about that little girl's disappearance. She told Tucker she was working something."

"You're sharing that a day late and a dollar short," Cohen said with real heat.

Time once again for the lying two-step tango. "It's not like that. Tucker figured she meant one of her charitable projects. But maybe he got it wrong."

"And she got killed to keep her quiet about this little girl? Meaning the original kidnappers are still around."

Just like the trouble Sherri Kane had implied. Her accusation that Elise was digging up dirt on people.

"Could be you're onto something, Parnell," Cohen said. "Any word on the German who gave Tucker his tattoo?"

"I've got a name and a call in to him."

"Oh," he said. "Good!"

"Don't sound so surprised."

"Not at all."

"Anything else?"

"Yeah. I need to get the sketch out among the hobos. Any idea where these guys scatter when one of their camps gets closed?"

"Hogan's Alley is still a crime scene?"

"The detectives have been working it around the clock, and they've probably pulled as much as we'll get out of there. But we're not ready to open it up yet."

"Some of the guys will hit the shelters. A few will go down to Taylor Creek. Most won't move far, though. They'll find spots in Darby Bay, up near 31st Street."

"Go with me?"

"I was figuring on doing it myself."

"I'm not feeling the love, railroad cop."

"Oh, for—" I stopped myself. "Fine. But if you want anyone to talk, then you've got to help these guys. Grease the skids. Bring some bribes with you."

"You mean like booze?"

"Your stereotypes are showing, Detective," I said. "I mean like winter clothes. Coats. Hats. Gloves. Try spending your life outdoors when the wind chill is below zero."

"Give me an hour. I'll bring the sketches and the clothes and meet you wherever you say."

"Corner of 20th Street and Market. We can meet up in the parking lot of the coffee shop on the southwest corner and make the rounds in my truck."

"Now I'm starting to feel the love."

"Just bring decent stuff, Cohen. These guys deserve it."

"Single malt?"

"Stop it."

But the weight on my chest had backed off a little, and I could breathe again. Elise's death was no easier if she'd been killed by skinheads instead of the Alpha. But it could mean everything for Tucker.

And for me.

I used the bathroom at the Happy Java, washed up, and ordered two turkey sandwiches, a Coke, and a large water. The girls behind the counter made a fuss over Clyde, and he preened.

"Don't get a big head," I told him as we walked back to the truck. "They just think all that hair means you're virile."

I lowered the tailgate and we sat together in the light wind, eating our sandwiches. The storm had circled around and wafted off to the east, and it was cold and sunny. The air smelled of diesel and chimney smoke and the ripe leavings of food from the bin behind the coffee shop. A crow fussed at us from atop a wooden fence. With my belly full, I was close to nodding off when my headset buzzed.

"This is Roald Hoffreider," a man said when I answered. "I got your message saying you needed to talk. Something I can do for you?"

"Thanks for calling me back, Mr. Hoffreider. And please, call me Sydney."

"Roald will do on this end."

"Roald. Do you remember running into a young vet a couple of days ago, name of Tucker Rhodes?"

"The Burned Man? Sure, I remember him. Seemed like a nice enough kid. Been through hell, that's for sure."

"You mean his injuries."

"'Course I mean his injuries. But the kid got jumped, too, day before I met him. Sporting some real bruises. Then he got robbed that night. You gotta ask yourself what the world is coming to when some snot-nosed punk thinks he can go after our wounded warriors."

"So you saw who jumped him?"

"Didn't see the guy in the act."

"But you have some ideas."

A brief silence. The crow stopped its fussing and cocked its head, eyes bright.

"I have an idea," Roald said. "The Burned Man told me it was a skinhead. There's been a big group of those punks making trouble on the line. Five or six main guys, but probably thirty others. Maybe more."

"That's why you gave Rhodes a tattoo?"

"Sure. Tat like that means he killed someone. Makes someone think twice before giving him hell."

"It also says he's a racist and a jailbird."

"Long as it keeps those punks off him, I ain't too worried about the message it sends anyone else."

"What did Rhodes say was stolen?"

"Beads. Hobo beads, they call them. Said the wife of one of his best friends made them for him. He was pretty damn mad."

"I'm going to text you a sketch of the man we think assaulted Rhodes. I'd like you to see if you recognize the guy."

"Sure."

"I'm going to hang up and send it. Call me back as soon as you've had a look."

I forwarded Cohen's original message to Hoffreider. While I waited, I cleaned up the sandwich wrappers and poured more water into Clyde's dish. A minute later, Hoffreider called back.

"Yeah, I've seen him," he said. "He's the leader, I'm pretty sure. A little older than the rest and ten times as mean. Goes by the name Whip."

"You know his real name?"

"No. Sorry."

"What about where he hangs out?"

"Aside from the camps, you mean?"

"Yes."

"Saw him at a biker bar in one of those little towns east of Denver. Don't remember the town, but the bar was called The Pint and Pecker. He was there with four or five other skinheads."

"Bikers and neo-Nazis? Odd mix."

"Not like it used to be. Word I've been hearing is that some of the skinheads are signing up with the hard-core motorcycle gangs. Hammerskins becoming Hell's Angels."

I didn't like the *Mad Max* visual that gave me. "Would you be willing to ask around your crew? Show them the picture and see if anyone can put a name on him?"

"You mind telling me why all this interest?"

"It's part of an investigation."

"Look, I know you're a cop and all. But do you have any idea what you're getting into?"

"What do you mean?"

"What I mean is, these guys are serious trouble. And there's a shit-load of them out there. The Aryan Nation, or whatever they call them-selves, they're on the move again. Last time was, I don't know, eight, ten years ago."

I got that feeling in my stomach, that warning flag I'd perfected in Iraq, that said I was about to roll into trouble. "What does it mean when these guys are on the move?"

"It means they're going to knock a few heads together. Or worse. The Burned Man got off light. His face makes him look like a victim, but at least he's white and clean-cut. Someone else might not be so lucky."

"You're talking murder."

"Might be. I've seen it before."

"Ten years ago."

"Or thereabouts. A group of these assholes were terrorizing the homeless. A black tramp in South Dakota ended up dead. And a little girl went missing from Denver. Final word was she was a runaway. But her brother never believed that, and neither did I. After the police started looking for her, the punks scattered. It's been a nice ten years."

"Jazmine."

"Jazmine Brown. That's right. You know about her?"

"Heard the story. Why don't you think she was a runaway?"

"I worked with her brother on the line. She was a good kid from a good family. You ask me, those punks took her and tossed her body somewhere no one would find it."

"You have any proof of that?"

"If I did, I'd've gone to the police when it all went down. All I got is my gut."

So we were back to that. Bandoni's gut. Mine. Now Hoffreider's. We needed less intuition and more facts.

"Do you know where I can reach Jazmine's brother?"

"It would take a Ouija board. Daryl died a year after his sister disappeared. Caught by a loose string in the yard."

The silent approach of uncoupled, rolling cars has killed more than a few employees and trespassers. The "midnight creeps" some call them. "What about other family?"

"Don't know. They scattered. She had another brother. A year or two older, I think. But I don't know what happened to him. Mom went back to family. Dad wasn't ever in the picture, far as I know."

"And the skinheads from back then? You ever see any of them?"

"Never knew who they were. Heard about 'em more than I saw them."

I looked up as Cohen pulled into the parking lot. He parked his car next to mine and got out. He tipped his hand to pantomime drinking something, then disappeared into the coffee shop.

"Can you ask around, Roald? With the sketch?"

"I will. Now, look, hon, I know it is not my place to tell you this. But you sound like a nice lady. Watch yourself around these guys. They play for keeps."

"This guy jumped an injured war vet and beat the crap out of him. I'm not going to pretend that didn't happen."

"Yeah, that pissed me off, too. But you get them riled up, the rest of us are still out there on the lines. We have to deal with the fallout. We get jumped in the middle of nowhere, you won't be able to do a thing to help us. And the tramps are sitting ducks."

"What if we just arrest them all?"

Hoffreider laughed. "They're mushrooms, Sydney. No matter how many you pick, there's always more come the next rain."

"Thanks for the warning."

"Poisoned mushrooms," he said as a final point and hung up.

CHAPTER 16

*You lie awake at one a.m., surrounded by people who
want you dead.*

*As you stare unblinking into the dark and finally give up
and go outside to have a smoke, they are half a klick away,
thinking how they will find a way to shoot you or blow you
up or cut off your head.*

*As dawn fans into the sky and you stumble in flip-flops
and sweats to the showers, they're thinking what they'll do with
your body. Burn it. String it up. Videotape it so your mother
back in Iowa doesn't miss a single moment.*

And you thought you were the hunter.

—Sydney Parnell, ANTH 2055, Cultural Studies

Cohen came out of the Happy Java with two steaming cups of coffee,
one of which he handed to me. We transferred the clothes he'd brought
for the homeless from his car to mine. Then he leaned against his car,
crossed his long legs, and hooked the thumb of his free hand into his
belt. He stared at the afternoon traffic streaming by.

"What are you thinking?" I asked.

"I'm thinking"—he turned his eyes to me—"that you don't look
half bad when you smile."

His comment surprised a laugh out of me. Before I could stop myself, I said, "Ditto."

"Yeah?"

No doubt I blushed. "Yeah."

He drank some coffee, looked around like he was taking in the day. "I'm sensing closure."

"How's that?"

"Cop's instinct."

I stood across from him and leaned against my own car while I watched Clyde explore the dirt field behind the coffee shop. "You and Bandoni."

"My gut isn't the sixth-sense machine Bandoni has," he said. "But a friend in patrol told me three guys have been terrorizing the homeless on the south end of town, near the tracks. Flashing steel and threatening to cut them. The description they got is white guys with shaved heads, steel-toed boots, and tats. Means these guys are around and up to no good."

"Still thinking Tucker Rhodes is a shoo-in?"

"I never liked that crime scene. Too . . ."

"Convenient?"

"Yeah. Maybe. I don't know. We still got a lot of evidence on him."

Clyde had his nose low to the ground. A scent-fest. I returned my gaze to the detective. The wind tugged his short hair sideways, worried his tie. Some of the tiredness had eased from his eyes.

"Is it just a job to you, Cohen?"

An eyebrow went up. "Are you asking me if the reason I'm feeling good is the prospect of taking a case off the board?"

"That's what I'm asking."

"Then let me answer by asking you something. Did you enlist because you needed a job? Or because you wanted to go to Iraq and fight bad guys?"

I debated not answering. This got too close to the things Nik had warned me never to talk about. But I sensed in Cohen a darkness that matched my own. "After what they did, I wanted to do a little whup-ass, same as a lot of people."

"It gave your life meaning."

"For a time."

"Then you'll understand when I say that with murder cops it's never just a job. I could give you some line about how we provide justice for the defenseless and restore balance in our society. And that's all true. It's why society pays us to do this job. But . . ." He swirled the coffee in his cup, staring down into the depths. "I'm not that noble. I do this job for my own sake. Because it gives *my* life meaning."

"God in his heaven."

He lifted his head. "Exactly."

"So I guess we're both just a couple of self-important assholes."

He laughed. "Could be." He tossed the dregs of his coffee into the dirt. "I like your Marine, Parnell. The guy's been shaved down to his essence by what happened to him in Iraq. Or maybe he was one of those old souls even before the IED. Either way, I'm struggling with the idea that, at his core, he's violent."

"He used to hunt. Before the war. Couldn't do it after. Couldn't hurt anything after the war."

"So war makes old souls."

"Or maybe just lost ones."

We stared at each other. I didn't know what Cohen was thinking about, but I was thinking about ghosts.

"He's still our best suspect," Cohen said after a moment.

I glanced at the sky, gauging the time. Or maybe checking the heavens. "Then let's go find a better one."

I took the wheel. While I drove, I filled Cohen in on what I'd learned from Roald Hoffreider.

"He's a line worker for DPC," I told him. "Those guys are the ones who know the tramps. He and Rhodes got to talking, and Rhodes told him his beads had been stolen. Hoffreider also verified Rhodes's story about being jumped." As had Jeremy Kane and his wife, Sherri. But I couldn't tell Cohen about that without revealing I'd talked to them.

Cohen wrote in his notebook. "He see it happen?"

"No. But he ID'd the guy in your sketch as the leader of a gang of skinheads. Rail name Whip, given name unknown. He says these guys are roughing up the tramps and even scaring Hoffreider and his crew. Rhodes was sporting some bruises when Hoffreider saw him. Could be part of that same group you heard about. Last time there was this much skinhead activity was ten years ago when—"

"When Jazmine Brown disappeared, last seen walking near the rail yard with a gang of neo-Nazis."

"Exactly."

"A friend in the Missing and Exploited Persons Unit pulled the case book," Cohen went on. "One Jazmine Anise Brown, age nine and a half, last known location the Colorado Front Range Trail, a half block south of Denver's DPC yard. She delivered lunch to her brother, Daryl Brown, then never returned home."

"Who worked the case?"

"Woman named Simpson in Missing Persons," Cohen said. "After one railroad employee and a couple of hobos placed Jazmine with the skinheads, her file was passed to Homicide. I haven't had time to do more than read the summary and skim some of the statements, but it looks like nothing linked her to the Nazis other than the eyewitness account by two men getting sloshed next to the South Platte River."

"And the railroad employee."

"Not much of a witness. He just got a glimpse. Wasn't even a hundred percent sure he saw the girl before the skinheads closed ranks.

He did pick three guys out of a mug book, but not with the kind of certainty that would stand up in court. And the punks' alibis checked out. They were home for dinner within an hour of the time they were seen with Jazmine. Then the two tramps recanted their stories."

"They were threatened."

"Or they sobered up. And there went all of our witnesses. A five-mile radius search turned up nothing. When detectives on the case learned there had been trouble at home, Jazmine was deemed a likely runaway. She'd threatened that before."

"She was nine," I protested.

He rested his arm along the top of the door panel. "A very mature nine, according to the detective's summary. Girl had been in some trouble already. The detective ruled her case INC and sent it back to Missing Persons. That was April of 2000. Jazmine Brown bounced around for a little while like a ping-pong ball that fell off the table. Nothing since."

INC, meaning Inactive, Not Cleared. Departmental PR people used the term "cold case," as if to imply detectives were still finding time to work them. But in truth, nothing happened on inactives unless a surprise witness stepped forward or evidence appeared from out of the blue.

"She was forgotten," I said.

"Cops don't forget." He drummed his fingers. "But we're realists."

I pondered the sadness of the world swallowing a nine-year-old girl whole, leaving behind nothing more than a vinyl binder that even the cold case detectives didn't have time for.

For the next two hours we made the rounds of the homeless shelters used by the hobos and showed everyone we could find the sketch of Whip. The response was universal. Everyone recognized the guy. And no one was willing to talk. Cohen made a quick call to his friend in patrol and got the same report from down south.

"There's nothing between them and the big bad world," I said when Cohen filled me in. "Of course they're afraid to say anything."

We stopped at Caring Hands, the shelter where I'd sent Melody Weber. When I'd fixed the cut on her face the previous morning, she'd seemed about to tell me why everyone in the camp was spooked. An opportunity interrupted by Cohen's phone call and the news of Elise's death.

But at the shelter, my friend told us Melody had checked out that morning, taking Liz with her.

"Said she was going home," Trish told me. "Took the little girl and hurried out of here in such a god-awful rush she left her daughter's backpack. I'm hoping they come back for it."

"You have an address?"

"You have a court order? C'mon, Sydney, you know the rules."

"Right. We'll go another way. Thanks for looking after them, Trish."

Trish puffed a strand of graying hair out of her eyes. "I didn't feel good about letting that little girl go. Seen a lot of sadness, that one."

Back in the truck, Cohen called Bandoni to track down Melody's address. I started the engine, wondering what made a woman like Melody go home so her asshole of a boyfriend could beat her some more. And so her daughter could watch. Was Melody afraid of him? Did she imagine she loved him? Or did she simply have nowhere else to go?

It's the ones who love us, hurt us the most, she'd said.

It was dinnertime, the sun a dull glow just above the mountains, when I pulled off the street and parked on a patch of dirt at Darby Bay, a scratch of land further north along the South Platte River. There, I expected to find most of the Hogan's Alley crew. I wasn't disappointed. Darby Bay was packed with people huddled in blankets, sharing bottles or food or sitting by themselves. Some of them talked to people only they could see; maybe I wasn't the only one with ghosts. Flames flickered in metal trashcans while the wind scratched through the skeletal cottonwoods. With afternoon pressing hard into evening, the light long and gray save for the sullen red eye of the sun, Darby Bay looked like a post-apocalyptic refugee encampment.

I got out into the wind and opened the back door for Clyde. I put him on his lead.

"You carry the clothes," I said to Cohen.

He snapped a two-finger salute. "Ma'am."

We made the rounds, Clyde serving as ambassador and Cohen dispensing coats and hats while I showed the sketch. Being around a dog drew people out, but a lot of them were beyond talking much, already sunk into a haze of drugs and alcohol. Those sharp enough to answer our questions were clearly reluctant. Just like at the homeless shelters, the most we got out of them were eyes widening in recognition and an agreement that the guy had been around here and there. Nothing concrete.

Trash Can was the most forthcoming.

"Saw him once, up near a camp in Powder River," Trash Can said. "Spooky dude. I was with Wicked Pete. We saw that dude in your picture there drinking with his buddies. They was sharpening knives like a group of whacked-out Boy Scouts. Pete and me, we got out fast."

I flashed to Elise's flayed skin. "How many of them were there?"

"That dude and, let's see, maybe five other assholes? Could've been six or seven. I didn't stay to do no count."

"You ever see them with the Burned Man?"

"Him? Nah. He keeps to himself."

"You catch any names?"

"We wasn't exactly introducing ourselves."

And that was that. Trash Can couldn't or wouldn't offer anything more. He took a scarf and a pair of gloves and we left him to his dinner of canned beans and Pink Lady.

As we worked our way down the line, I kept an eye out for Melody in case she'd chosen to come back here rather than face her boyfriend. Nothing. No sign of Calamity Jane, either, who might have more cause than anyone to worry about what the skinheads were up to.

Cohen and I looked at each other, mutually discouraged. Even Clyde had dropped his tail.

"Let's give it twenty more minutes," I said. "By then anyone who's coming in should have landed. We can call it a night after that."

We'd reached the southernmost end of the camp and were heading back north toward the truck when we found Calamity Jane. She'd come in after our initial walk-through and set up camp near the river. We found her sitting in a faded folding chair with her back to the water, swathed in an army blanket and smoking a cigarette. A small fire spit and hissed in a ring of stones.

"Hey, Jane," I said.

She lifted her head and warily watched us approach. Her eyes held a dull unease, as if she was too tired to be fully afraid.

I gave Clyde the command to lie down. He rested his head on his front legs and kept his eyes on Calamity Jane.

"Rough day?" I asked her.

She shrugged, let her gaze flick over Cohen. "He an asshole like the last cop?"

"This guy's all right," I said and introduced him.

"Murder cop?" Jane pushed herself forward and hawked into the fire. "What traffic I got with a murder cop?"

I squatted next to her chair and proffered the best coat from Cohen's stash. "He brought you this."

Her eyes fell to the coat, a beautiful gray parka with fake fur around the hood and a thick fleece lining. She stuck her cigarette in her mouth and stroked the fur with her thin hands.

Then she pulled her hands back. "I don't need the trouble that bring." She looked up at Cohen, narrowed her eyes with challenge. "You here 'cause the kindhearted lady?"

"What makes you say that?"

"We all done heard. Someone put a knife to her."

Cohen nodded. "I'd like to ask some questions about her. Mind if I sit down?"

"Sure, honey. You feeling the love seat or the comfy chair?" Jane laughed then coughed.

Cohen laughed too, a soft, rueful sound, and squatted on the ground near the fire, balancing on the balls of his feet with his hands dangling comfortably between his thighs. "I'll take the comfy chair."

They shared a laugh this time.

"So, Miss Jane," Cohen said. "What have you heard about the kind-hearted lady?"

"Someone cut her all to pieces."

"How does that make you feel?"

The detective as therapist.

"How you think that be making me feel?" Jane spat. "She one of God's people. Life all the harder, her gone."

"She took care of people."

"She tried. We didn't none of us make it easy for her."

I watched and listened as Cohen picked his way through Jane's fear and fury, getting to the place where he was ready to show her the sketch. I watched Jane, too, wondering about her way-back-when story and wondering what had happened since yesterday to drive her further into herself. She had fine features and a husky voice and a way of holding her cigarette, one hand cupping her elbow, that was both elegant and protective. In another life, on another stage, she could have been another Lauren Bacall.

"Elise come here much?" Cohen asked.

"Once a week or so. Like Special Agent Parnell. Brought us them food vouchers. Read the Bible."

"Anyone ever not happy to see her?"

Jane thrust a hand out from the blanket and used a stick to push the dying embers into a heap. "Not so's I heard. Anyway, why don't you be asking that PI about her? He know a lot more than me, them working together and all."

Cohen glanced my way, one eyebrow raised, then returned his attention to Jane. "A private investigator was working with Elise Hensley?"

"Didn't know till today he a PI. Seen him and the kindhearted lady talking to people the last few days. He come talking to me an hour ago." She pointed with her chin across the street to the Globeville Landing Park, where the homeless often spent the day. "Over there. That's when he told me he a PI."

"This PI give you his name?" Cohen asked.

"He done give me this."

She reached inside her coat, pulled out a business card and handed it to Cohen. He looked at it then passed it to me.

Thomas A. Brown. Brown Investigations.

Brown was a common last name. But still.

The only other item on the card was an email address. No street address. No phone number. Hard way to run a business. But maybe he didn't want anyone tracking him down.

"Black man?" Cohen asked, clearly thinking as I was.

Jane nodded. "Said I was on their talk-to list. But with Elise gone, it just him."

"What did he want to talk to you about?" Cohen asked.

"Some little girl died years ago. He all eaten up about it. Said he and Elise looking for people was around back then, people who might know something. He said time running out. But I couldn't help him." She studied the cigarette smoldering between her fingers. "Back then, I be in Louisiana with my little boy. Had a home with yellow curtains. And a garden."

I must have made some sound. She blinked up at me. "It's *hard* losing all that."

"I know." I was thinking of Malik. "Jane, why do you think he said time was running out?"

Her eyes came back to the present. She sucked hard on the cigarette. Coughed. "He sick, that boy. I seen that kind of sick, and it mean either God or the Devil be waiting close. He said he didn't have much time to find the men took that little girl. Made me sad for him. I told him how I'd heard the story, how it was skinheads done for her. And now them skinheads is back."

"You've seen them?" Cohen asked.

Jane blinked as if remembering where she was. She looked away. "Nah. Just heard."

Cohen and I exchanged glances. Cohen pulled out the sketch. "This one of them?"

"I told you. Haven't seen 'em."

"Maybe you could just take a look."

Her eyes narrowed. "Y'all should go now."

"You want to help find the men who killed that little girl, don't you, Jane?" I asked gently. "The man who killed Elise?"

"You think he killed the kindhearted lady?"

"We're looking into it."

With a snarl, Jane took the piece of paper from him and held it up to the dying light. After a moment, she balled up the sketch and threw it in the fire. Her hands were shaking.

"Jane?" I placed my hand on her wrist. "Who is he, Jane?"

She looked at me with a trapped wildness and shook off my hand.

"That ain't right. This ain't him. This man an asshole, but he and Elise had an understanding. They went way back, those two. Her trying to bring him God and him listening. She said I ought not to judge. Said that maybe his daddy beat him or his mama didn't want him and it turned him mean. Steer clear, she told me. But I ought not to hate him."

"Could be he and Elise didn't have the understanding she thought they did," Cohen said.

I stood. "I know you're afraid. But we can't help if we can't find him."

"Don't talk to *me* about being afraid." Jane clenched her fists. "You got *no* idea about what it means to be afraid, Mister and Missus Cop."

At the sudden rage in her voice, Clyde came to his feet.

Jane was shaking. "Them white fuck-ups with their tattoos and their shaved heads, they been coming around. Beating people, scaring the shit outta people. And what is it I ask myself? I ask where you be when they're here. You come 'round, asking our help. But where you be when *we* need *you*?"

"We'll find these guys," Cohen said. "And they'll be in prison a long time. They won't be able to hurt you."

"You gonna be arresting them tonight? Huh? Are you? Next thing, you be telling me to believe in the tooth fairy. You think I want to end up like her? Like the kindhearted lady? You turn your white asses 'round and get out of my camp. Talking to the po-lice ain't good for my health."

"Jane," I pressed. "This man might have killed a little girl. He might have killed Elise. You want him to walk?"

She snarled at me, her glare like a lash. It was all I could do not to take a step back.

Clyde growled, and I lifted a hand to silence him.

But Jane's next words surprised me.

"Ah, fuck. You always good to us," she said. "You another kind-hearted lady. For all I know, he go after you next. So—" She pushed herself upright. "What the fuck? The guy in your picture there, he ain't that good-looking in real life. But, yeah, I know him."

"You have a name for him?"

"He just go by Whip."

Cohen and I exchanged frustrated looks.

"You know anything else about him?" I asked. "Where's he from, maybe. Or when he might be back?"

"Didn't nobody share his travel plans with me."

"Okay. Thanks, Jane," I said. "You've been a big help."

Cohen handed her his business card. "You think of anything else or if he shows up again, let me know. Call anytime. And call me if Mr. Brown comes back, okay? I'd like to talk to him."

"Well, sure. They show up, I give you a jingle on my *eye-phone*."

"The Quik-Mart still has a pay phone half a block away," I said, giving her some quarters. I gave her a ten-dollar bill as well, which she slipped into her jacket. "There's phones at the shelters, too."

"Ain't going to no shelter."

"Yeah. I know. Thanks for your help, Jane."

I signaled to Clyde, and Cohen and Clyde and I moved away from the fire in the direction of my truck.

"Goddammit," Jane said. "Hold up."

We turned back.

"Whip don't tell me where he go," she said. "But I know where he from."

"Where's that?" Cohen asked.

"West. Past that big stadium where they be playing football."

"Where the Broncos play?"

She nodded.

"How do you know he's from there?" Cohen asked.

"'Cause that where Melody lives."

Cohen and I looked at each other.

"Whip," Jane went on, "he Melody's boo."

We must have looked blank, because she rolled her eyes. "Hook-up. BF. Her *boyfriend.*"

"Whip and Melody?" I thought of the bruises and the cut I'd seen on Melody the morning before. How uneasy she'd seemed. "Melody Weber?"

"The fat girl. The one got her own little girl. You done gave her a coat, too. She and Whip got a thing going." Jane shook her head. "Ain't a good thing. But it's a thing. Melody said how Elise was gonna help her leave Whip. Maybe he found out what they was planning."

"I'll see how Bandoni's doing on her address," Cohen said to me, reaching for his phone.

"You might better put some heat on finding her house," Jane said. "'Cause that PI said he knew 'xactly where she lived. Said he find her, he find that Nazi. Said he gonna do what needed doing. He didn't care what it cost him. He a dead man already."

CHAPTER 17

The American military has an acronym for everything from battle plans to report writing to taking a shit. Alphabet soup, we call it. But the acronym I keep going back to is the one that says it all: SNAFU.

Situation normal, all fucked up.

That's what we've got here in Habbaniyah. A total snafu. And I can't tell you the half of it.

—September 13, 2004. Letter to Gentry Lasko.

Cohen stalked the shoulder of the road as we waited to hear back from Bandoni. He prowled thirty yards down, about-faced, then stalked back, overcoat flapping, hands tapping at his sides, his face gathering darkness like a swelling storm.

A uniform helped Calamity Jane into the backseat of his squad car before he gave me a nod and got behind the wheel. He backed the car around, headlights sweeping the hobo camp. Jane's reproachful eyes met mine through the glass. But she couldn't stay in camp. Not after what she'd shared. She turned in her seat to watch me until the twilight swallowed her and her eyes and the blue Crown Victoria.

Promise me you come get me soon's I can come back, she'd said. *Stayin' in the shelter make me feel caged, like an animal.*

I promise, I'd said. *See the doc at the shelter, get some rest, and we'll talk.*

Cohen's phone rang, and he listened, said something at staccato speed, then listened again. He nodded at me—an assurance, I assumed, that we were getting the information we needed.

I sucked in air thick with the smells of smoke and diesel and damp, savoring February's icy burn. I stamped my half-frozen feet and rubbed my palms together, then bounced on my toes, surprised with how strong I felt. We might be within minutes of closing in on our killer. Soon—maybe in a matter of hours—I would be able to go to Tucker and tell him that he wouldn't be remembered as the beast who slew Beauty. And then to Nik to assure him that not only had we caught Elise's killer, we'd also cleared the man she'd loved. She'd still had Tucker in her heart when her heart beat its last.

Maybe finding Whip also meant that my fear of an Alpha was nothing more than paranoia. Maybe Habbaniyah would be allowed to bleach into the desert until the sand polished it to nothing.

Maybe some of the ghosts would go quiet.

Clyde pressed against my legs and together we watched the last blush of scarlet disappear from the sky. Night came on hard and sharp, bringing a kick of wind. Down in the hobo camp, someone laughed and other voices took up the boozy cheer. A semitruck roared by, heading north, brushing us with its wake. Then the five o'clock freight rattled past, its rumble swallowing every other sound before falling away.

Whip. Given name still unknown, but at this point I didn't care. I had enough names to walk him to the gates of hell. White power skinhead. Neo-Nazi punk. Gangbanger. Bonehead. Asshole. A racist little fuck filled with hatred and cunning and threats. He might have fooled Elise and even Calamity Jane. But not me.

If he was our killer, he would pay for what he did. To Elise. Maybe to Jazmine.

I don't give a fuck about justice, a Marine had told me after the FOB was bombed. *Don't give a fuck about hearts and minds. What I care about is running down every one of those ragheads and blowing their brains out.*

Not politically correct. Not my way of dealing with the world. But I kind of got it.

Picking up my mood, Clyde danced on his paws, looking in my hands for his Kong. The game was almost afoot, and he knew it. I gave him a predatory grin.

"Soon, boy."

Cohen came striding back. "We found her."

I put Clyde in his carrier and drove while Cohen gave directions. The address from Bandoni placed Melody and Liz Weber in a broken-down neighborhood in Jefferson Park, west of I-25 and the football stadium. I remembered it as a place where front yards devoured the wrecks of cars while sun-faded statues of Saint Mary guarded door stoops, the pale virgins nailed down or chained up against marauders.

Cohen's phone rang. Bandoni's voice boomed through the speaker.

"We got a possible ID on this douche bag from a priest who works with the homeless. Says he's seen the guy around with a woman and a little girl. Goes by Alfred Merkel."

The name rose with a dark and sudden push. "I know that name," I said.

"How?" Cohen asked.

"Let me think."

My fingers tapped the steering wheel as I chased Alfred Merkel along murky childhood tunnels to a summer when a gang of older teens took to congregating in the alley behind Joe's Tavern or sometimes hanging out on the picnic tables in the half-acre patch of grass known by locals as Royer's Hole. The boy-men wore military camouflage and

Doc Martens and went out on Friday and Saturday nights in their unmuffled Fords, cruising for trouble. They were known as the Royer Boys, although not all of them were from the neighborhood. They weren't all bad, I remember Nik telling me. They escorted Royer girls to and from parties or sleepovers, playing chaperone, talking about how white girls weren't safe anymore. And they took it upon themselves to be a sort of neighborhood watch, coming down like God's fist on underage drinkers and smokers or the perpetrators of any sort of crime, petty or otherwise. People might not have agreed with their politics—a few of them sported swastikas. But as long as you were white and law-abiding, it was hard to argue that they were bad for the neighborhood.

Bandoni's voice cut through. "I ran Merkel. No wants or warrants. All I got were some hits on contact cards. Trespassing on railroad property, mainly. A detective grilled him on a missing persons case a decade ago. Nothing came of it. Squeaky clean outside of that. Maybe our boy's too smart to get himself noticed. How do you want to play this?"

"We'll do a knock and talk." Cohen's eyes met mine when I glanced over, and I nodded my agreement. "See what he has to say, try to get a look inside. Could be a woman and child in there. And we may have Thomas Brown in the mix, if Parnell's homeless lady was right. Let's put a squad car on the street and have a uniform with us at the door. Anything spooks us, we walk away and call SWAT."

"Got it," Bandoni said.

Cohen touched my shoulder, indicated I should take a left turn.

"Anything pop up on the PI?" he asked Bandoni.

"One Thomas Aaron Brown, age twenty-two. Took out a private investigator's license three months ago. Kid files his taxes, drives the speed limit, and donates to SPCA. He purchased a handgun two months ago and got a conceal carry permit. That's all we got. No answer on his phone. Where are you? I'm five minutes out."

"Give us another five after that," Cohen said and hung up.

I told him what little I remembered about the Royer Boys. Their shaved heads and vigilante brand of law enforcement, and the fact that all of them had been cleared for Jazmine's disappearance.

"What happened to the group after that?"

"Never heard anything more about them until now."

The radio squawked. "I'm Code Six," Bandoni said. Cohen acknowledged.

"These assholes are a virus," Cohen said to me. "Just waiting for the ideal conditions to come back and destroy the organism."

Like Roald's poisoned mushrooms.

By the time we turned onto Melody Weber's street the clouds had lowered, reflecting back the glow from downtown and casting an oppressive illumination. Except for the lights at Melody's house and a handful of scattered porch bulbs shining further down the road, the neighborhood looked deserted.

I drove around the block at a crawl looking to see who was home, checking for dog-walkers and porch-sitters. People you didn't want caught in anything that might go down. But the entire area was dead. I pulled around front again, spotted a patrol car half a block down. Cohen pointed out Bandoni's Honda where it was parked in a deep pool of shadow across the street from Melody's. I pulled in behind the Honda so that my truck, with *DPC Railway Police* sprawled on the side, was hidden in the same inky darkness. Bandoni was nowhere to be seen.

"Reconnaissance," Cohen explained when I asked.

I studied Melody's house. Set far back on a corner lot and lit—in violation of city ordinance—with what looked like a two-hundred-watt porch light, the house squatted morosely amid the dirtied, hollowed drifts of the last snowstorm. A yellow two-level with a single-car garage, the house was a dreary dump of torn screens, packed-dirt yard, and flaking paint. The asphalt was so fissured that a knee-high forest of weeds had sprouted the length of the walkway. Weather-beaten trashcans looked like they'd been sitting at the curb since Christmas. I counted three cars in the driveway and four more in the street, all scabrous with road injuries and bad paint. Most of them looked to be halfway through some sort of repair work. Cohen called dispatch with the license plate numbers.

A solitary toy sat in the front yard—a purple plastic trike designed for a child much younger than Liz. A dog's rawhide chew toy dangled across the seat. From the house, the faint thump of bass music pulsed through the cold air.

To the north and east—the sides with neighbors—the lot and house were shielded by a thick screen of pine trees. The house directly across the street appeared abandoned—a foreclosure sign had been thrust into the dirt next to the cracked driveway. Maybe that was why no one had complained about the high-wattage porch light.

Suck of a place to raise a kid.

A single soft light shone upstairs at Melody's house, but the main level was well lit. Drawn curtains made it impossible to see what was happening inside.

I shut off the engine. A light wind with an edge to it cut through the pines, and from somewhere down the street a dog gave a halfhearted bark.

"We'll get feedback on the plates soon," Cohen said when he got off the phone. "Pretty quiet here."

"Not a good kind of quiet."

"Spooked?"

"Not as long as there aren't a hundred pissed-off Sunnis with bombs hiding in there."

"Right. A Marine." Cohen pulled at his tie. "I can be an asshole sometimes."

"Know thyself."

Bandoni appeared from out of the dark and rapped on the passenger window. Behind him stood a uniform. Kid fresh out of the academy, looked like.

Cohen rolled down the glass.

"Fucking slobs," Bandoni was saying as he swiped with a handkerchief at something on his knee-length overcoat.

"The hell you wearing your go-to-church clothes for?" Cohen asked.

"I have a date. Or I did up until you decided to play home invasion."

"In that getup? They offering free shrimp at the old folks' home?"

The kid snickered.

"Fuck you." Bandoni straightened. "There's another two-hundred-watt light in the rear yard. These guys really like to know when company is coming. Curtains mostly drawn. Two men and a woman in the kitchen in back. Maybe more out of sight. Beer bottles on the table. Couldn't hear shit over the music and couldn't see enough to tell if one of them is our perp. No sign of the kid."

"Layout of the back?" Cohen asked.

"Back door is maybe a four-foot dogleg left from the front. A window on either side of the door. Single window in the basement. Light's on down there, but I couldn't see anything. Heavy shrubs on the back walk, and all those trees." Bandoni rested his forearms on the door. "You're thinking this guy might be good for Elise Hensley?"

"Good chance of it," Cohen said. "Elise and the PI were asking around about these guys, trying to solve a cold case. One of Parnell's homeless confirmed the guy in our sketch has been around. She claims Merkel and the vic had an understanding. But she also says the vic was talking to Melody Weber about leaving Merkel."

Bandoni's gaze flicked to me then back to Cohen. "We got seven cars in front. Who knows how many assholes inside."

Cohen's phone rang. He listened for a couple of minutes, said thanks, and hung up.

"Plates don't match the cars," he told us.

The kid whistled. "They're *all* stolen?"

"Still want to go in nice and quiet?" Bandoni asked. "We got enough probable cause on our perp."

"The woman and child," Cohen reminded him. "And Thomas Brown. We don't want to spook these guys. And we don't want hostages. So we stick with our knock and talk, take Parnell and"—he peered at the kid—"Patrolman Schumacher with us. And call in the precinct car. We can put them around the corner in the back where they've got a line on the door. Whip causes any trouble, or his pals want to slow us down, the uniforms move in. Tell them not to let anyone run out the back. And make sure they've got their vests on."

While Bandoni radioed for another car and Cohen went with Schumacher to get some Kevlar, I stepped out and released Clyde from his carrier. I strapped his vest on him, snapped on his lead then reached into the truck for my own vest.

Cohen returned.

"Thanks for backing us up," he said.

"What did you expect?"

"Just didn't know you cared."

"I don't. Just don't want the paperwork if you trip up."

"Fuck you," he said, grinning.

I smiled back. "Ditto."

Another slap of wind swung down the street, herding dust and trash. A can rattled along the asphalt before banging into a curb. Overhead, hard clouds lowered like the lid of a trap, spitting a few drops of icy rain. I blinked sleet from my eyelashes and told myself my bad feeling was just a normal case of the jitters.

His eyes on the house, Cohen rose on the balls of his feet and dropped. Swung his arms. "What are things coming to when my backup is a railway cop and a furball?"

"Best deal you'll ever get," I said.

We stood on the street, sheltered by the truck and alternately look-ing at each other and at the house until the precinct car came up the street and parked around the corner. Two officers with shotguns got out and took up positions behind the car, one near the rear tire, the other leaning across the hood. From where they'd parked, they had a clear angle on the back door.

Bandoni returned with Schumacher.

"You and I got point," he said to Cohen. "Schumacher, Parnell—you two and the fleabag hang back a little. Give us room to work. We go inside, you guys move up to the porch and make sure no one else joins the fun. Things go to hell, Schumacher calls in backup and Parnell sticks with us."

Schumacher and I snapped a simultaneous "Yes, sir."

"Okay," Bandoni said. "Let's go before someone looks out the win-dow and realizes we're about to crash the party."

We jogged across the street and up the walk in a loose group. Cohen motioned for Schumacher and me to stay in the yard while he and Bandoni went up the stairs. Bandoni took a spot to the side of the door while Cohen rang the bell.

The music stopped. Cohen had his hand up as if to ring the bell again when someone shouted inside.

"Hold on. I'm coming."

A woman's voice. Strained.

Cohen dropped his right hand to his waist. With his left, he held his badge up to the peephole. The door swung inward, and Melody Weber looked out. The porch light lit her up like a battered diva. Her pale face sported a new bruise, and her eyes were swollen and red. The bandage was gone off the cut on her chin; the wound shone a vivid red.

Bastard had been at it again.

"Hello, ma'am. Detective Cohen with the Denver Police Department. Is Mr. Merkel at home?"

Melody's body twitched as if touched by a live wire. She glanced over her shoulder toward the back of the house, then faced Cohen again.

"Um, no?"

"Are you the owner of the home? Melody Weber?" Cohen's voice wore kid gloves. "Maybe I can leave a message for him, Ms. Weber. Can I come in for just a moment?"

Melody's face went ash beneath the bruising. "I don't think that's a good idea." She started to close the door.

Cohen stopped it with his hand and insinuated himself halfway into the room. "We'll just take a quick look around and be out of your hair, Ms. Weber. A simple welfare check. We do it all the time."

"No, I—"

But Cohen stepped the rest of the way inside. I couldn't see Melody's reaction when Bandoni loomed suddenly in the doorway to follow Cohen. But I heard her startled "Oh!"

Schumacher and I moved up the stairs to the porch with Clyde. The icy rain thickened, edging toward snow.

I wiped my face with the sleeve of my coat and peered through the open doorway at a cramped, filthy living room. Melody stood with Cohen in the middle of the room, her arms crossed over her chest as if to protect herself. Bandoni had maneuvered until his back was to the wall and he could see both the hallway leading to the back of the house and the stairs going up.

"You can't stay," Melody said, the words so soft they were almost white noise. "Whip won't like it."

"You're injured," Cohen said. "Did someone hit you?"

"Not like that," Melody said. "I mean, I had it coming. For being stupid, like."

"What he did is a crime, Ms. Weber. How about we take Mr. Merkel with us to the station, have a talk with him?"

"No. No."

"We can press charges on your behalf."

"No," she whispered. "That's not a good idea."

"Or we can escort you and your daughter to a shelter. He won't be able to reach you there."

"I don't need—"

Cohen and Bandoni stiffened as a large man with a bald head and tattoos came down the hallway.

"Slow down, pal," Bandoni said.

The man's glance took in the two detectives, then Schumacher and me with Clyde at the door. He glared at Cohen. "Who the fuck are you?"

"Mr. Merkel?" Bandoni asked.

"No, I ain't Mister-Fucking-Merkel. Who the fuck are you?"

"Detectives Cohen and Bandoni. And you are . . . ?"

"I don't have to answer that."

"You want to answer it at the station, asshole?" Bandoni growled.

"Where's Alfred Merkel?" asked Cohen in a reasonable voice.

"He ain't here. Come back next week or something."

"Frankie . . ." Melody said.

"Keep your trap shut, Mel," Frankie said.

"Did you hit Ms. Weber, Frankie?" Cohen asked.

"I don't hit women."

"But your pal Merkel does?" A cold threat had entered Cohen's voice, like a round being chambered. "You know where he is?"

Melody raised her hands in a pleading gesture. "He's just with—"

"Stow it, you cow," Frankie said, too stupid to hear the steel in Cohen's voice. "I look to you cops like a fucking babysitter? Try Tony's Bar."

Cohen ignored him. "Ms. Weber, is your daughter here?"

Melody sucked in a breath. "Why are you asking about Liz?"

"Merkel somewhere with the little girl, maybe?" Bandoni asked. "How about we ask your pal in the kitchen? You, Frankie. Yell at him to join us in here."

"Merkel ain't here," Frankie said. "And Petes don't know nothing I don't know."

"We need to see the girl," Cohen said.

"What's the fuck with some girl? I don't know nothing about some kid."

"You better figure it out," Bandoni said. "We ain't leaving till we see her."

From outside the house, in the back, a cop yelled. "Police. Stop!"

"Your pal Petes trying to beat feet?" Bandoni asked.

"You guys got a warrant?" Frankie had turned the corner from pissed to outraged. "I know my rights. You don't got a warrant, you gotta leave."

"Welfare check, asshole," Bandoni said. "We don't need a warrant. Now where's Liz Weber?"

From somewhere below our feet, a sound rose. A tortured moan that promised whoever gave voice to it was in unfathomable pain. The moan lifted to a cry then suddenly chopped off.

For a moment, none of us moved. The wind slapped the house. Trees scratched at the window. One of the garbage cans keeled over and rattled down the drive.

Melody sucked in air and fisted her greasy hair.

"The fuck was that?" Bandoni asked, his eyes drilling the floor as if he could see through it.

I signaled for Schumacher to radio for backup, then Clyde and I stepped into the living room.

"Melody," Cohen said. "Where's your daughter? *Where's Liz?*"

Melody looked at Frank as if for guidance. Frankie reached behind his back with his right hand.

"Don't even think it," Cohen said.

Bandoni lifted his gun. "Hands up where I can see them. *Now*, asshole."

Frankie brought his hand back around. It came with a .45. "You die," he said.

Bandoni fired a single shot with his service revolver, opening a hole in Frankie's stomach. Frankie crumpled against the wall and slid to the floor, leaving a dark trail on the dirty-white wall. He gaped at Bandoni.

"Damn it," Bandoni said.

Cohen kicked Frankie's .45 away, sent it spinning under the sofa.

The crack of a shotgun blast boomed behind the house followed immediately by three more.

Melody screamed.

Someone's emergency alarm began bleeping over the radio.

Dispatch came on. "Car 114, are you okay?"

The radio crackled. "Officer down! Officer down!"

Bandoni disappeared down the hall toward the back.

Dispatch was on the radio again. "Officer Wiley down. All units respond."

"You got Frankie," Cohen said to me before he followed Bandoni.

Frankie lay on his side against the wall, drumming his heels on the floor. He thrashed his bald, tattooed head. Blood seeped from his stomach. When his wild eyes caught sight of me, he screamed.

"They shot me! You stupid cunt, help me up! I'll kill those motherfuckers."

The dust of Iraq boiled up until I couldn't see. Shots echoed from somewhere beyond the road. Men yelled and dove for their vehicles.

"Maybe our day to die," Gonzo said from where he'd ducked behind the wheel of the seven-ton. "Ooo Rah!"

Clyde barked and barked, a steady beat that pulled me back to Melody's house.

"Help me, you bitch!" Frankie screamed.

I ordered Clyde to guard while I retrieved Frankie's .45 from under the couch, verified there wasn't a round in the chamber, then shoved the gun into my belt. I dragged a floor lamp over to Frankie and told him to shut up and hold still. As soon as he complied, I handcuffed both of his wrists to the floor lamp.

Fury boiled into his eyes. He tried to grab the lamp and swing it. Clyde bared his teeth and stuck his muzzle in Frankie's face.

"Lie down," I said to Frankie.

Frankie fell back, away from Clyde. The lamp crashed down beside him.

My radio flared in and out of life as dispatch handled the priority code. The second officer behind the house was still responding.

"Who's in the basement?" I asked Melody.

Melody wailed. "Make it stop! Make. It. Stop!"

Shouts and thumps came from the kitchen. Chairs scraped and something hit the floor hard.

"Bandoni's got one punk in the kitchen," Cohen said over the radio. "I'm going downstairs."

"Melody!" I gripped her shoulder. "Damn it, don't fall apart. Where is Liz?"

Melody dissolved into tears. I grabbed her wrist and pulled her toward the ratty sofa that ran the length of the room.

A door slammed in the back. A shot came from the kitchen followed by two more.

"Officer down," Bandoni said over the radio. He was panting hard. "Officer needs assistance." On our car-to-car channel, his voice weak, he said, "Parnell. Cohen needs backup."

Below our feet, as if rising from the depths of hell, came another long bubbling shriek that opened my stomach.

I pushed Melody behind the sofa and ordered her to lie flat and stay there until I came for her. In the doorway, Schumacher looked stunned. Like a kitten tossed into the lion's den.

Another round of shooting came from the backyard.

"Fuck!" someone screamed on the radio.

1662

4

"Schumacher!" I waited until his eyes met mine. "I'm going after Cohen. You need to clear the upstairs."

"I—"

"Backup is coming. But we can't wait. That little girl is still missing."

Something came back into Schumacher's eyes. "Yes, ma'am."

"Now!"

Without waiting for his response, I touched Clyde's lead, and together we headed down the hall toward the kitchen.

"Bandoni," I called. "You clear in there?"

"Clear," he said.

We paused outside the room anyway. I signaled Clyde to go through the doorway. He alerted, but his bearing told me there was nothing imminently dangerous. I followed him in.

A skinhead lay sprawled on his back across the kitchen table, handcuffs dangling from one wrist. A second skinhead lay curled on the floor. Both had a single bullet wound between the eyes. A Tek-9 lay nearby.

Bandoni sat in the corner near the back door, eyeing us blearily. Blood ran from his shoulder. His gun lay on the floor next to him.

I grabbed a dish towel and pressed it to his shoulder.

"Jesus, that hurts," he said.

The towel turned red.

"Guy on the floor came up from the basement with Merkel," he said. "Merkel shot me and went out the back."

I took Bandoni's good hand and pressed it against the towel to hold it in place. I pulled my gun and approached the basement stairs. "Cohen went down before those two came up?"

"Told him to wait." Bandoni panted. "Dumb kid thinks he's Superman."

At the doorway, I peered down. A single bulb with a pull chain lit a narrow wooden staircase. Something had set the bulb to swaying, and shadows bounced around. A charnel house odor wafted up, carrying the smells of urine and feces and the rusty-nail weight of blood.

"Cohen!" I whispered on the car-to-car channel.

Nothing.

"Anyone else go down the stairs?" I asked Bandoni.

He tried to keep his eyes open. "No."

I got on the radio, told dispatch I was going into the basement after Detective Cohen. I cupped Clyde's lead in my hands, one fist in front of the other, my thumbs on the lead to provide braking pressure if Clyde got too far ahead. Then I eased the tension on the leash, silently giving him the search command.

He went down the stairs light and quick. Unalarmed. I followed less gracefully, the wooden steps creaking beneath my weight.

When Clyde reached the bottom of the stairs, I used pressure from my thumbs to stop him. He looked at me for his next command, and I dropped my hand, palm down. He lay down.

As soon as I reached the base of the stairs, I crouched next to him. Cold air wafted over us from an open window at the far end of the room. Another bare bulb lit the immediate area. Nazi propaganda posters were thumbtacked to the tar paper on either side. A gun rack, holding a single shotgun, hung on the wall to my right. On my left, boxes of food and cases of bottled water were piled on the floor next to stacks of ammo boxes. For the coming Nazi apocalypse, presumably.

Beyond these items I could just make out similar stacks with hard edges and black recesses. Good hiding places. But Clyde gave no indication that anything threatened.

I strained my ears. Upstairs, men shouted, floorboards groaned. Ahead of us, wind whistled through the open window. Other than that, the basement was quiet as a tomb.

Gonzo's voice echoed in my ears. *Maybe our day to die.*

I gave Clyde the search signal with the lead, and he took off, tail raised. We leapfrogged forward, clearing the spaces between stacks of food and other supplies, stopping every few feet to resurvey the space until we were nearly at the far end. There, cold light from the back porch shone through the high window. A pool of wet glistened underneath, where the weather came in. A ladder leaned against the wall. Next to that, the room went right with a hard corner.

Again I downed Clyde and crouched next to him, listening for any sounds. Nothing. But a chill wafted from around the corner that had nothing to do with the sleet coming through the window. The skin tightened at the nape of my neck. Clyde pressed his ears back.

Someone had died down here tonight. Not in the way of the men upstairs in the kitchen. Those men had brought it on themselves.

This was different. This was evil.

I touched Clyde's back, willing calm through my hand. Clyde looked up at me.

"We're still good," I whispered. I pushed myself to my feet. But instead of signaling him to go ahead, I unsnapped his lead and pulled my gun. "We go together, boy."

I peered around the corner.

The faint light revealed a nude—and newly deceased—black man bound in a chair. From the looks of things, he had been stabbed, burned with something bigger than cigarettes, and bludgeoned. His fingers had been severed, as had his testicles.

He lifted his head and looked at me.

Ice went through my intestines. Clyde pressed against me with such force he nearly knocked me over. I looked away, sucked in my breath, and looked again.

The man was motionless. And very dead. I'd only imagined him looking at me.

I slid out my Maglite and flicked it on.

He was young. Early twenties. This had to be the PI, Thomas A. Brown.

My heart fisted. First his sister, taken by the skinheads. Then his brother in a rail yard accident. And now Thomas. Was there a mother and father somewhere to mourn the loss of their children?

Scattered all around the body, on the floor next to the knives and the lighters and the shears, next to a bloodied ice pick and several grill lighters, were empty beer bottles and bags of popcorn and crushed cookie boxes.

Nothing like a little torture to give you an appetite.

Beyond the dead man, the room continued into darkness.

Gingerly, Clyde and I skirted the chair and its gruesome burden and moved toward the back.

"Cohen," I whispered into the radio. No response. I softened my knees and pressed my hand to Clyde's neck. "Seek!"

Clyde moved ahead. Instead of bounding forward, he went slowly, as if sensing my need to touch him. Maybe he needed my hand, too.

More supplies were stacked in the back. Cardboard food boxes, mainly. Add it to what was in the basement's main room, it was enough to supply an army. Which was probably the intent.

The boxes stopped a foot short of the back wall. Clyde thrust his nose into the gap, then sat. I lifted the light.

Cohen. Lying on his side and wedged between the wall and the boxes. Hastily I set down the flashlight and holstered my gun, grabbed Cohen's feet, and pulled him free.

He was pale, eyes closed, bleeding from the back of his head. I touched my fingers to his neck. A strong pulse.

I tapped the radio. "Officer down," I said. "Request assistance. We're in the basement. To the right of the staircase and around the corner. We have a second victim down. My K9 and I have cleared the area."

I checked Cohen for other injuries, found nothing save the bloody lump on the back of his head. The skinheads must have figured he was dead and hidden him behind the boxes with the dumber-than-shit idea that he wouldn't be found. I took off my jacket and wadded it beneath him. Then Clyde and I sat with him in that chamber of horrors and waited.

While we waited, I touched my hand to my heart. Made Thomas A. Brown, Private Investigator, whole again in my mind.

Clyde and I stayed in the basement until the paramedics loaded Cohen onto a stretcher and carried him upstairs. By then he was starting to come around, glassy-eyed and pale but breathing. The EMTs carried him out to the front yard where Denver PD had set up a staging area beneath a canopy tent. The snow had turned to icy spitballs that rang against the trashcans, hissed on the ground, and pinged on the canvas. Beyond Melody's house, the street gleamed.

I followed Cohen's stretcher underneath the canopy, shrugged back into my coat.

He opened his eyes and looked at me blearily.

"What the hell were you thinking?" I asked him.

"The little girl," he said. "Is she—"

"We haven't found her."

Cohen closed his eyes. "Head hurts."

"What happened?"

"Went downstairs too fast, thinking maybe they had the little girl down there." His eyes widened. "Where's Bandoni?"

I spotted the huge detective in the back of an ambulance getting his shoulder looked at. When he saw Cohen stirring, some color returned to the big man's face. He blinked hard and then focused on whatever the EMT was telling him.

"Took one in the shoulder," I told Cohen. "He's going to be okay."

"And the patrol guys?"

"One down, I think. I don't know his status, but he was alive half an hour ago."

"Fuck." Cohen's jaw worked. "I walked downstairs and heard a bunch of commotion. I was afraid that whoever'd made the man scream also had the little girl. Went too fast toward the window. Someone clocked me from behind as soon as I rounded the corner."

"Not your smartest move."

"The man?"

"Thomas Brown. He's dead."

Cohen winced as one of the EMTs began gently poking around his wound.

"I'm going to check on Melody Weber," I said. "Don't do anything stupid while I'm gone."

Back in the house, I looked behind the sofa where I'd ordered Melody to wait for me. The space was empty.

Officer Schumacher was sitting on the stairs leading up, elbows on thighs, hands fisted under his chin. He looked like something important had emptied out of him.

"Schumacher?" I said. "You got anything?"

He startled then shook his head when he saw it was me. "There's a little girl's room upstairs. But no kids. No one at all. But . . . shit."

I sat next to him. Clyde took a lower stair.

"How can anyone live like this?" Schumacher went on. "That little girl's room is filthy. Like it's animals living here, not people. I have a little girl. Two months old. She'll never have to go through what Melody Weber's daughter lives with every day."

"If the world were fair, we wouldn't have our jobs."

"I'd be fine with that."

"I know." I stood. "We'll find her. Social Services will make sure she gets a new home. A much better home."

In the coat closet, I found Melody's ratty red sweatshirt balled up on the floor. Clyde picked up her scent, and together we trotted off, heading east down the street. Halfway down the block, he stopped and searched around, finally sitting down to indicate the trail had gone cold.

She'd caught a ride.

I stood in the dark with Clyde, and we stared across the highway at the lights of downtown Denver. At the amusement park, built on an old Superfund cleanup sight, the Ferris wheel was a silhouette against a sky the color of dirty steel.

We'd been so close to both Melody and her daughter. And so close to finding Thomas Brown before he walked into the lion's den. An hour earlier, everything might have gone down differently.

The adrenaline finished coursing its way through my system, and suddenly I was bone-weary. I waited to see if something else would fill me up. Determination or energy or just stubbornness. But all I felt was empty.

On top of everything else, we'd lost Whip and the others. A manhunt would already be under way, but it can be hard to find the rats once they've run to their holes.

Clyde and I made our way back toward the flashing lights, back toward the spotlights and the ME's van and the curious neighbors gathering outside the tape, despite the pelting sleet. When I flashed my badge and ducked back under the tape, I found Cohen sitting up, pale beneath his dark hair, purple bruises under his eyes. He looked as bad as I felt.

"Give me a ride to my car?" he asked as I approached.

"He refuses to go to the hospital," the EMT said, putting the final touches on a gauze bandage. He followed that with an ACE bandage he wound around Cohen's head. "As a city employee, that's strictly against protocol."

"I'll take responsibility," I said.

"He shouldn't be alone. And he can't drive."

"I'll watch over him."

The EMT looked at me closely, trying to gauge if I was trustworthy. After a moment he nodded, so I guessed I passed muster.

"He was knocked out, right?" the EMT said. "So keep him awake for eight hours. Watch for dizziness, slurred speech, pupils that don't match. You see any of that, you take him to the hospital, stat. He clears all those, after eight hours he can get some shut-eye."

"Got it." To Cohen I said, "We'll pick up your car tomorrow. Right now let's get you home."

"Watched over by Cujo and a railroad cop," he whispered as I loaded him into the passenger seat of my truck. "My lucky day."

"Could be worse," I said, thinking of Thomas Brown. "A lot worse."

CHAPTER 18

Part of our job was to search the pockets of the dead.
Marines carry all kinds of shit into combat besides the
required Rules of Engagement card. Bible verses. Good luck
charms. Cigarettes. Letters from home. Plastic coffee stirrers.
Pain pills. Photographs. Sugar packets. Poems. Affirmations.
Prayers to God.
One night, in a nineteen-year-old lance corporal's pocket,
I found a sonogram of an unborn baby. I pulled the image
out, studying it in the mottled light of the blood-smeared task
lamp. On the back, the baby's mother had written, "You can
see he's a boy!"
She'd drawn a smiley face. And a heart.
"We can't wait till you're home!!!"
—Sydney Parnell, ENGL 0208,
Psychology of Combat

Sleet continued to fall in a soft scrape against the truck as I drove over
icy streets, following Cohen's muttered directions until we turned south
on Monaco Parkway toward the heavily gated sanctuary of Cherry Hills.

"How does a murder cop score a home in Cherry Hills?" I asked
him once, trying to snap both of us out of the dark place we'd gone to.
"You and Bandoni doing things I don't want to know about?"

"Luck," he said. "Just dumb, fucking luck."

He'd been sitting bolt upright in the passenger seat since we left Melody's house, staring out the windshield with a gaze so far away he might have been looking at something on the other side of the world. I'd tried to engage him in small talk, just to make sure he stayed awake and that he didn't start slurring his words. But after a few feeble attempts, the talk died. The thought of the dead man and Melody's little girl sat like ghosts between us in the front seat—invisible, heartbreaking conundrums.

I turned west on Hampden. Kept my speed down on a road luminous with black ice.

Cohen made a sound in his throat.

I glanced over. "What?"

"I should have listened to Bandoni and waited for backup before going down those stairs."

"Every cop should have a crystal ball."

He met my gaze briefly, then looked out the window again. But I'd caught the anger and embarrassment in his eyes.

"Things just go wrong sometimes," I said. "Nobody's fault."

"When the people in charge fuck up, who is it pays the price?"

"When I was in Iraq, I used to ask myself that. I wanted to ask a colonel that question. Or a general. Hell, I wanted to ask the president. But I learned to shut up. Asking those kinds of questions was way above my pay grade."

"So then you know the answer," he said. "It's the innocent who pay."

I couldn't speak.

"You ever fuck up, Parnell?"

Flashing lights appeared ahead. I slowed to a crawl and steered the truck around an icy corner. A patrolman directed traffic through a raft of cars guttered by the freezing drizzle. He saw DPC on my truck and waved us through.

"Me fuck up?" I barked a laugh as I resumed our conversation. "Nah. I achieved perfection sometime between enlisting and throwing away a love letter I found on my first dead body."

"You threw away a love letter?"

"It wasn't written to her husband."

The lights of the patrolman flared on and off in the rearview mirror before falling away.

"Anyone ever tell you sarcasm's not the highest form of humor?" Cohen muttered darkly.

"Low is what I'm good at."

"Some war hero you are."

I almost found a smile. "Some cop."

Following Cohen's directions, I turned again, heading toward a gated community.

Cherry Hills is an ultra-exclusive community in a semirural area of southern Denver where the neighborhood is divided into two- and three-acre lots. The homes start at five million. Most people residing there either built on inherited gold-mining wealth created in the 1800s, or they earned it in oil. Or so I'd been told. Most everything I knew about Cherry Hills was just hearsay; our trains don't go anywhere near that rarified air.

"Why do you work as a cop if you can live in a place like this?" I asked.

"Fuck if I know."

I entered the code Cohen gave me at the first gate, then entered another code for the gate at the base of his drive. I drove for half a mile before a gray-brick, turreted mansion appeared on the hilltop, the drive and front yard lit by fifty or so globe lights, the house sprawling over probably twenty thousand square feet.

I tried not to gape. "Home sweet home?"

"Walker's Whim," he said.

"You fucking named your house?"

Although maybe anything with the bulk and heft of this house deserved a name. Plenty of large structures, like dams and mountains and the president's home, have names.

"It's a family name. Drive around to the west. I live in the carriage house."

"Main house not big enough for you?"

"Not until I have an army."

Which made me think of the food and water and ammo in Melody Weber's basement, and suddenly the distraction of Cohen's house was gone. I dove right back down to sorrow.

He had me pull into the single-car garage of the carriage house, a two-story affair that would have comfortably fit three houses like mine inside with room to grow. I shut off the engine and came around to the passenger side where I placed one of his arms over my shoulders and helped him into the house and up the stairs.

I flicked on lights. The main level consisted of a great room—living room and kitchen filling a single, immense space. Floor-to-ceiling windows lined the front of the room. Bare beams spanned the ceiling. Tasteful furniture was arranged in elegant groupings. Someone had mounted a basketball hoop at one end of the room. Probably in case the Nuggets dropped by.

"The couch," Cohen said in a whisper, indicating a leather sofa next to a coffee table the size of a door. The sofa was conveniently aimed toward a built-in television suitable for a drive-in.

"Sure you'll be comfortable here?" I asked. "TV's maybe a little small?"

"Sarcasm again," he said. "You got the pills from the EMT?"

"Hold on."

I deposited him on the couch with pillows and a throw blanket, then went back to the truck to get Clyde and his dishes and kibble along with the EMT's bag of bandages and meds for Cohen. Clyde and I walked out to the yard so he could do his business. Probably the first time a dog had dared to defile the manicured lawn. I cleaned it up with a plastic bag from the truck and tossed it in the trash. Then I closed the garage door and went back in the house.

In the kitchen—marble counters, custom cabinetry—I put down water and food for Clyde. I noticed that the trashcan was filled with empty Styrofoam containers and pizza boxes. Just like Sarge's apartment, minus the roaches. Cohen might be wealthy. But he was still a guy.

Next I opened the bag from the medic. Acetaminophen, I saw with disappointment. Four for him, three for me. I gave him water to wash his down with, then wrapped a towel around some ice and told him to put that on his head, near the wound.

Clyde finished his kibble and wandered out into the living room, his claws clicking on the hardwood floor. Cohen pressed a button, igniting a gas fireplace. Clyde took one look at the rug in front of the fireplace, looked at me for approval, then curled up. Dog heaven.

I returned to the kitchen. Since neither Cohen nor I would be allowed to sleep until Cohen made the eight-hour mark, I brewed coffee. I figured we both should eat, although I wasn't hungry and I doubted if Cohen was, either. But it was another thing I'd learned in the Marine Corps—eat when you can, no matter how you feel. Grams would have said it hadn't been working for me so far. But the Marines also taught me not to quit trying. Not until you're dead.

Maybe, if I didn't find any hope or ambition on my own, I could hang my hat on that. Trying had to count for something.

It took me a minute to locate the refrigerator, which looked exactly like the same dark wood as the surrounding cabinetry. I rummaged through the massive cold space, pushing aside beer bottles, lettuce and zucchini and peppers, jars of sundried tomatoes and artichokes and pesto. There was lots of fresh fruit and what looked like a nice bottle of French wine. Not that I could judge.

"You have all this and you're eating pizza?" I called.

I jumped when his voice came from right behind me.

"Expediency. But I also believe in the value of Maslow's hierarchy."

I backed out of the fridge and straightened. "Meaning what?"

He dropped the ice-laden towel into the sink and sank into a leather barstool. "You can't meet needs that are higher up on the ladder if you don't take care of those at the base."

"Pizza's at the base of your hierarchy of needs?"

"Quick nutrition, Parnell. It's about speed."

"Clyde and I prefer McDonald's."

We looked at each other across the gleaming span of the marble island. I read in the bleakness of his eyes that our attempt at humor wasn't working for either of us. Sarcasm, as humor or armor, sometimes simply can't do the job. Something in Cohen's face gave way, and he slumped in his chair. The purple bruises beneath his eyes belonged to a death mask.

"I called it wrong," he said.

"No. You didn't."

"I rushed us in there. Then I ran down those stairs when I *know* better. I put everyone at risk. And the guy in the basement—what if he was still alive until I went racing down there and got myself knocked out?"

I thought of the two screams we'd heard. "He wasn't alive."

"What if he was? If I'd been more cautious, waited for backup, maybe I could have stopped them."

"You could not have stopped them. And by then I doubt he would have wanted to be alive."

"What did they—?"

"You can learn for yourself later. Not now."

I didn't hold anything against Cohen for his decisions. My own, on the other hand, were giving me fits. If I hadn't let myself get sidetracked by my fears over Habbaniyah, if I'd looked harder at what Elise was up to, maybe Thomas would still be alive.

"Two injured cops," Cohen went on. "One critically. Not to mention the skinheads."

"Please stop." Driven by a trifecta of guilt and need and the desire to take away his burden, I moved toward him. The pain meds pulsed through my veins with a hard, rhythmic beat.

Cohen was still talking. "They tortured him, Parnell. To death. I can still hear him—I will *always* hear him."

The hair on my neck lifted. Deep inside, the monster I'd brought back with me from Iraq uncoiled. We, too, still heard the man's cry.

Cohen swiveled the barstool away. But I grabbed the leather arms and turned him back around. Slid myself between his legs.

He gripped my thighs but kept his eyes on the floor.

I gingerly touched his head near the wound. "You feel sick?"

"No. I just . . . Jesus, I can't stop thinking about him."

I took his face between my hands and gently tilted his head up. Grief shone in his eyes.

"Give me your sorrow," I said. "Just for a little while."

I moved my hands down his cheeks, caught his jaw in my fingers. Felt the roughness of stubble under my thumbs. Heat rose up in me at his weight. The realness of him. Not a ghost. Not a memory. Flesh and blood.

There'd been one man since Dougie. A fellow Marine I picked up in a bar for a one-night stand. When he came back the next day, I told him I'd shoot him if I ever saw him again.

I shrugged out of my coat, now tacky with Cohen's blood, and let it drop to the floor.

Cohen let my name loose with a sigh.

I undid the buttons on my uniform, my hands stiff and awkward. As if this were a performance I'd forgotten to practice for.

"No pity fucks, Parnell," he said, his voice ragged.

"No. Not with you. But we need—"

"In the bedroom. The nightstand."

I dropped my shirt on the floor, followed it with my bra. Shook my hair out. I leaned forward and kissed him again before pulling back.

In the bedroom, I found a condom and brought it back, set the foil on the counter.

He grabbed my wrists. My lips found his. His arms came up around me, yanking me against him, his mouth sucking the breath from me until I had to turn my head.

He groaned, and I turned back to him, holding my breath as if I would dive and never surface.

We undressed in a fury, molting our clothes as if they were on fire, shedding the guilt and grief and memory enmeshed in their folds. The air was warm, but I shivered. With sudden gentleness, he ran his hands along my hips and then up my ribs so slowly he might have been counting each one. My skin grew warm. I closed my eyes. His tongue found my breasts and then my throat. His fingers dove into my hair, twining there. He returned to the chair, pulling me with him. I placed my bare feet on the spindles and straddled him.

Icy pellets struck the windows, and for a moment the familiar darkness tried to claw its way free. The monster wanting to be fed. Wanting to go out into the storm and hunt down the men who'd killed Thomas Brown and return the favor.

I closed my eyes against the haunted faces at the window.

I am here, I am here, I am here. Nothing can harm me.

The monster fled, leaving only Cohen and me and Cohen's hands and hips and chest and cock and his lips against my skin, saying my name in a hoarse whisper over and over and over so that, for a short time, for a sweet, blessed time, there wasn't a thing wrong with the world.

Not a damn thing.

◆ ◆ ◆

After, we dressed like two pros, quickly and in silence. Cohen looked pale, and I steered him to the couch with a twinge of conscience.

For a moment we sat quietly, close but not touching. Then Cohen spoke as if our conversation had never been interrupted.

"We have to find Liz."

"How?"

"Where would Merkel go?"

"Cohen, think. There's an APB out on him. His face is on the news. Cops are checking out the homes of Melody's mother and Merkel's sister. My boss is sending the word up and down the line. We'll find him. And when we do, we'll find Liz."

"Promise?"

"Sarcasm again?"

"Hope." He shook his head. Winced. "Need."

"Then yes. I promise."

I followed his directions to the Scotch. I poured one finger for him and two for me, both neat. Then I found peanut butter, toasted some bread, dug out some baked chips with sea salt and a couple of bananas.

"Let's get something in you," I said. "Settle your stomach."

He said he would if I did.

I sat next to him on the couch and we ate. Maybe we made an okay team.

After I'd cleared away the plates, he said, "I'm going to think about things. Why don't you catch some sleep?"

"Where I come from, you get shot falling asleep at your post."

"So you are some fucking jarhead Marine warrior. Didn't they teach you to sleep when you can?"

"I'll sleep when I die," I said. "Same as you."

His smile offered both sympathy and commiseration.

"Jesus, it's a fuck awful job sometimes," he said.

"Yet here we are."

"Yeah." He blew out his breath. "Here we are."

We listened to the wind. To the ice. To the hiss of the fireplace. Clyde groaned in his sleep.

"Chasing rabbits?" Cohen asked.

"Insurgents."

"That's what he did in the war?"

"Clyde was a combat tracker dog. His job was to pursue insurgents back to their hiding places after they planted an IED or fled the battlefield. Clyde did some covert ops stuff, too. Even I don't know what that involved."

"So maybe I shouldn't have called him a furball."

I shrugged. "He may be a Marine. But in his heart, he's still a dog. I don't think you offended him."

Clyde moaned again, his legs twitching.

"Dogs get PTSD?"

"This one did. His handler died. He was transferred briefly to a second handler, but it wasn't working. Clyde had formed an unusually strong bond with his first handler. Then a bomb went off, and he took some shrapnel. It's been a long road back."

"He must trust you."

"He does. He trusts me with his life. But he also—"

I stopped at the sudden storm of emotion. Clyde trusted me. But there was also some part of him that held back, much as I did. Maybe he was afraid I would die on him as the others had. Trust is repairable. Faith maybe not so much.

"There's some part of him," I said, "that always holds back."

"You ever think that if maybe you open up, he will too?"

I let him see my eye roll. "Like I'm his role model or something?"

Cohen swung toward me on the couch, his face gray but his eyes filled with blazing intensity. That need to know. "Tell me what it was like. In Iraq. And coming home."

My gaze stayed on Clyde. "That's what passes for entertainment around here? Don't you have a bunch of TV channels on that monstrosity?"

"Parnell," he said softly.

"What?"

"I'd like to know."

I picked up my nearly empty glass and turned it in my hands, watching the leaded facets and the shallow amber liquid within catch the light. "Hemingway said that it's dangerous to write the truth in war. And that truth is very hard to come by."

"Somehow I think you're strong enough to be okay with the truth."

"No," I said. "I'm not. I don't have that luxury. And anyway, someone I trust told me not to talk about what happened in the war. Talking just churns things up."

"Let me guess. Nik Lasko."

I covered my surprise by finishing off my drink.

"Don't look so surprised. I'm a cop. And I've seen Lasko's type before."

I bristled. "Meaning what?"

"Sorry. Sore spot. It's just that men like Lasko confuse stoicism with strength. They're all about pretending we should be too tough for counseling. Fake it till you make it."

"You're a therapist now?"

He shrugged. "Got a problem with that?"

"Lasko's right. Some things are better left unsaid. Left behind. You let them out, and other things follow."

"Sitting on it isn't healthy."

My turn to shrug. I looked out the window where the sleet had switched to snow and begun to pile on the sill outside. "Maybe. The thing is, Cohen—"

"Mike. Haven't I earned that?"

I looked him full in the face. Something inside me tried to melt. To make its soft way through the marrow of my bones.

Marine up, Parnell.

"That was sex," I said, though that wasn't what it had been about. "It's not like we're engaged or anything."

He blinked as if I'd slapped him. I hurried on.

"Anyway, people say they want to hear it. But they don't. I mean there are a few sick fucks who ask you what it's like to kill someone. You've probably gotten that, too. But the truth is, no one really wants to hear the messy stuff. The dirty stuff or the immoral stuff or the just plain wrong stuff. The stories that might make them wake up in the middle of the night and ask what in hell our country is doing over there. So, no I don't talk about it."

Cohen stopped short of touching me. "But I *do* want to hear it. I want to know what's going on behind that stoic face you always show. I want to know who you really are."

"Bullshit."

"Cross my heart."

I let the temptation wash over me, waited until it passed. "Wow. Is this like a first date?"

"I think we went straight to the fifth date."

"Is that when you usually fuck someone? On the fifth date?"

I waited for his anger. God knows, I deserved it.

"You are a pain in the ass, Parnell," he said. But his voice was mild. "I get that you have to put the wall back up. But maybe give it a rest for a few hours?"

I said nothing.

"The first time I met you," he went on, "you quoted Shakespeare. I didn't expect that."

"Next time I'll try to drool and walk funny, like a real railroad cop."

He pressed gently on. "We're standing there next to the pieces of a jumper. I'm pretending to drink my coffee so you won't know how upset I am. And you're trying not to cry. Remember that? And then you start in with *King Lear*."

"'As flies to wanton boys—'"

"'Are we to the gods.'"

I finished. "'They kill us for their sport.'"

"So what I'm saying is, I don't know a single other cop talks like that. And definitely not a Marine."

I pulled the throw from the end of the couch and wrapped it around my legs, gave myself the momentary luxury of relaxing into the sofa's embrace to think about what it would be like to bare my soul. I'd tried more than once to talk to Nik about what had happened on the other side of the world. To free those dark things from my heart so I could get on with living. As if, once spoken, the words would free the memories, and the memories would lose their hold. The ghosts would go back to wherever they came from, and I could just be me. A twenty-seven-year-old cop with a dog and a handful of college credits and a dream about something more.

"Parnell?"

I looked Cohen full in the face.

"Talk to me."

I took a breath.

But *I see dead people* was a conversation killer. So was all the other crap I could spew. Things like, *I'm not over the war. I pretend I am. But I'm haunted. And I mean that literally. I have a dead private in my kitchen every morning, and only my dog and I can see him. Is he real? Or are Clyde and I both crazy? I did things in Iraq that no one—I mean no one—would forgive me for if they knew. I lost my lover over there. And the deeper truth? I was fucked up even before the war. My father walked out on us when I was ten and part of me hopes the only reason he never came back is because he's dead. My mother killed a man and was sent away for what amounted to life. I was raised by my Grams, who is the epitome of Appalachian tough-ness, and by a Vietnam vet who thinks that emotions are a sign of weakness.*

And half the time I think they're right. It's easier to zip it all up inside where no one can see it. It's safer. Because if they see it, if they figure out who you really are, they'll know that you are seriously fucked up.

"You don't happen to have Jazmine's file here, do you?" I asked.

He didn't move. But he went away all the same. "Okay. We'll play it your way." He picked up the Scotch I'd poured earlier and drank it down quickly. "It's in the study downstairs."

I found the white vinyl binder in the center of a massive desk in a room lined with bookshelves. A murder investigation would have meant multiple binders. But because Jazmine's case had been first handled by Missing Persons, then only briefly by Homicide before being relegated to the status of INC, there was only the one binder. I carried it upstairs and sat in a chair across from Cohen, opening the binder in my lap.

"Read the summary report," Cohen said. "And when you're done, start reading the rest to me."

I did as he asked. Read the two-page summary, then started in on the details, beginning with the first case report written by Missing Persons and then going on to the interview with Jazmine's mother and brothers. Her oldest brother had last seen her leaving the rail yard after bringing his dinner, heading south toward the bus stop around six o'clock on Wednesday, February 21, 2000. Her mother and the other brother hadn't seen her since breakfast, but both swore she had no reason to run away.

Cohen's cell phone rang. "It's Bandoni," he said and answered. "What?" Silence. "So nothing?" Then, "Shit, you're kidding me."

Cohen gave me an apologetic look then got up and disappeared into the bedroom, closing the door behind him. I frowned at that closed door, then continued thumbing through Jazmine's file, scanning quickly through sections labeled *Witness Statements, On-Scene Report, Continuation Reports, Vehicles, Medical, Neighborhood Surveys.*

I came to the list of persons of interest the police had interviewed. The list had only six names on it, given in alphabetical order. I recognized three of the names. Alfred Merkel and Peter Kettering. Both Royer Boys. Maybe the "Petes" Frankie had referred to had been Peter Kettering. There was a Frank Davis—the Frankie who pulled a gun on Bandoni and Cohen before Bandoni shot him?

There was another name I knew. It came before Merkel's name and after that of Frank Davis.

Gentry Lasko.

I made a small noise. Sweat popped out on my forehead. My mouth went dry. Across the room, Clyde lifted his head.

Gentry. Elise's cousin. Nik and Ellen Ann's son. Their golden child.

Gentry Lasko, at age seventeen a member of a skinhead gang, questioned in the disappearance of Jazmine Brown. Gentry, a neo-Nazi punk. I remembered Gentry hanging out with the Royer Boys sometimes, wearing the boots and the camouflage. But he'd been too much of a jock for them and maybe just too decent-hearted to be totally accepted. For him to be part of Jazmine's disappearance? It didn't seem possible.

Whatever he might have wanted to be then, he was now a kind and gentle man. A defender of the weak who took pro bono cases because he could make a difference. A brilliant lawyer trusted and loved by everyone. Including Clyde, whose standards were higher than most.

I stared at his name on the sheet in disbelief.

Hastily, I flipped to the tab labeled *Suspects.* The same list of names appeared. So somewhere along the line, the investigating detective had moved Gentry and the Royer Boys from witnesses to suspects.

Cohen's voice rumbled in the other room. On and off. On and off. Rising in both tempo and volume. I moved to snap open the binder's metal rings.

Then froze, my thumbs against the metal tabs.

I stared at the pages and, for a moment, the floor seemed to fall away, leaving me floating and rootless, wondering just who the hell I was. I am an honest person, I told myself. A cop. A Marine. *That's* who I am.

In the bedroom, Cohen's voice went silent, followed by the sound of running water.

But I was also family. Gentry was a brother to me. Nik a father. They had loved me and cared for me my whole life. They and Grams were all I had.

The floor settled once more beneath me. Fumbling in my haste, I snapped open the binder's metal rings and began lifting every page I could find with Gentry's name on it. Witness sheet. Suspect sheet. The interview. Chances were good that if no one had gotten around to scanning these pages to make an electronic document, this file was the only record in existence. I folded the sheets and hurried into the kitchen, stuffing the pages into the pocket of my DPC coat where it hung on the stool. I wondered how long it would take Cohen to realize the pages were missing. And what he would do when he found out.

At the sink, I poured myself a drink of water, trying to ease the nausea.

Cohen came out of the back room.

"It's Tucker Rhodes," he said. "He collapsed in his cell."

My hand shook on the glass. "What?"

"Something the doc missed. He's being transported to Denver General. I'm going in. You coming?"

"I—I. No. I'm officially on duty," I lied. "I need to check in."

"Okay." He came to me where I stood, lowered his head to kiss me. I backed away. Behind me, heat seemed to rise from the stolen pages.

"I'm sorry," I whispered.

His face went blank. "I'll keep you notified."

"Thanks."

"I want to see you again, Parnell."

"We're still working the investigation together."

"That's not—" His patience finally snapped. "Right."

He began moving around the room, angry, shrugging into a coat, digging gloves and a hat out of a closet. I stared at him, blinking, until he stopped again in front of me.

"But you're hurt," I said.

"I'm fine."

I couldn't move.

His face softened. "I'm sorry about Rhodes, Parnell. The good news is, he's stable for the moment. He couldn't have been lying there more than fifteen minutes."

The world was spinning around like a carousel. "You'll need a ride."

"A uniform is on the way."

The world didn't settle, exactly. But it backed off. I put on my coat, picked up Clyde's dishes, and Cohen and I said our good-byes, both of us brusque. He was still moving around the carriage house when I left. I passed the squad car coming in as I left Cherry Hills behind me.

I blinked back the tears.

Cohen had opened a window to friendship. Maybe to something more. And I'd considered it. I really had. I'd looked in his eyes and seen both understanding and forgiveness, something I'd not seen from anyone except Dougie and Nik.

The tears found their way free, splashed onto my coat.

But I knew in my heart that he would not care for me if he knew who I was. If he knew what I'd done in Iraq. If he knew about the pills and the drinking and the ghosts and the therapy and the nightmares.

And now, Gentry.

I'd done what I had to, stealing those pages. For all my high and mighty talk with Nik about choosing law and justice over what was personal, I'd apparently found my own point of no return with Gentry. We are defined by family before we are defined by anything else; they are our first and primal debt. But now I had to live with the fact that not only was I a thief, I might be protecting a child's killer.

And eventually Cohen would figure out my theft. Or at least he'd suspect it, which amounted to the same thing.

Whatever I might want, whatever we might have had, I'd just set it to flame.

CHAPTER 19

Morality? Go on, give me a black-and-white definition
for that one.
*   One man's sin is—by quirk of fate or need or desperation—*
another man's necessity.

                                              —*Sydney Parnell. Personal journal.*

Sleet had changed to snow, which fell steadily as I drove. White powder filled the hollows in the land, erased the gutters, piled on the fir trees like lines of cocaine. Everything—buildings, sidewalks, lights—turned blurry as snow enshrouded the city. Denver went silent under the soft, murderous weight.

At a traffic light I waited, wipers slapping back and forth, while a car heading the other way slid through the intersection. It skated through almost an entire three-sixty before the tires bit. The car righted itself and continued on.

I watched it disappear into the storm. The traffic light cycled through its circus colors of red, green, and yellow, and still I sat. Not another car in the world. Not a single pedestrian.

I huddled into my pain.

Older by a year and always protective of me, Gentry had been a stalwart friend through my stint in the Marines. Emailing me, answering my calls when I got my turn at the phones, telling me I was doing the right thing by fighting in Iraq while cowards like him were chowing down at Walter's Steakhouse and struggling through Constitutional Litigation Practicum. He told me I was a hero.

He kept me sane. And by keeping me sane, he'd saved my life.

I could not accept that he'd played any part in the disappearance of a child. Nor in Elise's death. I remembered the cry he'd given when Nik gave him the news about Elise, and I had trouble believing it was pretense. But the police would look hard at him because he, perhaps more than any other of the Royer Boys, had a lot to lose if the story came out. Gentry was in line to make partner in just a few years, a real coup for someone so young. But who wanted a lawyer with a little girl's blood on his hands?

The light cycled again and again, and still I did not move. I told myself that if just one car appeared behind me, if just one set of headlights broke the darkness, things would be okay. A superstitious game I used to play in Iraq. If we made it safely past the next heap of trash then there would be no bombs that day.

But no cars came.

Only the Sir, standing in the yellow glow of the streetlamp on the other side of the road.

I sat up higher in my seat, my shoulders at military bearing.

Clyde rose and put his paws on the dash. Panting softly, he too watched the Sir.

The Sir stared at us, expressionless, his ghost-gray head tilted ever so slightly. Waiting for me to figure it out, I guess.

"Talk to me, Sir. Tell me what's right."

He stood with his helmet in his hand, his rifle slung over his shoulder. In the yellow light, his desert camos glowed. His body from the waist down was a bloody mess.

He made no move.

"You used to talk about the slippery slope," I said. "Like it was a sheet of ice that, as soon as we stepped on it, doomed us to slide over the edge. We used to laugh about it. But then Habbaniyah happened, and we went sailing right into the abyss. So by that logic, it doesn't matter what I do about Gentry. Because I'm already gone. My life was over as soon as I burned Resenko's body so that no one would know how he really died."

He straightened his head. I thought maybe he gave me a bit of a nod.

"It was your job to be our moral compass," I went on. "We were just kids."

You want me to be your moral compass, Corporal? I could almost hear him say. *Not my job. You got to figure this stuff out for yourself. What's right and what's wrong. What's wrong and what's worse. You're a Marine. You can't count on someone being around to tell you how to act like a human being.*

"You sure as hell got that one right, sir."

The Sir turned and walked away, striding up the street on ruined legs. I watched him go, my hands lifted to my face as if holding my head together.

"Fuck you too, sir," I said softly.

Tiredness prowled up my legs like a tiger and tried to sink its claws. I rooted around in the glove box for my stash of Dexedrine capsules. I chewed up two—bitter but effective—then waited for the buzz. When the tiger loosed its claws and backed off, I put the truck in gear.

Maybe *I* couldn't accept that Gentry was guilty of anything more than keeping bad company. But for the police to believe that required proof. It was my job to find it. To save Gentry as he'd saved me. Just as I'd promised I'd save Tucker.

Then, when Gentry and Tucker were clear, I would feed Alfred Merkel and the Royer Boys to the monster.

At the Black Egg Diner, I hung my wet coat near the door then walked past the cherry-red service counter where a trio of men sat blinking at the lights as they tried to crawl out of the night's drunk. I went to a back booth, slid my bag across the seat, and tucked the end of Clyde's leash beneath it. Clyde paused in the damp and muddy aisle to sample the air, drawing in the smells of fried eggs and steamy water, disinfectant and the warm wool scent of drying coats. Finally he decided all was as it should be and sprawled under the table.

Suzie Blair appeared at my table with an urn of coffee. She took in my battered face without a word, poured my first cup of coffee then bent at the knee to fuss over Clyde. Clyde softened his ears and let his tongue unfurl. He knew Suzie as the source of All Things Bacon and accorded her proper respect.

When she straightened, Suzie said, "What can I bring you, honey? And don't you dare tell me 'coffee's good.' You look like something the bears hauled out of the dumpster."

I didn't take offense at anything Suzie said. She talked that way to everyone. "How you doing tonight, Suze?"

Suzie puffed a breath and tucked a graying strand of blond hair behind one ear. Her face was as flat and creased as an old pillow. But when she smiled, she was something.

"I'm fifty-three," she said. "Fifty-four in a month. I'm on my feet at two in the morning. That about says it all, don't it?"

"Prince Charming still a no-show?"

She laughed. "I'd take the devil himself if he'd rub my feet now and again. You're young enough to have a shot at Prince Charming, Sydney. So make it happen. Now, how you want your eggs?"

She'd bring food no matter what I said, so I ordered eggs over easy and toast. Bacon for Clyde. After she left, I took the folded papers I'd lifted from Jazmine's file and laid them on the table. I smoothed the pages out and started reading.

I stopped at the list of names I'd found under the heading "Suspect Interviews."

Peter Kettering
Frank Davis
Gentry Lasko
Alfred Merkel
Sean Sutherland

According to the investigating detective's report, all five men— Gentry was the only underage kid in the bunch—had been released for lack of evidence. But it was also clear from the report that to the detective's way of thinking, they were all as guilty as Cain. He just couldn't prove it. He'd poked around the case for six months, come at it from the front and back and sideways. Nothing ever broke. No witnesses could definitively place the Royer Boys with Jazmine. No bloody clothes or weapons. No body. And some of Jazmine's friends said she'd been talking about running away. The detective had no choice but to let the Royer Boys go. They no doubt went on to terrorize blacks and Jews and God knows who else in other cities and rail yards. Only Gentry stayed behind.

Suzie brought my eggs. She put a plate of bacon and sausage links on the floor for Clyde, refilled my cup, and plopped a fork down on top of the pages.

"Eat now," she said. "Work later. You work too much."

My mind elsewhere, I watched her leave. I pushed the fork aside and turned pages until I came to Gentry's interview. Because Gentry wasn't an adult, his father was present. As a police officer, Nik had known to keep his mouth shut during the interview. But according to the transcript, he hadn't managed very well. He was clearly pissed at the cop for considering Gentry a suspect. And furious with his son for getting himself into a position where he had to be interviewed by a homicide dick.

Nik and Ellen Sue had also been interviewed separately about Gentry's whereabouts that night. Both insisted that Gentry, after school ended at 3:30 p.m., had stayed for football practice and then been home for dinner by 6:15 p.m. Football practice ran until 5:30 p.m. Two of Gentry's friends vouched for his presence, but another boy insisted he hadn't been there. The defensive coach ran the practice that night, and he hadn't taken roll. He couldn't remember if Gentry, a third-string tight end, had been there or not.

The families of the other men, all from Royer, said their darlings were home in time for dinner at 5:30 p.m. The recanting witnesses—the two hobos—had no idea what time they might or might not have seen Jazmine and the skinheads. The railroad employee with the hazy memory guessed he'd seen the group around 5:30 p.m. According to the file, Jazmine's brother Daryl took his dinner break at 5:00 p.m., and Jazmine had arrived promptly on the hour with his meal, which she'd brought in her school backpack. She'd stayed until 5:15 p.m., then left to catch the bus home. The bus driver couldn't say if she'd been on the 5:35 p.m. or not.

Her backpack had never been found, either. Jazmine might as well have dropped in a hole to Wonderland. But it hadn't been the Queen of Hearts who found her.

Wearily I pushed the pages away. Nothing in there marked Gentry as a killer, just as the original detective had concluded. But nothing absolved him, either. Which meant that if Cohen and Bandoni linked Gentry to Merkel, Gentry would be a suspect in both cases.

And so what? Gentry wasn't a killer any more than Tucker was. Evidence against him couldn't appear out of the ether.

Suzie watched me from the counter. Obediently, I ate a few bites of egg. Drank more coffee and pondered my next move. The Dexedrine and coffee gave me energy I didn't know what to do with. I rifled through the pages again.

Across the table, Elise slid into the booth. Her sweet and bloody face looked newly struck by grief. Perhaps she'd gotten news of Tucker's collapse.

"If you'd tell me who did this," I said, "it would save us all a lot of trouble."

She, of course, said nothing. Maybe truly crazy was when your ghosts talked to you. So I wasn't completely gone yet.

I shrugged at her, then deliberately dropped my eyes. I could not deal with her right now. When I lifted my head, she was gone.

But she'd unjammed my thoughts. I needed a different approach. If I couldn't clear Gentry of having played a part in Jazmine's disappearance, I could focus on finding proof of Merkel's guilt for Elise. If he'd killed Elise to shut her up about Jazmine, then that would help seal his fate for both cases.

I hauled my camera out of the bag to look through the photos I'd taken at the crime scene. In addition to the shots I'd snapped in Elise's bedroom, I'd taken thirty-two more on my way out. Now I scrolled through them one at a time.

The crime scene was exactly as I remembered it: horrific. Blood everywhere. Hobo sign scratched in black atop the blood-spattered, white walls. The camera had caught the red-soaked curtain in mid-furl from the breeze entering through the open window. Elise a shattered doll in a bloody bed.

I forced myself to look past the wreckage of her death and search for details of her life. The nightstand held a lamp, a Bible, and a blue teddy bear. On a narrow bookcase were maybe twenty books and a startling collection of knickknacks. Bobbleheads. Ceramic figurines of pretty girls and mischievous boys. A wooden bowl filled with brightly painted hobo beads. And cats. A lot of cats. Maybe gifts for the kindhearted lady, whose hobo symbol was a cat? There were also a carved wooden box, candles, and a second bowl, this one filled with jewelry. On the top shelf sat a model of a steam engine.

I clicked on around the room. A large vase with dried flowers on the floor. A closet, partially ajar. Inside, shoes lined neatly on the floor. Hanging on the doorknob was a baseball cap with the DPC logo. Blood spattered the brim.

I set the camera down.

Nik had given one of those caps to me for my tenth birthday. As if to say that while I might have lost the tribe of immediate family, there was always him and Ellen Ann and the entire railroad community.

Gentry, also one of the tribe, had the same cap from his father. Presumably Nik had bestowed this one upon Elise, letting her know she was one of ours, never dreaming it would be witness to her death.

Our little tribe, shattered again. I closed my eyes.

Sensing my distress, Clyde came out from under the table and placed his chin on my thigh. I laid my hand on his head, spread my fingers through the thick fur between his ears. Clyde's solid, loyal strength passed through my skin in some sort of wonderful osmosis and eased the pain in my heart.

After a moment, I could open my eyes. Clyde studied my face and, apparently satisfied, returned to his lair beneath the table.

I kept clicking through the photos. Out of her room and down the hall. A shot of the room with the Tweety Bird and the empty night-stand. On through the kitchen, with its refrigerator covered with photos of hobos, and out to the living room. I scanned my shots, zooming in and out. Of all the photographs of rail riders in Elise's apartment, only one of them showed Merkel. The shot had been taken outdoors, a string of coal hoppers in the background. Merkel stood alone, his eyes burning into the camera, his tattooed face a series of hard lines and arid planes. A handsome man once, now corrupted from within.

Next to Merkel's picture, a miniature Confederate flag was thumb-tacked to the wall. I studied that for a moment before moving on.

I looked at the two glasses of milk on the dining room table and wondered how old they were. Given the general disarray in Elise's apartment, they could have been there for hours or for days. The sides were covered with fingerprint powder. I scrolled back to the kitchen. Dirty plates stacked next to the sink. A jumble of glasses, one of which was tipped on its side. A couple of drawers partially open. Mail in piles on the counter—envelopes and magazines and flyers. As if it had been weeks since Elise had taken care of anything around her home. The only things of beauty in the utilitarian kitchen were a painting of a mountain lake that hung between the refrigerator and the doorway and a lone ceramic cat on the windowsill.

Back to the living room. Three pairs of shoes neatly lined under a coat rack, which held four or five coats, a few winter scarves, and two woolen hats.

No sign of a struggle in the living room. Nor in the kitchen or second bedroom. No sign of a struggle anywhere except the hobo beads in Elise's bedroom.

I returned to the photo of Merkel and the red-and-blue flag tacked to the wall next to it. Was the flag something Elise had really wanted in her house? Had she used it to mark Merkel as a neo-Nazi? Or had someone other than Elise put it there?

I felt the first tickle of excitement. But just as suddenly it drained away. Merkel's photo and the Confederate flag didn't make him the killer. It didn't even place him in her home.

Something nagged at me. Something I was missing. But damned if I could figure it out.

I packed up the camera, pulled on my coat. What I had right now was a whole lot of nothing. Maybe something would show up in the autopsy or the DNA tests. Maybe one of the neighbors would remember something. All of that was now Cohen's purview. It was his investigation, and I had cut myself out of it.

For now, I was long past the point of being able to think straight. Time to go home. Sometimes my best ideas came while I slept. Maybe I'd wake up with an idea about where Melody and Liz might be.

I threw some bills on the table and nodded good-bye to Suzie as Clyde and I made our way out. Suzie blew me a kiss. Which only reminded me of the night's earlier kiss. And everything that followed.

Another broken tribe.

In the truck, Clyde and I gazed out the window as snow fell past a street light forty yards away, and the wipers scraped against the collection of ice. I pulled out my phone, saw that Cohen had tried to call more than an hour ago. I'd silenced my headset when we went to Melody's house.

I stared out at the winter bleakness for a time, then called him back. He picked up on the third ring.

"Parnell. I thought you'd be sound asleep around now."

"Sleep when we die, right?"

"Right." Behind him, other voices called back and forth, phones rang, and someone slammed a door. The homicide room in full what-the-fuck-just-happened mode. "It's the life we chose."

"How's Bandoni?" I asked.

"Doc patched him up and sent him home. Guy's a boomerang. Right back to work. Chief tried to put him on administrative leave, but that went over about like you'd expect. He says to tell you thanks, by the way."

In the background, I heard Bandoni say, "Fuck your mother."

"Grateful bastard," I said. "What about the precinct cops?"

Cohen's voice took a turn down a dark alley. "Officer Rossi is in critical at Denver General. We're working on IDs for the two punks in the kitchen. As for the assholes who started this shit, Frankie bled out before the EMTs got there. Petes is MIA. And not a goddamn whisper about Alfred Merkel. Frankie didn't have ID on him, and we couldn't find anything in the house or the cars. We're running prints."

Barbara Nickless

"My guess is Frank Davis and Peter Kettering. Both Royer Boys." The words were out of my mouth before I stopped to think what it might mean for Gentry.

"Okay." Keys tapped. "We'll look at that."

"And what about Rhodes? How's he doing?"

"Too early to tell. Subdural hematoma. They're just watching him now, taking repeated MRIs to see if the bleeding goes away on its own."

"Good," I said. "I guess."

"We got an ID on the civilian in Merkel's basement. You were right. Thomas Brown. Kid had just turned twenty-two."

I closed my eyes. Searched for words and came up empty.

"I gotta get back to work," he said.

Sometimes Weight comes without warning. "Yeah. Me too."

"Later then?"

I hesitated, on the verge of saying more. But I'd thrown that choice away. "Sure."

We hung up.

Dreams die hard, whether it's love or hope or money. We mean to live our lives one way, end up with something completely different. Thomas Brown had gone to Alfred Merkel's home to avenge his sister's death. But in the end, all it had gotten him was the same thing I had.

A whole lot of nothing.

CHAPTER 20

We all get our chance to sit alone in the dark, cheek by jowl with the devil.

          —*Sydney Parnell. Personal journal.*

At home, I parked on the street figuring I'd shovel the driveway once the sun was up. I let Clyde into the backyard so he could stretch his legs. In the harsh glare of the porch light, I used the broom leaning by the front door to sweep the stairs. Then I knocked the remaining snow off my boots and let myself inside.

The house was quiet and warm. The furnace hummed softly. I pulled off my boots and coat and went into the kitchen, where I flipped on a light, took off my headset, dropped my bag on the table, and hung my duty belt on a chair. I could sense the dead private's earlier presence in the room like a faint trail of burn in the air. But the man himself—or his ghost, rather—was absent.

The greasy diner eggs sat heavy in my stomach. I decided to try eating something else, then catch a few hours' sleep. After that, I would take another crack at finding evidence against Merkel.

Bent deep into the refrigerator, contemplating the contents of a ceramic casserole dish, I barely registered the warning squeak on the linoleum behind me. I grabbed the heavy dish, but before I could turn, something slammed into the back of my knees, buckling me. I crashed into the refrigerator door. Food and shelving rained down. Hands hauled me up, then someone kneed me hard in my lower back. The casserole dish flew out of my hands, spraying chunks of meat and potatoes in a sloppy arc before it smashed into pieces against the cupboards.

I didn't sail nearly as far but landed just as violently, smacking my face and forearms into the floor.

Outside, Clyde—alarmed at the sudden racket—launched into a five-alarm bark.

For a few seconds, I lay stunned. The linoleum squeaked again. I raised myself to all fours.

"Don't," said a deep voice. "I *will* hurt you."

Whip, I thought. Alfred Merkel. Come to do to me what he'd done to Elise.

I feinted a collapse, rolled to my side, and scrabbled toward the chair where I'd hung my gun. I made maybe six inches of ground before my assailant slammed a boot into my ribs, then gripped me by my shoulders and flipped me onto my back before bringing his boot down on my chest. A supernova exploded in my sternum. I sucked for air and felt nothing come through my windpipe. Black bloomed around the edges of my vision.

"If I'd wanted it to, that kick would have cracked your sternum," he said. "Now look at me."

My lungs opened enough to allow a thin slide of air. I hauled myself to a sitting position, hands clutched to my chest, and shook my head to clear it.

A man stood over me, dressed in filthy woodland camos, eyes as dark as his skin. He sported a month's worth of beard and a glint in his eyes like an unsheathed blade.

Not Whip.

This man was black. His face was vaguely familiar, but my rattled brain couldn't place him. He looked around forty-five, wore thin gloves, and had a Colt M1911 aimed at my face. If he fired, there would be nothing left of my head.

"Tell the dog to be quiet," the man said.

I tried to summon the air to say "Go fuck yourself" but nothing came.

"Tell him. Or I'll shoot him."

The man spoke with calm urgency. His hands on the gun were perfectly steady. There was enough steel in his eyes that I believed him not only able but willing.

My windpipe opened and my lungs filled. "Clyde, quiet!"

Clyde stopped barking and whined.

"Tell him again," the man said.

"Geh rein!" I said. "Be quiet!"

Clyde's whimpering stopped. But I could hear him on his paws, turning a tight figure eight outside the door.

"Good," the man said.

I had him placed now. From the photos in his apartment. Max Udell, aka Sarge. The man who, back in Habbaniyah, had notified the Sir when Tucker's unit found Resenko and Haifa dead in her house.

Sarge, who'd created a shrine to Iraq and been photographed with Malik and the CIA spook—the same dead spook who'd been hanging around in Sarge's apartment for whatever reason the dead hang around. Sarge, the alcoholic whom Jeremy Kane had to roust out of bed most Sundays to get him to his job.

This man looked nothing like an alcoholic with an on-again, off-again girlfriend and a roach-infested apartment.

He looked like a machine.

A terminator.

The first rule in a hostage situation is to avoid aggravating your captor. I kept my eyes on him but said nothing, doing my best to look scared and compliant. It really wasn't much of an act. My whole body felt as if I'd been dropped off a cliff, and an acetylene torch burned behind my breastbone.

Sarge backed off a couple of feet, but kept the gun trained on my right eye.

"My orders are to kill you," he said. "You think of any reason why I shouldn't?"

My body twitched and my eyes darted to my gun, hanging just out of reach.

"Next kick will put you out of your misery forever," he said.

Sarge hadn't been high on my suspect list. But now that I'd met him, the image of Elise, flayed like a sacrificial lamb, rose darkly in my mind.

I pushed the image away. If he simply wanted me dead, he would have already killed me. He was here for something more. I raised my hands, fingers spread in a conciliatory gesture.

"Max Udell, right? Sarge." Remind him that we're both Marines. "You want to tell me what this is about?"

He said nothing.

I drew a breath, winced at the pain, but kept my voice calm. "Sarge, let's talk, okay? Whatever it is that's on your mind, let's talk about it." My mind dredged up Tucker's nickname for Jeremy Kane. "Jeezer's worried about you."

He barked a laugh. "You think I don't know Jeezer's worried? Hell, he's the one gave me heads-up about you and all your questions."

Thank you, Jeremy Kane. "I'm guessing he didn't suggest you put a bullet in my brain."

"My orders to kill you come from higher up."

Panic later, I told myself. Panic kills. "Was it the Alpha?"

Another laugh. "The who?"

"The man who gave the order to cover up Resenko's death in Habbaniyah. I call him the Alpha."

"Like in a wolf pack." Sarge nodded. "It works."

"He have a name?"

"We'll stick with Alpha." Sarge pulled out a chair from the table and propped a booted foot on the seat.

"Look, I—what if I swear to you I'll never bring up Habbaniyah again? And that I'll never look for this Alpha? My bad for trying to dig up stuff that should stay buried. I get that. I'll stop."

He shook his head gravely. "The Alpha wants you taken care of."

"Then why am I still breathing?"

"You are just a child, aren't you?" He actually looked sad. "You are still alive, child, because the killing doesn't come right away. There are some things we have to take care of first."

My stomach lurched.

I am not here. I am far away. Nothing can touch me.

The smells of burnt plastic and charred flesh and the sick-sweet stench of rotten eggs filled my nostrils. Mortars whistled overhead. My body began to shake with adrenaline.

Not our day to die. Gonzo grinned at me as we lay side by side, holding our helmets tight against our skulls. *Not our day. Not yet.*

"Truth is," came a man's deep voice over the wail of the mortars, "I *don't* want to kill you. Got your whole life in front of you. Fellow Marine, gave a lot for your country. You got your grandmother to take care of. Your dog. But I got my orders."

Panic kills, Gonzo said to me, his face black with soot.

I began to count, just like the therapist had taught me. One. Two. Three. Breathe. Four. Five. When I reached ten, the bombs fell silent. The kitchen clock tick-tocked. The furnace whooshed.

Gonzo was gone. In his place stood Sarge. In my home.

I groaned, and Sarge shook his head at me.

"If you cooperate, if you talk, it will go easier on you."

"But you'll still kill me."

"I got my orders."

"Then why should I talk at all?"

Sarge grabbed my arm, yanked it straight, and slammed the Colt into my elbow.

I screamed.

Clyde barked once, a sharp, angry sound, then fell silent again.

Sarge dropped my arm. "Feel like talking now?"

I cradled my elbow. "You're no Marine."

"War does funny things to all of us." He studied me with something akin to pity. "One thing it does is make us want to live. Gives us that survival instinct. So think of it this way, Corporal Parnell. Every word that comes out of your mouth buys you a little more time on this filthy fuck-up of a world."

A shiver rattled through me. I might have had moments of doubt before, dark moments since the war, but now I knew that I did not want to die. Not today. And definitely not on someone else's terms. Buying time was all I had.

I said, "Tell me what you want."

"Who else besides Jeezer have you talked to about Habbaniyah?"

"Just him and Tucker. That's it."

"What about that detective you've been hanging with?"

"That would be stupid. Going public with Habbaniyah would hurt me as much as anyone. I'm still in the reserves. I can still be court-martialed. I swear to you—"

"Then why did you go anywhere with it, girl? You remember all of us talking afterward? How we each took an oath that we'd never talk to anyone about what we'd done, not even to each other. How your CO said *lives* were at stake. You remember that? Yeah, you're nodding now. So why the *fuck* did you show up at Jeezer's house with all this talk about Iraq?"

Clyde had stopped pacing outside. His dog tags jingled as he moved away. I had never felt so alone.

"To *protect* him!" I said. Helpless rage bubbled in my voice. "I made a promise to Tucker that I would try to find Elise's killer. I wanted to clear him, keep him from going to trial where the whole sorry story of Habbaniyah would come out. I was trying to help all of us. But in order to do that, I had to know if there really was any link between Elise's death and Habbaniyah. I had to find out who Elise might have talked to."

"The girl knew what happened in Iraq?"

"Some of it."

His eyes went to lasers. "What'd you learn?"

"That she'd been pushing Tucker and Jeremy Kane to come clean. But I didn't find any evidence she'd gone further with it. You'd be the next person she would have talked to, and if you're here asking me about it, I'm guessing she never approached you."

Sarge scratched his neck. "Fuck all. Then what did get her killed?"

"The police are still working the case. But Elise had also been working a little girl's disappearance from ten years ago. Elise tangled with some violent skinheads over it. That's probably what got her killed."

"Butchered is what it said in the paper. That true?"

I nodded.

"I don't know if it was skinheads who killed her, but I do know this. If she'd been killed over Iraq, it would have looked like an accident. Or suicide."

I remembered the arterial spray in her room and knew Sarge was right. If I hadn't been in such a panic after Tucker brought up Habbaniyah, maybe I would have realized that. Elise's death said rage, not expediency.

Gonzo's voice echoed in my skull. *Panic kills.*

The muzzle of the Colt moved from my right eye to my left and back, as if Sarge were trying to make up his mind which eye to use when he distributed my brain across kingdom come.

"Okay." I forced myself to ignore the gun and look him straight in the eye. "It wasn't you or your Alpha. Her death had nothing to do with Iraq. The police will find the skinhead who killed her and they'll release Tucker, and that will be the end of it."

He gave me a sad smile. "I'm here for the intel, girl. Then I gotta take care of you."

That one threw me. Intel? "You bastard. What danger am I to anyone?"

"You know things from Iraq that you shouldn't."

Panic kills.

I summoned a look of contempt. "What intel do you think I have? I worked the *morgue*, for Christ's sake."

"But you spent your free time fucking a spy."

"Dougie wasn't a spy," I said. "He was—"

"Hush." Sarge dropped his foot from the chair and crouched so that he was eye level with me, the gun between us. He took my chin in his hand, squeezed hard. "Lying won't get you anywhere. But coming clean will buy you a clean death. Answer my questions. Turn over whatever it was Ayers gave you, and I promise it will be quick. A single shot to the temple. Over before you know it."

If I fought back now, if I screamed, would a neighbor hear and call the police? I sucked in air.

"Nuh-uh." Sarge released my chin and pressed his finger to my lips. "Don't."

I released my breath. "No," I whispered.

"Good," he said. He stood and returned to the chair. "Where's Malik?"

"What?" My brain fumbled. "Why are you asking me about Malik?"

Faster than I thought anyone could move, he was back in front of me. His backhand knocked my head into the wall.

"I'm asking the questions now. Now tell me—"

The scrape of Clyde's claws on hardwood.

Sarge froze for a moment, looking confused.

It was a moment too long.

Clyde was already in the room. Sarge spun on his heel raising his gun as he turned.

"*Fass!*" I shouted.

Clyde leapt and grabbed Sarge's upraised arm in his mouth, biting deep. Man and dog went down in a flurry of fur and flesh, tangled up in a chair that toppled over with them. The revolver hit the floor with a thud.

Sarge bellowed in pain.

Geh rein. Inside. It had taken Clyde a while to find the narrow window in the crawlspace that I always leave ajar, and probably longer still to worm his way into the house then get himself through the defunct heating duct and into the hallway. Clyde and I had only run this scenario a few times, a year or more ago. But he'd done it.

I got my feet under me and snatched up the Colt. I yanked out the cartridge, made sure the chamber was empty, and tossed it out of reach on top of the refrigerator. I grabbed my own gun. The one I knew I could trust.

Sarge was still hollering.

"Out!" I shouted to Clyde. *"Aus."*

Clyde refused. He was in full-on devil mode.

"Aus!"

Clyde gave a final, reluctant shake of Sarge's arm then released him and dropped to all fours. He didn't back off.

"Get up," I said to Sarge, who lay sprawled on his back. The sleeve of his shirt was soaked with blood. More blood spattered his chin and cheek. At the sight of his blood, something cold and primal descended, something dark and dank, as if I'd pulled on a filthy coat.

I'd worn it before.

Sarge didn't move.

"Get the fuck up, Udell. Or I'll sic the dog on your face."

He rolled onto his side with a groan then got to his knees. He cradled his injured arm to his chest and gave Clyde a look of murderous fury.

"I hate dogs."

"Pass auf," I told Clyde. *Guard.* To Sarge I said, "Stand up against the wall."

"Bitch," he panted, still on his knees.

I grabbed my Sam Browne belt and pulled out three sets of cuffs.

"Get up, asshole."

"Fucker tore the shit out of my arm."

I kicked him in the ribs and knocked him flat, then kicked him again for good measure.

"Fucking cunt," he said.

"Now."

He grabbed a chair and tried to stand. As soon as he gained his knees and his head came up, I hit him with the gun. His left ear split open, spilling more blood. He bellowed with the pain and dropped back to the floor like the sack of shit he was.

"Try again," I said.

"Stop," he said. For the first time I heard a different note in his voice. Compliance.

Compliance wasn't what I wanted. What I wanted was an excuse to kill him. The monster, demanding to be fed.

I kept the gun on him, telling myself I wouldn't kill him. Telling myself we were both Marines, no matter how far he'd fallen. No matter that he'd intended my death. I warned myself to hold tight to the leash I kept around my rage and fear, for if I let go, something monstrous would emerge.

He found his knees. "You going to hit me again?"

"Knuffen," I snapped at Clyde. Clyde growled.

"Against the wall *now*," I said, "or I'll put him on your throat."

Sarge hawked blood onto the floor, but he dragged himself to his feet. I slammed him against the wall, punched him in the kidneys then pressed the Glock to the back of his neck.

"Hands behind your back."

His muscles coiled for a response. I hit him with the gun again, smacking the same ear. He screamed. I shoved him against the wall and stepped back.

"Hands."

He put his hands behind him, and I snapped the handcuffs on. I righted the chair and pushed it so it was a foot from the table.

"Sit," I told him.

He sank into the seat, his hands pulled tightly behind him. I pulled duct tape out of a drawer and wrapped it around his ankles and knees.

"Feel sick," he muttered. His face had taken on a chalky tone.

"You gonna throw up?" I asked.

He glared at me through his right eye. The other was swelling shut.

I braced my feet and leveraged the chair back against the table so that he was tilted at a twenty-degree angle. "You puke, you'll choke on it."

He rocked in the chair, trying to right it. I placed the muzzle of my gun against his temple.

"You want the dog in your lap?"

The steel was molten in his eyes now.

But he'd started this shit.

"The Alpha sent you here. Who is he?"

He gave me a stony face.

I put an elbow hard into Sarge's jaw. The chair teetered. "Who sent you?"

Silence.

I lifted my arm to hit him again, but his voice stopped me.

"I don't know."

Barbara Nickless

I followed through on the blow. His head whipped back then rolled forward.

"Who?" I asked.

"Goddamn it! I don't know. I've never met him. I work with some man calls himself Kevin. No last name. He sets up a meet and gives me the Alpha's orders."

"Kevin No-Last-Name. He works for the Alpha?"

"I don't think so. They're more like peers. Kevin is CIA."

"What the fuck is the CIA doing involved in this?"

"They're looking for the boy. And something else. I don't know what, exactly."

I stroked his cheek with the Glock. "You can do better."

"No! All I know is it has to do with something they started in Iraq, and Doug Ayers had some piece of the puzzle. It was a joint operation between military intelligence and the CIA. And some other group. A private contractor, from what I understand."

"Joint operation to do what?"

"Save the free world, Parnell. Jesus Christ. I don't know. Swear to God. It's a hundred levels higher than my pay grade. All I know is that the op went wrong. Was supposed to stay over there, in Iraq. But it spilled out over here."

"So where exactly do you enter the picture? A Marine sergeant working for the CIA?"

"Richard Dalton pulled me in. While we were still in Iraq."

"Dalton is the CIA guy in the photos on your wall?"

"Yeah. He was the one told me to hide what happened with Resenko and the Iraqi chick. When that went down like it was supposed to, he told me they'd need guys like me to track jihadists here in the States."

"Dalton is the one who gave the order? After he got the word from the Alpha, I'm guessing?"

"That's how I figure it."

"Why would the CIA be giving orders about a military matter?"

Sarge gave me a look that had "stupid" written all over it.

"Never mind that," I said. "Who killed him?"

"What?" Sarge looked genuinely bewildered. "Dalton ain't dead. He's still in that desert shit hole the rest of us left behind."

Interesting. So maybe I hadn't pulled up the memory of a corpse. Maybe I'd just taken a man I'd seen around the FOB and—in my rattled memory—mixed him up with the dead. Or maybe I really *had* seen him dead, and Hal and the Alpha hadn't gotten the word. "Why are they trying to find Malik? What could either the CIA or the Alpha care about an Iraqi orphan?"

"Nobody filled me in. But I'm thinking they wanted that kid for the op that went south. Maybe using him as a spy. That's as much as I know."

The slow burn deepened to reach bone. "The CIA is using a twelve-year-old as a spy? Do you know what al-Qaeda does to spies?"

"It's war, in case you hadn't noticed."

"What makes you think Malik would be here? Or that I'd have anything to do with him?"

"We know how close you were to the boy. He was brought to the States, I don't know when. Then, after those seven CIA agents were blown up in Khost—you remember that?"

I nodded. A Jordanian doctor named al-Balawi had pretended to be willing to spy against the jihadis for the Americans. Instead, he'd triggered a suicide vest and blown himself up along with the CIA officers, a Jordanian intelligence officer, and an Afghan working for the CIA.

"After that," Sarge went on, "using the boy became critical—losing al-Balawi meant we didn't have anyone on the inside. But then Malik went missing. We figured he'd show up on your doorstep."

"You sons of bitches."

"War, Parnell. War."

"Fuck you."

When I hit him again, it was really more of a love tap. Inside, my heart was almost singing. Malik was alive. And he'd made it to the States after all.

Sarge regarded me through swollen eyes. "You gonna kill me?"

"Depends. Tell me about Doug Ayers. What is it the CIA thinks he gave me?"

"I told you. Kevin wasn't too specific on that. I got the sense he was fishing. Like he doesn't really know."

"Is it Kevin who wants it? Or the Alpha?"

"Both, far as I know."

"If I let you live—and that's a big if—you tell those sons of bitches that Dougie gave me nothing. You understand? Nothing. No papers. No pictures. Not so much as an STD. Nothing."

To my horror, I was crying. With rage and with hatred and with the fact that what Dougie and I had once shared was reduced to this.

With Dougie gone, all I'd wanted when I came home was quiet. Clyde and me working together, trying to heal. Working the trains was a bonus. A way to flee into wide, empty spaces and feel in touch with my long-gone father.

It was all I'd wanted. And now this.

Nik was right. What happened in Iraq should damn well stay there.

"What does Kevin look like?"

"White guy. Over six foot, maybe two-twenty. Early forties. Soft looking. Dresses in nylon pants and polar fleece. Like he works for one of those fancy-gear outfitters."

"How does he arrange a meet?"

"Sends an email with the date and time and location."

I had Sarge give me the email address, and I jotted it down.

"What does all of this—Malik and Doug Ayers and this special operation—have to do with Habbaniyah?"

"Nothing. Habbaniyah isn't Kevin's deal. The Alpha's just cleaning house."

"Then tell me, Udell. Does the Alpha think he can kill everyone involved in Habbaniyah? Me? Tucker? Tucker's squad? Anyone else in the platoon who might have figured it out? Does he plan to kill everyone?"

"You're the only lucky one. Because you had to get nosy and start asking questions. The others are too smart to talk. They got too much to lose."

"And I don't? Where'd he get that idea?"

"I think he just needs me to explain it to him."

"What I'm wondering is if you could explain things better alive, or as a corpse?"

"You kill me, it's just gonna piss him off."

"So then he's going to, what, order me tortured and killed? How much worse can I make it for myself?"

"You kill me, you'll spend every minute looking over your shoulder for the next guy. Only you won't know what he looks like. And there's the cop, too, don't forget. The Alpha's got his eye on him."

A chill settled at the base of my spine. "I already told you, Cohen doesn't know anything."

"Who's going to convince your Alpha of that if you kill me? You kill me, you got no way to get to the Alpha. No way to communicate."

"But I do. I have Kevin's email address."

"Kevin won't respond. He won't care. Habbaniyah's got nothing to do with him so long as the Alpha keeps the sandbox clean. He sure as shit won't pass on a message to the Alpha."

"Oh, I think he would."

"Plus you gotta figure if you kill me, the next guy who comes knocking on your door won't be as nice."

"Because you're such a fucking prince," I snarled.

But Sarge was right about a lot of things. I had no way of knowing if the email address he'd given me was valid. And no other way to get to the Alpha, to warn him off. Most importantly, I now had Max Udell in my sights. The enemy you know is less dangerous than the one you don't.

"I let you go, you'd better sing to your boss like you've never sung before. You understand me? Because if something happens to that cop or my Grams or my dog or anyone else I care about, I swear to you I will cut off your balls and stuff them down your throat. And that's before I get really mad. Am I making myself clear?"

He nodded.

I reached over and brought down the front of his chair, then knelt so we were eye-to-eye.

"Okay," I said. "Here's the deal."

I watched Sarge make his way down the street through the snowfall, his dark figure disappearing and reappearing in the pools of light cast by the streetlamps. He moved with an upright bearing despite the beating Clyde and I had given him.

Maybe he really was a machine.

After I'd laid out exactly what Sarge was going to do for me—convince the Alpha to back off, convince Kevin I had nothing from Dougie—I promised I would drop the whole Habbaniyah affair and do everything in my power to steer the Denver detectives toward the skinheads. I didn't even have to cross my fingers while I said all this. Lying to a verifiable asshole doesn't count against you.

He'd asked if he could have his gun back, and I'd laughed.

Sarge turned the corner and disappeared. Maybe he'd circle back around with a different weapon and shoot me. But I didn't think so. Not while he thought I still had something he wanted. He'd talk to Kevin. Get his orders.

This bought me a little time.

I closed and locked the door and, as my knees buckled, I pressed against the wall to keep from falling. Hunched, every part of me in pain—my knees, my ribs, my back, my head, my elbow, and most especially my chest—I made my glacial way with Clyde to the kitchen where I grabbed Sarge's Colt, then through the doorway into the dining room. I eased to the floor in front of the liquor cabinet. Grams had poured out or given away the obvious alcohol, but a bottle labeled bitters held Jameson. I dragged myself into a chair and sat at the table with Sarge's gun and mine next to me. I poured myself a stiff drink, downed it. Poured another.

I had no fucking idea what to do.

With the whiskey warm in my belly, I leaned back and folded my arms as the shakes rattled through me. When I couldn't sit up any longer, I slid to the floor and pulled Dougie's ring free of my shirt, holding it tight. Clyde came and pressed next to me, licking my face over and over.

"I owe you one, buddy. I owe you big."

I wrapped my arms around him and wept.

CHAPTER 21

The body of a Marine who dies in Iraq arrives at Mortuary Affairs in a black human remains pouch. The Marine's body is placed on the concrete floor, and then one of our crew uses a metal detector to check for shrapnel.

We take turns using the metal detector. Because it isn't just shrapnel we're looking for.

It's unexploded bombs.

—Sydney Parnell. Personal journal.

Cohen called before I was ready for the world again. I let it go to voice-mail, but waited only a few minutes before I picked up my phone and listened to the message. I wanted to hear his voice.

"Call me soon as you can," he said quietly. "It's about Rhodes. You'll want to know."

I stared out the window to the gentle fall of snow glimmering in the back porch light. Beyond the halo of yellow, the trees shivered in a quick flick of wind, a nervous gathering of ghosts.

I tossed back the last of the whiskey and punched *Talk*.

"Parnell," Cohen said.

At the concern in his voice, I had to shove down the words *I'm sorry. I didn't mean to betray your trust. I didn't mean to betray* you.

"Is he okay?" I asked.

"He confessed. An hour ago. I typed up his statement, and he's signed it. The DA's office offered him a plea bargain—life in prison without the possibility of parole. With the death penalty on the table if his case went to trial, he took it."

My mouth worked, but I could not find air.

"I'm sorry," he said. "I know you didn't want this."

"He's lying."

"Parnell, let it go."

"Who came to see him?"

"Nobody." A pause. "If you think someone out there has the power to make our boy confess to something he didn't do, you'd better tell me what the hell is going on."

A movement beyond the doorway startled me into dropping the phone. Elise, shimmering in the kitchen.

Then gone.

"Parnell? You there?"

I picked up the phone, the movement making my chest explode all over again. "I don't believe it. He just—he's not a killer. Not like that."

"You're a good cop," Cohen said. "Don't confuse what you want with the facts on the table."

"A good cop doesn't make assumptions."

"I wouldn't call a confession an assumption. The ME has connected all the dots. The blood on his uniform is hers. The wounds were likely inflicted by a KA-BAR combat knife. The kind—"

"Issued to every Marine. You can buy them online, too. So the knife you found at the 7-Eleven wasn't the murder weapon?"

"No," Cohen admitted.

I roused a little. "This is bullshit. You were the one who said you didn't like the crime scene. That it was too convenient."

"That was before he confessed. Bandoni's list, Parnell. The blood on his uniform. The video of him at the convenience store. Multiple witnesses place him at or near her home around the time of her death.

No sign of a struggle and no evidence of a break-in, meaning she let her killer into her apartment in the middle of the night. That says to me it was someone she trusted."

"Or that the killer used the key under her mat."

"The *alleged* key under her mat."

"Rhodes never denied being there. That doesn't make him her killer. What about his stolen hobo beads? What about Alfred Merkel?"

"Merkel will have his own day in court," Cohen said. "But not for Elise's death. Rhodes now says he made up the story about his beads being stolen."

"He made up this story before he got to Denver? All the way back when he talked to Roald Hoffreider?"

"It just makes it—"

"I know." Weight settled. "Premeditated. I still don't believe it."

"And we have the confession." Cohen talked as if he had Weight, too. "We're still waiting on trace, and if that comes back with something different, I'll have another go at it. But right now we don't have anything that points to anyone *but* Rhodes. You were going to find me something else, remember?"

"What about fingerprints? You checked those glasses of milk?"

"No hits on any of the prints. The only ones we could match were Elise's."

I gave that some thought.

"It gets worse," Cohen said.

I waited.

"She was drugged. Enough oxycodone in her system to turn her into Sleeping Beauty. We found an empty bottle in Rhodes's rucksack. Tests show positive for oxycodone. So that, along with his story to Hoffreider, moves it from a crime of passion to premeditated."

"Rhodes is in constant pain. Of course he'd have something." I looked through the doorway to the pill bottle on the counter. "Everyone has something."

"Short of capturing it on video," Cohen went on, "things are about as clear-cut as they get. Unless trace puts someone else there at the time of her death." He paused as if waiting. When I said nothing, he went on. "Or unless you know some reason why Rhodes would give up his life for Merkel. What he said to me was, and I quote, 'Elise told me I need to come clean. So I am.'"

The weight in my chest grew until I felt my heart would plummet to my feet. I still did not believe Tucker had killed his Beauty. But a grand jury would look at the evidence and indict him. If he persisted in his claim of guilt and entered a guilty plea to the court, the judge would decide his sentence—minus the death penalty—and there would be no trial. No trial, no Habbaniyah.

Maybe he'd decided to sacrifice his life and honor for his fellow Marines.

Isn't that what you want, Parnell? said my survivor voice. *With Tucker guilty, you can walk away. You and Gentry.*

"Fuck all," I said.

We were silent for a moment, listening to each other breathe. I wanted to get up and find some cigarettes, but it hurt too much to move. I kept thinking of the photos I'd taken. Something continued to nag at me, just as it had at the Black Egg. But every time I tried to chase it down, whatever I sought vanished like smoke.

"And nothing on Melody or Liz?"

"We're looking. Nothing so far."

"Fuck all," I said again.

"Yeah." Cohen cleared his throat. "About last night. About us, I mean."

I closed my eyes against the tears, but they spilled out anyway. "Don't read anything into last night, okay? One cop helping another."

"Don't do that, Parnell. It was more than that."

It had been. But there was nothing I could do with that. "We wouldn't be any good together."

Another long silence. I gripped the phone like a lifeline.

"Fuck all. You're probably right," Cohen said and hung up.

I sat in the chair, staring at nothing, the phone dead in my hand.

Some part of me warned, *Get out of here. Sarge'll come back. And this time he'll kill you.*

But still I sat.

After a while, Clyde stood and nudged me until he—and the thought of Liz Weber out there somewhere—got me to my feet. I hobbled into the kitchen and grabbed the pain pills from the Laramie EMTs. I downed three and stuffed the bottle in my pants pocket.

Moving like a ninety-year-old, I tossed clothes and toiletries in a bag along with my camera. I placed Clyde's bowls and food into another bag. I watered Grams's plants, put a hold on the newspaper, and set the living room light on a timer. Just as if I were a normal person with a normal life, going away for a few days.

In the kitchen, I mopped up Sarge's blood and the worst of the mess that had spilled out of the refrigerator, tossing the dirty water in the backyard.

I strapped on my belt and added Sarge's Colt to my bag. Finally, I pulled my DPC coat on over my filthy clothing. Cohen's blood still spattered the front of the jacket, a weeping of red tears across the DPC logo.

At the front door, I paused. I looked around the worn-out living room. At the ancient furniture, the faded walls, the hardwood floor rubbed to dullness by passing feet. I took in Grams's sampler on the wall and the framed picture of my parents that Grams hadn't let me shove in a drawer. I stared at my textbooks piled on the coffee table, my spiral notebook still open where I'd been jotting notes next to a stack of books. *The Iliad, In Search of the Trojan War,* and *The Art of the Essay.*

I took it all in as if I'd never see it again.

Then I tugged on gloves, and Clyde and I walked out the door into the icy dawn.

At Nik's, I parked on the street. The snow had stopped, and I stared out the window. It had been less than forty-eight hours since I'd come to give Nik the news about Elise.

The house looked deserted. Curtains drawn, lights off. Harvey quiet somewhere—in the yard or maybe the house. The porch light still burned, and a couple of newspapers lay in the snow on the uncleared driveway. No one had shoveled the path or the stairs.

Just beyond the feeble reach of the porch light, a tiny amber flare came and went like a warning signal. Someone smoking.

I slid painfully out of the truck. Clyde hopped out beside me and we made our slow, limping way up the drive then up the porch steps toward the cigarette's glow. A low growl came from the porch. Harvey.

Clyde stiffened but made no sound.

"Sydney Rose," Nik said from the darkness. "Come sit with me."

I held my groan as I reached the last stair and stepped from the promise of dawn into the gloom. I eased my weight onto the plastic lawn chair next to Nik's and took the blanket he offered me, wrapped it around my legs. Harvey snarled again from his place beside Nik and Nik ordered him quiet. Clyde ignored Harvey and sat regally by my side. Score one for the Belgian Malinois.

"What are you doing out here, Nik?"

"There's so much pain in the house it's like being wrapped in plastic." He sucked the cigarette. "Man's gotta breathe."

I eyeballed Nik in the crackling light from his cigarette. His face was gray and sunken, red eyes heavily lidded. He looked half frozen in his jeans and railway jacket.

"You'll die of the cold out here," I said.

"No. I'll suffer a little. Seems like I should. Just so long as I can breathe." He nodded toward a box of donuts on the wrought-iron table. "Neighbor brought them. They're half frozen. Help yourself."

I was too nauseous. But I gave Clyde a glazed donut. He ate it politely, came back for more. Gently I pushed his head away.

Beyond the houses to the east, tentative sunlight infused the sky with opal. A splash of light splayed across the snow-filled yards. The air burned with cold.

Nik handed me a bottle of whiskey. I drank. Handed it back. The warmth crept into my stomach like an animal curling up in its burrow.

"You're hurt," Nik said.

"Some."

After a few times back and forth with the bottle, Nik said, "You want to tell me what's going on?"

I talked as the sun rose in a dead-white sky. I told him about the skinheads and the shootout at Melody's house and the missing little girl and Cohen getting hurt and Tucker's confession. I told him that despite those words, Tucker almost certainly hadn't killed Elise. Nik looked at me for a long time, then looked away, out toward a neighbor's yard where a pair of squirrels chased each other among the poplars, their crazy leaps dumping clots of snow to the ground.

"You sure?" he asked. "That he didn't kill her?"

"Pretty sure. Yes."

A pause. "Chief called me before you got here. I already knew he confessed."

"He confessed because he's a Marine who wants to protect other Marines."

"You're saying another Marine killed her?"

"It's more complicated than that."

"I got time."

"Forget complicated. It's irrelevant. And you said it yourself, Nik. What happens in Iraq—"

"Stays there. Okay. Who killed our Elise?"

"I don't know yet."

He kept his face toward the street and the yard. Seeing. Maybe not seeing. "But you got some idea, I can tell. So go on."

"It's about a man named Alfred Merkel."

Nik's face shifted. Went under, like the face of a drowning man. "Tell me."

So I did. I told him about the cops being shot and about Thomas Brown, although I didn't provide a name that would link him to his sister. When I got to the part about what the skinheads had done to Brown, I had trouble going on for a while. After I found my voice again, I told Nik about Cohen's home, a place the size of a small village, and even though it had nothing to do with the investigation, I wondered aloud what drove a man to have so much and yet turn around to risk his life for so little.

I ended by bringing it back to Alfred Merkel and the news that he had once been one of the Royer Boys. I didn't mention Jazmine Brown, or the fact of Gentry's name in her file. But I tossed out the Royer Boys like a piece of bait, wanting to see if Nik would grab on. When he remained silent, I ended my story with Cohen heading back into work and me needing some time and space to clear my head.

I didn't mention Sarge.

"You get hurt like that with the skinheads?"

"Partly."

"What's the rest?"

"Nothing to do with Elise."

The sun lifted over the houses, sent light like an ice pick stabbing across the porch. Nik squinted, took another sip, passed the bottle. His breath was a ghost in the morning air.

"It's good sitting here with you, Sydney Rose," he said.

"Yeah." By now I'd been shivering for some time. Despite the liquor and the pills, something mean and fanged had coiled up in the back of my head where Sarge had slammed me against the wall.

But I couldn't leave Nik.

He chose a donut out of the box, began tearing pieces off for Harvey. Finally he picked up the bait.

"Those Royer Boys." He cleared his throat. "Used to call them the Lost Boys. You know, like that movie about the vampire kids. Or Peter Pan, I guess. None of them with anyone to look after them. And all of them looking for something bigger than themselves to hold on to."

"You remember much about them?"

Nik shook a cigarette out of the pack on the table. He placed it in his mouth but didn't light it.

"Gentry got tangled up with them when he was still in high school," he said. "Kid wanted to join the Marines. We should have let him. The Marines would have given him direction like it'd done for me. Would've given him something to belong to. But Ellen Ann—" His voice broke a little. "She told Gentry that if he enlisted, he might as well put a gun to her head and pull the trigger. She'd be that dead. Said she'd never sign that release, not for love or money."

I wondered how my life would be now if she'd fought that hard for me back then. "So instead he hooked up with the Royer Boys?"

"Kid just wanted to be part of something. The Marines were his first choice, but he didn't have it in him to break his mother's heart. And he was seventeen, needed both our signatures to enlist. So he took to hanging out with those asshole punks down at the Hole."

"My dad always thought they were trouble."

Nik scooted his chair out of the dawning light. "Could be the one time your dad got something right."

Talking about my parents was the one place Nik and I had agreed—without words—to never go. I'd clung to the hope that my dad had a good reason for leaving. But Nik never forgave him for walking out. Who leaves their kid with a woman who turns out to be a killer?

"So how long was Gentry with them?" I asked.

Nik's eyes went small. "Not long. Those boys were older than Gentry, and mean. They got that way because of what they had to deal with at home. Parents missing or drunk. No one giving a shit about them. I promised I'd put him six feet under if I ever saw him with them again."

I said nothing.

"And don't take that personal, Sydney Rose. A broken home is just an excuse. You were always stronger than all of those boys put together. But for Gentry to hang out with them? He didn't have any good reason. His mother and I worked as hard as anybody ever worked to make sure he had everything he needed."

Nik finished feeding his donut to Harvey.

"And eventually it paid off," he said. "Away from them, and with the Marines no longer dangling in front of him, he decided he'd do something to make his mother proud. He studied for his SATs, finished school strong. And look at him now. He's going to make partner before he's much past thirty."

We gave Gentry's success a respectful pause.

"Worst of all," Nik said, "was when that little black girl went missing. The police came to ask Gentry about it. Was the first time the kid had to learn that it matters which toilet you do your business in. Ellen Ann was horrified, of course. But it was good for him. Taught him something."

"So you never . . ." I stopped.

"Never what, Sydney Rose?"

I could feel ice cracking beneath my feet. "You never thought he—"

He sucked in air like a man who hadn't drawn breath in a while. "No."

"I had to ask."

"No. You didn't."

I blinked. The flick in Nik's eyes was a blow, as sharp as if he'd really struck me.

I backed off. "How is Gentry holding up?"

Nik backed off, too. "He's hurting. Bad. He's taken himself somewhere, gone into hiding. Just like he did when he was a teenager. But he'll be okay. He has a future, that boy. And that's what he needs to focus on right now."

"What do you mean, hiding?"

"Means he was never the kind to fall sobbing into his mother's arms. He'll come around when he's ready."

"Did he and Elise talk much? In the last few weeks?"

"Those two always had something to jabber about lately, seems like. Dinners here. Heard them on the phone sometimes."

"And things seemed fine between them?"

That flick in his eyes again. I winced.

"It's not me," I said. "It's the police. If they start looking—"

"There's nothing to find. Gentry was cleared by the police back when that little girl disappeared. Anyway, why would they think there's a connection between that little black girl and—and what happened to Elise?"

"Tucker said Elise had started this thing where she was pushing people to come clean about their past. What if she thought the Royer Boys *did* have something to do with Jazmine's disappearance, and she was telling them to confess?"

"And they killed her for it."

I nodded.

He took the cigarette out of his mouth, rolled it between his fingers. "I don't see it, Sydney Rose. I wish I did because if Tucker didn't murder Elise, then her killer is still out there. But the truth is, no matter what Elise might have wanted them to come clean about, they didn't have anything to confess. Not, at least, when it came to that little girl. Those boys could be royal creeps. They terrorized her, I'd be willing to bet. But the police did their investigation. They pushed hard. They couldn't find anything."

"I read the reports. The detective seemed to think they were good for it."

"The report also mention that the lead detective was a drunk six months out from his retirement? Probably wanted to close the case and finish his career a Level Five. Probably would have arrested Santa Claus if he thought he could get a conviction." Nik rubbed a hand along his jaw, scratching at the stubble. "Nah, they didn't have anything on those boys. I wish they had. Maybe they'd have been put in prison a long time ago."

"So maybe," I said, "it wasn't Jazmine she wanted them to come clean about. Maybe there was another crime she knew about that involved those skinheads. Because Alfred Merkel assaulted Tucker in Wyoming and took his hobo beads. We found the beads near Elise's body. Or ones just like them, anyway. The theory is that after Merkel jumped Tucker in Wyoming, he got to Denver before him and killed Elise."

A muscle jumped in Nik's jaw. "What beads? What are you talking about?"

"There were hobo beads in Elise's room. Scattered. Like a strand had broken during a fight."

Nik tucked his chin down to his chest, hunched his shoulders.

"It looked like more evidence against Tucker," I said, "until we cross-checked his story about being jumped by Merkel and having his beads stolen. Now it speaks against Merkel."

"And you're just now sharing this with me?"

"Because your first thought is revenge. You're tough, Nik. But that gang is tougher."

Nik offered the pack of cigarettes to me, passed me his lighter. We lit up together, letting the smoke hang in the air with our breath.

"Funny the turns life takes," Nik said after a while.

"Or not."

"I've spent too much of my life trying to leave the past behind. But the past is a leech. Digs its head into you and sucks your blood until it leaves you dry."

"What past you talking about, Nik?"

"You sweet on that detective? Cohen, right?"

"What? No."

"You got all misty when you talked about him."

"That was just heart palpitations over the size of his house."

"I'm serious, Sydney Rose."

"So am I." I took a lungful of smoke, released it. My chest protested. "Okay. So maybe I thought about it. But it won't go anywhere."

Nik waited.

"He was asking me things last night," I said. "About the war. First time anyone's wanted to know. To *really* know. About me. Warts and all." I gave an elaborate shrug, kept my voice casual. "It counted for something, you know?"

"You want my advice?"

"You going to tell me anything I haven't already told myself?"

"Keep it close, Sydney Rose. About the war. He'll tell you that it doesn't matter what you did. That he'll love you no matter what, if that's what you two have going. But every time you break down or lose your temper, he'll start worrying that it's because of something you did. He'll start to wonder if you're really right in the head, worry that you're going to explode. First he'll hide the guns, then he'll hide the knives. He'll start to think you're broken."

But I *am* broken, Nik. Broken bad.

"My experience?" Nik went on. "Pretty much anything you've done you aren't proud of, whether it was in war or with something else, it's best to keep it close."

"I have."

"All that news footage they're blocking." Nik went on. "The videos that show the coffins coming back. People don't want to know. And you and I? We're part of what society can't bear to remember. Because if they really think about it, if they really look at us and realize the cost we've paid to keep them safe? They can't live with the guilt. They put up their ribbons and they give us fucking discounts at stores and they say, 'Thank you for your service' so they can go home and feel good about themselves. But if they really looked at what war does to us? Hell. They'd never let us come home."

"Stop it, Nik."

"And for what? What did either of us accomplish in 'Nam or Iraq? What, exactly, did the US achieve?"

The front door opened and Grams looked out. "Sydney Rose? And Clyde? What are you doing out here in the cold with that crazy man? Get inside."

I mashed out the cigarette and hoisted myself from the seat. "You know what Elise said to Tucker? She told him that a life's no good if it's a lie."

"What we did over there?" His eyes followed me. "*That's* the lie."

CHAPTER 22

There was nothing I could do for Dougie, the Sir told me.
Fate had dealt its hand.

But later, many hours later, after they'd taken him away,
I went back in. I knelt in his blood on the floor, and I prayed
for the last time.

After a long time, I stood. I swept the floor clean of saw-
dust dark with what remained of Dougie, packed the sweep-
ings into bags, and carried them outside.
—Sydney Parnell. Personal journal.

Grams drew me into the tiny foyer. She took in my battered face and filthy clothes and pulled me into her arms. I clung to her briefly then pushed away before the tears could start again.

"Don't go home for a few days," I told her. "You need anything, I'll get it."

"What are you talking about?" Her eyes went speculative. "How did this happen? Who hurt you like this?"

"Later, Grams. I need sleep. I'm dead on my feet."

"You'll be dead off of them if you aren't careful," she said. "Triage first. When I'm sure none of those injuries is going to kill you, then you can rest."

Grams had been an ER nurse all her adult life. Convenient in a place like Royer, where kids play chicken on the streets and the adults are into bar fights. Grams had always been popular, even after we moved away. Cheap, capable, and she never asked uncomfortable questions.

Now she took my arm, led me down the shadowy hall toward the warmth and light of the kitchen, Clyde trailing behind.

Ellen Ann sat at the table, staring into space, a cigarette smoldering in her hand. The light over the table carved such deep shadows on her face that her features looked as if they'd been stitched together by a child, and an awkward one at that.

"Ellen Ann?" I said.

Her gaze slid unseeing around the room until her eyes met mine. My presence registered with a shock that bounced down her body.

"Dear God, girl, what happened? Is that your blood?" She stubbed out her cigarette. "You need to go to the hospital."

"Is she right?" Grams looked me square in the face, assessing me in the brighter light. "You hurt bad enough you need the hospital?"

For my grandmother, coming as she did from the self-sufficient hollers of Appalachia, going to the hospital was a sinful admission of weakness. You went there if you were bleeding out or in full cardiac arrest. For everything else you had fortitude. And, hopefully, someone like Grams to patch you up.

I shook my head.

"But the blood," Ellen Ann said.

"It's not mine."

Both women took that in then let it go.

"Get a pan and some clean rags," Grams said to Ellen Ann. "Sydney Rose, go to the bathroom and strip."

While Clyde watched from the narrow space between sink and toilet that he'd wedged himself into, Grams tended me as if I were a child again. She drew a warm bath then had me swallow a couple of Vicodin before she helped me into the water. With the rags brought by Ellen Ann she wiped down my arms and legs and torso with hands as knotty and strong as tree roots. She removed the old bandages and threw them into the basin with the rags, then washed my face and neck and lathered and rinsed my hair.

I leaned my head back against the side of the tub and closed my eyes, surrendering to the cocoon of being cared for. The pain pills and the liquor slithered through my veins, a night train in my blood, rocking me to sleep. I dozed while Grams finished with my hair, then listened vaguely as she catalogued each wound, her voice raw with cigarettes.

When I was at last clean, she helped me stand up out of the tub and dry off. She wrapped an old chenille robe around me and pushed me gently onto the closed lid of the toilet.

"I'll be right back."

While she was gone, Clyde laid his head on my thigh and gave me his soulful eyes. I rested my palm against his head, scratched behind his ears. "We're still good, Clyde."

My eyes sank closed. Images of Elise swirled through my mind. The medical examiner washing her body free of blood. Washing her bright-blond hair. I thought of Melody, whose cut I'd treated only two days ago. And Liz, balled into herself. Where were they?

I jerked awake at the sound of the door opening and then closing.

Grams laid out bandages and ointment and hydrogen peroxide on the counter by the sink. She gave me a glass of water and a bottle of antibiotics and told me to take one now and put the rest in my pocket. Then she studied me under the light, gently turning my head this way and that, her fingers like feathers on the bruises left by Sarge.

"I'll stitch this," she said, lightly touching my cheek. "Give me your arm where he hit you."

I pushed up the sleeve on the arm Sarge had struck with the gun.

"This man, he really hurt you," Grams said. "Whoever he was. He knew what he was doing. Enough to hurt you bad without killing you."

Not right away, at least.

"That his blood on your clothes?"

I nodded. "Some of it."

"Is he still alive?"

"Jesus, Grams."

"Did he have anything to do with Elise's death?"

"I don't think so."

She made me hold ice on the elbow, then knelt in front of me to apply ointment to the cactus wounds, some of which had begun to ooze.

"I know Ellen Ann's a wreck," I said. "But how's Nik holding up? When he's not drunk, I mean."

The shake of her head was soft. "Oh, you know Nik. He's hurting, but he takes it out by getting mad at the dog and the paperboy and the poor girl who got stuck waiting on him at Denny's. He keeps saying he can't breathe and opens the windows, and I keep closing them. He's hard to live with right now. But that's men and women for you. We take to grief different. Who's to say his way isn't better?"

"What about Gentry?"

Her head shook harder this time. "He won't take my calls. Not his mom or dad's, either. Didn't answer the door when his parents dropped by. That poor boy does grief the worst of all. Always has."

Something sharp wriggled into my gut. "You think maybe he's home, just not answering?"

"Nik has a key. He and Ellen Ann went in."

"Nothing was gone? A suitcase or anything?"

She looked at me sharply. "Nothing except him."

"So he went somewhere to hide his grief?"

"Must have." She took away the ice and wrapped an ACE bandage around my elbow. "All the time you were in Iraq, Gentry worried for you. His worry made him restless. Fevered, almost. It was all Ellen Ann could do to get him to come around for a home-cooked meal and to sit still through it. When you decided to re-up, I thought he'd fly apart."

"He emailed me every day while I was over there."

"He's a good man."

"Any idea where he might have gone?"

She stepped back and looked at me, studying her work, checking for places she'd missed. She clucked her tongue.

"The bump to the back of your head is swelling nicely, so that's all good," she said. "Swelling out means it's not swelling in. That chest injury is the worst of it. How bad is the pain?"

"Fine as long as I don't move or breathe."

"You feel like you have to work for air?"

"No."

She put her hands on my chest. "Pain here?" she asked.

I gritted my teeth.

Her hands moved lightly along my ribs. "Anywhere here?"

"No."

Her hands moved around to my back. "What about here?"

"Just feels bruised."

She dropped her hands. "A blow to the chest can damage organs, Sydney Rose. It can kill you. So pay attention to what your body is telling you. You have trouble breathing or if the pain gets a lot worse all the sudden, don't wait. Call an ambulance. Don't mess around with this."

"Gentry?" I reminded her.

She laid out needle and thread. Numbing gel. "Ellen Ann says he always had secret places to go to. When he was a kid, she knew where those places were. But she hasn't known for years. He'll come home when he's ready."

"Friends? A girlfriend?"

"Ellen Ann tried. He was supposed to go into the office yesterday, some big trial they got coming. But his friends at work say he didn't show. I am—" She took a sudden suck of air. "I am a bit worried. He's a grown man and all, and he goes off sometimes. But this feels different. Not like him to walk out on his work, even with what happened to Elise. You find him, you tell him to call, okay?"

"I'll look for him," I promised.

We were silent for a short time while I thought about what Gentry's absence could mean.

"Grams, that man Ma killed, Wallace Cooper?"

She threaded the needle. Had me sit on the counter so we were eye to eye.

"What about him?" she asked. "Tilt your head up."

"You believed her when she said she did it in self-defense? That he was trying to hurt her?"

The needle bit. "She was my daughter-in-law. I believed whatever she believed. Sometimes self-defense isn't as obvious as someone having a knife to your throat or a gun to your head. Sometimes people got to take a wider view."

"What if Wallace Cooper had been family? What then?"

A distant tugging as the thread went through. "What is it you're saying, Sydney Rose?"

"What I learned in Iraq is that sometimes there's a higher truth than what we know. Or what we think we know. And sometimes—maybe all of the time—you've got to go with that higher truth." I rolled my eyes from the needle, let my gaze follow the trail of posies on the wallpaper up to the ceiling. "No matter what it costs."

"You're talking nonsense."

"I'm talking blood and water. Blood may be thicker, but that doesn't mean you have to choke on it."

The needle found a raw place. "You choke on it if you have to. Family is family. That *is* the higher law. Short of God's law, it's the only one that matters."

"How does that explain my dad?"

"Nothing explains your daddy." The prick of the needle vanished as Grams worked her way back to where my skin was numb.

"What if it's family *against* family?"

"Then you go after the furthest kin. It's how we've always done it. Now shut up and let me work. You're going to give yourself a scar, you keep yapping."

Afterward, Grams led me to Gentry's room, gave me some sweats to sleep in and more Vicodin, pulled the blinds against the growing morning, and left, closing the door behind her. When I climbed into bed, Clyde curled up next to me as if he sensed my pain and my need. I knew a lot of dogs slept in their owners' beds, but Clyde had always refused. The fact that he'd slept close to my bed the night we'd brought Tucker back had been a huge milestone.

And now this. Maybe not something we wanted to make a habit of. Or maybe we did. Today wasn't the day to figure it out.

Deeply grateful, I rubbed his face and his ears and gave him long strokes, head to tail, the way he loved. He licked my face.

"Easy boy. Grams just fixed that."

At last I lay back, my hand on his ruff.

"I won't die on you, boy. I promise. Third time's the charm. Maybe we both just need a little faith."

As if reassured, a minute later he was snoring, his weight warm and solid, pressed tight against my right side.

But I lay awake, wired and exhausted, seeing Liz curled up on that picnic table. I reached out my arm for the Vicodin on the nightstand then pulled it back. Later, I told myself.

Outside the room, the floor creaked. Clyde lifted his head. I closed my eyes as someone opened the door and the smell of cigarette smoke and winter trailed into the room. Nik. Needing the quiet of my own thoughts, I feigned sleep until he closed the door again.

"She's tough," I heard him say.

"Maybe not tough enough." Ellen Ann. "Lot of weakness in that family. I love her. But that girl will always be nothing more than middling."

"She just needs time," Nik murmured.

They moved away from the door. Clyde lowered his head.

But I opened my eyes, stared into the gray dimness.

Nothing more than middling.

Was Ellen Ann right? Were my parents and I the weak ones? My father abandoned his wife and daughter. Shortly after that, my mother threw me away when she murdered Wallace Cooper. At age thirteen, after a long period of furious, wounded rebellion, I'd buried my demons and set out to prove I was nothing like them. I became the good girl. In school. In sports. Good friend. Good granddaughter. Good worker. Trustworthy, reliable, obedient.

But I always stopped short of testing myself in full. I never earned straight As. Never took first place in anything. I refused to push myself because pushing myself and failing would be unforgivable. If I failed as my parents had failed, I'd have nothing.

I'd *be* nothing. I'd be like them.

Meanwhile, buried inside, that wounded child lurked.

I hadn't joined the Marines and the railway police out of courage. I'd joined out of a desire for security and stability. I'd wanted someone else to order and organize my life. To think for me and plan for me and tell me when I needed to be brave and when I could relax. I was the obedient soldier who did whatever she was told and never crossed the line until the Sir asked for my help. The men and women around me, the patriotic, high-energy, sometimes fearless Marines and police I worked with every day, proved to me that I was no warrior. But I played the part well. They never knew that inside I was still a thirteen-year-old girl filled with sound and fury.

Then Elise's murder landed in my lap.

Painfully, I rolled onto my side. Clyde groaned but didn't waken.

At the Black Egg, I'd been determined to find a way to prove that Gentry was innocent. Determined to find Elise's killer. But Sarge's arrival in my home had shattered me all over again.

Now I was at a crossroads. I had to choose between breaking the rules or guarding them. Between playing it safe and maybe playing it wrong. The hours with Cohen had made me ask how long I could keep running from what lay in my heart, keep hiding from the dark things that played in my head. Keep holding myself back.

I felt like Jekyll and Hyde. Simultaneously the person who always colored inside the lines and the monster who tore them apart.

Which one was I now?

I wrapped an arm around Clyde, buried my face in his warm fur.

It was safer to run. Running was how you kept the monster chained and quiet. Freeing the monster might be braver and more honest. But it could also get you and the people around you killed.

I should burn the pages with Gentry's name on them, claim ignorance of their theft, leave Melody and Alfred Merkel and even Liz to the Denver PD. Forget about Habbaniyah and Malik and go back to being a railway cop. Correction—to being a *lazy* railway cop. Keep the bar low. Keep the monster drunk on whiskey, high on drugs, soothed by routine.

It was safer that way.

And safe was all that thirteen-year-old girl had ever wanted.

Sometime later, I fell into the sleep of the dead. A sleep so deep and heavy that I might have been plucked from the world and banished into a dark abyss. I did not dream but once.

In the single dream, the ghost who had been at Sarge's apartment, the CIA spook named Dalton, came to me. With him was a young black girl, her clothes torn and bloodied, her body battered. Dalton took her hand and drew her forward until she stood in front of him. He gave her a gentle push in my direction, nodded at me, and vanished.

There would be time for him later, he seemed to say. First, this.

The dream-Jazmine studied my face, her expression grievous, her brow tight. As if she'd hoped to find that I measured up but instead had been disappointed. I shivered under her scrutiny, forced myself to hold her gaze. Did she see the monster and my best self? Did she see how I kept them both at bay so that I was nothing but middling?

At last she held out her arms, palms turned up in plea. Maybe I was all she had. Maybe middling would have to do.

The abyss dropped deeper, and I went with it. Safe for a time in that cocoon of darkness.

Just like I'd always wanted.

I awoke hours later with a clear mind.

I opened my eyes. The bedside clock ticked gently in the late-morning quiet of Gentry's bedroom. A murmur of voices came from beyond the door. Down the street, a neighbor shoveled snow, the metal scraping on the concrete. Cold breathed at the window. A thin line of sunlight fell through the gap in the curtains and set about capturing dust motes.

Jazmine Brown. Liz Weber. And somewhere, Malik. These children had not asked to be victims any more than I had when I was their age. It was just the luck of the draw that we'd pulled the short straws of poverty and violence instead of silver spoons and college trust funds.

My job—first as a Marine and now as a cop—was to be their voice. To stand up for them when they couldn't stand on their own. Whether that took my best self or my worst didn't really matter. Just so long as I got the job done.

Tentatively, I stretched one leg. Got one hell of a zinger back in return. Stretched the other. My body was a thrumming piano wire of pain. Made the job a little harder. But Marines love harder.

I relaxed my legs and groaned. Clyde lifted his head and regarded me with solemn eyes. I forced myself onto my elbows.

"Time to move out, Marine," I told him.

He hopped off the bed and went to stand by the door.

I slid out of bed and found my jeans and sweater cleaned and folded on a chair. I dressed as quickly as I could, given there wasn't an inch of flesh that hadn't been punched, jabbed, or scraped. I strapped on my duty belt and thigh holster then braided my hair and snugged it under my railway cap. Just as I finished, a knock came and Ellen Ann opened the door.

"Nap do you good, Sydney Rose?"

"It did," I said. "I'm feeling stronger."

A little light came into her eyes. Maybe she'd meant for me to hear her earlier words, hoped that calling me middling would piss me off enough to light a fire. No one had ever called Ellen Ann a fool.

"That's good," she said. "There's a woman here. Says she has something for you."

CHAPTER 23

- Do you believe in God, Corporal Parnell?
- Sure. I just don't like Him much. And I don't trust
Him at all.
—Kuwait, conversation with the Marine chaplain.

Sherri Kane, Jeremy Kane's pretty, pregnant wife, was not who I'd expected or hoped for. But I had to give her credit for finding me.

Dressed in a navy and white striped sweater, maternity jeans, and fur-topped snow boots, she sat in the wingback chair in Ellen Ann's living room. Knees and ankles together, legs tucked gracefully to one side. Her face was fresh and clean. Her hair, loosed from its ponytail, fell in a shining wave over her shoulder.

As Clyde and I entered the room, Sherri took in my wounded face and faltering gait. An unreadable expression flitted across her features. Satisfaction?

Maybe I was too harsh.

"Get you anything?" Ellen Ann asked me. She'd already brought tea for Sherri.

"I'm good."

She patted my shoulder, probably figuring I needed bolstering in the face of my visitor's wholesome beauty. After she left, I turned to Sherri. "What can I do for you?"

She set down her tea. "I am sorry to just show up at your uncle's house," she said. "But I have Tucks's beads. I tried calling the number on the card you gave me, but you didn't answer."

I didn't bother correcting her on my relationship with Nik. I pulled out my phone. Three calls from an unknown number. I really had been in the abyss.

"I called the railroad," Sherri went on, "told the man who picked up that I needed to see you. They gave me your uncle's name and number, and I figured out the address. When no one answered, I decided to drive over. I've made the beads, like Tucks asked. Now I want them off my hands."

Efficient. I remembered.

I lowered myself onto the chair catty-corner to Sherri's, next to a recently closed window where a chill still hung. Clyde stood next to me, tail straight. Probably he'd inhaled a snoutful of Ogre's scent. I wondered if he felt about Sherri's dog the way I felt about Sherri.

"Would you like me to take the beads to him?" I asked.

"Yes." Her voice was crisp. She rummaged through the purse in her lap. "You can do that, can't you?"

"Did you know he's in the hospital? He collapsed in his cell."

Her hand paused. "Is he going to be all right?"

"Too soon to tell. But I'll make sure he knows about the beads, once he's awake. I'm sure he'll be grateful to know you care."

She pulled out a drawstring bag. Wooden beads clicked inside. "You must think I just want to put all of this behind me."

"Never crossed my mind."

Her eyes narrowed, but she handed over the bag. "Please tell him we're thinking about him."

"I will."

She snapped her purse closed. "I should get going. I need to pick up Haley."

For a moment, I considered Sherri as a killer. She hated Elise, who had replaced her as the golden girl. A woman's choice of weapons is often poison, and Elise had been drugged before she died. Maybe the knife work was to mislead.

But I just as quickly dismissed the idea. The knife was too hands-on and messy for someone like Sherri, no matter how clever a cover-up it might have seemed. In Sherri's world, anger amounted to a door slam or maybe a burnt chicken. Not murder.

"Just one more thing, Mrs. Kane," I said. "When I was at your house, you mentioned that Elise was digging up dirt. You said you didn't know what kind of things she was looking for. But you're obviously a smart woman. And I'm guessing you're an astute observer of people."

Unimpressed by my flattery, Sherri sighed and glanced at her watch.

"So I'm a little surprised," I went on, "that you have no inkling what Elise might have been looking into. Surely she said something. Maybe you even asked her about it."

"Life can be bleak, Special Agent Parnell. I try not to bring in any more unpleasantness than I have to. But Elise did talk to me a little. If you think it will help, she said something to me at dinner one night. That she was dealing with a gang of skinheads."

If I was hoping for a new angle to pursue, I was disappointed. "What about them?"

"Elise was upset because they were coming around again. Hurting 'her' people, she said. There was one in particular she talked about. Blade, I think. Or Whip. Pistol, maybe. I don't remember."

I rose. "Can you wait just a moment? I have something to show you."

"I—"

"I'll be right back."

To encourage Sherri to wait, I gave Clyde the stay command. I found my bag near the front door and pulled out the sketch of Alfred Merkel.

I handed the paper over as I resumed my seat. "You ever see this man around?"

She took the sketch. Gave a startled little "Oh!"

I waited.

"Oh, my heavens, is he a criminal?"

"He's a neo-Nazi. You can decide if that makes him a criminal. You recognize him?"

"I made hobo beads for him. Last summer. I had a booth at a craft fair at Globeville Landing Park. He came up and admired the beads I had on display, but he didn't want any of those."

"What did he want?"

The expression on her face was a mixture of bemusement and disgust. "He wanted love beads. Hearts. Doves. The word 'Always.' As a gift, he said. I remember because it was so odd. This terrifying man wanting love beads."

"Did he say who they were for?"

She shook her head. "I took down his order, and he told me where to send them. Then he threw the money on the table and ran off. I saw him later with a woman and a group of men with tattoos like his. He was carrying a little girl."

"What did the woman look like?"

"Heavyset, but pretty. Dirty blond hair."

"Tattoos?"

"No." She shook her head, remembering. "I figured he took off so quickly because he didn't want his buddies to know about the beads."

Was this why Melody stayed with him? Because after he beat her, he tried to make up for it by giving her gifts?

"Where did he want you to send them?" I asked.

"It was a house. Or I guess it was. I can't remember the street."

I told her Melody's address, but Sherri shook her head. "I don't think so. It wasn't—I don't think it was in Denver."

"Mrs. Kane, I need that address. It's important. The woman and little girl you saw might be in danger."

"From whoever killed Elise?" Her eyes went wide. "You mean *he's* Elise's killer? That's why you have a sketch of him? You're saying that I made beads for a murderer?"

I let my silence speak for itself.

She went white beneath her delicate sprinkling of freckles. "The address definitely wasn't in Denver. It was one of those little towns out east. Wiggins, maybe. Yes, I think it was Wiggins. I remember wondering why anyone would live in a place like that where there's just nothing." She stared at me with huge eyes. "Oh, my God."

Roald Hoffreider had seen Alfred Merkel in a biker bar in a little town east of Denver. Wiggins was sixty-six miles out of Denver, right on a line run by Denver Pacific.

"Did I help?" Sherri asked.

"You helped a lot, Mrs. Kane."

After Sherri left, I used Nik's computer to search for an address belonging to any Merkels in Wiggins, Colorado. Nothing. I scanned the records of other small towns in case Sherri was wrong about the location. Brush. Fort Morgan. Points further east.

Nothing.

I looked at Clyde. "You're a tracker dog. Where does that son of a bitch go to ground?"

Clyde pricked his ears but had nothing to offer.

Today was February 21. Ten years to the day that Jazmine had gone missing. I stared out the window for a few minutes, thinking about Gentry and where he might be. For the heck of it, I looked online for milestones relating to the rise of Nazism.

Two things popped out. In February 1920, the German Workers Party became the Nationalist Socialist German Workers Party. Otherwise known as the Nazi party.

Then in February of 1933, civil rights in Germany were suspended, and the Nazi party was given emergency powers. The long, slow roll to genocide began.

For the first time I wondered if Jazmine's disappearance hadn't been a simple act of opportunity. Maybe the timing had been more significant.

I flashed to the swastika I'd seen on Nik's porch when I brought the news about Elise. The vandalized welcome mat. Had Alfred Merkel and the Royer Boys been sending Gentry a warning to keep silent? Had Gentry, with the anniversary approaching, given Merkel a reason to think he was going to go to the police with what he knew? Had he, along with Thomas Brown, been working with Elise?

Those two always had something to jabber about lately, seems like, Nik had told me.

Had the Royer Boys taken Gentry to silence him? Just as they'd silenced Elise?

I jumped to my feet and ran into the hallway. "Nik!"

Grams looked out from the kitchen. "What are you hollering about, Sydney Rose?"

"Where's Nik?"

"He's gone."

"What do you mean?" I followed her back into the kitchen. "Where?"

"You think he'd be bothered to tell us?" She picked up a knife and continued to chop beets. "Walked out like he had the devil on his back. Left his phone, too. Said he doesn't want to talk to anyone."

"Damn it. He's gone after the Royer Boys. He's going to get himself killed."

Grams lowered the knife and turned to me.

"What are you talking about, Sydney Rose?"

"Elise was trying to get those boys to come clean about something they'd done. I think Gentry was helping her. That's why someone spray-painted that swastika on Nik and Ellen Ann's porch. As a warning to Gentry to stay quiet."

"Elise said she was working with skinheads," she said. "And Gentry was helping her. I thought she was teaching them scripture, taking Gentry along as a bodyguard."

"Does Nik know how to find them?"

"The Royer Boys? It's been years, Sydney Rose. Those boys are long gone from these parts." She narrowed her eyes in sudden understanding. "You're saying they're back? Is this about that little girl disappeared all those years ago?"

I spun on my heel, headed toward the front door.

"Nik calls or comes home," I said over my shoulder, "you tell him I've gone to Wiggins."

Grams followed me to the front door. Outside, flurries spit from a leaden sky. Across the street, a neighbor worked a snowblower. I pushed my feet into my boots.

"We couldn't get your coat clean." Grams opened the closet door and pulled out a black wool coat, a hat, and a pair of gloves. "Ellen Ann says for you to use these."

I removed my railway hat, hung it on a hook near the door, and pulled on the stocking cap. Took the gloves and tucked them in the coat pocket. "Tell her thanks."

"Find her killer, Sydney Rose. Do what you have to do. And find Gentry and Nik. Bring those fools home."

"I will." Thinking of what Ellen Ann had said outside the bedroom door earlier, I blurted, "I'm not weak, Grams."

She squinted up at me through still-bright eyes, her sinewy body as solid and reliable as the oak she resembled. Years ago, when I was a child, she would take me on long walks in the woods. Out there, among the pines and aspens of the higher mountains, her eyes held a leap of wildness in them, as if she carried some elemental magic. I was a little afraid of her.

"You have both your father and mother inside you," she said to me now. "And Lord knows they had their share of weakness. But you're different. When the crap they pulled taught you to hold back, I just figured you'd step into yourself when you were ready." She tucked a strand of hair under my cap. "Leastways, that's what I thought until that damn war came along and took something bright and strong out of you. Maybe it's time to get it back."

"What if I'm like my ma, Grams?" I thought of Sarge's blood in my kitchen. Thought of Wallace Cooper and my mother, arguing by the train before the law said she pushed him. "What if something terrible happens when I stop holding back?"

"Could be your worst self is also your best." Gently, she pressed her palm to my heart, bringing both warmth and pain. "Maybe you shouldn't fear so much what you got inside."

I laid my hand on hers. She twined her fingers through mine and placed her head on my shoulder. I closed my eyes and breathed in her scent, the smell of mysterious things gone quiet with age. Like an old bear, hibernating under winter's depths.

Then she stepped away, and the moment passed.

"Be tough out there," she said.

She held my coat open. Painfully I twisted to slide my right arm into the sleeve and then my left. My wrist caught on the cuff, and a spark of pain radiated out from my elbow.

And at that very moment, thinking only of a coat, I had it.

Melody Weber.

CHAPTER 24

Hemingway said that in modern war, you will die like a
dog for no good reason.
    But sometimes you don't die. And there's no good reason
for that, either.
                            —Sydney Parnell. Personal journal.

I sat in the car with the engine off while snow feathered the hood. Clyde gnawed on his rawhide as I went through the photos again, looking for things I hadn't known to look for earlier.

Elise's bedroom and the wooden bowl of hobo beads. When I zoomed in, I could just make out a painted red heart on one of them.

Whip hadn't killed Elise. He'd had a crush on her. And Melody had known about it.

I flipped through to the front room. Two glasses of milk sat on the dining table, one untouched. Did it belong to Liz, who was unable to drink because she'd known what was coming? Or was it Melody's, who'd had other things on her mind? The crime lab hadn't gotten a hit on the prints because Melody and Liz weren't in the system.

The third glass was on the kitchen counter, tipped over and dribbling milk into the sink. Elise's. I'd missed its importance before, figured it for part of the general messiness in Elise's apartment. But now I had no doubt the crime lab would find traces of oxycodone there to match what they'd found in Elise's blood.

Finally, I zoomed in on the coats hanging by the door. I flashed back to my conversation at Hogan's Alley two mornings ago with Melody Weber. I'd asked her about the coat I'd given her, and she'd told me it was in the tent. But it had been damn cold at Hogan's Alley that day.

Melody's coat hadn't been in the tent.

She'd left it at Elise's.

Melody Weber and Liz had paid Elise a visit. Elise had offered her guests milk. Melody had slipped the oxycodone into Elise's milk, then dragged the unconscious woman into her bedroom, where—in her rage over Whip—she'd stabbed Elise to death.

All while her little girl sat in the next room, fingers curled around her phone. Cohen had told me it was someone young who'd called in Elise's death. Had Liz thought about calling the police while her mother was busy with Elise? Considered it again while Melody was in the bathroom washing up and staring at the cut on her face that I, a few hours later, would bandage for her? Had Liz finally summoned her courage once they were safely away at the hobo camp and her mother was sleeping it off?

It's the ones who love us, hurt us the most.

Almost certainly Whip had learned what his girlfriend had done and delivered the beating that Melody said she deserved. But he hadn't reported her. Instead, he'd scattered Tucker's hobo beads in the room, knowing—as he did—that Tucker was on his way home. He'd protected her.

I pulled on my headset, picked up my phone and dialed Cohen. It went straight to voicemail.

"Call me," I said. "Tucker Rhodes is innocent. I can prove it. And—" I hesitated for the briefest of moments. "I stole some pages out of Jazmine's file. To protect a friend. I was wrong."

I disconnected, my heart beating as fast as if I'd said the words to Cohen's face. *I am a thief. I am without honor.*

Seemed like I was getting pretty good at hammering nails into the coffin of everything that mattered to me.

I turned the ignition, and the engine roared to life. A sudden gust bitch-slapped the truck, and down the street a metal hubcap clattered along the curb. Clyde dropped his chew toy and rose fast in the passenger seat, ears and tail up, bumping into the ceiling.

Gently I pressed his rump down.

"We're still good, boy," I told him. "You should be happy. Today we're hunting bad guys."

Clyde eyeballed me for a minute then settled back into the seat and watched out the window. After a moment he retrieved his rawhide.

One more phone call, this time to the shelter where Melody and Liz had gone two days earlier.

"Trish, it's Sydney," I said when she answered. "I need to ask about that backpack left by Liz Weber."

"What do you need to know?" Trish asked warily.

"What's in there. I know, I know," I said when she started to protest. "Just accidentally spill it while you're moving it. Liz could be in danger."

"What? Sydney, what's going on?"

"I can't tell you anything right now. Just do it."

"Okay. I've got the backpack. Woops! Oh, darn, I dropped everything on the bed."

I waited while Trish listed the contents.

"A T-shirt and jeans. A Barbie doll in a tutu. A little ceramic cat with a broken tail. Let's see. A cell phone. Two pieces of candy. A feather and some pebbles. A key. That's everything."

I stared out at the fresh snow gathering on the grass, and I thought about the ceramic cats on Elise's bedroom shelf. A tide of ugly rose inside me. "Tell me about the key."

"Silver. Plain. Standard size. A single hole at the top for a key chain. A house key, I'd guess."

"Okay. Take a look at the phone."

"It's a typical flip phone."

"I need you to look at the list of calls."

"You're sure this might save Liz's life?"

"Your name will never come into this, Trish. Take a look."

"Hold on. Okay, there." A pause. "Sydney, the last number dialed is nine-one-one."

"When?"

"Two days ago at, let's see, seven thirty-one a.m."

How had that tiny stick of a girl screwed up the courage to call for help?

"Who does Liz have in her contact list?" I asked.

"Nothing. It's empty. And everything under recent calls has been deleted except that nine-one-one call."

Shit. "Thanks, Trish. You've been a huge help."

"Find her, Sydney."

"I will." Promises left and right. I hoped I could keep them.

I tried Cohen again, and again it went to voicemail. I opened my bag. Sarge's Colt gleamed within the dark confines. I removed it, chambered a round, and returned it, cocked and locked, to the bag.

"Looks like it's you and me, Marine," I said to Clyde.

Picking up on my excitement, Clyde barked.

"Game on," I told him, and put the truck in gear.

Wind shook the truck.

The snow had changed over to sleet as we left Denver behind. Now, ahead of us, the light lay flat and gray. In the rearview, storm clouds massed on a dark horizon. I switched on the radio.

". . . what may be the storm of the century. We're already seeing snow in some areas, sleet further east. Could be a foot or more of new snow on top of what the last two storms laid down. It'll be worse for you folks out east. Might be as much as three feet in Brush and Fort Morgan by the time this storm is done. Finish what you're doing, people, and get home early. We've got snowplows out there. But they won't be able to keep up with Mother Nature. Hold on to your hats."

I flicked off the radio and listened to the sweep of the wipers as chunks of ice gathered on the blades.

"Who'd we piss off, Clyde?"

Clyde let his tongue loll. Happy.

We headed east on a nearly empty highway toward Wiggins, the sun a rumor through the clouds, the tires whispering on glistening pavement. As I drove, I thought about the timeline for Jazmine's disappearance. If the Royer Boys had taken her from the yard at 5:30 and been home by 6:30, there weren't many options if they'd gone by train. Heading either north or south wouldn't have given them time to kill Jazmine, dispose of her body, and catch a train and get home; the Powder River train didn't come through often enough. West went nowhere. Wiggins was the next stop east. But an hour wasn't quite enough time to catch the 5:40 east-bound freight to Wiggins, jump out at the yard with Jazmine, then catch the west-bound back. An hour and a half would do it, though. If all the families had been willing to fudge a little about when their sons had returned home, it wasn't unreasonable to assume they'd taken her to Wiggins or somewhere near there. They could have shoved her out in the prairie and let the coyotes take care of the evidence.

The police had searched a five-mile grid from Jazmine's last known location, come up empty.

No one had looked at the trains.

I tried Gentry's number. It went straight to voicemail.

"We'll find him," I said to Clyde. "Don't worry."

Clyde glanced at me then returned his gaze to the window. Definitely not worried.

As I drove, the pain in my body returned like a series of light dimmers slowly dialing to bright. My chest was the first thing, then the burn in my cheek and elbow. Nik's whiskey and Grams's pain pills were wearing off. I reached in my pocket for the pills from the EMTs, glad Grams had transferred them to Ellen Ann's coat. I dry-swallowed four then popped open the glove box for something stronger. But I hesitated, my hand floating above the bottle of Xanax and the baggie filled with Dexedrine.

Thirty skinheads, Roald Hoffreider had said. Maybe more.

I closed the glove box and put my hand back on the wheel.

The truck slewed a few times on the slick roads before I reached the outskirts of Wiggins. By then the sleet was changing over to a wet, heavy snow as the temperature dropped and the wind kicked into a fury. Norway spruces, planted as windbreaks a decade or so earlier, shuddered in the gale. Plastic bags and other debris whipped past; bits of hay pelted the windshield. The snow flew sideways, as if someone had tipped the world.

Barns and ranch houses gave over to businesses as I drove into town. A single traffic light swayed forlornly above the empty street. I drove past a dry goods store, a saddle shop, and a single-marquee theater, all with *Closed Please Come Again* signs in the windows. Near the end of the block, red neon blinked through the snow. A grinning cowboy became visible, holding aloft a flashing beer stein.

The Pint and Pecker. The bar where Roald had seen skinheads and bikers comingling over drinks.

I slowed. The parking lot held four pickups and a rust-eaten van. As I rolled by, another car became visible, tucked halfway into the alley behind the lot. I touched the brakes, craned my neck. A cherry-red muscle car, all but lost to the alley and the snow.

Gentry's car.

"Jesus," I whispered.

On the other side of the intersection, I pulled to the curb. I called Morgan County Dispatch and learned that the lone officer on duty, Officer Markusson, was handling a domestic dispute. I identified myself and explained I was in Wiggins hunting a suspect. The dispatcher promised to put Markusson in touch with me as soon as he became available.

After we hung up, I considered calling the sheriff's office. I had no idea what I might be walking into. But a vision of Thomas Brown's tortured body put aside all thought of calling the cavalry. The kind of help the deputies would provide—the full-frontal assault kind—would be just as likely to get Gentry killed as rescued. It was how Merkel and his gang operated—kill the prisoners before you go down yourself.

I tried Cohen once more. When his phone went to voicemail again, I left him another message. I summarized my findings and said I believed Melody Weber was our killer. I told him where I was and what I planned to do in order to find Liz and Gentry and get them out of there. I told him I'd informed Morgan County Dispatch of my presence, but that the Wiggins on-duty officer was unavailable for the moment.

Then I hung up, turned the Explorer around, and headed back toward The Pint and Pecker.

Coming from this direction, I had a better view of the parking lot. All of the vehicles save Gentry's and one other had Confederate flags in their rear windows. The other exception to the southern supremacy rule was a blue Dodge Ram pickup with a *God and Country Will Prevail* bumper sticker.

Nik's truck.

He'd known right where to find the bastards.

I pulled into the parking lot, backed into a spot around the corner from the door, and took a quick minute to study the place. The Pint and Pecker looked to be an 1800s holdout from the days when Wiggins was established as a Denver Pacific railroad depot. One-story, built of peeling timber planks, with a pair of dusty windows set on either side of the front door. No other windows that I could see. A fence ran around the back of the property.

I slipped Clyde's Kevlar on over his halter, put my own vest on under my coat, and racked a round into the chamber of the Glock before returning it to the holster on my belt. I slid Sarge's Colt into my thigh holster.

Clyde and I stepped out into the storm's rage.

Eyes narrowed against the snow, we moved rapidly along the fence until we came to a gate. It was unlocked, and we slipped into a back patio area of maybe fifty square yards. A door led from the patio into the bar.

I gave Clyde the forward signal, and he and I made a dash for the door. Once there, we stopped, and I pressed against the warped wall, listening.

From inside came voices. Shouting. Angry. I reached over and tested the door. The knob turned easily. I peered in at a dimly lit hallway. Empty. Clyde and I slipped inside along with a confetti of snow, and I eased the door shut behind us. Immediately, I dropped to a crouch and downed Clyde next to me. I unholstered the Colt.

Voices fell like hammers from the front of the building, rising up and down with the tempo of the argument. Nik's voice carried above the others. Deep. Reasonable. Eerily calm in the way Nik had when the odds were stacked against him. For the moment, he had the upper hand. But I heard what probably no one else could—the thread of panic in his voice. He hadn't found Gentry yet.

Thirty seconds passed while my eyes adjusted to the gloom. The hallway was twenty feet long, with two doors leading to bathrooms and a third that said *Employees Only*. I signaled to Clyde and we went quickly down the hall. It took only a few seconds to clear each bathroom. The door marked *Employees Only* was locked.

Clyde and I reached the doorway into the main room and peered out.

Dark walls, dim lights, and a wooden floor dusty with crushed peanut shells. The tinted windows let in only a suggestion of daylight. The bar ran the length of the room to my left. A pool table and a series of two- and four-tops filled the remainder of the space.

Nik stood in the center of the room next to an overturned table. He had a semiautomatic rifle aimed at a skinhead in a leather jacket and heavy boots. The man had his hands up and was shouting at Nik.

"You are a stupid motherfucker," and "I don't know your son," and "Get the fuck out of my face."

Shit like that. He looked like he could keep it up for a while.

Behind him stood three of his pals, their hands at their sides, quiet. Too quiet. I looked for weapons, didn't see any. Guys probably hadn't figured on being disturbed in their home turf and had left the heavy artillery somewhere. But I was willing to bet they had knives stashed in their boots. Maybe handguns.

The bartender, judging by his white apron and the towel slung over his shoulder, stood in front of the bar with his arms folded. Well over six feet, with a shaved head, a swastika tattoo, and an expression of utter calm.

Which got me worried. Either he didn't care if anyone got shot, or he had a backup plan.

He looked like a man who always had a plan.

Next to me Clyde whipped around, hackles raised. I spun on my heel.

A man was just coming out of the employees' door. His eyes widened in alarm when he saw me, and I raised the Colt.

He opened his mouth, and I swung the barrel toward his face.

"Don't," I said softly.

He closed his mouth. I recognized him now. The tattooed kid I'd seen standing by my truck at Hogan's Alley back before all of this began.

With Clyde keeping watch, I stepped past the kid, hooked my arm around his neck, and held the gun to his head. The weight of the gun made my arm shake.

"Let's go," I said.

Together we shuffled to the doorway.

The bartender had gone behind the bar and was just coming back around with a shotgun.

I shoved the kid into the room, sent him sprawling into a row of barstools. The stools went down with a series of rattling clangs.

"Denver Pacific Railway Police!" I shouted at the barkeep. "Drop your weapon!"

The man froze with the shotgun half raised.

"Drop it now or I will drop you."

I watched in his eyes as he weighed the odds. A shotgun versus the Colt. I itched for him to go for it. But whatever he saw in my expression convinced him to do as I ordered. He lowered the gun.

"Set it on the floor. Good. Now kick it to me."

The shotgun came spinning in my direction. "Lace your hands behind your head."

"Good to see you, Sydney Rose." Nik. Still calm.

I didn't take my eyes off the bartender and the kid. "Where's Gentry?"

"That's what we're working on."

I kicked the bartender's shotgun down the hallway.

"Move," I told the barkeep and the kid, who was thrashing around in the tangle of stools. I gestured with the gun toward the center of the room where Nik had corralled the others.

Scowling, teeth clenched—the barkeep genuinely pissed, the kid looking more like he was trying to play the part—they obeyed. When they'd joined the others, I ordered all six men to their knees with their ankles crossed and their hands laced behind their heads. Clyde and I stood behind them.

"Bastards have Gentry," Nik said to me. "They're going to kill him if we can't find where they've taken him."

"You, barkeep," I said.

The bartender looked over his shoulder at me. "What, bitch?"

I pointed the .45. "Where's Gentry Lasko?"

"The traitor?" He locked his eyes on mine, drew back his head, and spit.

Sometimes your worst self is your best self. Sometimes not. I swung the gun into his jaw. The bone fractured with a loud snap.

The bartender and the kid started screaming at the same time.

"Shut up!" I moved the Colt toward the kid, who went silent. He stared at me, the whites of his eyes glowing in the gloom, lips back in a grimace of fear. Beads of sweat stood at his hairline.

He couldn't be past twenty or twenty-one, skinny as a rail. His ears stood out from his shaved head like the handles on a water pitcher. The tattoos made him look like a kid dressed for Halloween.

The bartender's sobs filled the silence.

"That was me being nice," I said. "I'm done with nice. Where is Gentry?"

"Tell her and you're a dead man, Jimmy," one of the skinheads growled.

"Don't tell me and you're still a dead man." I hefted the .45 and peered at Jimmy through the sights. "It'll just happen sooner."

"At the camp," Jimmy wailed. "They have him at the old Boedeker homestead near the tracks."

"What about Melody and her little girl?"

"Yeah," said the kid. "Yeah, they're there, too. I seen 'em."

Clyde growled a sudden warning and darted forward. I glimpsed a blur of movement as one of the skinheads unhooked his ankles and yanked a pistol free of his boot. I downed Clyde with a shout, and Nik's shot caught the man in the chest; the skinhead's back erupted in a spray of blood and tissue as the bullet exited.

Now the other three were coming up, weapons appearing in their hands as if magicked there. I took one man out with a round to the head. Nik fired on the other two in rapid succession. All three crumpled to the floor next to the first guy and lay silent, their blood soaking into the litter of peanut shells.

The echoes from the gunfire died away. I lowered my gun and stared at the dead men through the gentle float of dust.

"Four down," Nik said.

I looked over at the bartender and Jimmy, both of them still on their knees. The bartender, a shade paler than white, crumpled at the waist, grabbing for the nearest table. Nik spun and fired. The back of the barkeep's head exploded onto Jimmy.

Jimmy's shrieks sounded like the up-and-down wail of a siren.

"What the hell!" I yelled at Nik. "Why'd you do that?"

Calmly Nik walked to the table and kicked it over. A holster was fixed to the table's underside, the butt of a revolver clearly visible.

"Assholes like him always have a backup plan, Sydney Rose. Don't you forget that."

"You didn't have to shoot him."

"Yes," Nik said, his eyes a cold weight on me, "I did."

Something floated free inside of me, a tether cutting loose. As if by accepting Nik's words, all the principles I held no longer weighed me down.

"Get up," I told Jimmy, who was shaking like he'd grabbed hold of a live wire. "You're going to show us how to get there."

Outside, snow was coming so fast and thick, carried on the wind's banshee wail, that I couldn't keep my head up without being blinded. I insisted we take my truck, which had better traction than Nik's pickup. Nik kept the rifle on the kid while the two of them climbed into the backseat. I settled Clyde in the front, did a quick check to make sure he hadn't been struck by any shrapnel, then walked around to the driver's side, clearing windows as I went. In the cab, I started the wipers and the defroster. Nik snugged the rifle between him and the door and pulled out his service revolver. He shoved the barrel into the kid's side.

The kid didn't respond. Gore-spattered and pale, he gazed at nothing.

"Which direction?" I asked.

Nothing.

"Jimmy!"

He came back with a shudder.

"Left out of the parking lot," he said. "There's a road a mile east of town, goes south toward the tracks."

As I drove along Main Street, my headset vibrated. I glanced at the display on my phone. Cohen, finally calling me back. I debated, then returned the phone to my pocket. He was sixty-six miles away in Denver, on the far end of a killer storm.

No help to me now.

After the town fell behind us, the kid started to come to life a little. He craned his neck, trying to see through the falling snow.

"Drive faster," Nik told me.

I obeyed, fighting the Ford Explorer as if it were a roped bull. The road had been cleared after the last storm, the snow piled high on either side. But already another six inches had fallen on top of this morning's sleet, and the highway was an ice rink.

"What's the plan?" Nik asked the kid.

"Plan?"

Nik dug the barrel in. "What is it you assholes mean to do with my son?"

Jimmy moaned. "Shit, I didn't know he was your son. They told me he was a traitor. That he was gonna turn in Whip and me and everyone."

"So you figured on killing him," Nik said.

A quick glance in the rearview showed Jimmy's face going even whiter beneath the tattoos and the blood.

"Not me," he said. "I didn't plan any of this. It's not like I got a say in anything. I'm only a soldier. I just know they're planning something special."

"Special because it's February?" I asked. "Or because of who he is?"

The kid gave me an appraising look, like maybe I wasn't so stupid after all. "Both. February's when the Nazis rose in Germany. Back, you know, a long time ago. Whip could tell you when. That's how he got his name. 'Cause he's, you know, whip smart."

"That's why Jazmine Brown was killed in February?"

"Who?"

"Little black girl your buddies killed a decade ago."

The kid shrugged. "I dunno. We off someone every February."

Nik raised his revolver as if he meant to smack the kid.

"We need him cooperative," I said.

Grudgingly, Nik lowered the gun.

"Every single year?" I said to the kid.

The kid, to his credit, looked miserable. Although it probably had more to do with fear than a sudden conscience. "Yeah. A sacrifice to the trains. Just like the trains that took the Jews to the camps. Nazis and trains go together, you know? Usually we just push them off somewhere. Leave them for the animals. But this guy, this—" Jimmy glanced nervously at Nik. "The guy this year is special because he's worse than a Jew or a nigger. He's a traitor."

"How so?"

"He was working with that woman, the kindhearted woman, to get everyone to confess. Whip was hot for her, and I think she'd just about convinced him to go to the cops. But then Petes and Frankie reminded him: you don't betray the brotherhood. Especially not for some bitch."

"Isn't Whip the leader?" I asked.

"Even Hitler had Goebbels," Jimmy said. He'd obviously heard it a few times.

"How do they plan to kill my son?" Nik asked.

Jimmy glanced at Nik and hunched his shoulders. His knees jiggled. "They're gonna put him on the bridge over the canyon, chain him to one of the ties. They got a place where after the train hits him, he'll go flying off the tracks. But the chain, see, it'll keep him hanging off the bridge for everyone to see. Like a message. You don't betray the brotherhood."

The canyon. Devil's Gulch. A deep crevasse carved out of sandstone. I remembered it now from a comment made by one of the train crews. The tracks crossed over the gorge on a fifty-foot-high trestle, and the crew had to make sure to slow down before they hit the curve.

Ten to one, the ravine was where Jazmine's body lay. A lonely, broken thing at the bottom of the world.

"After that," Jimmy was saying, "we're clearing out. Whip says we're done with this place. He's found somewhere better."

"When are you putting my son on the tracks?" Nik asked.

Jimmy's knees jittered like machine-gun fire. "Tonight."

Nik looked like a bull tapped with an electric prod.

The kid glanced at him. "He won't know anything. They're getting him drunk. On account that, you know, he used to be one of us."

"We'll find him, Nik," I said. "We'll get him out."

"How?" he asked.

"What was your plan when you walked into The Pint and Pecker?"

"I was winging it."

"You want to call the sheriff?"

331

"What can they do?" His eyes met mine in the mirror. "Leave them for cleanup. Makes more sense to try and stop the train."

I pulled out my phone. One bar. I tried it anyway, hoping to reach the train dispatch in Fort Worth. Nothing but dead air. I didn't bother yet with trying to raise the crew on my railroad portable. The train wasn't in range.

When we were five miles east of Wiggins, the kid said, "The place is coming up. There'll be some trees and a fence with a gate."

Nik's finger went into the trigger guard. "Better get us there soon."

"There it is!" the kid yelled at the same time I spotted a clump of naked cottonwoods and a barbed wire fence.

I braked, skidded, then eased off the road.

Someone had propped the gate open; a heavy-duty combination padlock dangled uselessly off the latch. Beyond the fence, a narrow road curved south, away from the highway, winding upward into a series of low hills. Snow was starting to fill a set of tire tracks on the other side of the fence.

"You guys usually leave the gate open?" I asked Jimmy.

"Sometimes. When we know we got guys coming."

I put the truck in gear. "How far to the camp?"

"Three miles or so," Jimmy said. "Camp is right next to the tracks. There's a couple of old houses there from when that pioneer, Boedeker, used to ranch out here. But we sleep in the trailers."

On the other side of the fence, the snow was soft. The Explorer fishtailed a moment before finding traction. "How many trailers?"

"Seven. No, eight. Three for us, the rest for our stuff."

"And how many skinheads?"

The kid looked up and to his left, a sure sign he was preparing to lie.

"The truth," I said, "or Nik will hurt you."

He flushed. "Twelve. Thirteen with me."

"There a lookout nearby?"

"In weather like this? Anyway, that's what the gate's for." The kid snorted at the idea. Dumbest thing he'd heard all day, posting a lookout.

One point lost by the white-supremacist team.

I squinted through the windshield. The windows kept fogging and the wipers flailed against the snow. It felt just like the war days, rolling in for the bodies after the bombers had done their work, struggling to see through a sandstorm and praying the insurgents had all gone home. Hoping that what you found wouldn't be so god-awful that you'd lose what little breakfast you'd managed to eat.

With that memory, sweat beaded under my hat. I white-knuckled the wheel as my gut became a mess of sick energy. In the seat beside me, Clyde sat tense as an electric wire, humming with nerves.

I met Jimmy's eyes. "Where are they holding Gentry?"

"Trailer closest to the tracks."

"Is he tied up?"

"They got a manacle on his leg."

"Where's the key?"

"I dunno. The head guys like Whip carry a whole ring of keys. Must be one of those."

After two miles, the road narrowed to a track. Another half mile and it telescoped into a bumpy rut. The Explorer bounced and skittered.

I looked at my cell phone. No bars.

Nik pulled out his railroad portable.

"Senior agent DPC to westbound at Fort Morgan. Over."

Static.

He looked at me. "You got the train symbol?"

I'd checked earlier. "It's the Z train, Nik."

"Fuck me," he said.

A Z train is a high-priority run. This one was coming out of Chicago. It would be running fast, the proverbial bat out of hell, indifferent to the storm and caring only about velocity.

Nik hit push-to-talk. "Senior special agent DPC to Z-CHODEN5 22B."

All that came back was a burst of static.

Nik hit the PTT switch again, repeated his request. Nothing.

We got another quarter of a mile before the Explorer hit a pocket of deeper snow and skewed sideways. The passenger-side tires dropped off the road and the hood nosed into a snowdrift. I put the four-wheel in low and rocked the truck back and forth, trying to get the spinning tires to bite. I turned the wheel and tried again. The engine whined and the truck lurched, but I couldn't make it climb out of the hole.

"I have a shovel," I said. "There's cardboard in the back."

Nik got out, walked around back then came to my window.

"You're locked in good," he said. "And we're sitting ducks here. How far have we come?"

"Almost three miles. Quarter of a mile left, maybe."

"We'll walk."

I turned off the engine and pocketed the keys. I found my hat and gloves, then I cuffed the kid's wrist to the door handle to keep him from trying to steal the truck. Or walking into the storm. I dropped an army blanket over his shoulders.

"You can't leave me here," he said. "I'll freeze to death."

"Sheriff's men'll be along one of these days. After the snow thaws, maybe."

"I'll be dead by then!"

"Won't break my heart," I said.

He gave me the bird. Just like old times.

When I stepped out, I sank into snow halfway up my shins. I opened the door for Clyde. He'd picked up on my worry, and now he leapt from the truck like a cannonball before plunging through snow to his stomach. He gave me a look like I could've warned him.

"Let's check things out, boy."

We scrambled away from the truck and back onto the access road where the wind had swept the snow into hard drifts. Nik joined us, and we did a three-sixty scope of the area.

Not much to see. The snow had swallowed the horizon and rendered the hills into two-dimensional cutouts. A nearby clump of trees rattled like bones. The tire tracks we'd been following when we came in had disappeared. Our own tracks were filling fast.

"Thirteen with the kid," I said, thinking out loud.

Nik and I exchanged glances.

"Nothing for it," he said.

We returned to the truck and loaded up what we needed and could carry—weapons, radios, extra ammo, a flashlight and binoculars, and a compass. My phone in case we hit a sweet spot. I checked everything on my duty belt to make sure nothing had rattled loose, and we started walking south along the road.

Behind us, the kid shouted through the glass, his voice hollow with helpless fury.

I gave him the finger. Seemed only right.

CHAPTER 25

On my third day in Iraq, a lieutenant said to me: "If
there's no light to be had, immerse yourself in darkness."
"What does that mean exactly, sir?" I asked him.
"It means to hell with being a hero. To hell with worry-
ing about who's innocent and who isn't. Worrying whether the
guy's got a bomb or a bag of plums. It's your job, Marine, to
stay alive. If that means getting comfortable with your inner
darkness, then that's what you do."
—Sydney Parnell. Personal journal.

We'd gone only a short way through softening light when Clyde
dropped back beside me and pushed my leg. He must have alerted,
and I hadn't seen him in the snow.

I dropped into a crouch and Nik followed suit. Snow whipped into
my eyes, pelted the back of my neck. I tugged up the collar of my coat
and tried to see and hear anything more than ten feet away.

Then the wind shifted, and I caught it. The thrum of an engine
idling. Accompanying that, a faint ping like a door alarm.

I crab-walked to Nik and told him what I'd heard. He slung his rifle
to the front, and we eased around the bend between the hills.

Perpendicular across the road so that it blocked both entrance and
escape, a Wiggins police SUV idled, its headlights drilling twin holes

through the fog of snowfall. Exhaust streamed from the tailpipe, a gray cloud chuffing into the air. A dome light glowed feebly in the cab. On the far side, the driver's door was open, the alarm chiming.

There wasn't a soul in sight.

I pulled my Glock and told Nik to keep us covered while Clyde and I approached. Clyde let me know with lowered ears and tail that he didn't much care for whatever waited on the far side. He wasn't alarmed. Just unhappy.

A bad feeling wormed into my gut.

We circled around the rear of the cruiser and approached the open door.

The driver, a thirty-something man in a blue Wiggins Police Department parka, lay on his back, his spine arched over the console, his booted feet still tucked in the well beneath the steering column. The fingers of his right hand were curled around the radio mic. His death-white face was turned toward the dash, sightless eyes staring at nothing. A single bullet hole oozed blood from his temple.

Snow flurried in and settled along the man's feet and thighs. The wind tugged at his hair and coat. He hadn't been dead long.

I could just make out his badge through a gap in his coat. Patrol Officer Markusson. Maybe he'd seen the skinheads in town acting suspicious and followed them. Maybe the domestic call had been a ploy to lure him out. Either way, whoever was waiting for him at home—a girlfriend or wife, kids or parents—would wait forever.

I pressed my hands against his cruiser and closed my eyes. Mentally, I closed the wound in Markusson's temple. Returned life to his eyes. Breathed air into his lungs as he sat up.

Nik shouted over the wind. "They shot out the radio, too. No calling the posse. Let's go, Sydney Rose."

I touched my heart. "I'll hold you here," I whispered to Markusson. Then I opened my eyes and pushed away from the truck. "I'm coming."

Fifty yards past Markusson's patrol unit, Clyde's ears pricked and once more we slowed our pace.

Soon I heard what Clyde had—a rhythmic, metallic clanging. We came upon a Confederate flag whipping atop a pole. Just beyond, a barbed wire fence ran along the ground where the hills channeled into a narrow vale. We slogged up the nearest hill and dropped to our stomachs at the top. I pulled out the binoculars and propped myself on one elbow, using my other arm to shield the lenses.

The snow was too thick for me to see much. Eight broken-down trailers made a sprawling U-shape around a cluster of tumbledown buildings. Three pickups and an SUV sat parked near the gate; the beds of the trucks were covered with blue tarps. One of the trucks had an empty flatbed hitched to it. A snow-covered picnic table and a thrown-together outhouse completed the living quarters.

The only other signs of life were a pair of dogs roped up and howling forlornly and the rattle of a generator.

Nice advertisement for world domination.

"See anything?" Nik asked.

I kept scanning and was rewarded when a man appeared from behind one of the trailers.

"They've got a sentry. He's circling away from us, moving toward the south end of the camp." I used my sleeve to wipe moisture off the lenses and looked again. "He's taken a post on the southeast side of camp facing the train tracks."

I angled the binoculars beyond the trailers.

At the top of a rise on the other side of the camp, a wooden trestle hung against the snow-gray sky like the masts of a ghost ship. The bridge spanned a quarter mile and rode fifty feet over the abyss. The far side of Devil's Gulch winked in and out, a dark slash of rock in the swirling snow.

Off to the left, on the steep rise leading to the trestle, a cluster of lights moved up the hillside, weaving in and out among the rocks. I tightened the focus.

"A group of men heading up the hill toward the bridge," I said. "I count eight. Carrying rifles, I think. Hard to tell. They're wearing headlamps."

"Gentry?"

I squinted through the snow and the failing light until my head hurt. "I can't tell."

I passed the binoculars to Nik.

"Looks like they've got someone," he said after a moment. "But I can't be sure it's Gentry. Snow's too thick, and those rocks are giving them cover."

When he lowered the glasses, the look on his face made me glad he was on my side.

"I'll take out the sentry and head up the hill after the others," he said. "You clear those trailers. Make sure Gentry's not there. If the kid wasn't lying, should be three men down there."

Along with a murderess. And a child.

"Figure he was lying," Nik added.

I nodded, but it must not have looked convincing. The image of the dead patrolman kept floating in front of my eyes.

"What if I find Gentry?" I asked.

"Stay with him. I'll be back when I finish with the others." Nik gripped my arm, put his face close to mine. "You have to kill whoever's in camp, Sydney Rose. And fast, before they can get word to the group on the hill. Anyone left alive will come after us or notify the others. If we die, Gentry dies, too."

"The guys you're following will hear the gunshots."

"They won't know for sure what's happening. Assholes probably shoot off guns every time they take a shit. If they send someone to investigate, I'll be ready."

I nodded. Tried to ignore the fist clenching my stomach. It had been like this every time I went outside the wire. A shit-my-pants moment when I was sure I'd curl up in a ball on the ground and refuse to move.

In a shimmer of sudden light, Elise appeared behind Nik. Her face was worried, her arms crossed protectively over her breasts. As if she didn't like Nik's plan any better than I did.

Nik's voice pulled me back, his fingers digging into my arm. "You can't hesitate. You can't be soft. These guys are child killers. Cop killers. You understand?"

The world rushed in with a pop. My heart rate soared and my lungs expanded with an overdose of oxygen.

"I'm on it," I said.

He released my arm.

"Shoot to kill," he said, and disappeared with a long loping run down the southern slope of the hill. Clyde and I followed in the failing light, hurrying after Elise's ghost.

At the edge of the camp, she vanished.

CHAPTER 26

Bottom line, morality is different in war. And war doesn't always take place on a battlefield.
                                    —*Sydney Parnell, ENGL 0208,*
                                            Psychology of Combat

We moved fast.

The first trailer Clyde and I hit was padlocked shut. A smell like paint thinner oozed from the cracks. A quick shine of my flashlight through the window revealed tables laden with beakers, CorningWare, rubber tubing, large plastic tubs, and bottles of ammonia.

The next two trailers, also padlocked shut, held weapons, forty-pound bags of fertilizer, and gasoline cans. Empty boxes cluttered the floor and two loaded dollies stood near the door. Preparations for moving out.

We slogged through the snow toward the southernmost trailers and almost tripped over the body of the sentry I'd spotted through the binoculars. Nik had taken his rifle and left him on his back, throat cut.

I slowed as I approached the fourth trailer where a muffled diesel generator hummed. Light shone through partially drawn blinds, and men's voices rose and fell from within. Because of the dogs at the north end, I downed Clyde while I completed a circuit of the camp. The dogs went silent as I approached, then started up again. No one responded. Maybe none of them had read about the boy who cried wolf.

My reconnaissance yielded four more trailers, dark and empty, and two additional generators, both silent. Either the kid had been lying about Melody and Liz, or they were in the fourth trailer with the men. If Gentry was still here, he'd be in that trailer as well. The one closest to the tracks, Jimmy had said.

Back with Clyde, I stood in the snowfall and listened. With the howling of the wind, I couldn't make out the men's words. Couldn't tell if there were two men inside or five or seven.

I cocked my head at a sudden silence behind me. The dogs had stopped barking. I pulled the Colt free of its holster and wrapped both hands around the grip as two shapes hurtled out of the darkness trailing leads of rope.

The dogs separated when they hit the light spilling from the trailer windows; one launched itself toward Clyde, who leapt silently to meet it.

The second came for me.

I shot it through the chest and spun for the other dog. It had pulled away from Clyde, its black lips slicked back from long teeth, its haunches coiled for a second attack.

"*Steht noch!*" I yelled at Clyde. *Stand still!*

My second shot hit the dog in its hip. It yelped and pitched onto its side.

A man's voice cut through the ringing echo of gunfire. "What the hell you doing?"

I whirled to find the trailer door open and a man standing outside in the snow. He held an AR-15, the butt of the rifle tight against his shoulder as he stared down the barrel at me. A second man stood on the stairs, also holding an assault rifle.

"Hold off, Petes," said the man on the stairs. "Look. It's a woman."

Petes. The escapee from the shootout at Melody's house.

"A woman?" Petes lowered the rifle barrel. "What the hell you doing out here?"

"Them dogs must've broke their ropes," said the man on the stairs. "That's pretty good shooting, lady. Hell, I've been wanting to shoot those fuckers myself. They don't never shut up."

I tried to see into Petes's eyes, looking for evil. Looking for anything that said it was okay to put him down in cold blood.

But he was a cutout against the trailer lights, his eyes a riddle.

Nik's voice. *You have to kill them.*

I raised my gun and shouted.

"Special Agent Parnell with Denver Pacific! We've got your camp surrounded. Drop your weapons."

Petes's barrel came swinging back up.

"Fuck that," he said.

We fired at the same time. My shot punched a hole through his forehead. Petes folded at the waist and dropped hard, like a man trying to sit without a chair. The second skinhead had his gun partway up when Clyde flew out of the dark and knocked him back. Their combined weight carried them into the trailer's side. A vicious crack sounded as the man's skull hit metal. One glance at his face told me he wouldn't be getting up again.

I dashed to the trailer wall and flattened myself against it as a third man appeared in the doorway. He fired wildly into the dark. The Colt blew the side of his head off. His body hit the door frame and tumbled down the stairs.

I whistled to Clyde, shoved past the third man's body, and barged hard into the trailer, gun extended, shouting, "Hands up!"

Melody Weber stood near a curtained bunk bed at the far end of the single-room trailer, her hands raised high. When she realized I was the one who'd just shot her pals, her expression changed to relief. She started to lower her hands.

"Keep them up," I said, angling myself so I could see both her and the front door.

Her hands rose. "They've got Gentry," she said. "Up on the bridge. They're gonna kill him."

"Like you killed Elise?"

Hurt rose in her eyes like floodwater. She shook her head wildly. "I didn't. It wasn't me."

"Whoever is behind that curtain," I said, "I've got a .45 aimed right at you. Open the curtain and show me your hands."

"It's Liz," Melody said.

Hating it, I kept my voice hard. "Open the curtain. *Now*."

"I'll do it," Melody said.

"Don't move a fucking inch," I told her.

"Go ahead, Lizzie," Melody said. "Open the curtain. It's the nice Agent Parnell."

I'm sure we both enjoyed the irony of that.

A small hand grabbed the end of the curtain and dragged it open. Liz Weber looked out at me with terrified eyes. Her gaze took in first the gun and then the rest of me, no doubt seeing the blood on my face and coat from the men I'd just killed.

"I'm sorry, Liz," I whispered. I swung the gun back to Melody. "They took Gentry?"

She nodded. "To the bridge."

Liz's eyes locked on Clyde. She rolled out of the bunk bed and skirted past me to throw her arms around him.

"Agent Parnell—" Melody started.

"Keep your hands up." I became aware of a deep burn in my left arm. I glanced down and saw a hole in the sleeve.

"Mommy didn't do it," Liz said to Clyde.

I squatted next to her. "What, sweetie?"

"It wasn't Mommy who hurt Elise. It was the bad man."

The world went a little sideways. "Whip?"

The little girl shook her head. She was crying now, her face buried deep in Clyde's fur, her arms in a stranglehold around his neck. I touched her shoulder, felt her bones like those of a bird's beneath her pale skin. Her hair was a rat's nest. The faint scent of urine rose from her cheap nightgown.

I wanted to cry, too.

Outside, from far away, a shot rang out. Liz and I both flinched. Nik, I hoped, catching up to the skinheads.

"Who told you that, Liz? About the bad man?"

"We saw him."

I lifted my eyes to Melody, wondering if it could be true.

"Who, then?" I asked her.

"I don't know," Melody said. "We'd just gotten there, was standing on the porch. It was dark with only the light from the house. All I could see was his outline when he come outside. He was big."

"I know you were in Elise's apartment, Melody. Your coat was there."

Her chin came up. "It's true I went in, but I didn't kill her! After the man left, Liz and me went up to her place. I took off my coat before we knew Elise was dead in her bedroom. After I found her, I was scared. I sure wasn't thinking about my coat."

I stood and tightened my grip on the gun. "Don't you lie to protect Whip."

"I won't never protect Whip again. Not after all the hurting he did to Gentry." Fire entered her pale eyes. "Tonight he hit Liz. You was right about him. But he didn't kill Elise."

The clock was ticking. I would process Gentry's and Liz's pain later.

"Tell me about the man," I said. "Quickly."

"We saw a light moving in Elise's room as we come up to the house, so we hid on the porch. After the man left, we let ourselves in. Elise's bedroom door was closed, so I poured us some milk. The wind was rattling her door like her window was open, which was weird, it being so cold that night. We waited maybe fifteen minutes, then I knocked on her door. Elise was all—you know. I didn't know what to do. I worried the police might think it was me. So I called Whip and he come over. He thought I'd done it. On account of how he felt about her. He was really mad. But he went into her room and put some hobo beads there, said it would protect me. Said it would make the police think someone else had been there. Then we left."

Which didn't exactly exonerate Whip. And Melody could be lying about all of it. But I would leave that for later, too. For the moment, she had nowhere to go. Not in a blizzard with the road blocked by Markusson's cruiser.

I holstered the gun. "I'm going after Gentry. You and Liz stay inside the trailer. Lock the door and don't let anyone in until the sheriff gets here."

She looked like she'd throw up. "Whip'll kill you. Then what's gonna happen to me and Liz?"

"Maybe you should spend the time praying it goes the other way."

I took a rifle from the rack over the sink, checked that it was loaded, and slung it over my shoulder. Then I tried again to raise the train crew on my portable. Still out of range. Or maybe it was the weather and the hills and the gorge. Maybe I'd never get through. Not until it was too late to matter.

I stopped with my eyes on Clyde. Liz clung to him as if she'd just fallen off the *Titanic*, and he was her lifeboat. Which wasn't far off the mark, I figured.

For just a moment, I considered leaving him with her. I'd made a promise to Dougie to protect him, not walk him into a possible ambush. But I couldn't honor a promise if it meant treating Clyde like a lapdog. Clyde's work was his life.

Dougie would understand.

"I have to take Clyde," I told Liz gently. "He's my partner."

She dropped her arms and backed away without any argument. If there was one thing Liz had learned in her young life, it was that fighting back bought you nothing but a split lip or a black eye.

"I'll bring him to see you again," I said. "I promise."

She gave me a small smile. "'kay."

As Clyde and I headed toward the door, her voice made me turn.

"The bad man said something. On the porch. Like he was talking to himself."

"What, Liz? What did he say?"

"I think he was sick. Like I get sometimes."

"Was he coughing?"

She shook her head. "He said he couldn't breathe."

Outside, the snow had begun to tire. Slow, fat flakes swirled on the wind. A full moon glowed behind a thin haze of clouds. I could just make out the shape of the Boedeker home in the distance, leaning like a drunk in the silver light.

Clyde and I stepped around the men and dogs I'd shot. I didn't look at the dead. I don't think Clyde did, either.

The lights were gone from the hillside leading up along the gorge to the trestle. With Nik's first shot, I'm sure the skinheads had switched off their headlamps. No way to know what they'd done after that. If they'd kept going or hidden themselves or turned around. Together Clyde and I hurried past the southernmost trailers and made our way toward the incline. The wind turned and blew hard at our backs, carrying our scent forward and bringing nothing back. Bad news. If someone lay in wait, Clyde wouldn't pick up their scent until we'd gone past them.

As we cleared the last of the encampment, the abyss curved in from the west. Dank, cold air rose from its depths. As if Devil's Gulch really was a passage to the underworld.

Up ahead, another shot rang out. The echoes rattled through the gorge. Far away, a coyote gave a yipping bark and fell silent.

Jimmy had proven true so far. He'd said there were twelve skinheads in camp. The guard was dead, as were my three. That left the eight we'd seen heading up toward the bridge with Gentry. If the two shots I'd heard had been Nik firing, then six remained. Nik didn't miss his shots.

I found Nik's second killing another hundred yards up the path. The man lay on the trail, eyes open to the sky, his throat blown open.

Moonlight turned his eyes to silver coins, made him both more and less than human. I'd seen so many like this in Iraq. Held them. Laid them in bags.

My stomach clenched. Five corpses in, the death fear hit with a sick flutter in my bowels. The heat of Iraq rose around me and I was back in the seven-ton, driving into a bombed-out wasteland. A desert Charon collecting the dead.

The panic drove me to my knees.

Clyde nudged me.

The Sir knelt by my ear.

Our men are in danger, Marine. Get the fuck up.

I got the fuck up.

Night resumed around me with the jitter of the winter wind. Clyde and I kept walking. We were close enough now to the bridge for me to see the rails gleaming in the moonlight. On either side of us rose a jumble of sandstone rocks. Some no higher than my shoulders. Others the size of a house.

The potential for ambush waited at every bend. But the knowledge of the coming train rode my thoughts like a knife blade. We went fast.

Another fifty yards, another dead man. This one with his throat smiling. Nik had been close enough to the group with Gentry not to risk a shot. Or maybe it was just that he was good with a knife.

Man's gotta breathe.

Maybe all of us were half crazy. All of us former Marines, soldiers, pilots. Maybe we all came back from our wars infected with something dark and secret. Something that multiplied in the fertile silence of our hushed hearts.

Clyde stopped so suddenly I almost tripped over him. I crouched and watched as he circled back the way we'd come then trotted forward again, nose to the ground and then up in the air as he worked to pull whatever scent had alerted him. But the wind scattered the scent cone, spread the molecules to nothing.

He trotted back down the trail, and I followed.

The trestle bridge grew larger, filling the southern horizon. To our west, the gorge released a thin, chill breath of ice. Unease pricked at my skin. I crouched again and downed Clyde next to me. I looked up and down the hillside. The wind dropped, and for a moment the entire world lay wrapped in silence, the night a velvet glove.

Beside me, Clyde shivered. I felt it, too. A baleful presence. Someone nearby, their eyes on our skin.

I groped for Clyde's lead, intending to back us off the trail.

A burst of light hit my face. I pushed Clyde hard, trying to knock him back into the darkness.

His feet scrabbled on the icy ground and then he whirled and leapt into the space in front of me, a furious growl in his throat.

"Clyde!"

There came the flat report of a gunshot, and Clyde went down.

I rose and tried to run to him, but there came another crack, and something slammed into my chest with the heft and speed of a man swinging a baseball bat.

My rifle skittered away as I fell, the pain in my chest burning through my lungs until no breath remained. I skidded along the snow-packed slope toward the abyss. My right foot caught on something; the sudden braking spun me around and shoved me against a rocky outcropping.

Clyde, I screamed without a voice. *Clyde!*

A figure appeared above me, silhouetted against the moon-hazed sky. A man, tall and lean. He flicked a light on my face then flicked it off again. In the darkness, his breath hit my skin like the scratch of wool.

He reached out a hand and felt under my coat. Found the vest.

"Well, well, well," he said.

You're not breathing, Parnell, said the Sir.

I'm goddamn trying, sir.

"The lady cop, riding to the rescue," the man said. "But who's going to rescue the lady cop?"

The Sir squatted next to me. *Get. Up.*

A trickle of air slid down my windpipe. "Clyde?"

"What's that?" asked the man. "You got something to say?"

The light returned to my face, panned down my inert body. A headlamp. This time I caught a glimpse of the man behind it.

Narrow face, high cheekbones, a domed forehead. The face that had stared at me from a piece of paper until I'd memorized every feature.

Alfred Merkel, aka Whip.

In person, he was more imposing than I'd imagined from the artist's sketch. Violence sizzled off him with a chained ferocity. Muscled beneath his camos, his bare head smooth, he sat on his heels and regarded me with the languid confidence of a predator. His gray eyes held glints of amber, like sparks off flint.

Score one for the Burned Man, giving this guy his licks.

The light returned to my face. "That your pal up there, picking off my men?"

"My dog," I whispered.

"That your dog I shot?" He hawked up phlegm, turned his head and spit. "Looks like the fucker's dead." He swiveled his gaze back to me. "Was supposed to be you."

My face and chest grew hot with rage and grief.

"I will put you down," I said. "For my dog."

"That right?"

"And for killing Elise." Testing him. Testing my own theories.

Whip's eyes went to slits. His breath hung in a cloud between us. He seemed to be thinking. Probably not something he was used to doing in a hurry. He reached into his boot, came back with a knife.

I pulled my thigh to my chest then shoved my foot into him with everything I had.

He flew backwards.

I scrabbled to get my feet under me, thinking I would kill him. Then I would go to Clyde and fix whatever was wrong. Because Clyde couldn't be dead.

I made it to a half crouch before Whip came at me, swinging the knife in an arc. I feinted to the right and, as he followed, made a quick jag to the left. My foot slipped on the snow and went out from under me. Desperately I threw myself forward, grasping for anything to stop my fall.

My hands found Whip's coat, yanked him close.

The abyss opened behind us.

CHAPTER 27

Nietzsche said that whoever fights monsters should be careful not to become one.
I say, sometimes that's all you've got.
—*Sydney Parnell. Personal journal.*

We hit, bounced, caught air, hit and bounced again. Even as we went, Whip was trying to get the knife into me. The blade was the only thing that caught the light as we hurtled into the dark.

I let go of him, tumbling end over end as I descended, careening off snow-covered rock faces and tree trunks in an oddly weightless flight, the heavy snow and gravity carrying me like a wave past anything that could hit me with enough force to stop my downward descent. I heard Sarge's gun go flying. A second later the radio broke away and smashed against a rock.

And then gravity was done with me. It fetched me up against the trestle's base and left me there, stunned and panting, flung like a doll on my back.

With a groan, I lifted my head.

A little way north, where the ravine dropped deeper, a small light shone. Whip's headlamp. I watched it long enough to see that it was moving, but I couldn't tell if it was approaching or receding.

I dropped my head back and closed my eyes.

I had not known how much of me belonged to Clyde, how much room he had claimed in my heart. He was the one good thing, the one *living* thing, that had come back with me from Iraq. Clyde had held me together as we shared our grief over Dougie, our relief at leaving the war zone, and eventually our sense of purpose—muted though it was—when we returned to work.

From somewhere down the canyon an owl hooted, a throaty roll like water spilling.

I opened my eyes and turned my head, staring into the narrow gash of Devil's Gorge where the moon managed only a frail light. A little larger now, Whip's light continued to bob and weave, a ghost light making its way through the underworld.

My body was so filled with pain that I could not separate the hurt within from that without. And I was tired. Tired in Cohen's way, tired with the weight that makes your bones two inches shorter. I was tired of killing. Tired of death. Exhausted from scraping up against the kind of hatred that makes a man slap a little girl, slaughter a woman, shoot a dog. All I wanted was to lie in the snow and the dark and think about Clyde and Dougie and Cohen until I ran out of thoughts. Ran out of feelings. Until the wind abraded my skin to nothing and I was only disarticulated bones.

Cue the Sir. He was supposed to be here, telling me to get on my feet. Telling me that fifty feet above me, important things were happening. Gentry might be dying. Nik might be dying.

Perhaps the Sir was afraid of heights.

The thought made me laugh. Deep, aching belly rolls that brought tears to my eyes until the laughter began to hitch and moan and turn to a wild weeping.

Then the Sir *was* there. He grabbed my hand, hauled me up. I bit off a scream as my left leg buckled and sent pain rocketing up my thigh. The pain in my wounded arm flared like a beacon. The Sir held me upright.

Not the Sir. Whip.

He bared his teeth and snarled at me through the blood that ran down his face. "Not that it's any of your fucking business. But I didn't kill Elise. I loved her. Don't you fucking hang her death on me."

He reached for my throat.

I yanked the Glock free, shoved it into Whip's stomach, and shot him.

He went down, hands tight to his belly, blinking up at me as if he couldn't figure out how a woman had gotten the upper hand.

"You cunt," he said.

Something inside me snapped, like an elastic band under too much strain.

I shoved Alfred Merkel down with my bad leg, bent painfully to pick up a rock, and slammed the rock into his face.

Once. "That's for Liz."

He shrieked.

Twice. Blood flew. "That's for Thomas Brown."

A third time. Bones broke. "That's for Jazmine."

By the time I hit him again, his face was no longer human.

"And that's for Clyde, you fucking piece of filth."

I heaved the rock away.

I guess I believed him about Elise.

Focus, I told myself. That train's still coming. Gentry.

Then Clyde.

I limped to the trestle, hoisted myself onto the base of the bridge, and ignored whatever I'd done to my knee as I hobbled to the nearest sway brace. I grabbed hold of the brace and crawled up the eighteen-inch-wide span of wood.

At the top of the first sway brace, I pulled myself onto the sill and grabbed hold of the next brace.

Old timber trestles like this one had been built in the 1800s. Many of them had been replaced with steel or concrete or buried in enough fill to support the tracks. But a few of these old bridges remained, a series of vertical posts braced on horizontal sills and supported by angled sway braces. As a kid I'd climbed one, when I was too stupid to know better.

The trestle creaked around me in the wind. I clung to the brace and hauled myself up its length. My knee shrieked with every movement. My hands turned numb as I struggled to grip the weathered wood. The wind tore my hat free and tossed it into the darkness, sending my hair whipping about my face.

But I'd found my rhythm. Reach, pull, drag. Reach, pull, drag.

Then my bad knee gave. My foot slipped off the brace, swung in the emptiness. Before I could bring it back up, I began sliding back down the timber I'd just climbed, gravity tipping my body toward Devil's Gulch.

Markusson's ghost nodded at me from one of the sills, his Wiggins police jacket flapping.

Panic later, he told me. *Panic kills.*

I grabbed for one of the posts as I went past. Dug in my fingers and jerked to a stop.

"Is that what happened to you?" I snarled at him.

But he was right.

I pulled my foot back onto the brace and kept working my way up as the moon slipped in and out of the clouds like a ship in stormy waves. I didn't look down. When my feet slid, I brought them back. When my hands slipped, I pressed my body against the brace. I didn't think about falling. I thought of Clyde, maybe still alive and waiting for me to fetch him home. Of Gentry, hurt, about to die.

And of Nik.

Liz's voice whispered in my ear. *He said he couldn't breathe.*

Nik. Who would do anything for his son.

◆ ◆ ◆

The wind told me when I was near the top, its fury unabated as I cleared the sides of the gorge. Now I could see the actual railway, a latticed span of wooden ties set against an insubstantial sky. A few more feet, then I grabbed one of the ties, hooked a leg up, and peered over the edge of the rails just as the moon went dark.

I strained to hear over the roar of the wind and was rewarded with the low rumble of men's voices not too far off. A chain clinked.

"Hurry up," said one of the men.

"I'm trying, goddammit," came the answer.

I hauled myself onto the bridge. I drew my pistol and inched forward on my elbows and knees.

A little farther on, the forms of men became visible—shadows hunkered on knees or flat on bellies. Someone coughed, closer than the men I'd spotted, and I froze. Only ten feet away, two men lay propped on their elbows, guns snugged close. The wind had kept them from hearing my approach. I pressed against the ties and listened to the roar of blood in my ears. I could shoot them both where they lay. But I wouldn't get off another shot before one of the other men found me.

I had no idea where Nik was. If he was still in the picture. If he was still alive.

One of the men near me shifted. "Asshole'll start firing again."

"He can't see us, you dumb fuck. Anyway, I think Ty got 'im."

From the east, a mournful whistle floated through the night. The 1740 freight to Denver approaching a crossroads near Wiggins. Which meant it wasn't far off.

The sound created a flurry of panic and swearing among the men on the bridge.

I inched backwards, swung my legs out over the edge until I felt the end cap beneath my feet. I climbed back down the brace, went twenty feet to my right, and climbed back up.

When I peered over again, I was looking right at the other three men.

"Leave him!" one of them was saying. "He's not gonna wake up. Just put him on the rail."

"Whip wants him to hang. After. Like a message."

"Oh, Jesus, fuck that. C'mon!"

Chains rattled. "Got it. Let's go."

A pair of feet came in my direction. I grabbed an ankle and yanked. The man screamed as he catapulted over the edge.

Four to go.

"What the hell?" someone said.

I shot another man then dropped below the level of the ties. Up above, the three remaining men unleashed a panicked volley of shots. Rifle fire broke and echoed, but none of it came my way. They must have figured my shots had come from Nik. Now they were aiming for wherever they thought he'd holed up.

The moon hit a stretch of clear sky, bouncing off the snow and turning night into day. A rifle opened up from the east. A man screamed and a body tipped over the edge.

Nik stopped firing. The echoes died away.

I peered over the edge. Nothing moved. I pulled myself onto the bridge, hoping Nik could see it was me. Three dead men lay on their backs nearby. I limped over to Gentry. He lay unmoving, pale as death. Both eyes were blackened, his nose broken, the left cheek crushed. Lips like pulpy melons. Beneath a light jacket, his dress shirt and slacks were black with blood.

I knelt and placed my ear near his mouth, heard his faint breath.

I touched his hair, the only part of him that wasn't hurt. "We'll get you out of here, Gentry. Nik and I."

He made no response.

They had trussed him like a pig. Ankles shackled with cuffs. His wrists likewise manacled. A chain ran from his ankles to his wrists then up past his head, yanking his hands to his face.

The end of the chain had been looped around the rail tie and pad-locked closed. I cursed myself for not searching Whip's pockets before I left him. I knelt on the tie and tried to get my fingers under the chain. But the metal had bitten into the wood, and Gentry's own weight held it taut.

Markusson's ghost appeared, sitting on the end of one of the ties, feet swinging over the abyss. Like he didn't have anything better to do.

I scrabbled back to Gentry and shoved him toward the edge, trying to ease the tension on the chain. Then back to the tie, tearing against the wood with my fingers. The panic now a full-blown monster.

The minutes raced past.

Panic kills, Markusson offered.

I pulled out the Glock and fired at the padlock. The slug smacked into the housing, but the latch stayed firm. I fired two more times. Nothing. Fired at the chain with the same result.

Nik's voice came from behind me. "Stand back."

I stepped away. Nik raised the AR-15 and fired. The housing shattered.

"We'd better hurry," he said. Deceptively calm.

With no time to do anything different, I gathered the chain and laid it on Gentry's chest. Gentry's body bounced over the rail as Nik pulled him away from the edge. I lifted Gentry under his arms while Nik grabbed his feet. We stepped over the bodies of the dead men and headed west, walking between the rails. As I stumbled backwards in the dark, stepping from one snow-covered tie to the next above the gorge, I willed myself to look only at my feet. The standard span from rail to rail, an exact four feet, eight and a half inches, felt no wider than my shoulders.

"Whip shot Clyde," I said.

"Move faster," was Nik's reply. He was breathing hard, a strange, high whistle running through each inhalation.

Man's gotta breathe.

I focused on my feet again. Images flipped through my mind like a series of photographs.

Elise's open window, her hair fluttering in the breeze.

Nik rolling down the kitchen window after I'd brought the news of Elise.

Nik ordering me away from Tucker so he could shoot him.

Nik sitting on the front porch, claiming he couldn't breathe in the house.

Nik, who knew where to find the skinheads. Because he'd known all along who they were, what they were up to.

Nik, who'd lied to protect his son ten years ago. Who would risk everything to keep him from going down for that crime. Nik, who must have believed what I could not. That Gentry had played a part in Jazmine's death.

His voice brought me back to the bridge. "Don't slow down, Sydney Rose."

Beyond him, the train's headlamp appeared, the locomotive ditch lights joining it to form a brilliant triangle that hung bodiless in the night.

Far to the north, sirens rose and fell. The cavalry at long last. The sheriff. Maybe Denver PD. Maybe Cohen was riding toward me. Maybe he had forgiven me.

Nik stumbled. Held on to Gentry's ankles. Steadied himself. His breathing sounded like he was sucking air through a straw.

"It was you," I whispered, even as I was thinking, *Deny it, Nik. Tell me I'm crazy.* "You killed Elise."

Nik gave another wheeze. "Don't you slow down."

I stepped to the next tie, and the next, the ten-and-a-half-inch gaps yawning over something deeper and darker than Devil's Gulch.

"You knew Rhodes was coming into town," I went on. "You knew he'd be the first person the police looked at. Having Whip throw down those beads was just a lucky break."

Tell me to go fuck myself, Nik.

Nik said, "A man—" *wheeze* "does—" *wheeze* "what he has to."

His confession struck with such force that had the words been physical, they would have ripped skin, smashed bone, crushed organs. They would have killed me.

"It's not true," I said. I'd gone mad, and Nik was humoring me.

He faltered. Righted himself. "She threw her life away. On those hobos. Would have thrown his away, too."

"You *loved* her," I cried.

"Had to choose. Between a lawyer and a waitress. Between a son and a niece."

"And she loved you." Just as I always had. Loved you beyond reason.

The lights behind Nik swelled like a trio of rising suns. Now I could hear the steady thrum of the train wheels, feel the vibration beneath my feet. The world disappearing in an onrush of steel.

"Keep moving." His voice held the first metal-bright thread of panic.

Nik had never let anything stand in his path. Not the jungles in 'Nam. Not the Viet Cong sniper who had shredded his leg. Not Gentry's attempt to join the skinheads, nor my sudden orphaning. And I'd loved him for it.

Ten feet along, Nik went down on one knee. His other foot dropped between the ties. As he fell, Gentry's ankles slipped from his hands.

"Keep going," he told me.

The light grew brighter. The wheels thundered.

Gritting my teeth against the pain, against the weight, I walked. Gentry's feet bounced and dragged along the ties, his heels catching between the spaces so that each time I had to yank him free.

When I looked up again, Nik had gained his knees.

"Nik!" I shouted.

"You and I are just alike, Sydney Rose. Damaged." He got one foot under him. Then the other. Came to a crouch. "But strong as hell, too. We do what we have to."

I reached the end of the bridge, hauled Gentry to the side. When I looked again, Nik was back on his knees. His shadow stretched across the ties.

I put everything I had in my voice. "Nik! Come on!"

The lights of the train formed a supernova, filling the horizon.

I stepped back toward the bridge. "You told me. Never leave a fallen soldier behind."

The engineer saw Nik and sounded his horn. The brakes gave a wailing cry, a high drilling sound like a thousand voices calling in pain.

"Unless they've gone bad," Nik said.

Or I think that's what he said. Metal shrieked around the curve of the bridge. Sparks boiled under the wheels as if the train was on fire. I threw myself off the tracks and covered Gentry's body with my own, wrapping my arms around him and squeezing my eyes shut as the train hurtled past, tugging at us with its slipstream.

The pain in my chest burst into flame, burning everything.

The end of the world.

CHAPTER 28

*Cops and soldiers. We have a moral code that is too lim-
ited for what we face in the street or on the battlefield. Serve
and protect. Defend with honor, courage, and commitment.*
    *But the lines aren't clearly drawn. The bad guys don't
wear signs. And all of us are only human.*
    —Sydney Parnell. Personal journal.

I spent three weeks in the hospital. The blows to my chest had caused an arrhythmia in the upper chamber of my heart, which the docs thought would resolve on its own if they could get everything else fixed. I had two broken ribs, numerous lacerations, some serious, and a handful of hairline fractures, including one in my skull. My patellar tendon was shredded, my left bicep torn. So while I healed, the docs kept me afloat on a sea of artificial calm. Probably a good thing, since around me the world had erupted in a flurry of investigations, accusations, turf battles, and finger-pointing.

Throughout the days and weeks after Cohen pulled Gentry and me off that hill, the sheriff and a team of forensics experts spent long hours sorting through the dead. The last body recovered by the forensics team was the skeleton of Jazmine Brown, her bones sifted so deep into the soil at the bottom of Devil's Gulch that she would likely never have been found if Elise hadn't started the investigation. The team found nine other bodies in the gorge, as yet unidentified. All were disarticulated, gnawed and scattered by scavengers. One they thought might belong to a hunter—a man who'd stumbled upon the other bodies and been condemned to join them.

No one could accuse Whip and his gang of sitting idle.

The sheriff counted twelve recently deceased in the camp and on and around the bridge. They added that body count to the men Nik and I had killed at The Pint and Pecker and told me we'd done a good job. A bang-up job, I think the sheriff said, his tongue not obviously in his cheek. As if we'd done nothing more than clean up a rattler den. An internal investigation by Denver Pacific Continental cleared both Nik and me of any wrongdoing. Now it was up to the Colorado Bureau of Investigations and the DA's office to decide my fate. Cohen told me not to worry about it, and I didn't. Whatever the legal system decided about our actions, Nik would never face any sort of earthly trial. And I had done what I had to do.

Or at least, that's what I told myself. Killing is never easy to justify.

During those drugged-out days, I spent a lot of time staring out my tenth-floor window, working hard to keep my mind empty. Some days I was fairly successful. Other days, Nik and the rest of the dead crowded so close it was all I could do to breathe.

But the doctors said I was making great progress. By the fifteenth day, I was off most of the drugs. On the sixteenth day, I took myself to the bathroom. Brushed my own teeth. The morning of the seventeenth day I started physical therapy. And on the evening of the eighteenth day of my stay, I turned on the television and watched for fifteen minutes before turning it off again.

On the nineteenth morning I woke with a clear head, as if someone had finally switched on the light.

A nurse was bustling around my bed, poking and prodding.

"Aren't you bright-eyed and bushy-tailed today," she said.

"You got coffee in this place?"

"Welcome back, honey. Your detective coming to see you today?" She was cranking up the head of my bed.

According to the hospital staff, Cohen had visited me every day. Even before I was conscious. Even while I was drugged out of my mind. Probably I was easier to take in that state.

"Can you fix my braid?"

She patted my hand and stuck a digital thermometer in my ear. "You look beautiful."

"Maybe something to cover the bruises?"

She read a number off the thermometer, wrote it down. "You're a lucky woman. Having a handsome detective and his handsome dog looking out for you."

Clyde is *my* dog, I thought but did not say. *My* partner.

The nurse finished with me, patted my hand again, and left. A minute later, there was a knock on the half-open door, and Cohen walked in.

Or tried to. Clyde beat him to it then had to wait for the detective to lift him onto the bed. The nurses had been livid the first few times they'd come in and found a dog lying next to me, tangled among the tubes and wires. But Clyde wouldn't take no. They'd finally thrown up their hands, moved the tubing, and laid out a blanket for him.

I rested my hand on Clyde's head, felt the warmth of him, felt his strength pass through my skin in that wonderful osmosis we shared. Clyde opened his mouth and let his tongue hang down just about to the bed and watched me. He smiled like that every time I saw him. Judging by how much my face hurt, I was probably smiling, too.

"Fucking furball's gonna break my back," Cohen said, taking up his perch on the windowsill.

"You walking him every day?"

"Sure. Even though he barfed up a stolen steak on my rug."

When Clyde took that shot for me, he suffered three broken ribs and a bruise that began where Whip's bullet struck his shoulder and worked its way down almost to his tail. While Cohen and the police and deputies were swarming over the encampment, Clyde had hobbled through the mob to Cohen. Badly injured, in terrible pain, Clyde had nonetheless led Cohen up the trail and across the bridge to where Gentry and I lay unconscious. They had to medevac all three of us.

The nurses told me that when I learned Clyde was alive, I shoved a doctor hard enough to make her fall and tried to get off the gurney, rubber tubes and IVs be damned. I don't remember it. But it's still one of the best days of my life.

"How are things in the world of crime fighting?" I asked Cohen.

"Oh you know." His eyes were as dark and tired as I remembered them. "Days are never long enough."

"What are you wasting time here for, then?"

"Food's free."

"That's graft."

"More like perks."

When Cohen first came to the hospital, I couldn't look him in the eye. Not after what I'd done. Not with what I knew. But I came to realize that Cohen has monsters of his own. And if he suspected I knew more than I was sharing, he let it sit. He was plenty pissed about the papers I'd stolen. But he understood. He wasn't going to stay away from me because of that.

Especially since, he said in a moment of pique, I'd solved his crime for him. He might need me again.

Now, as we did every day, we talked about idle things. Gossip about some of the dicks Cohen worked with. How good the coffee was at the shop a block from headquarters. Whether or not I'd flunk out of school this semester from missing so many classes.

Denver PD closed the book on the murder of Elise Hensley with the identification of her killer as Alfred Merkel. Melody Weber's testimony, along with the fact of Tucker's stolen hobo beads at the crime scene, the presence of several of Merkel's hairs on Elise's body, and Merkel's possession of illegal prescription meds, helped convince Denver PD that they had their man. I didn't know why Melody lied, although I figured it was her one chance to give Whip the finger. Detective Bandoni kept giving me the evil eye about all of it, but in the end he said justice had been served, one way or another, and he let it drop.

I don't think Cohen bought it. I think the case remains open for him. But I also think he has no idea who her real killer was. And maybe not much inclination to pursue it.

Elise hadn't come by since the night we entered the encampment, so it could be she too felt that justice, however winding, had been served.

I thought about her and Whip a lot during the long, still nights as I listened to the beeping of monitors, the swooshing steps of the nurses, the occasional cry down the hall. Merkel had gone down for the one thing he hadn't done. And Nik had committed the worst sort of crime. He'd slaughtered a woman he loved, ripped her body apart to make it look like the crime of someone else's passion. Or maybe, once he started with the knife, he didn't know how to stop. Killing—in war or elsewhere—drives us mad. Death shoves its way into our nostrils and down our throats, filling us until there isn't room for anything else.

Nik had held his war inside for forty years.

No wonder he couldn't breathe.

In those long, quiet nights, I wondered about the dark things in my own future. The men I'd killed—first in Iraq, now in Colorado—had left marks on my heart. However justified the courts might rule it, killing is killing.

It does not leave us intact.

And now my silence let Nik get away with his crime. More than get away with it. Ellen Ann was keeping her grief at bay by raising money for a memorial fund to make sure no one forgot Nik Lasko's heroism.

"You miss him," Cohen said now, as if reading my mind.

"More than you know," I answered. But it was for the Nik I thought I'd known. Not for what he'd become.

"He died saving his son." Cohen looked at me as if waiting for some reaction.

But he'd tried this gambit before. I gave him nothing except a nod.

"Well." He stood. "Guess I'd better get back to work before Bandoni sends a hit squad."

"Wheel me up to see Gentry?"

Gentry had remained in ICU for two weeks before being upgraded to serious but stable and then to fair. He'd suffered a cranial compression fracture, a lacerated liver, a broken occipital bone, five broken ribs, and twenty-seven cigarette burns. His captors had done other things to him he wouldn't talk about and that his doctor said were none of my business. The physical recovery would take weeks.

I worried there might not be enough time in the world to heal the internal scars.

Cohen parked my wheelchair at the nurses' station on Gentry's floor. He gave me a chaste peck on the cheek. Clyde slobbered on my lap until Cohen bodily hauled him away.

"Your friend is taking in some sunlight at the end of the hall," the day nurse said.

Gentry's wheelchair was parked close to the window. The nurse rolled me up next to him. She adjusted the blanket on Gentry's lap, told us not to tire ourselves, and beat feet.

"They tell me you're getting better," I said.

He gave a slow, sad smile. "Rumor has it."

"You're looking good."

"You too."

Ah, the lies told to the hospitalized everywhere.

He returned his gaze to the window. "When are you going back to work?"

"Soon as they let me. 'Course, I'll be at a desk for a while." I fingered the brace on my knee. "What about you?"

"I don't know. I've resigned from the law firm. I'm thinking I'll start taking pro bono cases on my own. Or go to work for the public defender's office."

Outside, a bird hurtled past, flung by the March wind. It turned on its wing and swooped under the eaves.

Gentry shifted in his chair, sucked in his breath at the pain. "Your detective talked to me about Jazmine Brown."

"What'd you tell him?"

"The truth. I didn't hurt her, Sydney."

"I know."

"But I didn't save her, either. I knew what those boys meant to do, and I stayed silent. It's a hard thing to live with."

"I understand that, too."

After a while, his hand crept out from under the blanket and took mine. We sat that way as the sun faded and a winter chill took over the room. Spring was still a long way away.

On my twentieth day in the hospital, the ghost of the CIA spy, Richard Dalton, appeared.

I was furious with his intrusion. I'd half hoped that what I'd gone through had been payment enough to silence the dead. That after crowding me during my drug-hazed days, they would pack up and move out.

So when Dalton showed up, I picked up a vase of flowers and threw it at him.

A nurse came running, but Dalton just moved to stand by the window.

After an orderly had cleaned up the mess and I'd had some time to calm down, Dalton's presence forced me to think about things that, frankly, scared the shit out of me.

I still had the Alpha and Sarge to deal with. Whatever they thought I had, they'd be back for it.

More importantly, there was Malik. The boy was somewhere in the US with the Alpha and Sarge sniffing for his trail like a pair of jackals. I'd failed him in Iraq. I wouldn't fail him again. I had to find him before they did.

I pulled out Dougie's ring, held it up to the sunlight where it swung and spun on its chain, a gyroscope of promise and loss.

Whatever the Alpha wanted, whenever Sarge came back, I'd do my best to be ready. Given the level of alarm around what had happened in Habbaniyah, I figured there was a house of cards somewhere just waiting for a good breath of air.

Something that, maybe, Malik and I could do together.

On my last day, as I was packing up the flowers and stuffed animals that Grams and Captain Mauer and the railroad folk had brought me, someone rapped on the partially closed door.

Clyde lifted his head from his spot in the sun.

"Come in," I said, expecting Cohen even though he'd said he would wait for me out front. He had dropped Clyde off fifteen minutes ago and gone to bring the car around.

But it was Tucker Rhodes standing in the doorway.

"Ma'am," he said. "Hope I'm not bothering you."

He was dressed for the road in jeans and boots and an old army jacket. He had his ruck slung over his shoulder. As I came forward, he removed his cowboy hat. His eyes gleamed like emeralds in the wreckage of his face.

"Come in," I said again, glad to see him. "Sit down."

"I can't stay," he said. "Just stopped by for a second."

But he came on into the room, made his way over to the window. Clyde pulled himself to his feet, still moving a little slower than he had before being shot. He took a few sniffs then glanced at me to make sure we were good on this. No doubt he remembered the man he'd tracked through a snowstorm.

I turned my palm flat toward the ground. Satisfied, he returned to his spot in the sun.

Tucker said, "They told me you got busted up pretty bad. I felt bad when I heard."

I waved it away. "You doing okay?"

Always a stupid question.

He didn't take offense. "You talking my heart or my head?"

"Both."

He swung the ruck down on the bed, turned his hat in his hands. "Neither's been right for a long time. But I guess didn't any of us come back quite right."

The thought of Nik hit with fresh pain. Like it did a thousand times a day. No matter how much time I spent thinking about him, missing him, wanting to turn and ask him a question, the fact of what he'd done still surprised me with the suddenness of a knife going in.

"You're right," I said.

We looked at each other. The clock ticked on the wall. Outside the window, ragged clouds flew by.

He shifted. "Jeezer said you guys went looking for Sarge. Didn't find him."

"That's true." I didn't mention that it had gone the other way around.

"So none of this had anything to do with what we did in Habbaniyah?"

I shook my head. "That's behind us."

Down by the nurses' station, an alarm sounded. Footsteps hurried by.

"Elise—" he started. Couldn't finish.

"You loved her," I said. "She loved you back. That says everything about your heart and your head."

Grief swam into his eyes like a riptide. "She loved me even with all the war did to me. I never could understand why."

I couldn't think of anything to say that didn't sound trivial. Or patronizing. So I said nothing.

"Sometimes I feel like I'm tap dancing, you know?" he said. "Dancing right on the edge of some big pit that'll swallow me up soon as I slow down."

"What we did over there," I said carefully. "Could be it wasn't the right thing. Maybe we took a bad situation and fucked it up more. But we meant well. That's what you need to remember, Tucker. We meant well. That might have to be enough."

He nodded. "Guess it's what I got."

He patted Clyde on the head, picked up his ruck, and made his way toward the door.

"I'm catching out," he said, tugging on his hat. "Guess it's crazy to tell a railroad cop that. But I'm going to Montana to see my dad. He's not got long, is what the docs say. After that, I figure I'll just keep moving."

"You ever need help settling down," I said, "come talk to me."

"I will."

A nurse appeared at the door with a chair to wheel me out. Hospital policy.

I called to Clyde and took his lead in my lap as I sat. Tucker walked alongside us down the hallway. Someone would take the flowers and stuffed animals to the children's ward.

Downstairs in the lobby, through the glass of the front doors, I saw Cohen waiting by the curb. He leaned against his car, arms folded, his right ankle hooked over the left. The wind had caught his tie, blown it sideways. His hair still looked like he'd cut it with manicure scissors.

Tucker turned to me. "Me and Elise, we owe you a lot."

"I'll send you a bill."

"I still see her," he said. "Elise. Does that mean I'm crazy?"

"No, Tucker. I'm pretty sure it means you're sane."

He touched my shoulder. Then he put on his hat and pushed the door open.

"Semper Fi," he said and walked out of the building.

"Semper Fi," I murmured.

The door swung shut behind him.

I returned my gaze to Cohen. He must have felt my eyes on him even through the glass because he turned to look straight at me. Smiled.

I didn't know how things would work for us. Or if they would work at all. But I intended to try. As Dougie would have said, you gotta live a little.

The nurse opened the doors, and I pushed myself out of the chair. Clyde and I walked slowly out into the sunshine as Cohen came forward to meet us.

The day had been warm. Glorious for early March. But already the sun was tipping toward nightfall, the shadows growing. A chill wind ruffled my hair and Clyde's, and for just a moment, we hesitated.

Then I jingled his lead and he looked up at me, his brown eyes certain.

"Let's go, Clyde," I said. "We're still good."

ACKNOWLEDGMENTS

Writing this novel took a village.

To the members of my critique group and to my beta readers for their insight, talent, encouragement, and phenomenal editing skills: Michael Bateman, Patricia Coleman, Deborah Coonts, Ronald Cree, Kirk Farber, Chris Mandeville, Michael Shepherd, and Robert Spiller.

To my cheerleaders, Donnell Bell, Deborah Coonts, and Maria Faulconer, all wonderful writers in their own right as well as my go-to team on those tough days. Deb, I'm raising a glass of single malt to the brainstorming and laughter we've shared from New York to Jackson Hole to San Francisco. Good times, my friend.

This book would not have been possible without the knowledge and insight of retired Denver K9 officer Dan Boyle, Senior Special Agent Scott Anthony, Foreman General Edward Pettinger, and Career Intelligence Officer Steve Pease. A very special thank-you to retired Denver detective Ron Gabel for sharing his vast experience, his stories, and his time. The help I received from these gentlemen was invaluable; any mistakes in this book are entirely my own.

To my agent, Bob Diforio of the D4EO Literary Agency. Serendipity, indeed.

To Grace Doyle and the team at Thomas & Mercer who believed in a book about a railroad cop. And to Charlotte Herscher, Rick Edmisten, and Dan Janeck, who made it a better book.

AUTHOR'S NOTE

In writing this novel, I took certain liberties in how I portrayed some of the counties, cities, railroad tracks, military bases, and institutions described in this book. The world presented here, along with its characters and events, is entirely fictitious. Denver Pacific Continental (DPC) is a wholly fictional railway. Any resemblance to actual incidents and corporations, or to actual persons living or dead, is entirely coincidental.

About the Author

Photo © 2015 Jonathan Betz

Barbara Nickless is an award-winning author whose short stories and essays have appeared in anthologies in the United States and the United Kingdom. An active member of Mystery Writers of America and Sisters in Crime, she has given workshops and speeches at numerous writing conferences and book events. She lives with her family in Colorado. *Blood on the Tracks*, which won the Daphne du Maurier Award and was a runner-up for the Claymore Award, is her first novel.